THE
VANISHING
STATION

ANA ELLICKSON

AMULET BOOKS • NEW YORK

for Mom & Dad,
who would have jumped oceans for me

Cataloging-in-Publication Data has been applied for and may be obtained from the Library of Congress.

ISBN 978-1-4197-6422-6

Text © 2024 Andrea Ellickson
Book design by Natalie Padberg Bartoo

Published in 2024 by Amulet Books, an imprint of ABRAMS.

Printed and bound in U.S.A.
10 9 8 7 6 5 4 3 2

Amulet Books are available at special discounts when purchased in quantity for premiums and promotions as well as fundraising or educational use. Special editions can be created to specification. For details, contact specialsales@abramsbooks.com or the address below.

Amulet Books® is a registered trademark of Harry N. Abrams, Inc.

ABRAMS The Art of Books
195 Broadway, New York, NY 10007
abramsbooks.com

❧ PROLOGUE ❧

Montgomery once told me: the trains are always listening. But what about the rusted broken ones, the ones lost in the jungle under vines so thick they could swallow your arm? I don't know if I believed him—and maybe I still don't, even after everything that's happened—but I need to find my way home. So, I start talking, whether the rusted train can hear me or not. *Take me back. Back to Balboa Park. I'll trade my secrets if only you'll let me come home.*

I strain my ears against the buzzing-beating jungle, hoping for a sign, an answer from the twisted metal beneath me. Lush green vines sprawl across the railroad tracks, and a dark tunnel stretches into the forest. Wild ferns cover the steep hillsides, and bricks are overgrown with lichen. This is not a place for passengers to come and go.

Please.

I hear nothing except the slither of a red-striped tiger snake inching closer.

My blood thuds against my throat, and the secrets spill from my lips.

Are you listening?

⚹ CHAPTER 1 ⚹

My scooter can barely make it over Twin Peaks, but I spur her onward like a trusty silver steed. Come on, girl, it's only a hill. A winding hill I've crisscrossed a million times. We got this. As we crest the top, San Francisco's sunset skyline spreads before us, curving and starry-eyed like a van Gogh painting. Damp eucalyptus leaves fill my senses. I savor a deep foggy breath before charging down the other side. Wind snakes into my honey leather jacket, sending a thrill through my bones that I haven't felt in months. Ever since my mom died, there's a numbness that I can't seem to shake. But tonight is different. Tonight, I push the pedal a little harder than I should as we go shooting down Clarendon Street. There's no way I'm missing Diego's art show. Green lights all the way, baby.

There's a buzzing in my jacket pocket, but I ignore it. It's not safe to text and drive, and if I'm being brutally honest, it's Friday night and I know my dad always stops at the karaoke bar near 16th and Valencia after work. I know he's already downed three San Miguels, and it's only six P.M. Undoubtedly, he's singing Frank Sinatra, because every Filipino man over the age of fifty loves crooning "My Way" at the top of his lungs. Or if he's flirting with a new lady friend, he'll duet Disney's "A Whole New World" because he is the Sap Master. This would all be fine and great if my dad knew when to stop drinking. Otherwise . . .

A phone call from Balboa Santos always means trouble.

And I'm always the one to clean up the mess.

I push my sputtering Stella as fast as her tiny engine can run. We streak past Victorian houses that sparkle like amethyst and jade gems set into San Francisco's hillsides. My threadbare jeans are one wash away from splitting, but I still hug the seat tight between my thighs. I should slow down, but for once, this girl has Friday night plans. Diego Jose Alvarez's art launch— he's soon to be as famous as Diego Rivera and Frida Kahlo, I just know it. It's at an after-hours coffee shop on Divisadero where on Fridays and Sundays he works as an ever-broke and ever-forgetful barista. He even gave me a preview of his paintings—golden agave spikes and flower spires that reach into the sky. Agaves send up their tree-height flower stalks only *once* in a lifetime—talk about bittersweet beauty.

I can't not show up. Even if my dad calls, drunk and begging for a ride.

The phone gives one last kick in my pocket and then goes silent. Good—I don't want to hear the same old excuses.

Besides, I promised to help Diego hang the show's lighting. He insists I have an artist's eye, but he always says that sort of stuff. Diego Jose Alvarez is perfectly unable to keep a compliment to himself. The reality is: I haven't picked up a paintbrush since my mom died. Not once. Painting houses doesn't count—those are for cash to pay off endless hospital bills. Just because I have gallons of white paint splattered on every piece of clothing I own doesn't mean I'm an artist.

Whoa, Stella! I slam my horn at a car aggressively nosing its way into a right turn onto Carl Street. Not today, my friend. I'd like to keep all my limbs, thank you. As my Stella scooter speeds alongside the trolley tracks embedded in Cole Street, pinpricks tingle through my fingertips as if my hands have been asleep this whole time and are just now waking up. Blood surges into my palms, and I grip the handlebar firmly to keep from veering into the train tracks. Sometimes when I get too close . . . I don't know how to explain it. Something surges inside me.

I wish I could paint the feeling, get it out of my bones and onto paper.

But when would I ever have time to paint?

Divisadero Street is up ahead, almost there. I can't wait for the art show, even if I don't really know whether Diego and I are friends-friends or just coworkers who commiserate about being the hired help. Since I graduated high school a couple months ago, I barely know a soul in this city anymore. Everyone moved on to grander things like college or study abroad or coding bootcamp. I won't know anyone at the party, either, but maybe I can pretend to be a girl of mystery instead of revealing the truth: I'm a girl going exactly *nowhere*.

When I show up, sunlight steeps the sky in a rosy purple hue. I take a deep breath and run my thumb along the crumpled paper in my pocket. I don't need to open it to remember the exact details of my mother's bucket list, written in indigo ink with big looping *M*s and *R*s and everything in between. Her note gives me just enough courage to push past the CLOSED sign and poke my head inside. A bell rings above me.

"Hi . . . hello?" I say.

"Espresso?" Diego yells at me from behind the counter. "Single or double?"

"I want to sleep tonight. So . . . peppermint tea?" I step all the way inside, tiptoeing through the minefield of fairy string lights while trying to untangle my hair from the scooter helmet. I'm so glad to be able to move my jaw again without the helmet strap hooked under my chin. Not that I really know what to say now that I'm here.

"Sleep is for losers." Diego hops over the countertop and pulls me into a hug, kissing both cheeks before leaning back and yelling, "Make this girl a triple!"

I'm not usually one for physical contact (and any dirtbag who tries to grab me in a crowded bus better watch out), but I can never say no to Diego's hugs. They're epic. Imagine a warm caramel latte full of cinnamon spice. Don't let the skull tattoos on his deep brown forearms fool you—this boy has no idea how to pull off a death glare. I tried to teach him once, and he ended up summoning a boy to flirt with. Definitely not a death glare.

"But I'm so behind on sleep already," I groan.

"I can't have you fall off a ladder. Loretta will kill me if I mess up her coffee shop. And I'm too pretty to die this young."

"I've spent half the day shellacking a ceiling. I think I can handle a few lights and a ladder."

"My point exactly. Don't get me talking about the West Portal house. All those ornate bougie archways. My biceps are still sore. I mean, just look at this." He shows off his gorgeous muscled arms and wiggles his eyebrows. I can't help but laugh. They are rather impressive. I mean, after all the scrubbing and painting and rollering we do for Chen's Painting Service, my one-time chicken arms are now pure lean muscle, too.

I forget how much I miss these moments of "normal," and maybe one day I'll even be able to call Diego a true friend—without the weight of my dad's drunken Friday nights sucking the air out of my lungs, or a cobwebbed house crowded with all the things my mom left behind, a mountain of debt included. I can just be Ruby Santos, girl with a bright future . . . somewhere. The "where" is the tough part.

I pull my eyes away from his muscles and glance around the room. All the small round tables are pushed into a corner, and the floor shines with fresh beeswax. Diego already has an army of worker bees carrying out his plans. He'd make a spectacular general. He's planned it all: mini agaves in clay pots as giveaways, tip jars, and decadent Mexican hot chocolate brewing in the back kitchen. It makes me wonder if I'm needed at all. I fidget with my jean pockets, crumpling and uncrumpling my mother's last note. 623 days and it's still inside my pocket. But I haven't done anything on my mom's list. The guilt sneaks up on me, thick and sticky and here to stay. I clear my throat.

"So, you want all these lights on the ceiling?" I point to the bundles of white string lights scattered on the floor.

"My love ain't cheap, girl. Work your Ruby magic."

When Diego's boyfriend, Victor, floats over with a triple espresso, I gulp it down in two mouthfuls. I'll need my hands free, after all. I want my buzz from the scooter ride to last through the night. I want my fingertips to work magic, weaving the lights above our heads. I want to make something from nothing.

"Brava!" Diego yells at full falsetto, clinking his empty espresso cup with mine.

"I think someone needs to be cut off for the night," I say.

"It's just nerves," Victor chimes in, hooking his fingers into the edge of Diego's shirt as if he can tether him to Earth and keep him from floating off. I wonder what it would be like to have someone who cares for me like that.

"And four, no, no, no *five* espressos," Diego says, scrunching his man bun into a tighter topknot. "And complete strangers are about to come see my art and soul and judge me and tell me I'm brilliant, and then I'll have to fight off paparazzi and pretend I don't know you fools. It's going to be an epic night, just wait."

"I see someone has realistic expectations for his first art show."

"Ruby, you need to learn to dream bigger. When's *your* art show?"

"That would require making art. And this girl has nothing to show for herself."

"Little liar. I've seen the murals you've painted for Chen's clients. Go on, get up that ladder! Adelante!"

I stick my tongue out at him and climb up the ladder with a cape of lit fairy lights draped across my arm. My knees jitter as I cling to the ladder's metal steps. My biceps are indeed still sore from painting a ceiling this morning. They'd actually wanted clouds, which was a welcome distraction from the usual flat white, but that meant I'd had to paint layer over layer until the blues and whites looked natural. Let's just say my arms are now the consistency of gummy worms. The triple espresso might have been a mistake, too. I already feel the acid-fire caffeine worming its way through my belly. It's not even my own art show and I'm nervous. Nervous that I'll mess up the lights. Nervous that no one will appreciate the beauty I see in Diego's paintings. Nervous that I'll never be brave enough, like Diego, to show my nonexistent art to anyone.

Nervous that no one will care, anyway.

I check my phone and notice that Balboa Santos did indeed leave a message.

Lovely.

Not tonight, Dad.

Not. Tonight.

I shove the phone back into my pocket without a second glance.

My arms stretch across the bare white ceiling, pinning the lights without thinking, just driving in the hooks wherever it feels right. Pin, hook, string; pin, hook, string. A rhythm builds until everything fades away except for my fingertips and the web of lights emerging from the ceiling.

I startle when Diego gasps down below. Someone has turned off the overhead lights, leaving only my fairy lights and the glowing bulbs hanging over each one of the agave paintings. Diego wraps his arms around my knees and plucks me off the ladder, spinning me around the room and laughing like a complete and utter maniac.

The lights twirl above me like a web of magic. I feel like I can reach my hands up and press through into another world. I've always loved that about string lights—the way they can turn an ordinary room into a starry night or a glowing field of flickering wishes. My breath catches in my throat and my eyes feel too bright. My mom would have loved this, too—she'd done it to our dining room when the chandelier broke and we didn't have enough money to fix it. A dining room I'm no longer allowed in because we had to rent out our house and move into the garage. The renters took down her lights the week they moved in. Heartless fools.

"OK, OK, enough! Put me down before I knee you in the kidney!" I swat his head, long wisps of hair getting caught on my teeth. "Just because I'm small doesn't mean I like being carried."

He sets me down and bows before me on one knee. "Yes, my fairy queen."

"Dramatique." His boyfriend rolls his eyes. "I have to admit it does make the show really come alive." Victor reaches into his pocket and pulls out a wad of cash, and it immediately snaps me out of the moment. My gut knots. He counts out three crisp twenty-dollar bills and waits for me to hold out my palm to take them.

Right. So . . . I guess I'm the hired help? Was this all a business transaction? I try to tamp down the pride prickling up my spine. The puke-green from those twenties makes my stomach roil.

"Thanks for your help, Ruby. You've got such an eye for light and dark." Victor leans down awkwardly to whisper in my ear, and I wish he would stumble on his way down. Anything to stop this embarrassment burning in my chest. When he looks at me, does he see only the tattered jeans? The charity case? Is this the only reason I'm here? "Go on, take it. I know you need the cash, and I'm not taking 'no' for an answer."

I don't know what to say. I hate people knowing how much my dad and I are struggling to pay off my mom's cancer bills while still sending money back to family in the Philippines, while also scraping by in one of the most expensive cities in America—especially when my dad can randomly blow through a paycheck if he decides to drive out to the Reno casinos and binge for a whole weekend straight. I told Diego once how much I needed the painting jobs, how it was hard to find a job that paid more than minimum wage with only a high school diploma. Such a stupid mistake. I didn't think about the fact that he would tell his rich boyfriend.

I don't want friends who pity me. Who only want me around if I'm useful. Who tell me to host an art show as if it's the easiest thing in the world, as if I have time for anything more than survival right now. I'm trying, so, so hard. Tiny pinpricks come rushing to the edges of my eyes. Come on, Ruby, keep it together. Just take the money. It makes me feel even more pathetic if I cry over such a small thing. I force a smile and slip the cash into my pocket, before looking anywhere but Victor's eyes.

Diego hears another group of friends knocking on the door, and he rushes over, kissing them on their cheeks, waving them inside from the autumn chill. Their *oohs* and *ahhs* over the paintings echo through the room. I can finally release the breath I've been holding tight inside my chest. I hightail it to the door, slip out, just as more people push inside. Diego must know every living person within a two-mile radius of Golden Gate Park. They strut inside wearing glamorous embroidered jeans and velvet blazers and silk dresses. I'd never be able to pull off something like that. I'm a ghost in my own city. I glance back once more—soaking in the sight of his gorgeous agave paintings, his dreams lit up from the inside out.

I brace myself against a graffiti wall.

I hit play on the voice mail I've been avoiding all evening as the fog inevitably finds a way to sneak through the cracks in my jacket. A shiver jolts across my skin.

My dad's words are slurred, but it's a message I know all too well.

Help.

☆ CHAPTER 2 ☆

Ruby, give me ride. 26th ... aye, no, 16th! 16th and Valencia. You know, it's all the bartender's fault. He says sing "Don't Stop Believing," then they all laugh at my accent. Hurry up, OK? Hoy! That's my bag, hayop ka!

And that's the grand total of my dad asking "politely" to pick him up from his drunken stupor at the karaoke bar. When he says the word "fault," it comes out as "pault" because even after the last ten years in America, his Filipino accent is still going strong. Especially after drinking. He will never admit it, but this night is all his own damn pault. You know, when I'd agreed to let my dad buy me a Stella scooter in exchange for free rides, this is not what I'd had in mind.

Ever since Mom died, he's been ... different. Depressed? Guarded? I miss my old dad. The one who would fry up eggs over rice and Spam and make fun of my mom's pale Irish skin that would immediately burn when we'd go for picnics up in Bolinas Beach. Sure, he's always been a drinker. A mostly mellow one. Always a mug to hide the true contents. Always too rowdy at parties, apologizing to everyone afterward, but fun enough for everyone to forgive him. He didn't use to get drunk every single Friday night or binge at Nevada casinos or beg for rides home because his legs tripped him up. It wasn't "Ruby, help me, help me, help me," when I can barely keep myself afloat.

For a moment, I consider hugging Diego goodbye before jetting off, but he'll see the worry in my eyes. He'll ask questions. Back inside the coffee shop, his friends crowd around him, toasting with cinnamon-spiced cups of hot chocolate. Bet none of those people have to collect their drunk dads from the bar.

I grit my teeth and try to start my Stella. Again. She sputters and stops and refuses to turn over no matter how many times I try the key. Come on, girl, I know the feeling, but we can't let him sit on a street corner. He might get arrested. Or worse. Come on, start, start, start.

I should have checked my voice mail earlier. I knew it was going to be his slurred voice, his usual plea. But tonight . . . tonight was supposed to be different.

It never is.

Finally I stuff my key into my jacket and storm down the hill on foot toward Civic Center BART station. I pull my leather jacket tight around me, even though it means I'm swimming in cow hide. Still, I like the way it feels like a shield. Fog drifts in from the bay, and I glance back to see mist twisting through the spokes of my scooter's tires. The subway is the fastest way to 16th Mission. Stella can wait until tomorrow.

Appended to the "free rides for life" rule, my scooter came with another stipulation:

No BART subway trains. No streetcars.

It's not safe. Not ever.

I've never complained, because the scooter is damn nifty, and I can basically park anywhere in this city, even in those dreaded half-spots where no one can even squeeze their smart car. My dad told me it's because he'd witnessed a murder on a train once and never wants that fate for his daughter.

Only half of me believes him.

I know there's more to his obsession with keeping me away from trains. I mean, it's San Francisco. Everyone uses the subway. Commuters, parents, babies, students, they all zip around underground. With Mom gone, he's been extra protective. Which is ironic, since lookie who is going out of her way on a Friday night to rescue him from himself.

I hurry past Alamo Square, where the Painted Ladies parade their beautiful Victorian facades. People walk their corgis and mini Australian shepherds around the grassy square while sipping their expensive single origin coffees and talking into AirPods. This is where the opening for that old sitcom *Full House* was filmed. This is what tourists think of when they hear "San Francisco."

Here's the truth:

San Francisco is a shithole. I say it with love. I say it as the kind of person who roams the Mission, savoring the smell of grilled onions and chilies and melting ice cream. As someone who loves running through foggy Golden Gate Park and sneaking onto rooftops to catch the glittering cityscape. But what most people don't understand about this hippy techie mecca of San Francisco is that it's hard to scrape by for people like us. It's hard to make enough money to live here anymore. It's hard to hold on to what little we have left.

"Hola, perdóname, can I ask question?" A teenager stops me in the street, impeccably dressed in a black turtleneck and a messenger bag covered in Espania soccer ball stickers. He pushes the dark curly hair from his eyes and smiles. That look alone makes me melt inside. His friends hover back, glancing up at street signs and then back at their phones.

"We're looking for . . . uh, how you say, 'the hate'?"

"You mean the Haight-Ashbury?" A small smile escapes my lips. Ah, tourists.

"Yes!"

"Well, you're going in the right direction. Keep going another seven blocks, until you hit Masonic Avenue, then make a left. You can't miss it. There will be graffiti and incense smoke and white dudes with dreadlocks everywhere. Make sure to check out Amoeba Music. It's the best."

"You want to come with us? You can show us this Amoeba, yes?"

I can't help but imagine strolling through Gaudi's gorgeous orange-and-blue tiled park in Barcelona. How this could be me—in reverse. Discovering a new city. Meeting the locals. Taking college classes abroad. Finding the best art and music shops in the city.

My phone rings again, and I don't have to pick it up to know it's my dad wondering why I'm taking so long to rescue him.

"Maybe another time," I say, already walking away.

A quick goodbye is all I can give.

The shift between neighborhoods comes just as sudden. Alamo Square to Civic Center. Rich to poor.

I jog through the Civic Center neighborhood, careful to not step on wads of gum or half-eaten burgers or dirty heroin needles littered on the sidewalk. I always dread walking through this neighborhood. All the city's unhoused sprawl in the streets and storefronts, in contrast to our City Hall's golden dome. It makes my whole heart ache. I put up my leather collar and try to hide deeper in my coat. I can barely shoulder my own burden and can't take on theirs. I want to help, but I don't know how. I remember in high school, we'd volunteer at the St. Anthony's Soup Kitchen and attend masses in their chapel where a Black choir director sang hymns. But that was back when I could count on coming home to Mom, back when I wasn't the one keeping us from the streets. My dad says I worry too much, but I've seen the money disappear each month—and I don't know where it all goes.

I practically run down the steps into the BART Civic Center station, the heat and stench immediately filling my nostrils. I know my dad said I shouldn't be here, but who's to stop me? He's drunk on 16th and Valencia, awaiting his savior.

Down in the depths of the tunnel, passengers wait for the next train. Good, three minutes. Alone on the edge of the platform, I finally pluck the scrap of paper from my pocket. After seeing Diego's art show tonight, I feel my mom's words burning in there. She made me write a bucket list on a neon pink Post-It Note. I don't really remember if these were the items on her list, or if they were the ones on mine. The memories blur together, and I feel like I'm not even the same girl who stood next to her mother's hospital bed and wrote:

1. Volunteer at an elephant sanctuary in Thailand.
2. Hang an art show in my favorite coffee shop.
3. Study abroad in a country where art is hidden in every street corner and cathedral.

And lastly,

4. Live.

I can't help but feel like I've disappointed her on all counts. Even the last one, somehow. I mean, I'm alive. No thoughts of suicide, working a steady job, contemplating college. But I don't think that's what she meant. I think the true Meredith Murphy would say there's a difference between living and surviving. She'd also say I was overthinking everything. That I should jump in like I used to. Like the old Ruby who loved paint on her fingers instead of a delicate brush. Like the old Ruby who once told a boy that if he wanted to kiss her so badly, he'd have to leap over a beach bonfire first. The old Ruby who knew for certain she'd study abroad in Barcelona, so she could learn Spanish and soak in Gaudí's colorful architecture. Instead, my best (and only remaining friend) Claire left to study abroad in London last month, as part of her pre-freshman summer start at Stanford. We didn't even talk before she caught her flight. We don't have anything in common anymore.

Now, I'm not so sure how to live.

A stale wind gusts through the tunnel and the paper suddenly slips from my achy fingers.

No, no, no! I drop to my knees to reach for the neon pink paper, but then it drifts over the edge of the platform. Shit. I crawl on my hands and knees to the very edge. People are definitely staring. A kid with giant head-phones tilts his head at me and laughs. This isn't funny. I can feel every dirty footprint under my palms. I lean my head as far forward over the edge of the platform as I can without losing my balance. Half of my body lurches over the train tracks, and the other half clings to the grimy plat-form. There's a flutter of pink like a feather caught in a spiderweb below. I can reach it. It's teetering on the rough stone wall three feet below me. I lie on my belly; the stench of urine and melted chocolate and bleach nearly makes me gag. My fingers scrape across the jagged concrete. A rumble begins under my belly and the howling starts between my ears again. My palms feel hot, sweaty—and full of light. A train is coming. One minute. Please, let me just reach it. I have it memorized, but what does that matter if I'll never see her handwriting again, never see our dreams scrawled on paper like a spell that might actually come true one day, if only I could believe in it? If only I can reach it.

A horn blares, loud and deafening. It echoes through the station.

Someone grabs my ankles, and I struggle in their grip. A rip tears through my threadbare jeans, and cold marble snakes against my thigh. Wait, I can almost reach it. Almost there. Please. My belly drags against the stone floor, my shirt riding up, exposing my soft skin to the jagged warning line.

I glance up. The train stampedes forward—too, too fast—down the tracks. I launch myself back. Behind the yellow line. Away from the wave of metal screaming past my body. A gray-haired man hovers over me, yelling, but I can't hear the words over the squealing brakes, can't hear him over my own ragged cry.

I lost it. I lost . . . her.

I can't force my legs to lift me up, even as the train doors slide open. Passengers literally step over my body as they rush to catch another train or hurry toward the exits. The gray-haired man who held my ankles has finally shoved off. They probably think I'm a drug addict hallucinating.

I don't care what they think. I don't care about the grime clinging to my skin. I lost the list. Stupid slippery fingers. I start to wipe the tears from my cheeks, but they keep pouring out. Don't cry, not in front of everyone.

A hand taps my shoulder, and my fists clench.

"Don't," I growl.

"Let me help you up," someone says softly over the bustle of the station.

I shake my head and force my knees to move. I can pick myself up; I'm not that pathetic.

The train doors start sliding shut, but the person next to me reaches out a long arm to catch it. Metal twangs against his wrist, and I catch a glimpse of an intricate tattoo spiraling around his ring finger. The alarm bell blares through the station, and the doors slide open again. Hot air hits my face, like a giant beast ready to swallow me.

"Hey, we have a schedule!" the conductor hollers at us from the first subway car.

"Just a minute!" the stranger's deep voice hollers back. As if everyone wasn't staring at us through the thick scratched glass, he waits patiently by my side. "Is this your train?"

I finally glance at his face, and I'm surprised by how young he is. Nineteen, twenty, maybe. Wavy black hair, sapphire eyes, and wide lips that look like they were made for much more than talking. Heat flashes through me when I think about how much I'd love to paint that jawline. Even though I'm standing now, his tall, lean body towers over me. The stranger wears a crisp midnight blue suit that seems far too classy for a BART station.

The surreal moment stretches.

Then snaps.

When he meets my gaze, his eyebrows crinkle in surprise. Right, I must look downright awful from all the crying. Before I can make an even bigger fool of myself, I scramble aboard the train. For a moment, I wonder if I've seen him before, but I can't think of where. The doors slide shut. As the train lurches into the dark tunnel, I see my own reflection: wild long hair, dirty smudges on my olive skin, torn jeans, shaky fingers.

Did he see a ghost of a girl when he looked at me?

Or did he see something more?

⚹ CHAPTER 3 ⚹

Before I'm ready, the doors slide open at 16th Street Mission station. I force my legs to move before I miss my stop. A crush of bodies buoys me across the dirty tiled floor and up the escalator. I crane my neck back to soak in the last of the sweet sunset before night tamps it out.

I need to find my father. Fast.

Aboveground, it's a cacophony of fruit markets and rap music and tortillas fried by women with deep brown skin wrinkled from too much sun. I hurry toward 16th and Valencia, where I know my father will be waiting. I don't have to look hard to find him.

Balboa Santos always knows how to hold court.

His white sleeves are pushed up to his elbows, showing off his strong forearms. His black hair is slicked back like Elvis. A bunch of strangers laugh and joke around him as they toss dice against a blue-and-white tiled wall that belongs to a Walgreens Pharmacy. He better not be playing for cash. When his dice hit snake eyes, Balboa cheers and waves his arms around, nearly tripping someone with his cane in the process.

I ran all the way here, for this?

"You know, I was lucky once," he says to the man next to him. "Coming back from a game of mahjong at my Tito Conrad's house, I saw the White Lady in my mirror, her long dark hair and red eyes. No matter how fast I drove, she followed. Until I found a church to hide inside. In the morning, the Padre found me sleeping on a pew, and he said I had seaweed on my lips. Lucky, huh!"

"Not for long." A Mexican man leans back on his heels, blows on the dice, and rolls. They're about the same height, short and stocky, with incredibly muscled arms. I wonder if his new friend practices boxing as much as my dad does.

Despite his perpetual grin, my dad loves horror stories. It's like it's all one big joke to him . . . or maybe like he's seen worse in real life? One time, when I was eight, he'd swapped a hard-boiled egg my mom made with a balut egg. Apparently fertilized duck egg is a Filipino delicacy . . . yuck. Before taking a bite, he'd smeared red chili paste onto the translucent duck head. My mom had screamed, like top-of-her-lungs screamed. I'd become a vegetarian for two whole years because of that. Thanks, Dad.

I glare at him like I'm the White Lady come to claim his soul. My long black hair and bloodshot eyes might just do the trick.

Balboa startles when he finally notices me leaning against the wall a couple paces away. The alcohol makes him sloppy, so he tips back on his feet before steadying himself. When I was little, he could move with all the deathly grace of a boxer. I don't need to hear the grumbles as he struggles out of bed in the morning to know that his hip pain has gotten noticeably worse the past few months. Still, he storms toward me, his eagle cane pounding against the concrete with every limp.

"Did someone hurt you?" He scans my tearstained eyes, my ripped jeans. "You tell me who. You tell me where."

"I fell," I say. "It's fine." The lie comes too easily to my tongue. We're barely ever honest with each other these days. I'd tried my best to wipe all traces of tears off my face before I got here, but I'm sure my eyes still look bloodshot.

"If someone hurt you . . ." he says, stepping so close that I can smell the sour hops on his breath.

"I know, Dad. You'll go full Manny Pacquiao on their ass. Don't worry, I can fend for myself." I give him my best Ruby death glare and nudge him hard in the shoulder. "Too bad I can't say that about someone else I know." He isn't the only boxer in the family. My eighth birthday present from my father was a pair of matching boxing gloves.

"It's been a hard week." He sighs, exhaling stale beer too close to my nostrils.

It's always a "hard week." But I bite my tongue. We've had this same argument before. I don't have the energy to have it again.

"Let's go," I say.

"Where's Stella?" He searches the parked cars for my scooter. The busy avenue is crammed with dented cars and bustling food carts. A bus honks at a car idling in its stop, while another car honks at the bus for being a bus.

"Stella wouldn't start. So I figured we could just take BART."

He looks like I've told him that hell is real and now we have to take a leisurely stroll through it. I know it's against his stupid "rules," but it's his fault we're in this situation in the first place. BART made the most sense.

"No," he says, walking in the direction exactly opposite from the 16th Street station. I watch him limp along with his cane, his left knee barely bending.

"Seriously?" I yell. "Do you have to be so stubborn!"

He shakes his head, and his slicked Elvis hair doesn't move an inch.

"Fine." I turn my back on him and start walking in the direction of the BART station. The bustle of Mission Street stretches in both directions as I near the corner. Cars honk, and hip-hop bass thumps through my bones.

Faster than I thought possible with his limp, my dad yanks my elbow and pulls me back against the street corner. A surprised yelp escapes my mouth.

"I said no subway!" he says.

"Let go!"

His hand clamps even more tightly around my wrist. He never does this. I don't understand. What's so bad—

"Call a taxi!" he yells. "I'll pay for it."

"Nothing is going to happen on the subway! We shouldn't waste our money on a taxi."

I wrench my wrist out of his grasp and sprint toward the steps that lead down below the ground. At the top, a bicyclist shoves in front of me, hoisting his bike over his shoulder and blocking most of the stairway. My dad catches up, and before he can grab my wrist again, I spin on him.

"I won't take BART if you tell me the truth. Why won't you let me ride the trains? The *real* reason."

Our eyes lock on to each other, and it doesn't feel like the silly staring contests we used to play when I was little. Now, we're nearly the same height, and I'm tired of games. My jaw clamps tightly and my boots dig into the pavement. His hand wobbles on his cane, its sharp eagle beak pointed at me.

"So stubborn," he says.

"Just like you, Daddio."

He grimaces at the truth.

"It's a long sad story." He sighs. "I tell you at home. Please, Ruby."

My shoulders slump, and I drag my nails through my tangled hair. A streetlight flickers on overhead. The endless honking grates at my nerves. Thanks, Dad, for yet another disastrous Friday night.

"Fine, but that's a promise?"

"Yes, a promise," he says.

I pull up a rideshare app and type in our address.

"Done, it's coming in four minutes."

My dad leans hard against the concrete railing, swaying slightly from all the alcohol still churning in his blood. He looks like he wants to walk away from the station, but he's too exhausted.

Footfalls sound on the concrete steps behind us, and when I turn my head, a woman glares at my father. She looks somewhere in her early twenties with her hair chopped into a short blue bob and a silver chain spiked through her ear. The stranger wears a white sleeveless shirt with a fur collar that does a magnificent job of showing off her statuesque biceps. No goosebumps on her pale skin; she doesn't mind the biting cold. The lady reminds me of a snow fox, hunting for prey.

"So, this is her?" she says, towering over us.

My dad's handcuff grip circles my wrist again, like this stranger might drag me down into the tunnels if he doesn't hold on. He doesn't say a word. I've never seen his face this icy. Usually he's all smiles and stories and seconds on dessert.

"We're not interested," he says, as if the blue-haired woman is a random salesperson, when she obviously knows my dad from somewhere.

"*Madame* doesn't care who's interested or not. Just who's interesting. And *she* is very interesting." Her eyes rove over my hands like she sees something written on them. I look down at my olive skin, the dry and rough cracks from all of Chen's painting gigs. Goosebumps creep along my neck, sneaking through my leather jacket. I shiver in the sunsetting fog.

Clearly, this chick is mistaking me for someone else.

"Look, I don't care how you know my dad, but how about you two work this out some other time? We've had a long night."

"My name's Six," she says, as if I hadn't just spoken. "'Sixteen' just doesn't roll off the tongue. It's too . . . *tender* for the work we do. Don't you agree, Balboa?"

Fantastic, she knows my father's name. Her voice betrays a sharp-edged Russian accent. And is Six some sort of stripper name? Please don't be a stripper name. Please, *please*. Can this night get any worse?

She holds out her calloused palm for me to shake.

"Don't shake her hand," my dad says, still gripping my wrist. "We go. Now."

"But . . . the driver? He should be here any second."

"Chill, old-timer." Six flicks blue hair back behind her spiked ears. "Don't let me ruffle your plans with your daughter. Madame just wanted me to remind you of the debt. She's growing impatient, and she doesn't appreciate your sloppy work lately. You know she'll collect. She especially likes collecting *interesting* things." She winks at me before swinging around the concrete barrier and strolling back down into the tunnels' depths.

Before I have a chance to say another word, a silver car swerves into the spot in front of us.

"Hurry up," the driver hollers, typing something into his phone. "Traffic is about to peak." He doesn't bother to turn down the thumping electronica spewing from his Honda's sound system. Nor does he help my dad hoist his cane and aching legs into the cramped backseat. With the doors shut inside this tiny space, the frantic techno beats pound and pulse against my skull.

"Can you turn that down?" I say.

The driver ignores me and swerves into traffic. My shoulder lurches into the hard door panel. I want to pepper my dad with questions, but he goes stone-faced before eventually resting his flushed forehead against the window. He looks nauseous, and I can't tell if it's from the drunken kara-oke, or the lady named Six, or the fact that when we get home he promised to tell me the real reason I'm not allowed on the BART trains. The driver glares at him from the front seat.

"Open the window if you're going to puke," the driver says.

My dad's eyes sharpen when we pass the next subway station along Mission Street—the blue-and-white BART sign like a beacon in the night—and he doesn't relax until we finally roll up to our house. Grandma Murphy bought the house back when this was a poor Irish and Italian neighbor-hood, and she then passed it on to my mom, Meredith Murphy, who then passed it on to me. It's all we have left. My mom poured her heart into the murals inside the house, and every growing crack in the lavender exterior walls reminds me how far we're behind.

My phone buzzes with a message from Diego:

"Where'd you vanish? Everyone is in love with your fairy lights!"

Part of me aches to turn back, to see their glowing faces when they see Diego's agaves illuminated by my web of lights.

But I need the truth.

Tonight.

Because I don't know how long we have before the truth finds us.

⚘ CHAPTER 4 ⚘

When I swing open the door to our makeshift garage, only the spiders greet us. A red tea kettle topples off a mountain of boxes and crashes to the floor. We should have plastic-wrapped it like the rest of our furniture, but I always crave mint tea in the autumn fog.

I'm tired of this garage.

I'm tired of always feeling hungry for *more*.

I'm tired of being walked over.

Lo and behold, twenty seconds later, I hear feet stomping on the ceiling above my head. Tiny splinters flake down on my forehead and hover in the dust-speckled air. That's Shannon or Dorothy, the renters–probably Dorothy. She works remotely for a tech giant and guards her quiet like a hungry badger. It's impossible to keep the ceiling clean, since it's made of unfinished wooden beams and heating ducts. God, I hope those aren't lined with asbestos.

The last time I'd had a remotely meaningful conversation with my dad, he'd said:

"One day, anak, we go upstairs again."

I hadn't said anything in return.

We've been promising ourselves for months now that we'll pull in enough cash to move back upstairs. That we won't have to rent it to strangers anymore. But Mom's hospital and funeral bills weren't cheap. And money keeps "disappearing" and my dad won't tell me why. I might be an art kid, but even I know that the math doesn't add up.

One of the last things my mom said before she died was how happy it made her to know that we'd still be surrounded by her murals. I miss seeing them every day. Sure, I could break all sorts of privacy rules and sneak upstairs when the renters aren't home. I could lose myself in her jungle murals from her Peace Corps days—sunlight streaming through feathered wings, monstera leaves bigger than my face, the whole scene grander than life itself—except my mother actually lived it, and here I am living in a garage, and she's gone.

It's all sour luck, no way around it. And I'm not asking for pity, just for a break. For a tiny bit of freedom.

Quiet smothers our small space. It feels too much like we're living in a crypt with concrete walls and a complete lack of natural light—except two slatted windows in the garage door that look like eyes. I can't tell if we're living inside of a giant beast or staring one down.

Balboa pushes past me, snags his sloppy arm on the laundry rack, and collapses into his creaky mattress. He groans into his pillow and drops his cane to the floor. He looks like an overgrown child.

"Dad," I growl. "You promised."

He swears into his pillow before slowly rolling onto his back. The eyes staring back are bloodshot and unfocused. I sigh and squeeze my eyes shut. I'm so tired of this. How many more of these Friday nights can I withstand? When I open my eyes again—there, right in front of me, as if he truly is a five-year-old who believes that I won't catch him—my dad pulls a Jack Daniel's flask from his jacket pocket and tries to take a swig. It makes me want to scream. I snatch the bottle out of his hand, open the garden door, and chuck it as far as I can. I hear it crash against a neighbor's wall before falling into the dirt. Coffee-colored whiskey has soaked into his white shirt. He doesn't bother to wipe it away. The heavy stench of alcohol fills our garage.

"You promised," I say, again. "You've always said it's because you witnessed a murder on the trains . . . but that's not the real reason, is it?"

His dark brown face hardens. I feel like I'm staring at a rigid mahogany mask, taunting me with its silence.

"Dad, tell me." I squeeze his hand and realize his fingers are trembling. It makes my heart shudder, and I swallow hard.

Balboa digs his head back into the pillow. He closes his eyes, and it takes me a few seconds to realize his lips are moving. I can barely hear his words over the renters' footsteps above. I crouch closer. The concrete feels icy against the bare skin along my ripped jeans, sending shivers down my legs, and I wrap an arm around my knees to keep from running away.

"When I was young, I was desperate to come to San Francisco," he says, in a scratchy slurring voice. "In the Philippines I come from big family. And there was never enough for everyone. So, when you are desperate, when you will give *everything* for something in return—you give away too much. You make deals with beautiful devils. Anak, I do not want you to ride the trains because I do not want them to steal what is not theirs. Please listen to your father. I'm afraid to lose you." A tear escapes down the side of his cheek and hangs stubbornly on his jaw before falling. He still refuses to open his eyes, as if it's too painful to look at me. Arms resting at his sides, body deathly still—his corpse-like image makes my throat knot.

"Dad," I whisper, unsure of what his story even means. "You're not going to lose me. I'm right here."

An Our Lady of Guadalupe candle sits near his bed, so I light the flame. Every morning at dawn, he diligently surrounds it with bright purple agapanthus flowers and orange nasturtium petals. Flowers that always manage to grow even in the poorest soil. I always appreciate how the Virgin Mary's arms are open and outstretched—like she's always there for a hug if you need her. But even she can't turn back time. These petals are already shriveled and rotting.

I want to grill my father for more details. What exactly did he trade? And he doesn't really mean a devil, does he? It's true, he grew up as a devoted Catholic in the Philippines, and he's not great at expressing himself with English as his second language. But devils in the subway, what the hell am I supposed to think of that?

Slowly, his hand releases mine, and labored snoring fills our makeshift sanctuary. I sit by his side, mesmerized by our Mother Mary candle—lit bright for Mom, for him, for everyone who's feeling just as lost as we are. For everyone who is searching for *more*. And I know, even as he's warned me to stay away from the trains, there's something deep in the tunnels that we need to face if we want to break this curse.

❧ CHAPTER 5 ❧

Balboa always sings a kundiman while he's shaving, crooning to his own reflection in the mirror as he swipes a sharp blade across his chin—and I'm not talking Gillette razors, I'm talking a blade sharpened to perfection. A blade he keeps tucked away in his boot for emergencies. A similar blade lies hidden in my backpack, because there's no way my father would let me wander San Francisco alone at night without a chaperone—even if that chaperone is a blade I've named Miss Marybeth.

I only know a miniscule fraction of Tagalog (yes, shame shame), but my dad has sung that kundiman love song enough times for me to know the lyrics backward and forward. It's called "Dahil Sa Iyo," and back in 1961, Nat King Cole came to Manila and sang it in Tagalog instead of English. It blew my dad away, hearing a Filipino ballad sung by *the* Nat King Cole. Like something in his own language was worth sharing with the whole wide world.

I wish he'd tell me more about his homeland.

Hell, I wish he'd tell me why we're sinking further and further into debt.

With the secrets he spilled last night, I need more answers.

As the sun begins to peek through our slatted garage windows, I pretend to sleep. My dad sings to himself in the mirror, the usual kundiman. With all his rambling about deals with the devil and Six mentioning a debt,

I refuse to blindly wait for him to tell me what's wrong. What if he's been gambling? He obviously already has trouble with addiction—what if he's taken it one step further? What if I can stop him from making an even bigger mess? I need to know why we're falling behind on my mom's medical payments when he says that he's working a full-time job. The rent payments are taking care of the property tax, house repairs, and funeral expenses. I'm taking on as many house-painting gigs as I can get, so I'm able to cover my own expenses and save a bit for when Stella breaks down. But somehow, we're *losing* money. I've seen the overdue statements. It's just not adding up.

The moment Balboa closes the garage door, I leap out of bed. I wrangle my arms into my backpack straps—all the extra clothes I'll need for Chen's Painting Service on this fine Saturday.

It's not hard to follow him. I keep a block between us, ducking below trash bins when it seems like he'll turn around. But he doesn't turn back; he's only ever trudging forward. At the station, my boots clamber down the stone steps until I'm deep below the earth, sucking in stale air and listening to the whirl of ticket turnstiles.

I pull a shimmering blue-and-white ticket from the machine. Dampened sunlight streams in at the far end of the platform where the concrete opens into air. Behind me, people speak in Spanish, Chinese, English, Hindi, and all sorts of languages mushed together. Balboa hovers a few yards away, far enough to not notice me with an inevitable hangover pulsing inside his head. My heart thuds when the sign flashes SAN FRANCISCO AIRPORT TRAIN: ONE MINUTE. I stop listening to the cacophony of voices and the rustling of wings.

Instead, I'm listening for the train. I'm trying to feel its rumble in my bones.

When I was eight—before my dad came to live with my mom and me—I played this game where I tried to see how close I could get to the train as it ripped through the station. The conductors hated it. My mom freaked out on multiple occasions. But every time I was down here, I always ached to get as close as possible to that roaring wind.

Now, I feel that same urge thrilling through my veins. My eyes electric, my lungs savoring the intoxicating smell of metal burning bright. Wait—wait until the train comes howling into the station; wait, pressed up to that yellow warning line, until I'm only steps away from the roaring hot metal. I feel as if it's a wild horse that I can snatch hold of and swing myself atop of in one daring leap. The train's wake shoves me back, and I hold my ground against the wind, hold my eyes open to the silver rushing blur, hold on to the heartbeat hammering in my chest. I don't even flinch.

And then, the doors open.

Hot air blows out with a flurry of passengers going about their boring lives at Balboa Park station. Their hurried footsteps add more layers of grime and scuffs to the tile floors. I swallow down the pulse pounding in my throat. Every day these trains race below our city, nothing more than metal and electricity.

I hover on the platform and watch as soon-to-be travelers board the airport-bound train. They wedge themselves into the narrow blue vinyl seats, balancing suitcases and backpacks on their laps, cursing the fact that they brought too many pairs of shoes and books they'll never actually read on their beachside adventure. A pang of envy rumbles deep inside my gut. What would it be like to have the freedom to go where I want, to follow my dreams?

A kid stares up at me when I stagger back from the yellow line. He saw, of course. In vain, I try to tamp down my wind-whipped hair. He tugs on my paint-splattered backpack, and his mother doesn't notice.

"What did that feel like?" he says, little kid mouth agape.

"Like I was flying."

He smiles.

"But don't try it. It's dangerous." I wink. I really shouldn't have winked. The last thing I need to do is encourage a seven-year-old to do harebrained stunts. But I can't stop the adrenaline flooding into my chest. And I lied. It feels less like flying and more like I've jumped off a cliff into the roaring wind and I'm trusting that I'll have wings.

It is dangerous. One wrong step and I'd be clobbered by 110 tons of metal.

Trust me, no one who knows me would ever call me a daredevil. I'm actually known as the Responsible One. The one who took care of her mother all through sophomore year of high school while she was battling breast cancer. The one who didn't go away to college or travel abroad because too many people needed her here. I promise I'll always keep those two steps between me and death. I swear it.

It's just—I don't know what makes me want to leap into that blur of blue and silver. It feels like I could leave this all behind and wake up somewhere else entirely. Somewhere brighter, bolder. It's almost like there's a wild heartbeat under the iron and steel, and all I need to do is reach out and grab the reins.

A horn blares.

I jump aboard before the doors slide shut, and the train shoots forward through the maze of tunnels twisting under San Francisco. I hide behind a thankfully large man and scan around his shoulder to see where my dad is sitting. Correction, standing. Leaning hard on his cane, but not wobbling an inch on this bumpy train. He stands beside the exit door on the opposite end of the car. The minutes tick by. Am I more nervous about him catching me on a BART train—or about finally finding out the truth? As we wait for the next station, my eyes roam across my fellow passengers. It calms my hammering heartbeat to imagine how I'd sketch their faces. Reality flips on full blast: the kid snoring beside me with a face like melting candle wax, the old man stuffing French fries in his mouth, making my stomach growl from no breakfast.

And a voice.

"Dahil sa iyo!" The Filipino words come swaggering down the aisle, an aisle so thick with passengers, I can barely see who's singing.

But I don't need to see.

I know his voice.

It's the Sap Master himself.

My dad sings a wicked kundiman.

But why is he serenading an entire train car? I inch closer, still out of his range of sight among the crush of passengers. My legs wobble as the train curves underground, and I cling to a metal pole to keep from falling. Dried paint sticks under my nails. It's been so long since I've walked on a train that my knees tremble with the effort.

Still, the song lures me across.

Dahil sa iyo . . .

Because of you . . .

His words come softly now, sweetly melancholy. His rich honey voice fades into the sound of brakes squealing against metal rails—*dahil sa iyo, nais kong mabuhay.* "Because of you, I want to live." Something isn't right—this isn't the way he sings when he shaves in the mirror. His voice sounds mournful, broken at the edges.

A chill drips down my spine as I push faster through the crowd, the lonely words echoing in my ears. Is this really my father? It's his voice, that much I know; but I've never heard this pain crackling down his throat. I shoulder through the crush of passengers blocking my way.

A flash of movement up ahead. His eagle cane, his shiny Elvis hair slipping away from the crowd toward the dark shadows. The train car's connecting doors creak open. A blast of roaring wind pierces my ears. Am I the only one to hear it? None of the passengers flinch.

"Dad," I say. "Dad, wait!"

The glass doors separating the two train cars begin to slide shut. I still can't see with the last two passengers blocking my way. Through the crevice between their elbows, I catch my dad's eagle cane as it disappears behind the doors. Fog swirls on the glass, and a spark of cobalt flashes across steel, rippling out like dewy spiderwebs.

"Hey, how about an 'excuse me'?" a bald man grumbles as I shove past his shoulder.

I yank open the doors.

The heavy plexiglass slides open and leads into a space that reminds me of an old phone booth. An icy blast slaps my skin, as if the conductor has cranked the AC to max capacity. But that's never the case on a BART train. It's always too hot. Always too many people breathing in your ear, elbows out and sweat stains under armpits.

My breath leaves a mist on the glass, and I touch my fingers to the water droplets to make sure they're real. A whiff of my dad's coconut aftershave, his cracked leather jacket. He was here a moment ago. The two accordion walls crunch together as the train lurches to a full stop. It wouldn't be able to turn inside the dark tunnels without these flimsy rubber walls bending with the curve. I don't stay long. There's nothing like imagining the train splitting into pieces while I'm standing on the bridge connecting the cars.

My eyes frantically scan the passengers' faces before the doors open at Daly City station. Not-my-father, not-my-father. No! No slicked-back hair, no eagle cane, no leather jacket. Not on this train. It wouldn't have been possible for him to push his way through all these passengers to the exit.

The conductor gives one final call.

Doors closing.

A warning beep blares into the tunnel.

"Dad?" I holler into the train.

Heads snap in my direction as if I'm a lost toddler. My cheeks redden at the sudden attention. I'm too old to be a little girl calling for her father. But I'm not worried about myself—I'm worried about *him*.

Before the doors slide shut, I gaze up at the ratty pigeons clinging to the ledges of the train station even though they've added spikes to scare them away. The train starts to speed down the tunnel in a blur of blue and silver. It scatters newspapers and feathers into the air.

In all the magic tricks, a dove always disappears and reappears.

We all know what really happens to the dove.

That will not be my father.

⁂ CHAPTER 6 ⁂

can't afford to miss a day of work.

So after about twenty-seven unanswered phone calls, I hightail it to Chen's latest house in the Haight and chase away my questions with a million brushstrokes. My dad has been keeping secrets from me for ten years—he's not going to give them up so easily now. I need to—

"Hurry it up, Ruby! Some of us are starving for McMuffins." Diego stares up at me as I'm perched on the top ladder rung. Paint fumes clog up my lungs, and my biceps are begging for a break. From this high, I have the perfect view of the thick man bun knotted atop his head. The skeleton tattoos on his deep brown skin are covered over with white-splattered cloth.

"You can't hurry a masterpiece," I say, waving my paintbrush at him like a magic wand. White paint is so thickly caked on my fingers that I'll have to scrub them bloody to get it off.

"Mamacita, it's white and more white."

"You'll see the brushstrokes if you don't blend the roller and the edging together perfectly."

"This Ruby—she always does her best work. Even if it's all white paint," Chen says as he tucks an envelope full of twenty-dollar bills into my open backpack. I nod at him, grateful that he's never once tried to short me. He smiles, and the deep wrinkles under his eyes lighten for a moment. From this height, I can see all the gray streaked through his thinning hair. Chen used to bring me on board as my mom's assistant. She was a master at trompe l'oeil–imitation brick, herringbone, sponge press. Now, I'm desperate for money. Now, white is my new palette.

"There's only one way to breakfast," I holler at Diego, nodding toward the bucket of eggshell white. Diego rollers like his life depends on it. Oh, the things you can get a man to do if you promise breakfast sandwiches. I'm just thankful he hasn't brought up the fact that I ghosted him at his Friday night art gallery.

When we've finally packed up Chen's truck, Diego and I sit on the stoop to catch our breath. The truck is piled to the brim with all the spare paint cans and canvas sheeting he reuses over and over for each job. Ancient dried paint flakes off the fabric's creases. Chen waves goodbye before driving up a dizzying San Francisco hill. His truck sputters once, sending a plume of exhaust into the overcast sky.

"Breakfast!" Diego hollers as he slips into a fresh T-shirt. I catch a glimpse of long-ago scars on his abdomen. I've never asked, but I know there are secrets he carries, too.

Neither of us touches today's paycheck. We need it to pay the bills. Instead, we scrounge our pockets for enough spare change for McMuffins. I know it's horrible for me, but it's warm and cheap, and I need the calories. Frozen eggs be damned, I could eat three of those. Hooray for dollar menus and all-day McDonald's breakfast. T-minus two blocks to go.

Diego starts to croon the lyrics to "Ruby Tuesday" as we stroll along.

"Not you, too. I don't think I can handle all the crooning old men in my life." My stomach twists at the thought of my dad's forlorn kundiman. Call back, please call back. I glance down at my phone, and still nothing.

"I'm twenty, not seventy," Diego says. "Get it straight, or we're no longer friends."

"The Beatles are old, and I still love them."

"That's not helping," he grumbles. "Plus, it's The Rolling Stones, not The Beatles."

"You're not old, anyway. I'd murder you for your eyelashes. Happy?"

He flutters his eyelashes at me and nearly topples off the narrow curb, as usual, pretending to be a ballerina while traffic zooms by. I have to resist the urge to tell him to be careful.

"Miss Ruby, I'd be much happier when you finally decide to apply to art school and stop wasting your talents on eggshell white."

"I will. So quit pestering me!"

"When?"

"When my dad . . ."

Diego stares me down with those ridiculously gorgeous eyelashes. He knows there's no "when" written in my brain. How can I possibly apply to something as wasteful as art school when we already have a mountain of debt? How can I even talk about my dad's alcoholism, without pity filling Diego's eyes? So I don't say anything.

"Take it from someone older and wiser–"

"Hold on, you said twenty wasn't old?"

"I'm only going to bring this up once–because your business is your business, *chica*–but I wish my eighteen-year-old self knew not to give up his Friday nights for someone who needed to be carrying their own shit."

"Are you done with the lecture?" The words snap from my lips before I have a chance to school them.

He sighs and starts walking toward the McDonald's down the street. Paint chips flake off his jeans and flutter into the sewer drain. This is why

I shouldn't have friends who ask questions. They'll never understand how everything will crumble without me holding it up. The corners of my eyes sting as I take a shaky breath. Think about breakfast, think about now, think about the dirty pigeons dodging my footsteps.

Relief washes over me when my phone starts vibrating in my back pocket.

It's the Sap Master himself. Finally. I need to know what happened on the train. His message reads:

"Embarcadero West. 117th floor. Come soon, Cutie."

Cutie?

It makes my heart stop.

My dad never says the word "cutie." It makes us both want to barf when we hear it. He's not cute; I'm not cute; we're annoyed by all the people whose sole adjective is "cute." The train that's about to hit you is, like, so cute! We always said it would be our code word in case one of us was in trouble. It means "come now!" Or maybe "run away now"? We probably should have specified that part.

Come soon, Cutie.

Something's wrong.

My feet freeze in the middle of the sidewalk, and a pedestrian nearly barrels into my shoulder. Diego doesn't even bother asking what's wrong.

"Where?" he says.

He's probably one of the few people in my life who knows how many times I've had to run home for "family emergencies." He never asks questions. Only: *where do you need to go?* He always hands me his phone, and I type in an address from anywhere in the city. Diego's boyfriend foots his rideshare bill. It's one of the few bits of "charity" we'll accept, and it's only because it's practical in emergencies.

"Thank you." I have to delete and retype the letters, my fingers are shaking so terribly.

When I hand it back, he stares down at the unfamiliar address.

"Embarcadero?" he says.

"Don't ask."

And he doesn't.

I should let him ask. Diego offered me a ride, didn't he?

I try to stretch out the tension in my neck from all those hours rollering the ceiling. My family drama isn't anyone's business. Friends or not. Blood comes first. That's what my dad always says.

One time, Balboa let it slip that his boss ran the business out of Embarcadero. He's never said what business. He always says he works in transportation. He says it like the mob says they work in waste management. Like he could be a mechanic or a ticket operator. But I know mechanics don't get bruises on their fists.

§

Before I know it, the car drops me in front of a steely skyscraper.

Tall towers crowd around me, forcing me to crane my neck back. It's daylight, but the sun can't reach through the spires of concrete and glass. Shadows swallow the sidewalk as I hurry my steps toward the Embarcadero West tower. Seagulls scavenge a nearby garbage bin and shred trash with their sharp beaks. Two of the biggest gulls start a fight, and their ungodly squawking chases me down the street. The Ferry Building's bells chime furiously as fog rolls in from the ocean.

Dad, what mess have you gotten yourself into? I shouldn't have let him disappear on the train this morning.

When I walk into the building, the security guard doesn't bother to hide his disgust. Let's be real, I came from a painting gig, so ratty sneakers, faded jeans, and an old Hello Kitty turtleneck seemed appropriate. It was also laundry day. I'm also dying for a shower.

I don't belong here. The security guard knows it; everybody living in this skyscraper knows it. The lobby itself is bigger than my entire house. A statue of Achilles rests in the far corner, and jagged crystal chandeliers dangle overhead. Who in their right mind would install crystal spikes in a city of earthquakes? Rich fools.

"Hi, there," I say as I approach the security desk.

The guard stares.

"Uh, I have an appointment?"

"With whom?"

"That's a good question. The text only gave me a number. 117th Floor."

"That's it?"

"That's it."

He stands there for a minute like he's not going to let me in. Like he doesn't believe me. I wouldn't believe me if a scraggly person came up in my hood with just a number. No name, nothing. The sweat pools in my palms, and I grip my paint-spattered bag.

"Miss, I don't have time for–

"Look, it's important." My hand smacks against the marble ledge. "Can you just do your job and let me up to the 117th floor?"

Judging by the look he gives me, that was perhaps the wrong thing to say. The security guard picks up the phone, and for a moment I think he might call the cops. My dad told me once that courtesy and manners go a long way, but it's hard to be polite when your dad's in trouble, and you're hungry, and all you've eaten all day is string cheese because that's all you had in your backpack. Because you didn't have time for McMuffins because it's an emergency. Because that's life. Good luck, *Cutie*.

"Name?" he says.

I swallow down my frustration and fear and tell him. He leans into the receiver.

"Madame, there's a guest here to see you. Her name is Ruby Santos."

He nods at me and points toward the elevators without another word.

"Can you tell me her name? Madame . . . ?"

"M," he says.

"M, like the letter *M*? Like Madame M?"

The elevator doors ding open, and I rush over to them because who knows when they might slide shut. Black velvet covers the elevator walls, and the bronze ceiling has a phoenix unfurling its wings etched in gold. I hit the 117th floor. OK, I'll be honest, I hit all the numbers to slow down my heartbeat before I have to face whatever is up there, but only 117 lights up. I try to rip the Hello Kitty label off my turtleneck, but no such luck. Seriously, Ruby, why must you inflict your fashion choices on the world? Not now, think, just think, prepare for . . . for what? I try to straighten out my hair before I meet this infamous M, but the golden brass distorts my reflection.

The metal box lifts me 117 stories into the sky.

I feel the gravity in my gut, creeping into my throat.

Oh, Dad, what have you done?

The doors yawn open like a dark beast.

And I step into a room filled with silver stars.

⟨ CHAPTER 7 ⟩

t's a dim entryway, all cold hard marble. Spiked star-shaped lights dangle from the ceiling on invisible wires. It looks like it's raining light. It would be gorgeous if it wasn't so unsettling. A shiver runs down my neck, seeping all the way down to my toes. No one greets me, except two grim guards who stand frozen on either side of the elevator doors. They're dressed in satin suits, blending into the shadows. A cacophony of voices echoes down a high-arched hallway, but I can't pick out the words. Slithering snakes and shooting stars are carved into the thick marble archway. This elevator is the only way in and the only way out.

The metal doors slide shut behind me before I have a chance to step back into safety.

Breathe. Get in, get out. Where's Dad?

I expect one of the guards to escort me to where I'm supposed to go, but they leave me standing under the spiked stars. I take a step forward, and another, and another, my paint-spattered tennis shoes squeaking along the polished marble. Still, no one comes for me. The candlelit entryway leads into a grand hall, where color and light come blaring like a movie flicked on in a dreamless midnight.

I've officially stepped into *The Great Gatsby*. Never have I seen such glittering fringe and silk and sculpted honeyed skin. It reminds me of

Diego's art opening with his fashionista friends, but amped up to full blast decadence. If I felt out of place at the art show, I feel like a Hello Kitty–obsessed alien here. I glance down at my ratty sleeves and try to tamp down the panic. You're not here to party; you're here to find Dad. I hurry into the crush of laughing, drinking bodies, as a woman in a leopard-print dress almost spills her champagne on me. Pomegranate seeds float on top, reminding me of bloodied teeth.

I'm too short for this. I can't see over the crowd to find my dad's slicked-back Elvis hair, his eagle cane. I need a bird's-eye view of the place; I need–whoa . . . I crane my neck back. We're in a skyscraper, not even on the top floor. So how is there a basilica dome? I gaze closer at the ceiling and realize it's all an illusion of gold and ivory paint and curving alabaster. Clever lighting and an artist's touch. My mouth drops as I crane my neck farther back, to see how they managed to paint the ceiling in wonderous three-dimension.

A shoulder knocks into mine.

Shoot, I've jammed up the flow of bodies shimmying across the grand hall. A guard pins me with his glare. Everyone acts like they've been here before. A series of smaller alcoves surround the hall, like we're inside a cathedral. Except instead of statues of saints, each alcove showcases a table covered in black satin. Lamplight illuminates the contents on top. I slow my gait, force myself to roam the tables while panic pulses behind my eyes. This is . . . a marketplace? Currencies from around the world float through the air on whispered breath. Guests pick up items, examine them, and then an unnamed servant rushes out from the shadows to draft an agreement. Maps in thick gilded frames line the walls. Peculiar maps, maps with golden ink connecting points across the world.

"Enjoying yourself?" a woman's raspy voice hisses into my ear. My whole body jolts. Her eyes stare at my hands as if there should be marks there. Without looking, I reach for the closest object on the table. Anything to distract her from the fact that I don't belong here.

"Uh, yes, these pieces are quite—"

It takes me one long, startling second to realize that the thing I picked up is a gun. Cold hard metal, with a silencer on the barrel. This whole table is smothered with guns of every shape and size and style. Ones that would be too heavy for me to even hold upright.

"Oh my god." I drop the gun and back away. It clatters against the polished marble floor.

The woman howls with laughter. She's familiar—short blue hair tucked behind her ears, a silver piercing that glitters under the dim starlight. I rush out of the alcove, and she doesn't follow. I can still hear Six's laughter hounding me. I need a moment alone, time to catch my breath. Time to think. To come up with a plan. For Dad.

There—an alcove with only a couple people standing in front of the table. My shoes squeal on the glossy marble, but the couple doesn't turn around. Their eyes are fixed on a wall where a single painting hangs behind glass. My curiosity pulls me forward; there's something unique—and oddly familiar—about the brushstrokes. Postimpressionist, that's for certain. Like it could have been snipped from my mom's Vincent van Gogh book. We always talked about saving up to visit the Van Gogh Museum in Amsterdam. To see firsthand his mesmerizing pinks and yellows, his startling Japanese blue ink. In this painting, a whole forest landscape is lit from within. Brushstrokes that won't hold still, as if the painting is coming alive before you, over and over with each sidelong glance.

A notecard reads: STONE STEPS IN THE GARDEN OF THE ASYLUM

No.

No, this can't be true. I must be the one going insane. This can't be a real van Gogh from when he was at the asylum in France. It belongs in a museum. It can't—

It must be a reproduction. An art forgery. An imitation. Or maybe these people are rich enough to host a private showing of his work, on loan from the museum in Amsterdam? I inch closer to the glass-covered frame, until my nose is practically touching. I've never seen a van Gogh in person before, but it looks so convincing. Those unbelievable brushstrokes.

A man clears his throat behind me, and I nearly knock my head on the glass. He holds a white slip of paper that glows against the darkness.

"The bidding starts at fifty-six million. The seller also allows a comparable trade from your line, but it must link to Tokyo or Amsterdam. He has no interest in other portals." The man pulls out a gold fountain pen, ready to jot down my request.

"From my what? I mean . . . I'm not . . . Sorry, I need a moment."

I back away slowly, my knees shaking. How in the hell is my dad involved with this? I need to find him. *Focus, Ruby.* In the grand hall, I catch sight of a hallway directly opposite the entrance. No guards. Good. Maybe there's a ladies' room where I can think for a second without eyes crawling all over me. I leave the alcoves behind and hurry into the empty hallway, where illuminated portraits line the walls. They're mostly white dudes who look spectacularly proud of themselves. Under each one are the same two names: MONTGOMERY and EMBARCADERO, but with different numbers attached. MONTGOMERY I. MONTGOMERY II. MONTGOMERY III. EMBARCADERO I. EMBARCADERO II, like there's a special succession line. The faces share the same dark wavy hair, same blue eyes, same wide lips.

At the end of the hall stands a man—a real live man—with a face like the rest.

He wears a midnight blue suit that makes his serious white face stand in contrast to the darkness. Almost like a Caravaggio painting. I forget to breathe. All I can think about are my charcoals and pastels. Which obviously shouldn't be my first thought in this dangerous place, but I can't help it. He looks lost in thought, framed in the perfect light to capture his long chiseled face. My mind starts to soak in the details, memorizing them for later.

"What are you doing here, Ruby?" His voice suddenly rumbles down the hall.

It feels like a painting has just woken up and addressed me.

A painting who knows my name?

He strides down the long hallway, his shoes silent on the Persian carpet. I should flee, but I know him . . . somehow? Concern flashes across his face, like spilled ink muddying up his sapphire eyes. Civic Center station—*the boy who'd caught my train*. He's much taller than I remember.

"Are you Embarcadero or Montgomery?" I whisper.

He arches an eyebrow and smiles, unexpectedly. When he smiles, his whole face changes, like a marble exterior has melted away. And then his face snaps back to stone. He tugs on his blazer with its perfectly ironed sleeves—like his stone expression, the suit is another mask to slip on.

"I'm Montgomery," he says.

"The fourth?"

"You're a quick one."

"Bullet train, that's me."

"Then I need you to listen very carefully. You shouldn't be here. Leave now, before she sees you."

"But my dad . . ."

"Balboa will figure a way out of this. *You* won't."

"Excuse me? You don't even know me."

Montgomery takes my hand like he's known me forever and drags me down the hallway toward the elevators. I shake out of his grip and grind my heels into the rug.

"I'm not going anywhere without my dad."

"Can you stop being stubborn as hell for one second, and–"

"How do you know me?" I dig my nails into his palm, and he finally stops. "Were you following me on that Civic Center train?"

"There isn't time. Sneak out, now."

"She already knows I'm here."

Wait–I've seen his face, even before Civic Center station. A hazy memory forms out of the fog, from when my mom was sick. Almost two years ago. A cute delivery boy who I kept hoping would drop off the pineapple fried rice. We'd had so many nights where we were too exhausted to cook. I remember swinging open the door, hoping it was him again. He'd hook his chin on the top carton to keep everything from falling and always brought extra mint-and-basil spring rolls. I wouldn't forget his face, not after I'd felt so guilty for crushing on a boy while my mom was fighting cancer. Who is this stranger? He can't be a delivery boy if he belongs in this grand gallery of Montgomerys and Embarcaderos.

"You were the one who brought the pineapple fried rice," I say.

"You actually remember that?"

"Why–"

Footsteps snag on the rug at the end of the hall, and he rushes me toward the elevators, back into the grand hall.

"I promise to answer all your questions if you leave right now," he whispers.

For a moment, I stare into his bright ocean eyes, and all I see is sincerity. It's not enough though—my dad is in danger. Real danger. He called me here. I have to find him. As I pull out of Montgomery's grasp, another voice startles us.

"I see you've found our lovely guest."

A pale woman in a black dress stands at the center of the room. Her hair is tied up in a loose bun fastened with a dagger. It's startling how much she reminds me of John Singer Sargent's *Madame X* painting. I'd read once that the painting sparked a scandal at the Paris Salon. Madame's graceful neck, her pale bare shoulders on display. The way she turns away from the viewer, daring you to look.

Now, everyone in the grand hall turns to stare at us.

I've never been more painfully aware of my ratty Hello Kitty sweatshirt and paint-splattered jeans.

The woman glides flawlessly toward me, with my father's eagle cane in her fist.

"So you've finally arrived," she purrs the words, tongue sticky with delight. As if she's caught a bird in her claws—and I am that bird.

⟨ CHAPTER 8 ⟩

"Didn't your father teach you that it's rude to keep your host waiting?" she says.

"You're Madame—"

"Call me M."

"As in . . . *Em*. You're Embarcadero the III?"

She smiles, all teeth and crimson-painted lips. Skin so pale, she must spend most of her days inside this skyscraper, never bothering to associate with the street rats far below. Madame Em is near my mother's age but with none of her honey-bread warmth.

"And you—*Ruby Josephine Santos*—do not belong here." She leads me toward the elevator doors. Montgomery backs away from us, not a trace of concern left on his face. He blends in with the statuesque guards stationed in the shadows.

"Wait, but he called me here. My dad—"

"Is a fool. Merritt, bring him." She snaps her fingers and a burly guard rolls a slumped body in a wheelchair through the crowd of onlookers. One of its wheels squeaks against sticky spilled champagne on the floor.

"Dad?" I step forward, but Em links her arm through mine as if we're schoolgirls.

"He's coming, darling. In the meantime, we should have a little chat."

The elevator doors slide open, and we step inside its golden cage. Merritt rolls my father's body inside; his slack knees knock together. Madame Em punches the button for the ground floor. The doors start to slide shut, but a hand juts into the crack. The doors ding open again, and Montgomery's chiseled face stares Merritt down. The resemblance between them is so startling that they must be family.

"I'll take him," Montgomery says.

Merritt gives him a knowing smirk and grips harder onto the wheelchair handles. Neither moves as the seconds tick by and the silent crowd watches. Merritt is, undeniably, more built, but with the determination sparking in Montgomery's eyes, it's a fight I wouldn't want to bet on.

"Do as your brother says," Em commands, coolly.

Merritt whispers something sharp into Montgomery's ear before stepping out. Finally, the bronze doors shut, and I can breathe again without all those staring eyes.

"What did you do to my dad?" I say.

Em laughs. "Darling, he did this to himself."

"Balboa!" I grab his slack hand, but he doesn't squeeze back.

"Your father won't hear you through his painkillers."

The floors tick downward, 117, 116, 115, as we plunge back down to Earth. The phoenix wings shimmer overhead, reflecting our tangled bodies on its feathers. My heart hammers inside my chest, but it somehow feels safer in here with Montgomery instead of Merritt. Even if he only stands in silence.

"I'll be blunt," Madame Em says. "Your father owes us a great debt. He has been paying his debt through the years; however, in his current state, he is useless to us. One of my men found him on the train like this when he was supposed to be completing a job. A very *delicate* job. Unfortunately, this is not the first time. Nor the second. The last incident, he reconciled his mistake with your house as collateral."

"Wait, collateral? My dad wouldn't trade our house . . ."

"If there's one thing you should know about me—I am *not* forgiving." She leans closer, and her charcoal eyes feel like thorns against my throat. "His debt will be paid. Your house has been forfeit due to his incompetence. He's useless to me if he is drunk or drugged on the job. It should come as no great surprise to you that your father has made foolish choices. Consider this your notice. You have one week to vacate your house before my men come for it."

"But where will we live?"

"That is none of my concern."

The elevator doors snap open, and I stumble into the desolate lobby.

"It was my mom's house," I say. "It's *my* house!"

"And he is your father. If you would rather that he pays his debt with broken bones, then that can be arranged."

A blacked-out Mercedes rolls up to the curb, and I'm nearly blinded by the glare on the glass skyscrapers along Market Street. Reality hits me in the gut, thick and heavy. I'm going to be sick. Brakes squeal as a white limousine jolts to a stop at the streetlight. The seagulls are gone, leaving trash and French fries spewed on the street corner. I plant my palm on the shiny black hood of the Mercedes to steady myself. It leaves behind a sweaty handprint, the lines in my palm leading to a barren future. Montgomery gently hoists my father's body into the backseat. His head hangs backward, eyes fluttering open and closed for a moment. *Was it worth it, Dad? Was our house worth the painkillers?* Montgomery walks around to the driver's seat and slips dark sunglasses over his eyes. I can't read his expression.

"Wait! How much does my dad owe?" I grab Em's arm, and it feels like I'm clinging to a statue.

"Four more years."

"I asked how much."

Madame Em twirls my dad's eagle cane, eyeing it as if she's debating whether to steal it. A smile plays along her lips.

"Darling, it's not a number—it's *time*," she says. "He signed a contract to work for fourteen years. He has four years remaining."

"I can work."

She barks out a laugh. "You don't know what he does. You don't know how much he has paid to keep you away from this life."

"I can learn. You can't take Mom's house. Please . . ."

With that, I feel Montgomery's firm grip around my shoulders as he leads me into the backseat. I shove my shoulders into the plush leather to keep from screaming. Madame Em spins my father's eagle cane and disappears into her skyscraper.

The air tastes thick, stale and drowning.

I throw open the windows and let the San Francisco clamor fill my ears.

Even with the painkillers, my dad flinches when we jolt over a giant pothole. His limbs splay out at all the wrong angles. His hand instinctively reaches for his hip. I know his joints have been giving him grief. Bone grinding on bone. The doctors had recommended surgery, a hip replacement to combat the arthritis. But we're still paying off my mom's cancer bills. We kept saying we'd hold off for another year. Save up. Almost there.

Almost.

But never there.

"We're here." Montgomery's voice jostles me from my thoughts.

My house. It's all we have left. I gaze at the lavender paint with white trim. My mom and I had painted the house all by ourselves, the two of us perched up on impossible ladders. She'd even planted delicate blue roses that I couldn't manage to keep alive. A decoy owl lives on the redwood tree in the back garden. This is the only home I've ever known.

Montgomery walks around to my father's door. I hurry to unbuckle my seatbelt.

"You don't have to . . ."

But he's already lifted my father's body out of the car and has started walking toward our doorstep. Montgomery grunts under the weight, but he doesn't complain. He's not as muscular as Merritt, tall and lean instead. When he starts to climb the stairs, I stop him.

"No, we have to use the garage door." I fish the keys from my backpack and fumble with the lock. My nerves zap through my fingertips. He's going to think we're nutjobs the second I open this door.

"You can leave him right here," I say. "Really. I've got it."

"I won't leave him in the street," he says with surprising tenderness— at least for an asshole whose business trades in broken bones and stolen houses.

"You're taking away our house. Now you care?"

"That was Em's choice, not mine."

"You just stood there, didn't you?"

Montgomery glances away, and I know I've stung him. Part of me wants to do worse. Part of me wants to rail at him. For being part of all the lies and letdowns. For letting this disaster happen, even if he warned me to run away. But at the end of the day, it's my dad who made the choice to trade away our house. Not Montgomery.

"You can't lift him," he says. "Let me carry him to his bed. It's the least I can do."

I sigh and push open the door. It opens only about halfway because of all the furniture crammed into our garage. Dining chairs and coat hangers jut into the narrow walkway. Books pile toward the ceiling, and a toaster balances on top.

"You know, we get earthquakes here," he says.

"Well, if I die in an avalanche of junk, you can be the first one to tell me I told you so."

"What's wrong with the upstairs?" He groans as he tries to maneuver my father's body through the mess. His leg catches on a pile of art books, and I have to unsnag it before the whole stack falls on us.

"We had to rent out the upstairs to pay for my mom's bills...and apparently my dad's debts. It's temporary, OK."

It was meant to be temporary. Now, it's been almost a year of this mess.

Finally, the narrow walkway opens up to the laundry room, that is, my bedroom. A twin bed rests against the side of the washing machine. Stupid hopeful fairy lights twinkle overhead. Paintings of ballerinas cut from an old Degas calendar hide the cracks in the drywall. My mom's old paintbrushes sit unused by my bed. I don't know why I keep them; they've turned hard as stone without use. I know she would have wanted me to keep painting, but when would I even have the time?

"I didn't realize it had gotten this bad," Montgomery says.

Everything is covered in dust, and the silverfish feast on our old books. I wonder if his skin is crawling. It's so much worse to see it through a stranger's eyes. A blush blooms along my neck. We're trying. We're trying so very hard.

We move farther back, past the concrete sink and hot plate. Past the giant furnace that heats the upstairs (but not our garage) to the twin bed that belongs to my father, wedged between the garden door and the antique upright piano.

"There. You can drop him there."

Montgomery rests my father's unconscious body on the bed.

When he stands back up, his head nearly hits one of the ceiling beams. I bet his claustrophobia has kicked in. I can see his Adam's apple bobbing as he gulps down a stale breath. I miss the high arched ceiling of our living room. I miss sunlight and curtains.

Montgomery glances at the old piano as if he's tempted to try the keys; instead, he starts toward the front door. I grab his sleeve, but he shakes me off like I'm a beetle clinging to his expensive blue blazer.

"Save your breath," he says. "I can't save your house. Once Em makes a decision, she doesn't turn back. She's already been lenient with your father. If it had been anyone else who'd broken the terms, she would have taken the house *and* broken his bones."

I take a shaky breath, bracing myself for the stupid thing I'm about to say next.

"What would it take to pay back his debt? Em said four years. I can do four years."

"You have no idea what you're asking. You don't want to do what he does."

"But I could, couldn't I?"

Montgomery sighs and sits down on my bed. It makes me cringe. What he must think of our house compared to the grandeur of their Embarcadero skyscraper. Marble and crystal and champagne and fireplaces and pomegranates—everything this place is not. He stares at the Gustav Klimt art book on my bed. It's open to *The Kiss* painting with its intimate golden lovers entwined. I quickly shove it under my pillow.

"What are you doing?" I say.

"There's nowhere else to sit, and I was starting to get spiders in my hair."

Before I can stop myself, I start to pluck the cobwebs from his black waves. I can't help it; I need to fix it. And for some strange reason, he lets me. His hair is so silky that I have to stop myself from being a creep. I shake the spiderwebs from my fingers, and we linger in silence for a moment longer. It's like we've stepped out of time to take a breath. I want the moment to stretch longer because I'm afraid of what comes next.

"Please, just tell me how to fix this," I whisper, even though my dad is passed out. "I can't lose everything. My mother's murals, our home, you don't know how much they mean to me."

He glances around at our depressing garage, until finally our eyes meet.

"Please," I say. "If the tables were turned, wouldn't you want to know how to stop your life from being ruined?"

"Ruby, I know you don't think this is a lucky break, but it is. Yes, you've lost the house, but the debt is done. Get him the hip surgery. Get out of the city. Start fresh."

"How could you possibly believe we can let go of this house? This is all we have. Don't you understand?"

He shakes his head.

"There's a whole world of possibility." His voice rises against the clatter of footsteps over our heads. "Don't go back to Embarcadero. I know it's hard, but you have to let go. Look around you—you're living in a *garage*."

Shame sucker punches me straight in the gut. Damn it, we're doing the best we can. What would he know about losing everything, about trying to survive? He can gaze out over the city in a glittering skyscraper. He was born a Montgomery in a long line of Montgomerys, and that's the way of the world. My dad and I, we scrape by and never get ahead. Start fresh? What a joke. It's impossible. An absolute lie.

"We're trying to survive." I rise up from the bed. "I'm trying to hold on to what's left."

"Sometimes you need to let go of the things holding you back. You're capable of so much more."

"Like making a deal with Em. Like . . . *jumping the train portals*. I can do it, too, can't I?"

Montgomery doesn't speak.

"Is it magic?" I say.

He sighs and stands up. Even though his body towers over mine, I hold my ground.

"Show me how." I don't even attempt to keep the begging out of my voice. It's our house on the line. Our future.

"I can't," he says.

"You can't, or you won't?"

"Your dad kept this world from you for a reason."

"My dad messed up, and now I have to fix it. Please, show me how to fix it."

He shakes his head and leaves through the cluttered hallway. The door swings open, and sunlight pierces through the whirlwind of dust. Montgomery gazes back, and I can't see his shadowed face with the light streaming in.

"When you open the doors between the trains," he says, "imagine where you want to go. Then, take the leap."

"That's it?" I holler.

But he disappears without another word.

⚹ CHAPTER 9 ⚹

My dad sleeps and sleeps, tossing in fitful dreams. I don't know what makes me do it, but I pull out a blank canvas and wipe away the dust. I squirt crusty oil paints onto a pallet and soak Mom's paintbrushes in hot water to loosen them up. I roll my shoulders and massage my wrists.

And then I grab a paintbrush.

We can't lose our house. There is no safety net—*I am the safety net*. Painting always helps clear my mind, and I need a plan. For three hours, I lose myself in the brushstrokes, trying to sap a little extra mileage from these worn-out brushes.

I try to paint from memory, try to mix the perfect emerald for our living room's jungle scene. Lush vines reaching for the ceiling. Curious elephants ready to spurt water at me. A toucan we called Tommy. My mom's murals made you feel like you could teleport into the jungle, the sea, wherever her mind wandered.

Maybe I can recreate it somewhere if we lose the house. The very thought sucks the air out of my lungs. *Lose the house. We're going to lose the house.* I gulp down the panic and force my fingers to keep moving. I have this stupid childish hope that if I paint, maybe Mom will send me a message from wherever she is now. Tell me how to keep from losing everything.

When I stand back and stare at my poor imitation, it only makes me angry again.

The green is wrong.

The elephants are stiff and stilted.

Tommy looks like he's trying to dodge a speeding windshield.

It's all wrong.

Where's the magic? Where's my mom's perfect brushstroke? Her paintings felt dreamy, alive, like a page out of a John Singer Sargent book. When she was my age, she volunteered at elephant sanctuaries in Thailand and taught English to kids in sunny rice paddies. She'd always told me that elephants and rhinos were disappearing at an alarming rate. The idea of extinction, the fact that a creature could never come back—it scared me, and still does. People say that elephants never forget, so I like to think that her painted elephants will never forget her, that *I'll* never forget her.

But my weak imitations are nothing compared to hers. I bend my crappy canvas in half until the wood frame snaps, the wet blues and greens and yellows smearing into each other. I throw it in the trash bin, where it belongs. I'm wasting precious time painting. I'm wasting my breath trying to talk to someone who is dead and gone.

Montgomery's wrong.

I can't dream up anything new.

This house is all we have left.

I need answers, and there's only one man who can tell me.

ဒ

For real, I didn't think a grown man could sleep this long. When he finally pushes himself up to his elbows *seventeen hours later*, guess who's glaring at his groggy face.

"What do you remember?" My voice is colder than the icebox between the trains.

"That you're my sunshine, my only sunshine, my Little Hamboorger."

"Cut the shit, Dad."

"Hoy, language! Ang tigas ng ulo mo."

"My shitty language is the last thing you should be worrying about right now. What. Do. You. Remember." I pace the room, my arms itching to grab something to break.

"I just woke up. Give me minute. Some coffee. Some tink-juice."

"You have no idea what happened yesterday, do you?"

He limps toward the toilet, painfully slow. I can't even watch. I want to rush over and give him a walking stick, but then I remember that Em stole his eagle cane. That greedy witch. Balboa shuffles through the medicine cabinet. A second later, he swings the bathroom door open.

"What did you do?" He shakes an empty pill bottle at me.

"Don't bother looking for your painkillers. They're gone."

"Susmariosep!" he groans.

"Don't you realize how addictive those are? You're already hooked on alcohol. Those are ten times worse!"

"I need those for pain."

"You know what Embarcadero and Montgomery need? Someone who does their job as promised."

He stares at me like I've said a holy incantation. Like I've called down Saint Anthony and Archangel Michael and the Knights of the Apocalypse, all in one foul breath.

"They said it's the last time they'll let you mess up a train job. They said . . . They said they're taking the house." At this my voice finally breaks, and I slump onto my bed. All the anger that's been fueling me for the past twenty-four hours finally drains from my body. What does any of it matter if they take away the house?

"I'll fix it." His body is already shaking without painkillers or alcohol to tide him over. He slumps onto the bed next to me and holds his head in his hands. Sweat smears onto his fingertips, and his gelled hair sprawls at jagged angles.

"Em said she doesn't forgive," I say.

"She doesn't," he mutters.

"I can find a way to pay it back. You need to show me how to jump the portals."

"Over my dead body will you work for those mga demonyo. You got a million doors, Ruby. Not this one!"

My dad snatches the coffee pot and limps out to the back garden. As I watch from the doorway, he slumps into the dirt beneath the redwood tree. He gulps cold coffee like there might be answers at the bottom of the pot.

But there's only one answer.

I steal his train pass and run out the door.

⁘ CHAPTER 10 ⁘

I let two trains streak past before I finally work up the nerve to board the next one headed toward the Embarcadero. It still reeks of day-old deodorant and smelly socks and someone eating seaweed crackers. Station by station, I inch closer to the heart of San Francisco. It's evening on a Sunday, so there's hardly anyone here, at least not compared to commute time. This will make what I'm about to do more discreet.

When you open the doors between the trains, imagine where you want to go. Then, take the leap.

Bastard made it sound so easy. For some people, maybe life is easy.

Embarcadero. I want to go to Embarcadero station. I close my eyes and hold my breath and wait for something to happen.

What actually does happen is that we pull into 24th Street Mission station, and a bunch of people push past me to board the train. One of them fills the space with a skunky weed aroma that makes me cough. This is impossible. I pace the train aisle and pull my navy coat more tightly around myself. This time, I left the Hello Kitty turtleneck at home and came prepared in my leather motorcycle boots.

I have to do something.

They'll take the house. And then we'll go from barely enough, to not enough, to never enough.

Couldn't my dad or Montgomery have at least given me the key to jumping the trains?

I swear under my breath, and an older Vietnamese woman clutches her purse. Wrinkles tighten around her eyes as she stares at my frenetic footsteps. I'm mumbling to myself, aren't I? We arrive at 16th Street Mission station. Four more stops until Embarcadero. There's no time.

I stand in front of the train doors and stare down my refection.

Ruby Josephine Santos, you can do this. *You are the safety net.*

A street performer hops aboard and blasts hip-hop music.

"Little help goes a long way!" he hollers into the train. His younger brother passes around a donation hat, while the boy dances Michael Jackson blended with acrobatics. He glides across the aisle, leaps and spins in his knockoff Nike sneakers. His locs twirl around him, and he seems free for a moment. He deserves Juilliard, not begging on the trains.

I can't concentrate with all this noise. I can't.

We pass Civic Center station.

Three more stops.

Shit.

I shove open the sliding doors and step inside the no-man's-land between the two trains. Please just give me a minute of muffled quiet. This closet-sized crevice between the train cars feels like my saving grace. All I hear is the train—its rumble and howl—and my own frantic heartbeat. It looks like a moving phone booth, except the word "saddle" pops into my brain. My knees and thighs tense as if I'm trying not to fall off of the back of a wild beast. Yes, "saddle," I like that. It makes it feel more real. I breathe in and imagine that I'm calling Embarcadero station. Like it's a real live beast to be called. I think about the day I'd once spent hours waiting there, wondering what my dad did for work, and now I'm so close to knowing, so close

I can reach out and smell the seagulls and hear the Ferry Building bells chiming deep down into the underground. All those hours waiting for my father stitched under my skin, soaked into my lungs.

Embarcadero.

When I touch the door handle that leads into the next train car, blue light sparks from my palm. Darkness presses in around me. Everything turns crisp icy cold, and I can barely push the air through my lungs. I can't see my reflection in the glass anymore. My shaky hand struggles to yank open the door. Sapphire streaks still swirl around my palms, and it burns like ice held against my skin for too long. Finally, I stumble forward into the crowded aisle, as the train jerks to a stop. The world spins and twists. As I try I shake off the dizziness, the conductor broadcasts the call for "Embarcadero station" through the speakers. At least I think he said Embarcadero. I don't have time to question it; the exiting doors are already sliding shut.

I make a run for it.

My boots hit concrete. Loud beeps squeal around me; the motion detectors hollering that a human body is caught in their metal muzzle. The conductor yells at me from the first car, but I can't really hear him. I did it. I really did it.

This is Embarcadero station.

Technically, I should be at Powell station right now.

I jumped clear across Powell and Montgomery stations and landed at Embarcadero. Two stops. That's almost two miles. It isn't much, but it's something. It's real. It's magic.

My magic.

I take a step—and fall down to my knees.

The dizziness threatens to spill the contents of my stomach onto the concrete. I rest my palm on the disgusting sidewalk, where thousands of footfalls touch daily. I need something to ground me. Something to stop the spinning. Pink bubble gum jams under my fingernail as I try and fail to scramble up. My teeth are chattering.

"Oye, lady, are you OK?" a man with a Spanish accent says from above me.

I want to say something, but the nausea claws at my throat.

The train slides away, preparing for its dive underwater toward the East Bay stations. My ears feel clogged shut, as if I've been riding the train underwater. I slouch back onto my ankles and take deep slow breaths.

"Fine," I say with as much of a smile as I can muster. "I'm not used to the trains."

The man nods and helps me to my feet. I force my legs to move, to take me toward the escalators. I'll feel better with some fresh air, not this sour underground. With each step, I find my strength returning. I hurry along Market Street, toward the Ferry Building and the smell of the sea.

I can jump portals! I almost start skipping. Me, skipping. I know. It's ridiculous, but I haven't felt this excited in years. Chirpy blackbirds scatter out of my way like I'm the queen of concrete.

It's not long before I'm in the same lobby. Fire glowing under the mantle, Achilles statue watching from the corner. I'm ready to sneak on to the elevator if the guard won't let me up, but oddly, he smiles at me this time.

"I'm here to see Madame Em." I grip the desk to keep from toppling over when another wave of nausea hits me. The chandelier lights blur and spin in my vision like fireworks.

"She's expecting you. 117th floor, ma'am."

It's ma'am now, is it?

I slog over to the elevator on my sea legs. The burst of adrenaline is already starting to fade. How long is this portal hangover going to last?

I need to focus. I need to convince Em to make a deal with me. Montgomery and my dad warned me to stay away. But what other option do I have?

The elevator shoots me skyward. Star-shaped lights twinkle overhead. No one greets me at the entryway. No one greets me in the empty grand hall or in the long hallway of dead ancestors.

"Hello? Madame Em? Montgomery?"

I hear chatter and classical piano in a room farther down another hallway. This place is a labyrinth. Despite being in a skyscraper, it feels like a castle that's been here hundreds of years, a fortress in the San Francisco fog. It takes me a moment to grope along the wall and find the light switch. Electric candelabras line the thick adobe walls. One of my favorite movies growing up was *Beauty and the Beast*. That moment when Belle wanders the castle looking for help, and Cogsworth and Lumière whisper about her in the shadows—it seemed so fun in the movie, stumbling upon a secret magical castle, even if it had a beast inside. This is just annoying. Turn on the lights already. People have places to be.

I hurry down the hallway and finally turn into a dining room. Black-and-white checkered marble floors, ornate statues of Atlas holding up the world on his shoulders. Four people sit around a huge mahogany table. Madame Em, Montgomery, and what must be his two brothers. Same black curls and wide lips. It takes me a moment, but I eventually remember the burly one from the elevator standoff. Merrill—no, wait, Merritt.

"Good, you've arrived—we wouldn't want dinner to go cold." Madame Em takes a sip of her wine. Her lipstick leaves behind a crimson smear. "Have your sea legs adjusted to steady ground yet?"

"Yes," I lie.

"Well, I'd suggest taking a seat regardless."

I pull out a heavy chair, and the instant I sit, I feel like a child. I'm much too small for it, or it's much too big. Either way, I stretch my back upward to at least appear more like someone who belongs at the grown-up table.

"Powell, mix our guest a Last Word," she says.

"I make a divine Last Word." Powell winks in my direction before popping up from his seat and perusing the alcohol bottles lit up along the wall. He relishes in making us wait, fingers brushing along the glass, leaving his fingerprints on every bottle, until finally he chooses the brightest chartreuse he can find.

"Just mix the drink, fool." Merritt leans far back in his chair, and then lets the front legs slam against the marble floor. The sound echoes through the hall.

"You make such a wonderful host, dear brother." Powell shakes the metal cocktail canister over his shoulder, but it looks like he might rather hurl it at Merritt's head.

Right.

So, we have three squabbling, hungry brothers.

Hold on, could Em be their mother? Her blond hair and charcoal eyes don't match theirs, but there's something protective in the way she watches over them.

"Ruby, you'll have to excuse them," Em says. "We rarely have guests during our Sunday supper."

Montgomery is silent through all of this. He stares at his plate like he wants to disappear into the mashed potatoes. My stomach grumbles. The portal jumping has made me ravenous. Besides, I've only had toast and coffee all day, and their feast smells like gravy and roast beef and everything I wish I could shovel into my stomach.

"Won't you join us?" Em says.

"I'm here for—"

"Darling, of course, I know what you're here for."

"How did you know I was coming?"

"Only a foolish woman would not watch her trains," she says. "I know all who pass through my portals."

But it's more than that, isn't it?

She knew I'd come back.

She knew I'd make a deal.

This is what she wants.

She smiles and passes me a carving knife. The steaming roast sits next to my plate.

I hear ice shaking in a bottle, and then Powell returns from the bar with a cocktail in hand. He practically glides across the floor and does a tight spin without spilling a drop. Show-off; he'd give Diego a run for his money. Jade green liquid hovers inside a precariously thin cocktail glass.

The Last Word. Ominous much?

"What's in it?" I say.

"If you could pick your last words, I wonder what they would be?" Powell muses.

"If thou poison'th us, do we not see it coming?"

Powell laughs and nearly spills the cocktail on my lap.

"I like this girl. Cheers." He winks and takes a sip of the cocktail before placing it in front of me. "Voilà, it's not poison."

I still stare at the green liquid.

Montgomery pipes in. "It's gin, maraschino, chartreuse, lime. And you don't have to drink it if you don't want to."

"It was in such demand in Prohibition times," Powell says, not bothering to settle back into his seat. He seems to enjoy standing above us, gesturing wildly with his arms. "You know in the 1920s, speakeasies were All. The. Rage. The dancing, the parties. The government tried to crack down on alcohol, but look at us now. Our vices always find a way to thrive."

Merritt grunts and continues to shovel food into his mouth. So far, he is the only one eating. I guess with that much muscle, the boy must eat his weight in beef every day.

"You'll learn soon enough that our family business is like a speakeasy of sorts," Powell says.

"That's enough business before dinner." Em passes me a heaping platter of mashed potatoes, the smell of butter drifting up from the bowl. "Help yourself. Our chef knows what Sunday supper means to our family, and she skimps on nothing."

I can't stop my arms from reaching for the plate. It smells too good. Gravy and mushrooms simmered in red wine. I heap roast beef, asparagus, and mashed potatoes onto my plate. And a roll, two rolls. Butter, too.

"I didn't realize a little girl could eat so much," Merritt says with a smirk.

"Race you to seconds." I don't miss a bite. The meat is so tender it practically melts on my tongue. For a moment, I think of prisoners and how they're allowed one last meal of their choosing. This one would have been a fine choice.

We eat mostly in silence, except for the piano sonata in the background. It's not until we're done and the chef clears the plates that Madame Em begins to talk business. I notice that Montgomery's plate is still mostly full when it's taken away.

"So you wish to take over your father's debt?" Em says.

I nod.

"May I be excused?" Montgomery interrupts.

"No," she says, the word heavy as a railroad spike. She turns to me.

"You may have an affinity for jumping due to your father's bloodline, but this is no easy job. It requires discipline. Running highly sensitive errands. Utmost loyalty. No questions asked."

"I can do it." What other choice do I have? I can't lose Mom's house. It would only be for four years. And it can't all be bad, can it? My dad did it for ten years; he's not a bad man.

At least, I don't think he is.

"Well then, Powell, draft the contract. Montgomery will train you."

"Can't Powell train her?" Montgomery says.

"I'd be a very good teacher." Powell leans close and gives me a devilish grin. "Trust me, Montgomery is a bore. He's all about rules, rules, rules. You'd have much more fun with me."

"No, she will learn from our best jumper. Montgomery will do it. We want no weak links in our trains. Do you understand?"

Montgomery nods, his lips pressed into a grim line. He stands up from his chair and leaves the room without looking at me. Great, I'm the weak link, and my trainer already despises me.

Powell glares at the silver knife on his napkin before finally rising to retrieve a pen and paper. I've never had siblings, but even I can feel the undercurrent of tension sparking between them.

Powell drafts the contract with a glorious gold fountain pen and a hand that looks like it's never dished out a beating. Soon, the swirling cursive letters fill the page almost as if it's an intricate pattern meant to obscure the real meaning underneath. I scan the words when he's finished writing. It says all the things Em has already stated, and more. Four years of servitude to the Bartholomew line (i.e., BART). A flat fee of $2,000 for each package that I myself jump across the portals, and $200 per day for when I'm only there to receive packages. Commission bonuses for highly sensitive packages or particularly far jumps. The rest goes to paying my dad's debt, and of course, to the Bartholomews. It's more than I make with Chen's Painting Service, that's for sure. There must be a catch.

Complete confidentiality. A breach of confidentiality, disregard of duties, or unauthorized portal exchanges will result in forfeiture of our house and termination. Though they're quite vague about what "termination" entails.

"Can I see my dad's contract?"

"Why, darling?"

"I want to know what he got in exchange for fourteen years of service."

Madame Em's lips flicker in amusement. "You'll have to ask him. I'm not in the business of sharing secrets, not when my business runs on utmost confidentiality."

I stare at the words on the page again. Four years of my life in servitude to the Bartholomew line. We can keep the house, my mom's murals. It sounds like I'll even earn cash every week, so we can finally finish paying the bills and move upstairs. If it sounds this simple, why was my dad failing so miserably after ten years of it? And then I remember all his drunken Friday nights, his broken promises.

I can keep a promise. I can get us out of the garage.

My signature scrawls across the bottom of the page—long looping R and S for Ruby Santos. Madame Em snatches it across the table before I can take a second glance. Merritt grabs something from a drawer and then scooches next to me, rolling up his sleeves. He can barely slide the shirtsleeves up his thick arms.

"Welcome, Balboa," he says.

"But . . . that's my father's name?"

Em laughs. "Do you really think my name is Embarcadero, or his name is Merritt, or Powell, or Montgomery? We are our stations, and you are now Balboa."

"As in Balboa Park station?"

"Yes, you are now responsible for Balboa Park station and all the transactions that pass through those gates. I recommend leaving 'Ruby' behind you. This is your life now. BART always comes first. You are the gatekeeper, the jumper, the watcher of our trains. You work for the Bartholomew line, and it's best you never forget this fact, *Balboa*."

It's so obvious now that I think about it. Powell, Montgomery, Embarcadero, Merritt, all BART stations. "So, my dad's name . . . it's . . . it's not really Balboa?" The question strains through my tight throat. I don't even know this simple fact. My father's real name.

"Curious." Em leans close, as if she's savoring the aroma of my pure foolishness. "I would have thought by now you would have learned to see through your father's lies. But blood does make it difficult to see clearly."

My cheeks heat. Dad had always told me that the nickname came from Rocky Balboa because he was good at boxing. When Manny Pacquiao made it to the championships, my dad wouldn't take off his lucky boxing gloves, not even to shower. He used to practice every day before the arthritis kicked in. He hits like a champ. Scratch that, he hit like a champ, past tense.

He's such a liar.

It's not fair—why do we always believe the people we love?

I push back the chair to leave, but Merritt grabs my wrist. I wince at how tightly he grips my skin.

"We're not done yet," he says. "You'll need this for the portals."

"This might hurt a bit, darling," Em says, without a trace of sympathy on her pale face.

Merritt swabs my left hand with rubbing alcohol. He peels back my ring finger until it's pointed toward the ceiling. I squirm in my seat. The tattoo needle hovers over my hand for a moment.

"Ready?" Merritt says, switching the machine on. It rumbles above my skin.

No, I'm not—but I nod my head and bite back a scream when the needle pierces my finger.

⚝ CHAPTER 11 ⚝

When it's finished, I expect something badass like jagged teeth or claws or dragon flames. Instead, the cursive blue letters spell BART around my ring finger, circled like a wedding band. It looks like I'm some sort of transportation fanatic. No one likes BART trains *that* much.

My skin stings, red and sore. Merritt hands me a bandage. I wrap up my finger and start toward the door.

"You start tomorrow," Em says. "Meet at Montgomery station. Take the five A.M. train." With that, she leaves the room along with Merritt. As Em walks, she leans heavily on his shoulder. Her spike heels clatter against the black-and-white tiles.

Powell lingers, watching me gaze out the panoramic skyscraper windows. Both the Golden Gate Bridge and the Bay Bridge reach through the fog into the distance like a dousing rod. Twinkling car lights stream across the bay. If you tried to take a picture of it, the lights would blur into brushstrokes.

"Have you had that ocean view your entire life?" I say.

"Oh, yes."

"Do you still see it, or is it like a painting blended into the background?"

He says nothing for a few moments, his teeth chewing on his lower lip. Then, a sly smile appears. "My stop comes before Montgomery station. You know where to find me if you grow tired of my brother's rigid teaching methods."

Ha, right. Because I need to add sibling rivalry to my list of concerns. No, thank you.

Powell station is in the heart of downtown San Francisco with glimmering cocktail bars with names like Novela or Redwood Room, world-class theaters, and all manner of decadent shopping surrounding Union Square. The perfect place for a guy who enjoys wearing a velvet dinner jacket trimmed with blackened leather. I have a feeling we have absolutely nothing in common. At least with Montgomery, I'll learn the rules of the underground.

I take one last glance at the foggy bridges and catch Powell gazing out the window as if he hasn't seen the world outside in a very long time.

On the street, I pull my coat tight around me as I head toward the station. San Francisco wind is no joke. Doesn't matter if it's winter or summer, it bites through anything. My newly tattooed finger throbs in the chill. I feel older after everything that has happened tonight. After Mom died, I thought maybe I could go away to art school and have a couple years doing all the ridiculous things college kids do. It was a stupid, impossible thought.

But now . . . I can do an even more impossible thing, can't I?

Inside the train, my heartbeat thunders and the blood thrills through my veins. A tart-sweet energy coils inside my chest, tighter and tighter, craving release. *I can jump portals.* A devilish smile crosses my lips. *I can jump home.* It's official. I'm part of this now. I squeeze the BART tattoo on my finger and close myself inside the narrow space between the train cars.

As we race along the tracks, my palms throb and spark. I feel like I'm holding on to the reins of a giant beast.

Balboa.

Take me to Balboa Park station.

Take me to where I first met my father.

§

When I was eight, my mom finally decided to tell my father that he had a daughter. The story goes: My backpacker mom met my dad in the Philippines in a lush mountain town called Baguio while she was on a break from her Peace Corps assignment. It wasn't love. It wasn't marriage. It was just a particularly fateful (and rum-infused) night. My mom didn't sugarcoat it. Sure, she left out the racy bits, but she didn't say I was a blessing or a delivery from a stork or whatever things people say to little kids without fathers around. She just said it happened. And she wouldn't ever take it back. Over the years, they kept in touch, sending letters across the great ocean dividing them.

Then, one day, Mom told me we'd meet him at the Balboa Park station. We sat on the concrete benches, waiting for the next one arriving from San Francisco Airport. We waited and waited, wondering if maybe his flight was delayed. I kept wanting to stand on the edge of the tracks (big surprise), but she kept dragging me back to a safe distance. Pigeons landed on the ceiling above, even though the station had installed spikes to drive the birds away. I wanted to feed them cheesy crackers, but my mom said they'd follow us home if I did. I snuck them crackers anyway. My dad promised he would be on the first train car, so we waited at the end of the platform in a patch open to the cloudy sky.

My mom didn't have to tell me when it was him.

The train doors opened. I saw the face from the photographs.

I ran to him, and the pigeons flew wildly into the sky.

"Ruby," he said, swinging me up into his arms. "You know where to find me now."

From then on, he would visit a few times each year. The Philippines was a faraway place both in reality and in my imagination. A place that was part of my blood; a place I hardly knew anything about. Eighteen hours, seven thousand miles. It was an expensive flight. But he kept coming. Birthdays, random Sundays when the two of us could button up and stroll along the San Francisco beaches. He'd bring me my favorite treat— Ube Kalamay, a sweet sticky glob of rice, coconut milk, and purple yam; and then we'd play a game of who could stuff the most purple ube in their mouth and still be able to talk. I should have known something was off when he refused to take the trains with me. Always walking everywhere or shelling out cash for a taxi. *"You don't want your daddy turning into a lazy pig, na?"*

My dad knew how to keep secrets. But even he couldn't keep everything hidden.

It wasn't until five years later when my mom was dying of cancer that my father actually moved into our house to help care for us. Still, he refused to say a single word about what he did for work. I caught them arguing once while waiting outside her sickroom door. My mom begging for answers. *"When I'm gone, who will watch Ruby? You leave for long stretches and don't tell us anything about your other life? Who will be there for her?"* Sometimes when I feel like we're strangers living under the same roof, I think back to that first day in Balboa Park station. That instant I knew when he stepped off the train: *This is my father. This is my train station. This is my home.* For better or worse, this is it.

Now, letting the memories and magic burn through my fingertips, I think again of meeting my dad for the first time at Balboa Park station. The pigeons, the crackers crumpled in my palm, the squeal of metal brakes.

Take me home.

Darkness tugs at the edges of my vision, and an icy breeze claws up my legs. The next stop should be Montgomery Street station; but when I pull open the doors, the conductor yells, "Balboa Park." I push through my heavy sea legs and bolt off the train. A sliver of starless sky opens up above me. I can't help but feel the high of streaking seven miles clear across San Francisco.

Flash, just like that.

But the feeling doesn't last long.

This time I don't fall to my knees, but I do lurch over to the trash bin and throw up all the decadent roast I'd eaten at Madame Em's feast. Saliva drips from my long black hair, and something sticky coats my hand from grabbing the trash lid. The pigeons start circling me, hoping for spilled dinner, which just makes me want to throw up more. People wince and make a wide berth, like I'm drunk and deserve my misery.

"Ma'am, y'all right?" A BART security guard walks up to me.

"Fine. Just getting over a flu." I stumble toward the escalator. Thank god for escalators. I nearly face-plant when it dumps me aboveground. Cars honk along the boulevard, and someone is speaking Cantonese really loudly behind me. I should have taken the train home like a normal person. The dizziness feels worse this time. Was it because I crossed a greater distance? Was it because I'd already jumped portals earlier today? Will it be like this every time?

I don't know how I make it home, but I do.

My fingers slip and tremble on the garage door keys. The metal bites into my thumb until, finally, finally I pound on the door and lean my head against the wood. I can hear my dad limping to the door.

When he opens it, he looks angrier than I've ever seen him. He also smells like whisky. I'm about to say something, but my knees buckle beneath me. Despite his limp, he picks me up and ever so slowly carries me to my bed. His hot, bitter breath presses against my forehead. I'm not a kid anymore. I'm not. I should carry myself to bed.

"You didn't sign, did you?" he says. "Please, Lord."

"Someone had to save us."

He drops me on the bed, and I knock the top of my head on the washing machine. Stars flash behind my eyes. When he tears the bandage off my ring finger, he swears and prays, and prays and swears all in the same breath.

"Tanga! Tarantado ka!"

Stupid! Foolish!

Don't I know it.

A little before my mom died, she told me that the two things she was most proud of in her life were me and her murals. I might be a lost cause, but at least we still have the house.

When I drift into fitful sleep, I dream of the rooms upstairs. The brilliant murals she'd painted in the bedrooms, the kitchen, even the mermaid in my closet. In my dream, I keep moving from room to room, looking for her. A flash of her long red hair in the doorframe. I reach out to grab it, to make her hold still, to make her give me a hug because life's too hard—but all I'm left with are giant clumps of coppery hair.

⚜ CHAPTER 12 ⚜

've never been on the very first train of the morning.

When I step aboard, it's cleaner than I've ever seen a BART train. And that's saying a lot. This time, I ride the train like a normal passenger. Balboa Park to Glen Park, 24th Mission to 16th Mission, Civic Center to Powell, and finally Montgomery station—nothing fancy, no magic. My eyes slide shut as station after station passes; passengers crisscrossing the city, daydreaming about how good it would be to take a lavender bubble bath, how good it would taste to bite into the morning's fresh baguettes—and then opening my eyes like I actually did teleport here by magic.

A hand snatches my forearm and pulls me off the train.

I'm about to land a hard one on the dude's face but then I see that it's Montgomery.

"You were about to miss your stop," he says, as I relax my shoulders.

"I was gonna jump off."

"You know, daydreaming can get you killed in this job."

"Are you always this serious?"

"It's my job to take things seriously."

"Then what's my job?"

"Staying awake."

"Done and done."

He looks me up and down, dubiously.

"Did you get any sleep at all?" he says.

"Enough." I cross my arms over my crumpled shirt. My eyes feel dry and puffy. No one said anything about looking presentable for the job.

"Let's get coffee." He sighs. "You need to be awake."

"I promise I will never argue with you if you mention the word 'coffee.'"

"Mm-hmm, I'm not so sure about that."

"OK, you're right. I'll probably always argue with you, but I'll be nicer about it. A blonde roast instead of a French roast. Not a hint of bitterness, I promise."

My part of the city might be janitors and landscapers getting ready for their long mornings, but down here, businessmen are already barking orders into their cellphones. They walk with purpose. Like those tin toy soldiers that you wind up and let loose, long legs scissoring across the sidewalks. Montgomery fits right in with his midnight blue suit and his impossibly long legs. I hurry to keep pace.

We roll up to a hole-in-the-wall diner near Montgomery station, and it feels as if we've time traveled back to the 1950s. I have no idea how a place like this survives surrounded by twenty million Starbucks and Blue Bottles and hipster coffee shops. When I walk inside, I realize exactly why.

"Are those powdered sugar donuts?" Before he even has a moment to answer, I'm at the counter ordering three. Two for me, one for him, and only if he eats it fast enough.

I reach into my pockets and realize that I don't have any spare cash. I'd used the last of it yesterday, and since my dad botched his job he didn't bring anything home.

Montgomery throws down a twenty and scoops up the donuts and coffees and motions me over to a back booth. We slide into the red vinyl seats, and I inhale both a donut and the coffee.

"So how do I get paid?" White powdered sugar sticks to my chin, but I don't bother wiping it off. There's more where that came from.

"After you complete a jump, you get a cut of $2,000. The rest goes to the business. For days when you're just waiting to receive packages, it's only $200. We pay in cash. When you bring over more *sensitive* goods, then you get a bonus. Bigger distance, bigger cut. Some things are more taxing to move across the portals, and then distance just multiplies it."

"Is that why I felt so terrible after my second jump yesterday?"

He frowns and glares at my sticky fingers. as I savor my next lucky donut.

"You just had to jump home," he says. "You didn't even bother checking the rules first."

I waggle my sore tattooed finger at him.

"I thought this was the only ticket I needed."

"Next time, *ask* before jumping. Besides, you should have ridden the train home like a normal passenger instead of wasting your energy on a nothing jump."

"A nothing jump? Well, thanks."

"Trust me, when you're done training, it'll feel like a nothing jump."

"OK, fine, important question number three: are you going to eat your donut?"

His eyes rove over the powdered-sugar state of my face.

"I'll pass," he says.

I snatch the paper bag and dive into donut numero tres.

He tries to hide his smile, but I see it lurking. The corner of his lips tip up even as he fights it. OK, I'm making a fool of myself with this third powdered-sugar donut, but he's serious enough for the two of us. I might as well enjoy my sugar rush before work burdens my shoulders again.

"So, why are we up at five A.M. if we're just sitting around drinking coffee?" I clean my sugary face and wash down my throat with dark, rich coffee. If Diego were here, no doubt he'd be scolding me for not ordering a triple espresso instead. Will I even see him anymore with my new job?

"You'll need to be on the trains early. The time zones compound the lag from the portals. Jumpers don't always step in one place and out the next a minute later. Sometimes they're basically . . . nowhere? It'll feel like seconds for the jumper, but for those waiting for the package, it can take minutes or hours. It's unpredictable. And each jumper has a different speed depending on their skill level. Sometimes someone will leave Tokyo or Budapest or Mexico City, and we'll expect them at ten A.M., but then we won't see them for another couple hours. I try to take notes on particular jumpers and routes, so we know what to expect. But it's not an exact science. Hence, we need you to be there to pick up the package. Whenever it arrives. No sleeping, no wandering off, no unnecessary attention from bystanders. Discretion is key. Do you understand?"

"So, I just wait on the trains twiddling my thumbs."

"Balboa." He sighs.

"Yes, I understand; I'm not stupid." I throw my hands up in surrender. "What are they bringing across?"

"Don't ask them questions; don't ask yourself questions. Just keep it simple. It'll be better if you think of it as a bank transaction, except in physical space. Our clients demand complete and utter confidentiality."

"So, I'm, like, aiding gangsters, terrorists, and businesspeople to skip law enforcement borders for a commission? Is that basically it?"

Montgomery stares at me across the table, his jaw clenched tight. He glances around the room before he leans close.

"Balboa." His voice is a low rumble. "You might think this is a game or an adventure that you've stumbled into, but it's real. It's messy and dangerous and mundane work. I told you to stay away from this, but you signed the contract. And now here you are. If you think this is going to be a problem, I'd suggest backing out now, before you get too involved."

I lean forward, until my face is only inches from his.

"I signed a contract. I'm true to my word. But I don't like lies. If we're the bad guys in this, then I'd like to know that."

"We're the bad guys," he says without flinching.

"Got it," I say. "What are we doing for lunch?"

He grimaces, and I can tell he needs zero lessons on how to perfect his death glare. Powell was right about his brother's serious side. Montgomery's hands clench on the tabletop as if he's a parent who has lost all patience with his toddler throwing applesauce on the floor. Give me a break. I've signed away the next four years of my life to ferry packages across a magical train system. I may as well get used to it.

"What?" I shrug.

"I don't think you're understanding the danger of the situation you've put yourself in." He stands up and throws away our donut wrappers. He even tosses my coffee cup, which I was most definitely not done with.

"The deadly situation that *I* put *myself* in. Are you kidding me?" I wave my glaringly blue BART tattoo in his face. It's still swollen and pink around the edges. "I'm pretty sure I didn't do this to myself."

He storms toward the Montgomery BART station, summoning me to hurry up without a backward glance. I dust the powdered sugar crumbs from my jeans and rush down the station stairs. Damn his long legs. It's too early in the morning for man-trums. Montgomery steps aboard the nearest train and pulls out a palm-sized leather-bound notebook from his inner pocket. The pages are filled with neat lines of times and locations and amounts. I grab it out of his hand. I bet it's a ledger of everything owed, and everything to come.

"Let's get something straight." I grip the metal bar to keep my balance as the train rockets forward. Montgomery looks ready to throw me off a moving train for swiping his precious notebook, but I need him to listen to me. "I'm not here because I want to be. I'm here because your family made me sign a contract, so I wouldn't lose my dead mother's house. So how about you cut me some slack while I get up to speed?"

Passengers turn their heads to stare at us. OK, maybe I shouldn't have been talking so loud about "the business," but fury beats my heart into a frenzy, even as I try to gulp down stale subway air. I'm stuck. For four years. Montgomery's eyes flash, and he's obviously tamping down all the words he wants to spit at me right now. He snatches his notebook out of my hands and stalks toward the car's connecting doors. Each footstep seems solemn and resolute, like he's treading upon a holy place. This creaking train, this shaking beast. I force myself to follow him, my own knees wobbling as the train twists through the underground tunnels.

When I reach him, Montgomery leans close to my ear, so that the other passengers can't hear. His voice comes out in a jagged murmur. "When I say 'no unnecessary attention on the trains,' I mean it. When I say 'your life depends on you following our rules,' I mean it. When I said 'you had a choice to *not* sign the contract,' I meant it."

"Don't you dare pretend to know about the choices I've had to make because of my dad's addiction."

"There was an out . . . and I wish you'd taken it." For a moment, he looks sorrowful—and so, so young—but I don't care. I can't listen to this bullshit for another second. As if giving up my mother's house was an actual choice.

"I'm out. I need air." I rush toward the exit.

"You can't leave the trains when you're on duty. This is your job, *Balboa*." He says my new name in a thundering voice as if it's a spell to command me. Guess what—these are my own legs, my own arms—and I need fresh oxygen. Not this regurgitated air with everyone's germs weighing on my lungs.

The train screeches to a stop at Embarcadero station, and passengers hustle on and off the platform. A bunch of boys in green jerseys hoot and holler and whip a soccer ball back and forth across the aisle as they chase each other out of the train. I wonder what it would be like to have a soccer game as my biggest worry. Amid the chaos, Montgomery grabs my elbow and leads me back toward the connecting doors. No one is watching.

"Would you lighten up and just be a human being for one damn second?" I try to wrench my arm from his steely grip.

He doesn't listen. Instead, Montgomery throws open the connecting doors with a flash of blue sparks.

A blast of icy wind hits my cheeks, and I stumble back.

And back.

And back.

And realize the ground is gone beneath me.

⟩ CHAPTER 13 ⟨

The back of my legs hit a ladder—hard. My palm slams against a metal rung, shooting pain up my forearm. I groan, clutching my forehead as the dizziness threatens to bring me to my knees. What the hell was that? I force my eyes open against the blinding fluorescent lights.

This is *not* San Francisco.

This is . . . another train. The window shows me nothing but a black concrete wall blurring into tar as we speed ahead on the tracks. It's crowded full of people speaking rapid-fire Spanish. I grew up in the Mission and can handle myself in basic conversations, and maybe even Spanglish my way through a situation, but I can barely keep up with the cacophony of words around me. A bright orange train flashes past in the opposite direction. I cover my ears. The portal jumping has turned all my senses to full blast. If I'd known Montgomery was going to toss me like a hot potato across the train portals, I'd have prepared with a couple espresso shots. Or maybe a pack of ginger candies to keep this nausea in check.

His silhouette stalks down the aisle away from me. Midnight blue suit, black wavy hair, and enough haughty attitude to expect me to chase after him. I guess that's part of my job now? If he thinks he can just boss me around all the time—

The train jerks to a stop.

La Raza station.

Next to the words, there's a symbol of a pyramid-shaped temple on a bright yellow sign.

Montgomery hurries off the train, and I follow him before the doors shut. I wobble like a newborn fawn. I tell my feet to get a grip, tell my throat to tamp down the seasickness burning up my esophagus. Rush hour, just my luck. As I step onto the platform, Montgomery disappears around a corner without a backward glance.

Jerk.

I bet Montgomery has been jumping since he was a kid and probably doesn't even remember how massively disorienting the portals can be for newbies. I jog along the platform, bile slick and disgusting at the back of my mouth. Come on, Ruby, forget the ache in your knees. This is your job now. You signed the stupid contract, and Montgomery is going to rub it in your face any chance he gets.

"Señorita, are you OK?" A man around my father's age stops me. Concern crinkles his deep chocolatey eyes. He's short with a shaved head and sinewy arms, all muscle under his jeans and crisp white shirt. His leather boots are shined to perfection, and I wonder if he has a young son somewhere who helps keep them polished.

"Sorry, my stomach. Duele." I keep walking down the gray checkered tiles. I need to find Montgomery and figure out what the hell is going on.

"Lo siento," he says, shaking his head. "Señorita, espera. El baño está aquí." He swings open a door along an endless hallway and waves me inside. My head pounds, but maybe if I splash cold water on my cheeks, it'll stop my vision from blurring around the edges. The last thing I want is to black out. As I slip past his outstretched arm, I notice he has a tattoo woven around his thumb, train tracks shaped like curving *M*'s molded into a blazing orange sun. Wait, is that—

He slams the door shut.

The two of us alone.

Inside the cramped handicap restroom.

Nightmare of all nightmares. My hands squeeze into fists. Panic and adrenaline quickly replace my nausea. Only a dim light glows overhead, and water drips from the sink in loud plunks. Crumpled paper towels are scattered across the floor like dead pigeons.

"State your purpose." The man has an edge to his voice, and now he speaks in perfectly crisp English.

"Open the goddamn door. Right now. And then we'll talk." I hate the waver in my voice, but I need him to know I'll do whatever it takes to open that door.

He shakes his head. "We'll talk now. There are no freebies on the trains, kid. You have cash?"

"Is this some sort of test?"

He sighs like his time is a crumpled hundred-dollar bill and I'm setting fire to Benjamin Franklin's face.

"Look, I'm in on the secret. The underground. Whatever you guys call it." I wave my ring finger at him; my BART tattoo is a deep underwater blue in this feeble light. I feel like I'm sinking with every passing second trapped in here.

He grabs my outstretched hand, twists it behind my back, and slams me against the wall. My cheek presses against the cold, hard tile. White stars flash behind my eyelids. I swing my free elbow back, and he dodges to keep it from slamming into his nose. It gives me two seconds to grab my butterfly blade—my father's balisong blade. Miss Marybeth, don't fail me.

He backs up slightly when he sees it flash silver. But his muscled body still blocks the door.

"I don't care who you're working for. The Bartholomews don't own these trains. This is Colectivo territory."

"Where are we?"

He laughs, and it echoes loud inside this hollow space.

"Come on, niña, it's been a long shift. I'm tired of tourists. Put away the blade, hand over the cash, and let's get on with our day, okay?"

"I don't . . . I don't have any cash. Let me out of here." The claustrophobia gnaws at my skin. I grip hard onto my switchblade, daring a step forward. He still doesn't flinch.

"I had a friend with a blade like that," he says.

"Was his name Balboa?" I whisper.

The man smiles, a gold-toothed grin so much like my father's that I ache for him to be here, to guide me through his world. To tell me secrets about how to survive the underground. Was my dad once friends with this man?

A knock pounds against the door. Two rapid taps, followed by five more.

I'm about to let out a yell for help, but then the door swings open and Montgomery leans against the wall. He looks . . . impatient? Bored? Like he's been waiting outside the door for the right moment to knock. That bastard. What is this insanity? I rush into the endless hallway. Montgomery tries to call my name, but Balboa isn't my name, not yet—I need air, fresh air. I need out. I don't want to be Balboa.

My boots pound against the tile floor, and bodies jump out of my way. I slide my blade back into my pocket before the authorities see it; otherwise, I'll have even more trouble chasing me. I can't outrun Montgomery, though.

I risk a backward glance, and he's moving through the crowd jungle-cat-quick without drawing any attention to himself.

At the end of the hallway, a mural startles me. A giant with an ax chops into a tree shaped like a man while a cloaked woman cries into her hands. Another giant bites into a man's thick thigh flesh while a crowd of peasants fights and screams. Jarringly, Superman stands in the middle of it all with light or flames coming from his lips, and I can't tell if he's hero or villain. What is this fresh hell?

My boots squeal around a corner, and I stagger into a glowing cobalt-purple hallway with constellations painted on the ceiling. I brace myself against a wall to catch my breath. It smells metallic and sweaty and oddly like burnt corn. On the ceiling, the words CASQUETE ESTELAR SUR are scrawled across the night sky. Something . . . south star? I nearly tip over craning my neck back, until I feel Montgomery standing beside me.

"Where are we?" I whisper, not caring that I'm leaning my shoulder into his chest. I can barely stand, all my adrenaline sucked out of my veins. I need something, anything, to hold on to before my body floats away.

"This is La Raza station," he whispers. "This part is called 'El Túnel de la Ciencia.' The Tunnel of Science." He glances upward at the glowing ceiling. "Those are the southern constellations. It's an art and education piece installed by the University of Mexico."

"We're in . . . *Mexico*?"

He nods. "Mexico City."

Amaranthine and ultramarine darkness wraps around us, reflecting off of the shiny metal walls and floor, so I feel like I'm suspended in space, falling and floating at the same time. I can't see the details in the dark faces gliding past us. Which probably means they can't see the horrible state of my face. I let out a long breath.

The constellations Carina, Centaurus, and Crux hang above us in shimmering green ink.

It makes me feel slightly less alone.

"I know this is hard," Montgomery whispers. "My job is to prepare you for what's to come. The most important lesson is how dangerous the trains are. If you're not on a Bartholomew line—trust no one. It's a cutthroat Wild West of territories, and you'll be navigating it alone. Always know where you're stepping; never let someone drag you across the lines, like I did. Never let someone trap you in a station. I was hoping you weren't going to step into that restroom with Ángel."

"My brain has been run through a trash compactor. My whole body aches—"

"It doesn't matter how much it hurts. Never let anyone close, not on the train lines. Especially when you don't know where you are. There are only ever three options: you pay a price for stepping into someone else's territory, you get 'recruited' to work their lines, or they make sure you never . . . return."

"So, you just left me in that bathroom?"

"I didn't leave you. Not long."

"What if that guy . . ."

"Ángel is a decent man. He's like your father. He does only what's necessary, so I knew he wasn't going to hurt you."

"That was a lousy power play, and you know it." I lean away from his shoulder, my strength seeping back into strained muscles. "What if I'd hurt him? What if he'd hurt me? All for a 'lesson' on train jumping." Anger churns inside my gut.

"I didn't realize you had a blade."

"My dad always made sure I never left home without one."

Montgomery turns my chin up, so we can lock eyes in the inky night sky. "Ruby," he says, softly. "I need to prepare you for what's to come."

"You could have just told me."

"Well, all I have to go on is our coffee break this morning–where you promptly disregarded everything I said."

"Well, if you'd just stop being so–"

"Rigid? Serious? Call me whatever you want. As Montgomery, it's my duty and responsibility to look after everyone on the Bartholomew lines. And yes, I take it very seriously. I'm going to make sure that you'll be the best Balboa you can be." Montgomery takes a deep breath, the strain in his shoulder blades dissolving into the constellations surrounding us. "I'm sorry, the locked bathroom was . . . too much. I'm worried about the dangers you'll face. That you won't be ready." He chews his lip like he's not used to being this honest with his recruits.

"I'm listening now," I whisper.

I take one last glance at the endless starry sky before we jump back.

⚕ CHAPTER 14 ⚕

For hours, we ride the trains all across the Bay Area. He explains the protocols. What I do with packages when they arrive. What I do with people when they materialize. The drop-off points. The pickup points. Which train cars. The security cameras. The best way to stage distractions if needed. The best bathroom breaks. The best coffee shops. The best views—hands down, the Oakland shipyards are a Lego enthusiast's dreamscape. Stacks and stacks of shipping containers swinging from mammoth cranes. Montgomery laughs when I tell him this. Apparently, he was a Lego fiend when he was a kid, too.

He doesn't laugh when I call him Monty, though, which means I'm going to have to do it from now until eternity. It's a shame it bugs him so much. I actually much prefer Montgomery to Monty.

He introduces me to the goon posted at each station, so that they can recognize me if I need to jump their trains. I hadn't realized there were far more operators out there than Montgomery, Powell, Merritt, and Embarcadero. Their network of henchmen, called the Bartholomew, stretches all across the BART rail lines. It makes sense, but who knew so many people could jump trains like this? I've known about the subway all my life, and I've never heard about anything this weird. Let me clarify: I've heard of too many weird things, from furry assless chaps during the Pride Parade to a tulle-tufted ballet troupe on their way to Union Square and a man who talked to his bicycle, but nothing weird in the magical sense. I guess Montgomery wasn't kidding about discretion.

He goes on to tell me the specialties of each station: his station in the financial district handles businesspeople, who, of course, want to make their money "disappear." Powell station handles celebrities and politicians who want to move incognito across the globe. Merritt station handles illegal weaponry and other illicit goods.

Apparently, Balboa Park specializes in South Asia and Latin America.

That's about all Montgomery will tell me.

"You're not allowed to ask questions," he says.

"Fine, fine, for the hundredth time, fine!"

We're on our way back to Balboa Park, done for the day. It's nearly one P.M., and my body aches from so much sitting and surfing on the train cars.

"Here, you might need this." He discreetly hands me a wad of cash for today's cut, along with a small red book the size of my palm. White chickens strut across the cover.

"William Carlos Williams? What's *The Red Wheelbarrow* got to do with trains?"

"Everything." His smile sends a small thrill down my fingertips. He steps off the train. Even after a long day, his silky suit looks flawless. As the train pulls out of Montgomery station, I catch his aquamarine eyes through the window and watch him disappear into the blur. Stop staring, Ruby. We're not even remotely in the same league. But at least looking is free of charge. Verdict: he'd be quite handsome if he smiled more.

On the way back to Balboa Park station, I start to read the little red book. It turns out to be poetry. No joke. Or maybe it is a joke? Some kind of highbrow version of hazing? Or maybe a puzzle? He's scribbled in the book with a pencil, circling certain passages. I can't discern if there's a pattern or not. It mainly looks like he's circled some of Williams's pretty-sounding lines. Stuff like: Icarus falling, and farmers not noticing, and melting wings.

Am I supposed to learn something from this? My time would be much better spent with a *How to Jump Portals* mechanics manual, or a map, or something remotely useful. I flip through the pages until I come across one poem that I vaguely remember from a high school English class:

```
so much depends
upon

a red wheel
barrow

glazed with rain
water

beside the white
chickens
```

That's it. That's the whole poem. I remember reading it in English class and thinking—*this dude* won all those awards and praise and a spot in the canon of fine literature? Thinking, hell, no shit, a lot relies on a red wheelbarrow. That's the whole point of owning a wheelbarrow.

But what's this got to do with trains?

The conductor spouts the usual "Balboa Park station" announcement, and I stuff the book into my pocket. I stop at the Mexican market on my way home; stock up on ground beef, tortillas, rice, eggs, beans, and limes; and even splurge on some blueberries and a pineapple. I can't resist a couple tins of Spam, too. There's nothing I'm more grateful for than a full fridge. I hurry home with my arms heavy. The closer I get to home, the more my stomach gnaws at me. What will my dad say now that I've seen into his world?

I find him sitting in the back garden, staring at a blank blue sky. He sips from a coffee mug, and I know there's no coffee in it. He never drinks alcohol in clear glasses. Tucked behind his leg under the bench lurks a box of cheap wine. I don't know why he bothers half-hiding it. He must know I'm not blind. But maybe it's for himself to pretend.

I stare at our little greenhouse still dripping from a dewy morning. My dad built it from giant window panels a neighbor was throwing away. It's a simple cobbled-together A-frame, but it does its job. It reminds me of that red wheelbarrow glazed with rain. I don't know how I'll manage to have time to tend the bok choy and herbs anymore. So much depends on me now.

"I bought a bunch of food," I say, still leaning against the doorframe, half-inside, half-outside. The autumn fog slips between the houses, an ever-present cat nuzzling between our rooftops. There was a T. S. Eliot poem about fog, right? The words echo from a long-ago literature class. Darn Montgomery and his poetry.

My father sits in a puffy jacket and an orange Giants baseball cap.

He doesn't say a word.

I'd almost prefer if he were mad and raging at me. This silence is worse. The late afternoon light starts fading behind the neighbor's house, silhouetting our apple trees in a desolate rosewood haze.

"So, now you don't listen to your father?" he says, finally.

I stand corrected—the slurred alcohol-heavy words are worse. He turns and glares at me with bloodshot eyes.

"You're one to judge," I hiss back. "You were stupid enough to trade away our house. And after all this you're still drunk?"

"You think I chose this? My joints on fire from all the portal jumping. They're going to use you until there's nothing left."

"Yeah, well, *you'll* use me until there's nothing left!"

I slam the garden door. He switches on the radio to a deafening volume. If you don't think The Beatles are capable of screaming through speakers, you're sadly mistaken. It turns to static noise as he churns through the radio stations. The upstairs renters start pounding on the floor above my head, and I can't take it. I can't. I wish I could go upstairs and lock myself in my mermaid closet and disappear.

Instead, I rush through the front door and out onto the street. My chest swells. All I can think is to run to Cayuga Park, a little baseball field surrounded by a hodgepodge of carved wooden statues. The BART trains roar overhead, but it's oddly soothing. It's something you can count on every six minutes. Like church bells on the hour.

My brain is a tangled mess, and I bury my face in my arms. What else was I supposed to do? Let them take away my house? His words echo inside my head: *"They're going to use you until there's nothing left."* Is that how my dad ended up an alcoholic? I always thought it was because of losing Mom to cancer, but it's true that he always drank a little too much even before then. I think about his hip pain, his joints aching in the San Francisco cold. I squeeze my knuckles and wonder if that will be my fate, too, eventually.

When I flop down on the dewy grass, a sharp edge digs into my ribs. I reach into my coat and pull out the little red book. I flip the pages, scanning for pencil marks, anything to blunt my brain. Baseball bats clink in the distance, and footfalls tamp down the grass. When I read a poem, the words' cadence sucks me in. Even the cars driving on the boulevard disappear. It's just me and the poem, "Landscape with the Fall of Icarus" by William Carlos Williams. The last two stanzas hit me straight in the gut. His words conjure up the Brueghel painting from my mom's art books. Icarus falling, drowning—and no one notices. All he wanted was to reach for more.

A giddy ragged, laugh escapes my mouth. Poor Icarus. And life just goes on. Isn't that the truth of it?

A baseball lands near my head and pulls me back to reality.

"Sorry, that almost got you!" the kid hollers as he runs toward me.

"Watch it, muskrats!" I chuck the ball in their direction, and a kid snatches it from the air. They keep playing their game, and life goes on. I stuff the poetry book back into my pocket and breathe in the dewy grass. I let myself lie there, rolling the words over my tongue.

Eventually, I come home to the smell of fresh rice and meat grilled in onions and limes. My dad has set our makeshift table—a plank latched onto the upright piano. We sit at the counter as if it was a bar with stools and ignore the fact that it's actually a piano bench.

He has been waiting for me to return. I can tell. He's straightened up the garage. The house sits quiet, except for the footfalls of the renters upstairs and a bird squawking over its nest in the garden. My dad lifts the lids on the pans, and savory steam rises up. The hot plates sizzle as water drips from the lids. For someone who's "on the road" a lot, my dad can cook up a feast. He basically learned four recipes to absolute perfection.

"Patawarin mo ako," he says.

I don't know many Filipino phrases, but I know this one. I've heard it too often. It basically means "forgive me."

I know he's sorry. I know this isn't how any of us expected our lives to turn out. Poor old Icarus can tell you about that shit. Funny how it's been thousands of years since the Greeks told the Icarus story, and it's all the same drama.

"I know, Dad."

He serves us each heaping scoops of spicy meat and rice and stewed bok choy. I flip on the fairy lights, and we sit side by side on the piano bench. He smells like mint and coconut, his face freshly shaven.

He's trying. He's always trying.

"I need you to focus on getting better," I say, after I've taken my last bite. "While I'm working for Em. I need you to be working on you. They host Alcoholics Anonymous meetings over at St. Thomas More Church. I want you to check it out. Tuesday nights."

He squeezes my hand to keep his from shaking.

"Please don't stop believing in me," he says.

I squeeze back. It's a miracle that we're both staring straight ahead at the sheet music, because I don't think I could look at his face without tearing up. I know I'll never stop believing in my dad, but I don't know yet if that's a good thing.

❧ CHAPTER 15 ❧

A t the crack of dawn, I'm out the door running back to the train station. This will be my life now. Every day. Trains. I catch the five A.M. I meet Montgomery, and today we ride out for another round of Teaching Balboa to Be a Henchwoman. Today, he stares straight ahead like maybe he's the one who had a sleepless night. After a couple stops, his head drifts toward the window and then straightens, swaying slightly.

"So, is the trick to serenade the trains with poetry?" I raise my palm to my chest in mock Shakespearean seriousness. *"So much depends upon a red wheel barrow."*

"Memorized it already?" He smiles, some of the tension dissolving down his neck.

"Come on, what's it for?"

I catch him sneak a glance at the security cameras overhead. How much is the Bartholomew line watching us? Montgomery looks like he stops himself from saying something important, instead shrugging his shoulders.

"It's for you," he says, eventually. "So you don't get bored on the trains. You'll have long hours waiting between jobs, and it can fit neatly in your coat pocket."

"But isn't that what my phone is for?"

He looks a little disappointed when I say this, and for some reason, I feel bad for disappointing him. I could have said any number of clever things. Or even honest things. Why can't I tell him that the Icarus poem saved me from shedding more tears yesterday? Maybe even thank him for the book.

"If you don't want it, it's fine to give it back to me." He holds out his hand, and I clutch my arms tightly around my chest. I can feel the little red book cocooned between my coat pocket and my stomach. The pages are probably as warm as a baby bird.

"No, I want to keep it. I just . . . want to understand."

He doesn't say anything. Like he doesn't believe me. Like I'm being polite or something. He should probably know by now that I don't waste my time on false niceties.

"Like that Icarus poem . . ." I say, drumming my fingers on the train railing, nervous to admit I want anything. Nervous to even talk about the mysteries of poetry aloud. "I want to see that Brueghel painting one day. In real life." It's not the whole truth, but it's something.

"It's in one of the Royal Museums of Fine Arts in Brussels. They've got incredible collections." He stares out the window at the black tunnel walls and won't meet my eyes. Maybe he's nervous to show how much he cares about all this artsy stuff too? I don't know why he should care—his family is rich enough to host an art auction with a real van Gogh, for god's sake.

"Well, when I find a few grand lying around, I'll be sure to take the vacay." I scoff and watch the passengers squeezing aboard the last stop in San Francisco. I picture Madame Em gazing down on us from her skyscraper, sipping champagne, surrounded by all the paintings she could ever want. I bet you she has an entire fridge devoted to champagne, an entire wing devoted to oil portraits of her ancestors.

Montgomery tosses me a playful smile. It's a great smile–the kind you only catch small flickers of, which somehow makes it all the more dazzling. Do they teach guys how to do this in those fancy prep schools? A class on "How to Pull a Mona Lisa." A class on "How to Pull a Ruby Santos" would be a far easier lesson to learn–always bare your teeth.

"You know, there are trains in Brussels." He looks like he's itching to jump the train and dash over to Brussels this very second. I can't say I blame him.

It suddenly dawns on me that this portal jumping could mean a lot more than working as a henchman for Madame Em. It could mean the Royal Museum of Fine Arts Antwerp. It could mean the Louvre and the Metropolitan Museum of Art. I pinch my wrist to stop myself from getting too excited. I'd still need to find the time between jobs and taking care of Dad and the house and everything. Dad never took me outside of San Francisco–and he could have. Why didn't he?

"Hold on, don't get any bright ideas yet." All the seriousness returns to his chiseled jaw and eyebrows. "You'll need to know which train lines are friendly. We have tenuous truces with some of the lines, and others will happily toss your dead body onto the tracks. It's important for you to know all the rules before you start jumping. There's always a price. Always."

"What if someone doesn't pay the price?"

"That will be today's training."

He doesn't look happy about this. Not that he's a chipper person in general, but at this he closes down completely. I'd much rather go back to that glow in his eyes when he talked about Icarus and art. I want to say more about the William Carlos Williams poems, but I also don't want to make a fool of myself. That's the problem with talking about poetry–I'm always afraid to say something stupid because someone else might have no idea what I'm talking about. Though I have a feeling that Montgomery would understand me.

We get off at Ashby station near the border between Berkeley and Oakland. An unhoused man greets us, his fingers wrapped in thick, ragged gloves. A cardboard sign sits next to him, scrawled with the word VETERAN in messy black ink.

"Good day, y'all. It's a good day. Ma'am, sir, good day." The man holds out his hands, begging for cash. Montgomery drops in his spare dollars.

I wonder what this man's story is, what bad fortune brought him to the streets. Guilt and fear twist in my gut—I have no idea how to solve this man's problems. And, worse, I pray that it's something my dad and I never face if we lose our house.

Aboveground, the light is blinding. It's always sunnier in the East Bay than it is in San Francisco. They don't get the same insistent fog. Montgomery slips on his sunglasses to shield his blue eyes. In the sunshine, my steps feel light, bouncy; that is, until we descend another set of stairs a couple blocks away.

"Are we always going to be underground?" I groan.

He doesn't bother answering me. He knocks on the door five times, two fast, three slow. Someone opens the eyehole, takes a glance, and lets us inside.

It smells like feet down here. Dirty fungus feet. Discarded socks. Locker-room funk. You get the picture.

"Hey, Monty, can I vote for a change in scenery?" I say.

"Oh, *Monty*! I'm so glad you could drop by," Merritt hollers from across the empty room. I barely recognize him in the padded headgear and boxing mitts. He puffs up his chest and saunters over in a shirt that reads "Two Words One Finger" in an angry red scrawl. Well then, tell me how you really feel.

Montgomery doesn't wince at the nickname, but I can feel him coiling up beside me. His hands turn to fists. He stands taller if that's even possible, but Merritt has at least thirty pounds of muscle over him. Brothers. Pfft, like I need this kind of drama in my life.

Though, to be fair, I should have left the Monty nickname out of the mix. My mistake. One day, I promise to learn my manners.

"She's training today," Montgomery hollers back. "Keep your guys out of the Blue Room."

He leads me back to a room that lives up to its name. It's completely bright blue, including the ceiling. It's disorienting. Like I've walked into the sky. At the side of the room lies a regular old sparring mat. Here we go, something familiar. But is that a moving walkway? Like the rubbery kind you see in airports where passengers are zipped across long terminals? Except this one leads only from one end of the room to the other.

"Change into workout clothes, and gear up." He points to the padded gear on the opposite wall. "There's a changing room with fresh clothes over there."

I nod and brace myself for more aching days.

"And, Balboa . . ." I turn to catch his eyes. "Don't feel like you have to be nice if any assholes come up to you."

"Don't you know me by now? I'm never nice."

"I know." He smiles.

In the mirror, I try to pump myself up, remind myself that my dad has given me boxing lessons since I was eight years old. Punk music blares from the Blue Room, and someone whistles and hollers. Curiosity wins out, and I sneak a glance outside.

Powell saunters out in a bath towel, his pale skin damp and glistening.

Montgomery and Merritt exchange a look before bursting into laughter. It's only the three brothers in the Blue Room, and they've each smiled more than I've thought possible for a Bartholomew.

"Ten minutes of training, and this one thinks he's earned a sauna break?" Merritt scoffs.

"Who needs training when *someone* had the absolutely brilliant foresight to bring a tray of carne asada burritos to feed the barbarians and, thusly, has *earned* a sauna break." Powell nods over to a silver tray that smells like heaven wrapped in avocado and beans. It takes exactly two seconds for Merritt to lunge off the wall and dive into the foil tray. He tosses one to Montgomery and chucks another one at Powell's head before snagging two more for himself. Powell leans up beside Montgomery and glances up and down at his impeccable navy suit.

"Do you own nothing else?" Powell says.

Montgomery shrugs, half a burrito already stuffed down his wide mouth. A smear of pico de gallo and cilantro hangs on to the corner of his lips. "I finally found a suit that fits."

"Look inside his closet," Merritt says, unwrapping two burritos at the same time. "He owns five of this exact same outfit."

"Seven." Montgomery grins.

"Sweet mercy, how are we related?" Powell grimaces as if it's an affront to humankind to wear the same outfit every day of the week. I'm sure it probably saves precious time not having to choose an outfit—especially when your days are overrun with making life-or-death decisions for a crime empire.

"I ask myself that every day," Merritt mumbles, playfully knocking Powell—hard—in the shoulder. Powell gives him a withering look.

"Play that game and you'll never find out where I get these burritos from."

"Come on, man." Merritt eyes the silver tray and licks his cut lip.

It all feels so ... normal. I wonder what their family would have been like if they'd never had a Bartholomew crime legacy hanging over their heads.

And then a pack of henchmen creaks open the basement door.

It slams shut.

The sharp clang echoes down the string of rooms like a warning bell.

Montgomery wipes any trace of cilantro from his face while Merritt slips on his boxing gloves and pounds his fists together. Powell throws on an oxford shirt and black jeans before hightailing it for the nearest exit. All trace of brotherly love collapses under the sound of boots marching toward the sparring mats.

"Let me guess, you find them all dashingly handsome." A woman's voice teases against my ear, and I spin around. Six unknots a towel tangled in her blue hair. She shakes her head and throws her hair back. Every move is pure confidence, from the way she holds her shoulders tall to the way her smirk dares you to say more. I wonder if I'll ever be able to move like her.

"The Bartholomew Brothers have certain *reputations*," she teases, arching her finely plucked eyebrow. "Maybe if you tell me which one is your favorite, I could help you out?" Six winks, as if we would ever be the kind of girls who gossip with each other in a bathroom. Her eyes scan my face for any trace of weakness.

"None," I say. "I don't have time for silly crushes. What about you?"

She watches Montgomery disappear into the men's locker room.

"None worth pursuing." A tinge of bitterness laces her words, even though she tries to hide it. "I've been bound to a BART contract since I was thirteen. And they don't dally with the hired help." She plucks a loose thread in my shirt and watches as the cheap fabric unravels. I smack her hand away, and she laughs. "Lesson for the wise: the Bartholomews are obsessed with bloodlines. The only reason Em was allowed to marry their father was because she is an inordinately talented jumper . . . with a rather unique *gift*. They don't let trash muddy up the bloodlines."

Heat flushes my cheeks, and I try to keep my expression neutral. I know she's just trying to get under my skin. I throw on a pair of leggings and tie my hair into a firm braid. No distractions, no boys—but secrets, on the other hand . . .

"So, what's unique about Em?" I say.

"Your father really told you nothing?" Six scoffs and flings her towel into the bin. "Let's just say she's not the kind of jumper you ever want to cross. Montgomery, either."

"Speaking of Montgomery, I need to get back to training."

I push past her into the Blue Room. I don't need Six weaseling her way into my head. I slip on the helmet and padded gloves while Merritt saunters over, leaving behind a batch of jumpers who I've never met before. They look rough around the edges, like their line of work happens only under the cover of night. I stretch my arms from side to side, waiting to see what Merritt's move will be.

"Montgomery might be a good train conductor, but he doesn't know shit about fighting. He should leave this part of the training to me. Though I guess he doesn't have much to work with in your case."

"What makes you think I need training?"

Merritt laughs.

"Come on then, let's see it." He steps onto the moving walkway and pounds his padded fists together. His feet scissor in constant fluid motion, but you would never guess it from his perfect balance.

Me and my big mouth. I roll my neck and shoulders out.

"On that moving walkway?" I say, trying to keep the panic from my voice.

"Any time you get into a fight, girlie, it'll be on a moving train. With a confined walkway as your only playing field. That a problem?"

I step toward the moving sparring mat, and a crowd of burly henchmen start to gather around us. Stupid dirty smirks on their faces. My heart pounds inside my chest, and my palms sweat inside the gloves. Montgomery comes out from the locker room, confusion darkening his features. He wears black sweatpants and a Nirvana T-shirt. It's the first time I've seen him in anything but a sleek blue suit. So he does have serious muscle under there. I mean, focus, Ruby . . . uh, Balboa. Get your head straight.

Rubber slides beneath my worn-out sneakers as I step onto the rotating walkway. I rush to find my balance, fists up and legs gliding across the slowly moving "ground."

"What are you doing?" Montgomery yells at us. I can't tell if he's scolding me or his brother. Very likely both.

"She said she doesn't need training." Merritt smirks. "I thought I'd see for myself."

"I'm fine," I say, sidestepping into a fighting stance while still cognizant of the rapidly approaching treadmill ledge. "Let's go."

We dart and retreat, testing our footing, testing each other. It almost feels like what I would imagine fencing would feel like . . . while on a treadmill. Merritt has significantly more muscle and an arm radius that could snatch me up if I let him get too close. I make sure to keep out of reach. That's my only advantage. I'm smaller, quicker (maybe?), and my dad's a real-deal Rocky Balboa. If Merritt doesn't think I can punch, then he's in for a rude awakening.

I flick my arm out for a quick jab, a test to his reflexes. Elbows close, legs strong, none of that sidewinder junk in the movies. He blocks it like swatting a fly.

"Nice form," he says though the face mask. "For a girl."

He throws a punch my way, and I barely dodge it in time. We dart and dodge like this for a few minutes, the constant motion of the moving walkway wearing down my thigh muscles. The crowd looks bored.

"Come on, Merritt, quit playing with your food!" one of the guys yells.

At that, he comes at me quick, too quick. I can't dodge back without toppling off the walkway. I swing back, but he knocks my shoulder, and I go stumbling to the side. My shoe snags on the line where treadmill meets solid ground, and I crash down onto my right knee. Before I have a chance to back away, his hands clamp around my throat and shove me to the floor.

"Girl, maybe you should have stuck with Pilates."

I kick at his groin, but he doesn't let go. Panic rises in me, acid-hot through my chest. I try to get my knees up to pry him off, but it's a lost cause. My face goes red and splotchy; it's hard to breathe.

"One!" yells the crowd.

"Two!" I struggle to slip the glove off my hand.

"Three!"

I hold a thin blade to his throat.

The crowd stops making noise.

"That's cheating," he growls.

"It's all cheating," I rasp through my burning throat. "This, your job, your portals. You're going to get picky now?"

Merritt grins and lets me go.

"She'll do well," he says.

Finally, the crowd disperses, and it's only me and Montgomery left in the Blue Room. He doesn't help me up, so I drag my sorry ass back to my feet. I don't have to look at his face to feel the anger radiating off of him. I pull the padded mask off. Lord almighty, my shoulder aches; my face and neck are probably lobster red, and I'm dying for some water. I fold Miss Marybeth and tuck my blade back into my boot.

"Are you always this reckless?" Montgomery says.

"The first thing you should know about me is that I'll do whatever I need to to survive."

"Like provoking my brother into a fight for no reason?"

"He provoked me! You think I'm just going to lay down and take it?"

"You want to go around throwing yourself into danger, go right ahead. It sounds like Merritt would be better suited as your trainer." He snatches his bag with his blue suit in it and walks away.

"She's all yours!" he hollers to Merritt on his way out the door.

⚹ CHAPTER 16 ⚹

Hey, hold up!" I chase after him as a cold sweat races down my spine. I catch Montgomery before he disappears underground. The sound of passing trains echoes up the staircase, and scraps of trash twine with the maple leaves caught in the gust. We linger on the sidewalk, both unwilling to disappear into the underground quite yet.

"You're my trainer," I say.

"Not anymore."

"I don't want to train with Merritt. I want to train with you."

"What happened to 'I don't need training'?"

"Look, if I'm going to face those guys, I'm going to make sure I can stand there on my own, OK? I've had boxing lessons since I was eight. You know my dad–he would never let me wander San Francisco on my own without teaching me basic self-defense and then some." Here I thought he was being a good dad, but I guess the joke's on me. He just worked for the bad guys.

"Is that why you have that blade?" he says.

"My dad brought it from the Philippines. It's called a balisong, like a butterfly knife. No big deal, OK?"

"Have you ever actually used it?"

"What is this, Twenty-One Questions?"

"Have you?"

"No!" I look away and cross my arms. I hate feeling small. "But I would if I had to, OK."

"I'm glad you haven't had to."

Departing passengers flood up the stairs, and we stand at either end of the tunnel, waiting for them to leave. I stare at the cracks in the staircase and wonder how an earthquake might rip this all apart one day. I hate when my father's lies seep through the cracks. Sure, he wanted me to be able to defend myself—and don't get me wrong, I'm grateful—but what are all the things he's done over the years? Was he only defending himself? Or was he the man you had to be afraid of in the dark?

I hear Montgomery's footsteps approach me. He hovers a foot away, looking much younger in his Nirvana T-shirt than in those immaculate blue suits. We look like we belong here, like we might go to the movies or grab a pizza at Jupiter's like normal Cal college kids. We don't look like the kind of people who would have switchblades in their boots.

"Last question," he says, softly. I almost have to lean forward to hear him. "Why do you stand inches from the trains when they roar into the stations?"

My mouth goes dry.

"You . . . see that?" I say.

He looks away now, blushing slightly. Even the tips of his ears go pink. "If I'm going to train you, I want to know who I'm dealing with."

"I don't know how to describe it." I shove my hands into my pockets to keep them from shaking. "It feels . . . when the train comes, it feels . . . like it could take me somewhere. Like it's a wild beast, and I want to grab hold of its mane and leap on. It sounds silly, I know, but I can't explain it any better. It's like I could feel the trains were alive even before I believed in the portals."

"OK." He nods, staring at me for a moment longer. "Let's go."

"Wait," I say. "I have a question for you. Something I don't understand yet."

He looks at me warily, eyebrows scrunched together.

"I know, I know, no questions. But like you said, if we're going to train together, I have to know who I'm dealing with."

"Fine," he says. "Ask your question."

"Why do you care so much? About me. And my dad."

Montgomery sighs before glancing away. As if kindness could be a weakness. Maybe in his line of work it is. Sunlight streams through the maple tree overhead, casting us in zigzagging shadows.

"I've known your dad for ten years. Ever since I was nine and Merritt wouldn't quit beating the crap out of me. My dad was gone, so your dad showed me how to fight. He . . ." Montgomery stops and glances around for security cameras before continuing in a whisper. I lean in close to hear him, and some silly part of me wants to lean in closer. People pass us in the street, but it feels like we're alone, together on the edge of the underground.

"Your dad showed me how to jump portals to places I hadn't ever been before. Secret places." He clears his throat and steps back. "A few years ago, when I'd started overseeing some of the lines, I'd see you sometimes. When I'd drop your dad off at the house, after he'd had a bad night. Or those Thai food deliveries. I . . . your dad . . . He talked about you a lot. He loves you, you know, even if he's done some stupid things."

This time, I'm the one to step back.

It hurts too much to think how little I know about my dad sometimes. How much he's hidden from me. How he could have been there for me and my mom more if he didn't have this secret life. How much he still makes terrible choices that impact me, even though he loves me.

"It doesn't excuse the lying." I fold my arms across my chest. "Or the drinking."

"He said you were a tough cookie. He's not wrong about that."

"Actually, he calls me his Little Hamboorger, but you probably already knew that."

"Actually, I didn't. I'll trade you—stop calling me Monty and I'll keep your little nickname under wraps."

"But Mr. Monty fits you so perfectly."

We stand smiling at each other in the last patch of sunlight before stepping into the underground. I trail him down the echoing stairway. Not long after, a train heading back to San Francisco squeals into the station. We board it and sit side by side in the blue vinyl seats. The silence between us feels comfortable. I can finally let my shoulders relax after being in that man pit reeking of soggy socks and too much testosterone. I can finally breathe again as long as we avoid talking about my dad anymore. It hurts too much.

"We should have gotten you some ice packs," he says. "How's your throat?"

"Your brother has a mean grip."

"Tell me about it."

"So, who's the older brother, you or Merritt?"

"Merritt," he says. "By a year."

"And Em put you in charge. I'm sure that went over well."

"When Merritt found out, he started a new hobby called Dead Rats in Montgomery's Bed."

"How imaginative."

"That's exactly Merritt's problem, though. He doesn't have enough imagination to be truly great at portal jumping. He wears the same cargo shorts and muscle T-shirts every single day, and I still find dead rats inside the sock drawer of my Embarcadero apartment. When I was thirteen, I started jumping farther than him, like San Francisco to New York far, while he could barely make it across the Bay. Speed and distance vary among jumpers, even in families. But I tried to teach him. Tried to tell him that I think the trains actually listen. So he decided to throw my violin in front of an incoming train. That was Merritt when we were kids; that'll be Merritt twenty years from now. He can only see the tracks in front of him, not where they lead."

"Do you two still fight a lot?"

"Not as much. At least not on a sparring mat. Not since your dad taught me some tricks."

"OK, just tell me." I sigh, picking at a scab that hasn't healed yet. "What's my dad really like?"

"Come on, you live with him. You know what your dad is like."

"I keep finding out more and more lies about him. How do I know the real him?"

"He'd die for you. That's how much he loves you. Isn't that enough?"

"The one thing I know for certain about my dad is that he'll go down swinging." I say it lightly, but I already feel my chest tightening around the words. Often, I worry I'll come home to find him fallen. I worry that he won't wake up from one of his binges. I worry that he'll limp, stumbling and drunk, into an oncoming truck. I worry he'll never make it to old age. And that was before I knew about his work in this crime underworld.

I try to steady my breath, but I can't stop the messy tears that start to blur the edges of my vision. *Don't cry, don't you cry. Not here. Not in front of Montgomery.* This is why I never talk about my dad's issues with anyone. I can't help the burst of emotion clawing up my throat. I try to tamp it down, deep inside where I bury it. I clench my teeth together and look away. I will not cry in front of this stranger. I will not cry in front of my boss. I will not. You're Balboa now. Stop it. You've already buried Mom—you survived—you can—god, a wet messy sob escapes my mouth.

He'll die, just like Mom.

Too soon.

And he'll rage against it, because that's what my father does; and I'll rage against it, because that's what I do, but it won't matter in the end.

"I'm sorry," Montgomery says. "I shouldn't have said that. Your dad will be fine."

"Shut up, it's fine. I'm fine." I shove away the hand he's awkwardly reached toward me as if he doesn't know whether he should touch a wild animal. A few people glance our way, and there's nowhere to hide myself on the train, nowhere except the space between the trains. I bolt up and shoulder people out of my way. I slide open the train doors and shut myself inside like it's a coffin. Like I can bury all the feelings inside this box and close the door and climb out without them. I have to; it's the only way to survive.

Suddenly, the train's electricity flickers.

I squeeze my eyes shut, and then open them again.

Still, flickering.

Am I causing it? I'm not doing anything on purpose. But I can't even think straight, not right now.

The lights black out. Through the glass door, bright phone lights shimmer across the train car. Passengers, no doubt, panicking that they might get trapped in the middle of a dark tunnel.

The smell of cedar and spice fills my nose. Montgomery opens the doors and squeezes his tall body into the cramped space with me. He keeps coming farther inside until the door shuts behind him.

"What are you doing?" Panic rises in my throat while my shoes slide.

He grasps the door handle, and a chill floods into the small space. Now all I smell is the sharp tang of metal and ice; all I hear is the train's deep rumble. Blue cracks form on the glass doors. The fluorescent lights flicker on for two whole seconds. His eyes are closed, and he mumbles something that sounds like poetry. Pinpricks shoot across my spine as the train squeals to a stop.

⚡ CHAPTER 17 ⚡

The first thing I think—did all the parts of my body come through in one piece? The second thing I think—*is that snow?* I tumble onto a red carpet and clutch at a wooden pole to regain my balance. The whole world spins and tosses and swallows me whole. Until finally, my hammering heartbeat slows to a crawl and my hands feel solid again. Montgomery slumps onto a red velvet bench and pinches the space between his eyebrows. I try to shake off the dizziness while I scan the train for clues about what the heck just happened.

My mouth drops.

Dorothy, we've officially left San Francisco.

Beautiful white mountain peaks glide by our windows, along with waterfalls taller than I ever imagined. Glistening railroad tracks cut through valleys. Red and blue A-frame houses freckle the hillside below, and kids play some sort of game involving snowballs and nets. And it's snowing, lovely and white and glittering.

No one else is in our train car. The comforting sound of wheels gliding on tracks calms my heartbeat. Heat slowly returns to my fingers. Montgomery opens his eyes and watches me cling to the window.

"Sorry," he says. "I should have warned you. I thought you could use a distraction."

I press my palm into the glass, and the wind howls alongside the train. Icicles cling to the window ledge. I trace my fingertips along the dewdrops. It's real. It's all real.

"This train line has been around since the 1940s. It's called the Flamsbana. Its cuts through Norway's mountains and fjords between Oslo and Bergen."

"We're . . . we're in Norway? Like *the* Norway? Like the snowy country halfway around the world?"

He smiles as if he's pulled off the greatest magic trick in the world. And he has. We're in Norway! A world away from San Francisco. I want to hug him. I don't hug him. Instead, I slide into one of the red velvet seats across from him and press my face against the glass. I have to keep wiping away my steamy breath to catch every glimpse out the window. The train chugs through tunnels carved into the mountains, past misty waterfalls and icicles dangling on light posts; its green tail wags into view on the wide turns through the valleys.

"You jumped us *thousands* of miles," I say.

"About five thousand, one hundred miles, give or take."

If he's still catching his breath, he's doing a good job of hiding it. He can do this. No sweat. With me in tow. I can't even imagine how much energy that takes. I, on the other hand, was left breathless after jumping seven measly miles across San Francisco. I turn to face him. He leans back against the plush headrest and looks as enamored with the passing landscape as I am. I'd been expecting a smug told-you-so smile, but honestly, he just seems happy to be here. It makes me grin right back.

"Can I say for the record that I'm glad you didn't take me to Narnia," I say. "The last thing I need right now are talking lions."

"Had enough magic already?"

"Back on the BART train, was I messing with the electricity?" I say.

"No, I have a special device. For distractions," he says. "A guy disappearing into thin air with a crying girl would raise far too many questions. We only needed to buy twenty seconds."

"I wasn't . . ." I want to say crying, but I can't deny the remnants of tears still smeared on my cheeks. I quickly wipe away the last of the salty evidence.

"Is that device even legal?" I say.

"Of course not, but Merritt has some interesting clientele. It comes in handy sometimes."

A hulking blond man approaches us. His hair is shorn, and his lips are pink from the frost outside. He wears a navy vest with an official train emblem stamped across his chest. The vest looks a size too small, but only because his shoulders are so wide. A whistle dangles from his throat, and his hands are wrapped in leather gloves.

Oh god, I don't have a passport. Or a train ticket, or an alibi, or anything.

"God dag," he says in greeting. He scowls at our seats, where he probably knows there were no passengers a few minutes before. My mouth churns like a fish caught on a hook. Thankfully Montgomery jumps in, since I don't know a drop of Norwegian.

"Hvor kan jeg kjøpe en vikinghjelm?" Montgomery says.

"Up your ass," the man says in perfectly crisp English.

They stare at each other for a long moment until they finally burst out laughing.

"What? What's so funny?" I say, glancing from face-to-face.

"So, who's your girlfriend?" he says.

"She's not—"

"I'm not—" we say in unison, both eager to jump out of this velvet bench.

"Yah, yah," the man says, waving away our discomfort.

"She works for Em now," Montgomery says eventually.

"I'm Håkon. Hyggelig å treffe deg." He reaches out a hand, and I shake it. I notice a tattoo around his wrist, an intricate Viking design that looks like inter-looping train tracks. I was hoping for my tattoo to look daring or iconic like that instead of this measly BART logo.

"I'm Balboa." When I say it, I sound like a liar. I'm not used to calling myself Balboa aloud. It suddenly makes me miss my old name.

"Are you stopping at Myrdal?" Håkon says.

"If you don't mind," Montgomery says.

"Yes, go. I have a girl who wants to visit San Francisco next month."

"Hit me up when you're passing through. I'm sorry this was so . . . sudden."

Håkon waves away the apology. Thank god Montgomery doesn't mention my crying spree. Though I bet my face is still a red splotchy mess.

The conductor continues down the aisle, across the hallway to another train car with a set of tourists chattering away in German. That much I recognize.

"I thought we couldn't cross without a price," I say.

"Uh, well. It's like . . . There's this . . ." Montgomery stutters and stops, and I can tell there's something he doesn't want to tell me. Something about our jump. His lips do this cute quirky thing when he's nervous. I try not to notice. "Basically, Håkon and I are old friends. Sometimes I let him through San Francisco when he wants to impress a hot date."

"Is this a date?" I flutter my eyelashes in a way that would make Diego proud.

"No! I'm not . . ." He looks more flustered than I would have expected.

"Relax." I slip out of the red velvet seat and stretch out against the train door. "I know why you brought me here. Thank you, I appreciate the distraction. Truly, I do."

See, I'm getting better at my manners. I owe him a little decency even if it was trying to talk to him about my dad's secrets that made me cry. There's just . . . so much to process. As if my brain isn't fried enough learning about this train portal magic, now I need to figure out my family drama, too.

"You're welcome," he says. "I thought Norway would be a good place to start."

To start. I giant grin blooms on my face. All the new places to explore, and this is only the start.

"So, what did you ask him before?" I say.

"Ah, you mean: 'Hvor kan jeg kjøpe en vikinghjelm?'"

"Yeah, that gibberish. What does it mean?"

"Where can I purchase a Viking helmet?" A boyish grin spreads across his face again, and I wish I could get him to smile like this more often. "Besides, I don't think Norwegians would appreciate you calling their native language gibberish."

"Maybe if they didn't wear those Viking helmets, then people could take them more seriously."

He joins me by the window and points out a deer peeking from the edge of the forest. Our shoulders touch, and I try my best to ignore the heat whirling down my arm. Wispy white mountains glide past us like a dream. Icy streams reflect the train, a green streak painted on their surface. I nestle into the red velvet seats and feel my troubles melting away. Five thousand miles away from home, five thousand miles away from all my worries. I almost feel high. Or maybe it's the portal jumping, or the altitude. Does my father feel this way every time he leaps across the world to the Philippines?

"In all seriousness," he says. "If you can jump trains to foreign countries, you should start learning some key phrases."

"Such as?"

"Man er ikke norsk med mindre man kan navngi fem typar snø."

"Which means?"

"You are not Norwegian unless you know five names for different textures of snow."

"Man, what kind of trainer are you? First you give me poetry, now we're going to have deep philosophical debates in Norwegian."

He smiles and cracks open a window. The fresh air smells too good to be real. It's crisp and refreshing. I wish I could bottle it and bring it home.

"Come on, give me something useful," I say.

"Ever the survivalist."

"Always."

"I need your help," he says. "Jeg trenger din hjelp."

"Jeg trenger din hjelp," I repeat after him.

"I need a doctor," he says. "Jeg trenger en lege."

"Jeg trenger en lege."

"Again," he says.

"Jeg trenger en lege," I say with slightly better pronunciation. My tongue feels sloppy and thick. "Why a doctor?"

"Your feminist sensibilities will probably bristle at this, but if you find yourself alone and caught on a foreign train, I'd lean into the helpless act. While they're busy trying to get help, it buys you some important seconds to escape."

"Jeg trenger din hjelp."

"Good, you're a natural."

"Maybe it's in my blood. Supposedly, my grandpa on Mom's side came from somewhere in these icy fjords."

"Maybe, but you don't resemble your mom."

"God, can I say how creepy it is that you know so much about my life, and I know practically nothing about you except you jump trains and read William Carlos Williams and have two annoying brothers? Tell me something about you. Right now."

"You already know more than you should."

"Afraid to level the playing field?"

"Fine." He muses for a moment, eyebrows quirked. "I play music."

"Piano, guitar, violin?"

"Yes to all of the above. I play trumpet, too. And I dabble with mixers."

"Show-off! Am I allowed to throw you off the train for being so ridiculously talented?"

"I've been lucky enough to have time to practice. And tutors. And any instrument I can get my hands on. I don't know if I can call that talent."

"Is that why you like poetry? The rhythm?"

"Maybe. Who knows why anyone likes poetry." The edges of his mouth quirk up in a stifled smile. "This is going to sound silly," he says, tapping his long fingers on the windowpane. "But I have this theory that the trains are drawn to poetry and music. Like maybe they can hear us calling to them more strongly when we whisper a melody instead of a memory."

It's alluring to see more of this music and poetry side of Montgomery after spending so much time with the strict no-nonsense version of him on the trains.

"Can I hear you play sometime?" I say.

"Nope."

"Bastard."

"I don't like to play in front of people. Especially audiences of one."

"I'll hide in the closet."

He grins, and I can't help but feel like time has slowed down to a butterfly stroke.

The conductor says "Myrdal" on the speakers. The train slackens, brakes grinding on the tracks. Snow gently flakes down from the sky. It melts off the windows and leaves behind silvery streaks. The sunlight dances and dodges through the water droplets.

"Do you want to get off the train?" he says. "It'll stay at this station for a few minutes."

The train jolts to a full stop. The doors open, and icy air sweeps inside.

"Of course." Who cares if it's freezing outside and I'm wearing only a sweater. What if I never make it back to Norway again?

We step carefully onto the grated metal platform. A couple of German tourists follow us with giant cameras dangling from their necks. After this train ride, I wonder if they'll adventure farther north in search of the northern lights. My shoes crunch across the snow. I feel giddy. Like a schoolgirl. I have never, ever been a giddy schoolgirl. But this is my first time in the snow. So, of course, I resort to the most cliché thing possible—I stick my tongue out for a passing snowflake. It tastes like a sliver of . . . snow. Some part of my brain told me it would taste like cotton candy. Our brains are such liars sometimes. Still, I can't help it. I run through the snow with my arms out, mouth open, tasting the cold. The Norwegians stare. Let them stare.

"Don't tell me this is your first time in the snow," he says.

"You know, it's rude to make fun of virgins."

"I'm not making fun."

"Because, man er ikke norsk med mindre man kan navngi fem typar snø."

"I don't believe you know all five yet."

"I will. Give me time. I'll learn the flavor and texture of each type of snow."

"I don't doubt it, Ruby."

"It's Balboa now, remember?"

At this reminder of my new name, a little of the lightness fades from his eyes. Curse the gods, this snow does wonders with that blue. The sapphire held in contrast with the white; it's striking. My fingers want to reach for invisible paintbrushes. Instead, I scoop up a handful of snow and cup it into a perfect sphere.

"No snowballs, or I'm leaving you here," he says.

"What makes you think I'd do something like that?"

"Everything."

I juggle the snowball between my freezing fingers, loop it around my back, then up in the air and back into my palm like I'm a circus magician. When the whistle blows and Montgomery glances toward the train doors, I make a toss for his wavy hair. He ducks before it hits him.

"Someone's not fond of listening," he says.

"I listen quite well, in fact." I nod toward the hole in the snow and squeeze the snowball still here in my palm. On the ground, a bright orange ball peeks through the white. He leans down to pick it up.

"An . . . orange?" he says with a laugh. "I'm going to have to keep an eye on those hands, aren't I?"

"It's a Cutie, as a matter of fact. And yes. You are."

He looks like he doesn't want to get back on the train. Or maybe I'm making that up. I don't want to leave, not yet. The horn sounds again, and I can see Håkon in the first train car waiving us aboard. There's a smug smile on his face, like he won a bet with Montgomery.

"We better run, before he leaves us here," he says.

"What would happen if he did?"

"Come on, Cinderella. You know what happens when it strikes midnight. Besides, my fingers are frozen."

We sprint toward the train, and the doors close behind us in a whoosh.

I want to say, *let's stay.*

I want this lightness to last.

I want to be a normal girl, who can flirt and laugh and taste snowflakes.

But if there's anything I know about life, it's that you can't run away. It'll be there waiting for you when you return.

❧ CHAPTER 18 ❧

That's why, when I finally walk away from the train station back to my house, I expect the absolute worst. My dad hungover on the mattress, vomit coating the stairs, sticky beer spilled on the sink, broken piano keys and raging music.

Instead, I come home to an immaculate abode. Well, as immaculate as a concrete room full of furniture and silverfish could be. My dad has wiped away the thick layer of dust on everything from the washing machine to the piano keys. It smells like beeswax and honey and lemon. He's even rolled out one of my mom's bohemian rugs to cover the concrete. The bright greens and oranges make the place feel alive. It resembles a slice of our old home. For a second, I breathe in the smell of her, my mother, the cloves and vanilla, and then it's gone. I could have imagined the whole thing, but I'm still glad to have a moment with her.

In the garden, my dad sits on a bench under the redwood tree, sipping a mug of mint tea. I know because I can smell it when I sit down next to him. It's not the stale hoppy aroma of beer or the rank toilet bowl from cheap vodka. No, this is mint tea.

This is my father.

"Balboa," he says, testing out my new name, his old name.

"Dad."

I realize with a jolt that I still have no idea what his real name is. If he's not Balboa, then who is he? I'm afraid to ask him, afraid to lose what little sparkling pieces I have of him in my memories. For now, and forever, he is *Dad* in my mind.

"How did it go?" he says. It sounds almost hopeful.

It was . . . exciting. Exhausting. Raw. Everything all in one.

I relax into the bench beside him, so illogically happy to see my dad again. Even if I don't know his real name. This is my real dad. The dad who gives me boxing lessons while singing karaoke, who cooks up the best chicken adobo; the dad who would step off the train and take me to Golden Gate Park to name the ducks silly things like Dalloway and Mozart and Manny. The dad who would jump thousands of miles to see me. I want to tell him all about Norway, about the snow, about the waterfalls that cut through the mountainsides, but I don't want to betray Montgomery's hideaway.

Instead, I tell him that Montgomery is teaching me the ropes. That I haven't really done anything yet. That I'm excited to learn more.

His calm vanishes. Tension creeps into his neck, and he twists to stare at me.

"Excited? Excited. Ruby, this is dangerous!"

"It's Balboa now."

"Be careful, anak." My dad stands up and hovers over me even though his hips ache. "You will open and close doors. You do not know what will come through the lines."

"I can handle it."

"I tried so hard to keep you away from this." He takes a long gulp of his mint tea as if he wishes it was alcohol instead.

"Well, it's too late now. Besides, Montgomery is a good teacher. He'll teach me everything I need to know. It's amazing how far he can jump across the portals. He really seems to care, and . . ." I feel like I've said too much already. My dad knows me too well to not notice when I'm rambling about a boy. A blush creeps across my cheeks. I lean against the tree and pick at the redwood bark. My fingers smell raw and earthy.

"Thank you for cleaning the house," I say to break our awkward silence. "It looks great."

I wish I could fully express how much it means to me to come home to this instead of his usual messes. How much I've missed the real him. How glad I am that he no longer risks his life on the trains with his bad hip, even if it means I have to take his place in the Bartholomew contract. He squeezes my hand and pulls me into a hug.

"Montgomery is a good boy. But you must still be careful. Family always comes first."

"Dad, you know I'll always put family first."

"No, I mean the Bartholomew family. Montgomery will always be a Bartholomew. You must remember that, even if he cares. One day, he will have to make a choice he does not want to make. One day, anak, *you* will have to make a choice you don't want to make."

"Dad, I've been doing that for a long time already."

He sighs and pulls me more tightly into his hug.

ᥫ

Inside the house, we try to put aside all our dark thoughts. He marinates the chicken legs while I chop bok choy and carrots. My dad slathers on the soy sauce, vinegar, and peppercorns. It'll make a delicious adobo when it's done. A rice cooker steams up the room. It feels warm. Safe. It feels like home again. While we wait for the meat to simmer, my dad oils his old leather boxing gloves. I pull out my phone, half-itching to tell a friend about my snowy adventure with Montgomery. I scroll down my contact list and realize I haven't talked to any of these fools in months, years, even. Except Diego. And I'm always afraid I'll ruin things with him. With Mom's chemo, I'd pushed everyone away. It was too hard to face "normal." Gossiping over boba smoothies, planning the next road trip to Stinson Beach to catch the nude sunbathers in action, braiding Claire's hair into the tiniest braids possible. Normal, all normal. Worse yet, I couldn't face their grating optimism that a bright and sunny future awaited me once I'd gotten over the grief.

I couldn't breathe around it.

My friend Kayla used to send me the funniest memes with cats curled up in unlikely places, along with persistent questions about when I was going to apply to art school, travel, get on with life. I got fed up one time and told her another unlikely place she should go and shove her freaking cats. I agree, I could have been less of an asshole. But chemo. And debt. And my dad. And it was too much. It was a moot point anyway; we all graduated high school and went our separate ways. I'd heard Kayla went to NYU, and Jessica went to some engineering school, and Gretchen went on a gap year to find herself. Everyone left, moved on with life.

Except I'm still here.

I feel like I'm caught in a weird purgatory between high school and college, as if I'm caught in a gap year with no beginning and end.

I hover over Kayla's phone number and feel the urge to send her a meme with a cat startled silly after its first encounter with snow, but I stop myself. Why would she want to hear from me? She's already moved on to a new life.

I consider maybe telling Diego, but he'd probably hear about my snowy crush and bust out laughing. Sometimes I think Diego might actually have something helpful to say about my dad's addiction. It seems like he has experienced a whole lot of life already. But how do I even bring it up? And what if he tells me that I'm failing my father, or that my father is failing me? God, what if I start crying and he gives me that disgusting pitying look? What then? Imagine how awkward it will be when we have to paint our next house. I love painting with Diego and the crew. I can't risk it.

This is my life now. Why bother thinking about what could be?

There's no time to waste on impossible things.

Well, except the trains.

⚹ CHAPTER 19 ⚹

Do you feel that?" Montgomery says.

"Yes," I lie.

"Balboa," he grumbles.

"OK, no! I don't know what I'm supposed to feel."

"A rumble, like the edges of an earthquake. It's subtle, but you need to feel when someone jumps the trains. It's our job to keep outsiders off our lines unless they've paid the fare. But you can't keep someone off unless you know they're there."

"Isn't that what security cameras are for?"

"Too slow. You need to be there in a flash."

I close my eyes and try to feel the train ripple as one of his henchmen jumps on and off our line. All I feel is Montgomery's body heat next to me, his long legs pressing into the seats in front of us. Does he have to be so darn distracting? We've been trying this for hours, and I still can't feel anything remotely magical.

"Man, this ain't worth the sore knees." The henchman drops into a BART seat next to us. Sweat drips down his Black skin, and he runs his hands over his knees like they ache all the way down to his bones. Joint pain, one of the perks of the job. He's too young for that, probably only in his twenties. Montgomery told me his name is Dublin, but that's all the information I'm allowed. Dublin / Pleasanton station, all the way across the bay. Just another henchman in the intricate Bartholomew web. Like me.

"OK, let's go." Montgomery jumps up. "This isn't working."

I try not to let his disappointment bring me down. Maybe I won't be any good at this. Maybe I won't be able to fill my father's shoes. Will Madame Em still want me to be Balboa if I can't do my job? Even though Montgomery far outjumps Merritt, Em keeps Merritt around because he's her blood—and we've all seen how much muscle that boy brings to the table. What if I didn't inherit the jumping gene from my father as strongly as Em had hoped? What if I can't jump beyond San Francisco?

Montgomery glances back and waves to me to follow him toward the Saddle, the plexiglass space between the train cars. He closes the doors without letting me inside with him. His breath fogs up the glass.

"Catch me if you can," he says with a playful smile.

And then, he's gone.

Flash, just like that.

I rip open the sliding doors, and an icy blast hits my face. I blink away the frost and I wave my arm through the Saddle to make sure this isn't some sort of invisibility trick—as if that would make any more sense than teleporting.

How can he vanish that fast?

I didn't even see his limbs dissolve or fade away.

One second there, the next second gone.

Whenever I've jumped trains, it feels like time slows down and frost slips in between the cracks. It feels like I'm an ice cube melting into something else.

Dublin strolls up behind me and laughs.

"Good luck catching *him*. That man is fast."

"How do I find him?"

"Call to the trains, they'll hear ya."

Right. Because that makes complete sense.

I hurry into the Saddle and close my eyes, try to feel for him in this web of train lines. A well-worn map of the BART system hovers in my mind. I know every city in the Bay Area. But how is it possible to pick out an individual among all the jumpers? How can I feel something that happens miles away? There's no choice—this is my job now. I need to prove myself, or else Em could break the contract. Take the house. Come on, *you are Balboa.* I can still smell Montgomery's rich cedar and spice cologne, but I'll need more than that to carry me across.

Dublin said to talk to the train. That it will listen.

"Uh, hello . . . train. It's Balboa here. Do you, uh . . . have a name? Never mind. Look, I just need you to help me track down Montgomery, OK?"

Dublin watches me talking to myself through the plexiglass doors and bursts into laughter. Real funny. So much so that he doubles over into an empty seat next to him and keeps on howling.

I flip him off and twist in the opposite direction. My reflection stares back at me.

"Look, real talk," I say with my hands balled into fists. "This is the red wheelbarrow. This is the end all. I need this, please. Everything depends on this." I start to recite the poem that Montgomery shared with me in case the trains can actually hear me. In case the poem's melody calls to the magic inside the trains. Like a spell, an incantation, a plea to take me where I need to go—all wrapped in a poet's words. Hear me.

```
so much depends

upon


a red wheel

barrow


glazed with rain

water


beside the white

chickens
```

As the words fly out of my mouth, an impossible wind rustles through the plexiglass booth. It feels like something is listening in the brush, its ears perked up in curiosity. I squeeze my eyes shut. Nothing will break my concentration. Not Dublin's laughter, not the fact that Montgomery's spicy cologne is fading fast, not the *clu-clunk* of wheels on the tracks.

Inside my hazy head, I can see Montgomery pushing open the Saddle doors—*somewhere*—glass squealing against metal. I grip onto the door handles in front of me and push them open. Ice pummels my lungs, and I can't breathe for a minute. The train hits the brakes and I go toppling backward—into something solid and warm. Laughter fills the small space, and at first I don't know if it's my own. Or Dublin's. Or someone else's. Strong arms steady me, and I open my eyes. I see our reflections wrapped around each other in the glass doors. We're inside the Saddle—together.

"You did it," he whispers into my ear.

For a moment, the train stands still.

It feels like we're free-falling.

Silence wrapping us in its secret cocoon.

It smells like cedar and a warm crackling fire. He stands behind me, his arm wrapped around my waist, even though my feet are steady now.

"It was the William Carlos Williams poem," I whisper.

"I told you it was key."

"I thought you were joking about serenading the trains with poetry."

"Well, it doesn't work for everyone that way. It works for me."

"And me."

I catch his smile in the glass reflection.

"I think the magic in the trains understands poetry better than commands," he says. "I think something in the rhythm calls to them. As long as they can feel your intention."

The train speeds up again, and the momentum presses my back into his chest. He lets me stay there until we reach the next stop. He wraps a hand around my hip to keep my shaky legs steady. Minutes fly by too quickly. Our inhales twine together into the same breath, and it's hard to admit how much I want to lean my body into his.

"Dublin / Pleasanton station," the conductor announces.

Did he say, *Dublin / Pleasanton?*

Holy smokes, I jumped all the way across the bay. By myself. And the trains heard me. Maybe this means that I'll hear them better, too.

Once we arrive in the station, Montgomery sees Dublin smirking in the aisleway and quickly drops his hand from my waist. He snaps open the doors and hustles me forward. I wish I could take a minute to celebrate. Instead, he strides down the aisle. It feels like an icy frost follows his every step. I wrap my arms around myself and try to shake it off, but I can't help feeling like he has dumped a cold bucket of water over my head.

What's the deal? One minute, he's hot; the next, cold. As if the train jumping wasn't dizzying enough. I don't know where my footing has gone. He storms down the aisle without a backward glance to make sure I'm OK. A teenager retracts his leg from the aisle, afraid Montgomery might trample it in his rush. Jerk.

Dublin arches his eyebrow like he knows a secret.

How much did he see?

"Back to work," Montgomery snaps at Dublin before stepping out onto the platform.

I catch him sneaking a glance at the security camera on his way out. It's a shiny orb that resembles a cross between an obsidian marble and Sauron's evil eye.

Montgomery stands on the platform while passengers rush past him into the train. Sunshine dapples his face as he grimaces at the waiting train. I shiver. He's a Caravaggio painting all over again.

Unsure of what to do next or if we're still training, I take a step toward him.

"No," he says when I'm about to follow him off the train. "We're done for today. You can go home. We'll start again tomorrow. Dublin, take her home."

I want to tell him it's fine. I can find my own way back; I know this city. No need to make Dublin's knees ache anymore, but Dublin does as he's been ordered. A frown spreads across his face as he escorts me back to Balboa Park, quick as a bruise. On my way out, I take one last glance at the security cameras guarding the station. I wonder who else is watching and how much they've already seen. I wonder if I really know Montgomery at all.

⚡ CHAPTER 20 ⚡

I wake up to tapping on our garage door. My dad grumbles in his sweaty sleep, though he doesn't wake. I throw on a wool sweater, my boots, and grab the baseball bat resting by our door. The tapping sounds again, more insistent this time. My heart thunders inside my chest. Is this part of the job? Did some shady gangster follow me home from the train station? My hand shakes as I turn the knob, slowly, and peek outside without removing the chain lock. A shadow towers over my door.

"Balboa," the voice says.

"Montgomery? It's midnight, what are you doing here?" I lower the bat to the floor but keep the chain in place.

"I'm sorry I left you like that on the train," he says through the crack.

It's hard not seeing his face, but his voice sounds sincere. We really should install a motion sensor light in our driveway. Especially now that I know about my dad's line of work. I pull my sweater more tightly around my chest. Fog wraps around the chimneys, smothers out the moonlight.

"I know it's just business," I say, even though it still stings to realize how quickly he can freeze me out, how suddenly he can transform into someone else. "We should keep things more professional."

Montgomery leans his head against the sliver of space open between us. I can see his eyes glowing in the streetlight. The smell of cedar and spice sneak through the doorway.

"No, it's not OK. I wish . . ." He looks like he wants to say so much more. I hope he doesn't. I need this job. I can't risk anything going wrong, and the last thing I need are more complications in my life. But I can't resist—a small hopeful part of me wants to know.

"What do you wish for?" I whisper into the darkness. He hovers by the door in silence, his fingers picking at his coat sleeves.

Finally, he says, "I wish you hadn't signed the contract."

Anger rises up in my throat, bitter and scalding hot.

"Yeah, well, your family didn't give me much choice, did they?" I glance back at my father sleeping in his bed, afraid I might have woken him with my sharp voice. His fitful snoring echoes down the dark garage.

"There's always a choice," Montgomery says.

"So what are you doing here?"

When he doesn't say anything, I step back, ready to slam the door shut. I don't have time for this. I don't get enough sleep as it is.

"Please," he says. "Let me take you somewhere."

"The only place I'm going tonight is my bed, thank you very much."

I shove the door shut, but he stops it with his palm before it slams. A thin crack lets in the streetlight. Montgomery continues in a whisper that barely sneaks through the heavy wood.

"When I was nine, Em rushed my brothers and I into a safehouse after my dad was gone. She refused to lose Embarcadero station. While she was fighting off our rivals, she'd come back to our snowy safehouse, and she'd say, 'Let me take you somewhere. Somewhere special.' And no matter how furious I was that she'd leave us with a nanny for weeks at a time, I'd take her hand because she always knew somewhere special to take us. Somewhere only I'd wish for. I'd close my eyes and wake up somewhere I thought I'd imagined in a dream."

My breath fogs into the cold night, and I realize I've let the door swing open as far as it will go while on the chain.

"You said you like van Gogh?" he says.

ς

Montgomery hops over the ticket turnstile with all the grace of someone who has done this many times before. Sneaking into an empty BART station; the rattle and bustle of trains gone. The trains stopped running at midnight. He continues down the dark walkway, and I follow, hesitantly at first, and then swiftly because I can't bear the thought of getting lost down here in the shadows. His sneakers are surprisingly silent on the tile floor. Train stations are always filled with endless chatter, tunnels echoing and candy wrappers crinkling. It's never this:

Pure silence.

And footsteps.

Only ours, I hope.

As we rush down the metal escalator stairs, it feels like we're descending into a crypt. It's colder down here without the train engines and hundreds of human exhales to keep the tunnels warm. It smells dank; sweat and spit clings to the walls. It's hard not to imagine strange beasts in the shadows. Every once in a while, I hear small feet skittering. Rats or pigeons, or worse?

Finally, we come to the edge of the platform. Eight feet below, the iron tracks stretch to the edges of our city and beyond. I hear wings flapping farther down the platform, and it sends a chill across my neck.

"Montgom—"

He leaps down into the pit.

His shoes hit gravel, and he disappears into the shadows.

Suddenly, I'm alone. In the darkness.

Wind whistles through the tunnels. Where does the wind come from if there are no trains snaking underground? I call out his name again, but I hear only my own echo. I pace back and forth along the platform. I'm about to call out again, but then I hear his voice in the darkness.

"Don't try jumping down," he says. "Dangle your legs over the edge, and I'll help you."

I can barely see the outline of his body. This far down in the labyrinth of the train station, there are no lights. It's obsidian darkness. I've lost all sense of depth or texture. A dark beast could be watching two feet away, and I wouldn't know it. The only reason I know Montgomery is still down there is the crunch of gravel under his sneakers. Or maybe there's more than Montgomery down there? Maybe . . . *Stop it, Ruby. Not tonight.* Tonight, I'm walking into a deserted train station with a boy I kind of like, and kind of work for, and kind of trust, and kind of want to follow into this dark tunnel.

I want to see where it goes.

"Are you coming?" he says in a low rasp.

My heart hammers as I kneel down to the rough edge. Plastic bumps rest below my palms, markers telling me where the edge is, so I know when I've crossed it. So I know when I've gone too far into danger's path. It's as if the ground is covered in goosebumps. I swallow a breath and swing my legs across the edge. Across the yellow line. It's like dangling bare toes off a boat, and I can't see the sharks circling below.

A hand clamps onto my calf, and I let out a small scream.

He immediately lets go.

"Sorry, are you OK?" he says.

"It's just . . . dark."

I hear the crunch of gravel again, and then suddenly light shines up. Blinding me. When my eyes finally adjust to the brightness, I see his cell-phone beam and his smiling face gazing up at mine. For once I'm taller than him.

"Can I help you down?" he says.

I nod and wiggle closer to the edge. His arms wrap around my knees, and my body slides into his embrace as he slowly lowers me to the ground. It could have been awkward and wobbly, but it isn't. I feel weightless, free-floating. Honestly, I wish he hadn't let go so soon. My feet hit the rocks, and everything is heavy again.

"You've had that flashlight the whole time!" I smack his arm. Chivalry or not, there's a thing called common sense.

"Even if the train station is closed, I don't know who's watching."

I peer up at the security cameras hovering over the train platform.

Montgomery flicks off the light, and again we're standing in the pitch dark. I can hear our heavy breathing. It feels like the tunnel breathes alongside us, though that's impossible.

"Can't we leave it on?" I hate the waver in my voice, but Montgomery or not, I don't completely trust the situation.

"Scared?"

"Clumsy."

"Liar," he says. "I've seen you move, and it's ballet."

I let a shy smile cross my lips. Not that he can see it, anyway. I take a breath and finally let my shoulders relax. I press a palm to his chest to ground myself, the thin cotton sweater, the warm heartbeat stuttering beneath my fingertips. He flinches beneath my touch. Come on, Balboa, what happened to personal bubbles? There's something about the dark that makes me too daring. I pull my hand away, but then, he brings it back to the spot where I had rested it. I can feel the rise and fall of his shallow breaths. His warm fingers twine with mine, and heat sparks down through my core, melting into my toes. I want everything and nothing, all at once.

"Are you OK if we walk a little farther in?" he says.

I nod, but then realize that he can't see me.

"Yes, I'm fine," I say, stepping back. "There's just . . . I don't know what to expect anymore. A couple weeks ago, your magic train portals didn't exist. All of you, Madame Em, my dad, everyone takes this magic for granted. You've always known it was there and how to use it. I'm still learning what's possible. How far I can go, how far this magic extends into real life."

"I won't let you get hurt," he says.

I want to believe him, but my dad says that kind of thing all the time.

But my father isn't Montgomery, and Montgomery isn't my father, and maybe just maybe, I can trust this boy.

Montgomery takes my hand and leads me farther into the tunnel.

I tap my toes along the iron tracks to keep me grounded. I've been to this train station a million times before, but never like this. Inside the trains, it's urban; it's everyday steel and one-sided phone conversations and scheduled stops along a route. *This*—this is primal. This is rock and dirt and darkness. The air is damp. Clean, though. Nothing like the dingy tile platform. Here, we're inside a cool cave. I keep my hands up in front of me to shield my face from industrious spiders, or worse.

Suddenly, Montgomery stops, and I almost knock into his back.

"Here's as good a spot as any," he says.

"You still haven't told me what we're doing here."

"Didn't I promise van Gogh?"

"But there are no trains to jump."

"It doesn't mean the magic isn't here."

We carefully avoid the third rail, and Montgomery crouches down to rest our palms on the twin iron tracks.

They're worn smooth to the touch.

Miraculously, incredibly, impossibly, they're *warm*. And not just from the heat in Montgomery's hand. They're warm like skin after a day on the beach. The trains stopped running hours ago, so it can't be residual heat from all-day use. I press my hand into the gravel for comparison, and it's frigid cold rock. I run my finger along the iron beam, and a tingle ripples through me. I take a leery step back.

"Feel that?" he says.

"Yes," I say, no lies this time.

It feels the same as petting a cat, that ripple of pleasure that you can tell zips across its arched spine. I wouldn't be surprised if the tracks started purring.

Ruby, do you hear yourself?

This is impossible.

"Not everyone can feel the trains when they're not running," he says. "Something about the electric current makes it a thousand times easier to jump. Most jumpers can't jump when the trains are at rest. I don't know why. Maybe not enough energy to harness the portals? I can't claim I know anything about how this magic works, or physics, or whatever. But when I first came here at night, I knew in my bones that I could jump these lines.

That they weren't dead at night . . . just sleeping. They only need something to rouse them."

"So, you bring a lot of girls down here for midnight practice?" I say before I can clamp my mouth shut.

"No. Only . . . you."

I let out a shaky breath, afraid to hope that there might be something sparking between us.

"Are you sure?" I say.

Montgomery takes a step closer, and my whole body flares to life. His hands are inches from mine, his lips within reach. He leans to whisper in my ear. Maybe it's the darkness that makes me bold, but I lean closer as if I don't know where his body ends and mine begins. The toes of our shoes touch. My fingers brush against his sweater, and they ache to explore the warm skin along his hips. Our bodies hover inches away, and the tunnel wind weaves between us as if it wants to push us closer.

"You keep making me wish I didn't have to be *Montgomery* anymore. That you could be Ruby, and I could be—"

But he stops before he says his real name, swallowing the words before they can escape his throat. The wind howls through the desolate tunnel. It's as if the trains are aching to hear his real name, too. Disappointment digs into my throat, but I don't press him. Those are his secrets to keep. What makes me think that I deserve to know them? We hardly know each other, and yet . . . I constantly feel like we're old souls, lost and found. Maybe it's because we've both had to grow up too fast. We've had to bear burdens that shouldn't have been ours to bear. Maybe we can help each other reach for more. It's a ridiculous thought. A cliché that's more daydream than reality. But I can dream, can't I?

"Have you ever been to Amsterdam?" he says, breaking the silence stretched thinly between us. A flutter of wings echoes down the dark tunnel.

"No, I haven't been anywhere."

"Do you want to go?"

"Yes," I say immediately, afraid he might take back his offer if I wait even a second to consider what's about to happen.

"I've never done this with someone before," he says. "Not when the trains aren't running."

Gently, he pulls me downward onto the tracks, our knees crumpling, until we're both lying side by side. We're pressed together between the rails like perfect piano keys. Gravel scratches beneath my jacket, but his hand is warm around mine. I hear him whispering beside me. It takes me a moment to realize it's another poem he has memorized. I catch a few scattered words, blurring into the impossible wind.

"*Vermilion . . .*"

"*Orange . . .*"

"*He cut off his own ear.*"

The train tracks start to rumble beside me, even though there are no trains. Iron turns to ice, blue sparks snapping and popping around us. My vision swirls even in the darkness. Montgomery squeezes my hand tightly.

Then the ground disappears beneath our backs.

⚡ CHAPTER 21 ⚡

We open our eyes inside an abandoned train car. A patch of blazing sunlight streaks across our chests. My leg jams against a metal pole as I try to stretch out my aching knees. Horns blare in the distance, and it smells of rust and metal and forgotten things. Dust creeps under my nose, and I sneeze halfway because of the dust and halfway because it's too darn bright outside.

"It's . . . daylight?"

"There's a nine-hour time difference between San Francisco and Amsterdam."

Right. Because we're in Amsterdam. Halfway around the world.

I quickly drop Montgomery's hand. I can't believe I was thinking about kissing him. At least in broad daylight, I won't be tempted to do anything quite so foolish.

Montgomery hops up and brushes off his sweater. Then he reaches his hand down to help me to my feet. I shake my head—I'm Ruby Josephine Santos. Balboa, now. I can't rely on anyone else to pick me up. My aching joints protest as I stand. Dizziness hits me the moment I'm vertical, and I latch onto a metal pole to keep from falling.

"Hurry," he says. "We don't want to be caught here."

I stumble onto gravel. We zigzag our way through a maze of train tracks, busted engines, and shipping containers. A train boneyard, that's what this is. In the distance, I can see the real train station with its Gothic clock towers and a sign that reads AMSTERDAM CENTRAAL STATION, where trains zip passengers all across the Netherlands and farther across Europe.

"Why didn't we jump to the actual station?" I say.

"The Amsterdam jumpers are not nearly as friendly as their city promises. Their price is steep. Besides, word might get back to my family. Better to take the back entrance."

"You're full of secrets, aren't you?"

"Unfortunately."

We step onto the sidewalk and instantly we're caught in the flow of people moving across the city. We walk parallel to a canal filled with dark, glittering water. A boat splashes below, and bicycles glide along the opposite side. Crimson tulips sprout from a window box, and I want to crane my neck to see all the lovely architecture. Everything is at least three or four stories high, brick facades crowned with Dutch curving eaves and tiny rooftop windows. I've always dreamed about a little library attic, warmth wrapped up in the rafters and a Georgia O'Keeffe art book spread across my lap.

"Did you write that poem?" I hurry to keep up with his long strides. "The one you used to jump us to Amsterdam."

"Nope, not a poet."

"What about music? Ever serenade the trains?"

He shakes his head. "I'm not that talented."

"You seem like the kind of person who works hard to be good at something, talent be damned."

"I always find time to practice—in between running the trains. And school. And family. Honestly, it doesn't really leave time for moments like this." He gives me a gorgeous smile, and I want to ask him—*moments like what?* But then the streetlight turns red, stopping us in the middle of a tourist horde.

"I can't believe you have time to study!" I have to yell to be heard over their excited chatter. Yes, yes, we're almost to the Van Gogh Museum.

"Technically, I'm not in college to study music theory." Montgomery leans close, so I can hear him better. "I'm there on official Bartholomew business. A lot of rich kids go to Stanford, which feeds a lot of business into Montgomery station."

"But you study music anyway?"

"Any free minute I get."

We wait at a streetlight as scooters and cars zoom by. On the other side, a wide grassy field awaits us. In the distance, I see the cluster of museums surrounding the park. A giant sign reads I AMSTERDAM with the "I" and "AM" in bright red, and the remaining letters in white. A few teenage tourists climb on top of the enormous letter E and dangle their feet off the edge. Their mother snaps a photograph and waves to her kids to climb down.

"And what does Em think?" I say.

"Em wants me to focus on the family business."

"You seem very focused. At least when you're training me."

"I wish I could pour that kind of focus into music. And the other things I love. Instead of ruling an empire."

I've never heard such honesty and intensity in his voice before. He gazes down at me, and I can't help but blush and wonder what other things he loves. Outside of the trains, outside of his family's watchful eyes, Montgomery seems so much more free.

"Sorry, I'm being too honest," he says. "Sometimes it feels like I've known you for a long time. Even if it's mostly because of your dad's stories."

"It's OK. I know what it feels like to be trapped."

When the light turns green, impatient tourists push at our backs, and we're forced to march forward across the street.

"I don't mean to be rude, but you're not locked into a debt like mine," I say. "You haven't signed a contract. Why don't you just *leave*?"

"Not all debts are contracts. Some debts are bound by blood."

"Wouldn't your mom want the best for you, though?"

"She does. To her, that means the trains. And only the trains."

"But your brothers could run things instead, couldn't they?"

"Look, let's just enjoy the day!" He jogs through the grass toward the Van Gogh Museum. "We came here to get away from San Francisco."

"Speak for yourself. I came here for sunflowers!" I run to catch him, and we race toward the museum steps.

Time stretches as we wander through van Gogh's masterpieces. Bright orange and vermilion and starry blue burst from the paintings. I hear you, van Gogh, I hear you in my bones, my fingertips. I even drag Montgomery through the Rijksmuseum to catch the Rembrandts and the Vermeers and all the Dutch artists of the Golden Age. When I grab his hand to rush to the next painting, he lags behind me. His sneakers drag along the wooden floor. Oh no, jump-lag is finally catching up with him. He tries to hide that he's massaging the pain in his knees when he thinks I'm absorbed in a painting called "The Threatened Swan." It doesn't help that it's actually around four A.M. in San Francisco.

"We can jump back if you're tired," I say.

I keep my eyes pinned on the painting so Montgomery won't see the sting in my eyes if he says *let's go*. What if I never make it back here again? It's so different from gazing at paintings in books. In real life, you can see every brushstroke; you can stand at all different angles and see the magic an artist wove into the paint.

Montgomery leans down and rests his heavy chin on my shoulder. Now, we're looking at the painting from the same angle. The same swan, fiercely protecting her nest with pearly wings outstretched.

"How about I find us some coffee?" he says. "Triple espressos?"

I squeeze him into a tight hug before I bolt toward the next painting. His laughter trails me down the hallway. That boy better keep up.

Once we're sufficiently caffeinated, Montgomery lets me gaze at each painting for as long as I want. I keep reaching for his hand when I see a painting I'm particularly enamored with, and he squeezes back.

I don't feel like Ruby Santos here. Or Balboa. Or a girl with an alcoholic father. Or a tiny cog in the Bartholomew crime network.

I feel like I could become a whole new person. Someone who chases her dreams.

But I know it's all temporary. I'll wake up in San Francisco and have to go back to work, back to the garage, back to my dad's addiction.

Finally, Montgomery says we should head home before the first BART train starts at five A.M.

We're walking across a canal bridge when I stop to examine a giant clump of locks attached to the railing. I graze my hand across the smooth hooked metal and peer at our reflections in the water below. The breeze brings the smell of weed smoke and blooming algae and baked bread. I want to savor our last moments here. I have to say something before we're frozen again under the security cameras' watchful eyes. Say something, anything.

"I meant to thank you." I don't dare look him in the eyes. "For sharing this with me. I know it's not easy to hide things from your family."

"You're worth the trouble," he says.

Heat rises to my cheeks when he says it, but the moment doesn't last long. Next to us, a man clinks another lock onto the bridge and runs across to someone waiting for him. He lifts her up and spins her in a circle, nearly wobbling into a passing bicycle in the process. The man left behind a lock as big as my palm and bright sunburned orange. A van Gogh type of orange if ever there was one.

"Hey man, you left your lock!" I say.

Montgomery grabs my arm before I can holler after him again.

"Whoa there." He laughs. "It's meant to be romantic."

"Littering a lock on a bridge?"

"You've never seen one of these?"

I shake my head at the clump of forlorn locks. They come in every color and size, latched onto the chain-link, no keys in sight.

"They're called 'love locks.' Supposed to be an expression of eternal love. This is the Staalmeestersbrug bridge. A lover adds a lock, and then throws the key in the canal. I thought you knew this when you decided to stop here . . . Not that I thought . . ." His voice comes out flustered.

"That's ridiculous! Why waste a perfectly good lock? So, you're telling me that it's going to sit here and rust away on a bridge all because some dude wants to make a grand romantic gesture? Look, if you want to show me your love, give me a lock—*for my bike*. I'll treasure it every time my bike doesn't get stolen. Not that I have a bike . . . And by 'you,' I meant the universal you. Not you, as in *you*. And I'll stop talking now. OK."

His face looks horrified.

I spin around and hurry across the bridge.

Ruby, stop making a fool of yourself. I can't believe you stopped at a love lock. Can you be any more ridiculous?

Montgomery runs to catch up.

"We're going to be late," I say.

"Don't worry, I'm a quick jumper."

We sneak aboard the abandoned train car and catch our breath in the dusty light. He pulls me close to him, and I wait to feel the icy blast, the dizzying jump, the vertigo hitting my chest. Instead, we stand there for a moment, with only the trains rumbling in the distance.

"Isn't something supposed to be happening?" I say.

Montgomery leans down and leaves a soft kiss along my cheek until heat blazes all along my skin. He rests his forehead against mine and I soak in his heady cedar scent.

"I just wanted another minute before going back," he says.

Without another word, I reach up on tiptoes to meet his lips. His mouth is all cinnamon spice and warmth and sweet honey, the kind of lips you can sink down into. We don't have darkness to hide beneath, but it makes it feel more real that way. My fingers graze along his neck, along his broad shoulders. He slips the hair away from my face, and I pull him closer until every inch touches. Until we're breathless. Our fingers tease across bare skin, trailing the edge of his jeans, until I snag on something cold and metal in his back pocket.

At first, I wonder foolishly if it's a lock like the ones on the bridge.

But no, it's the handle of a blade.

A knife.

A reminder of our real lives.

I pull away to catch my breath. This isn't a game. This is the underground. The blood keeps rushing to my heart. His shoes squeal back onto rusted metal. We stand there reeling in silence for a few long seconds.

Then, he takes my hand and jumps me back to San Francisco—where we belong.

⁑ CHAPTER 22 ⁑

The next day, and the next day, and the next day, it's more trains. It's picking up packages from silent train jumpers while Montgomery eagle-eyes me from the opposite corner of the train. I think he's only there to make sure I don't ask questions. Not that the train jumpers offer any answers. They hand me a package, and I accept. End of transaction. He doesn't even let me see inside the packages. He checks inside each one, counting or eyeballing that whatever is supposed to be in there matches the agreement. I wonder what he will do if there's ever a day when those two don't match. It makes me cringe to imagine what *I* might have to do if that ever happens.

This morning is all waiting.

Two whole agonizing hours of it.

Are you still excited for this adventure?

I should be grateful for the quiet, but I've never been one to handle stillness well. Especially since Montgomery and I haven't been "alone" since that night in Amsterdam, and I can't stop looking at his lips. It's all business when we're on the trains. It's like he's Dr. Jekyll and Mr. Hyde—there are two halves of him, and they're not allowed to be on the same train. Except sometimes . . . when we're together, I can see the two halves become whole. I'm being ridiculous, aren't I? It's just a passing flirtation between us. That kiss didn't mean anything, even if I can't stop thinking about his fingers dancing along the small of my back. Even in this dingy fluorescent train, a delicious shiver travels up my spine when I think about that day in Amsterdam.

Focus, you're on duty. And Montgomery is late.

My legs can barely keep still. The nurses must have hated my frantic pacing when I used to wait in the hospital lobby for my mom. Sneakers squeaking on the linoleum, back and forth, back and forth. One of the nurses started calling me Zippy. *"Zippy, sit down!"*

I try people watching—and that's when I see them. Through my window. Standing still as my train drifts into Embarcadero station.

Madame Em and Montgomery.

This time, she wears gladiator sandals that spiral up her calves like snakes. The train rattles to a stop, and I twist my neck to spy on them.

Montgomery carries a plaid messenger bag on his shoulder. Oddly, he looks like a schoolboy as his mother hands him a paper bag. He reaches inside. Is he really going to pull out a wad of cash in the middle of the station? He unwraps the white paper, and inside sits a simple peanut butter and jelly sandwich in a sourdough muffin. Through the glass, I can see his smile, those bright Montgomery eyes. He digs into the bag again and holds a handful of gold foil-wrapped chocolate coins. A rare smile plays across Em's face. She waves him goodbye as he boards the train. I wonder, when he was a kid, did his mom link arms and pull him through his first portals?

The doors slide shut, and I pretend to stare straight ahead while Montgomery plops into the seat next to me.

"Hey, stranger," I say.

He smiles and tucks the paper bag between us.

"Hungry?" he says.

I pluck a single chocolate coin from the bag and peel away the foil. I let it melt on my tongue as I try to keep my questions at bay. What's it like to have a mother who rules a train empire? A woman who demands that you face danger every day to protect her empire—and yet, sends you off with homemade peanut butter and jelly sandwiches?

As the train accelerates, I keep my gaze on Madame Em while she watches the train leave Embarcadero station. Her blond hair flutters in the breeze, giving an unexpected softness to her otherwise brutal black dress and gladiator sandals. She refuses to tamp down her bangs in the train's gust. She lets them fly wildly around her face, never once breaking her gaze. In that moment, I wish I had an unrelenting stare like hers. The world wouldn't dare say no to my dreams.

By the time I turn back around, Montgomery already has half the muffin inside his wide mouth. A heavy textbook sprawls across his lap.

"Sorry," he says, dusting the crumbs from his pressed-and-ironed suit. "Late night. I have something I need to read. For school."

I tip the front cover, so that I can read the title.

"*Music Theory and Composition*?"

"Exam coming up," he says through peanut butter teeth.

"Seriously, how do you find time for all this?"

"By not chatting on the trains." He playfully bumps my shoulder with his, but the lightness doesn't last.

Montgomery sighs as he pages through the dense text, obviously stressed. From his messenger bag, he pulls out a mini energy drink with a lightning bolt on the bottle. He takes a slug and doesn't even grimace at the taste. Habits of the stressed and sleepless.

I lean back into the seat and try to busy my mind, but curiosity gets the better of me.

"Why was your mom in the station?"

"Ruby, please. What did I say about questions?"

He glances up at the video camera in the corner of the train.

"Are they always watching?"

"Yes. Always. Mainly, they watch the security cameras to make sure you don't skim off the top, or if trespassers are jumping borders without payment."

I graze my thumb along my shimmering BART tattoo. I'm connected to this train network now, no longer a trespasser in my dad's hidden life. "How long before I can start jumping portals like you? You know, across the world?"

"Patience. Your job is to wait." He frowns, shutting the textbook. I should let him study, but this growing curiosity makes my hands itch, like when I can't wait to dunk a paintbrush into fresh paint.

"Your job is the packages," he continues. "You have no idea what you're doing yet. Sure, you've made it between San Francisco stations. You've lived here your entire life. You know these stations. It's near impossible when you're trying to jump onto trains you've never been on. Most can't do it in one leap. I'll start taking you on some of our regular routes soon, so that you can begin to know them. Trust takes time; show us you can complete these jobs first—*no questions asked*—then, we can start jumping portals."

He glances at the train doors and then at his watch.

"What's taking so long? Shen left Shanghai at ten A.M. I have too many things to do today."

"You can leave it to me."

He doesn't say anything and instead glares at the doors. Like a grown-up. Like a giant man-boy. It's not a good look.

"Explain this to me," I say, twisting toward him. "When we'd jumped to Norway, it took seconds. *Seconds.* What's the deal with Shen? Is he not as good a jumper as you? Or is Shanghai harder to jump from?"

"Most jumpers have to leapfrog long distances, stopping at stations along the route. The farther away, the longer the lag. The better the jumper, the less lag time. We wait."

He opens the textbook on his lap and jerks through the pages until he finds the one he's covered in pencil marks. I glance at my watch.

"Bet you'd make it in half the time Shen takes to get here."

"True," he says. "I'm not saying this to brag, but I can jump farther and faster than most people on these lines. It's why I'm Montgomery, and not Merritt or Powell or Balboa."

"Oh, is that so? But you haven't seen what I can do yet."

"We'll see." His lips perk up at the corners, and his shoulders relax a tiny bit. It's too tempting to knock my leg against his and feel the warmth tingling up my thigh.

I lean back and try to summon a sense of serenity. My life as a monk, starting now. Except all I can think about is jumping somewhere, anywhere, seeing how far I can go, how fast, how much I can push the boundaries of my magic. It isn't helping my case for monkhood.

The days have been passing quietly at home, too. Maybe quiet isn't the right word. My dad mainly lies in a ball of his own sweat, while he's slowly weaning off alcohol and whatever vile painkillers he's ingested. Sometimes I hear him groan in the night like a bear with an arrow in his chest. He grinds his teeth in his sleep. Otherwise, he spends his days resting in the garden, drinking gallons of dandelion tea, threading and unthreading his boxing gloves. Sometimes he stops by the AA meetings at St. Thomas Church, and it seems to help, a little. We don't talk about what's happening. The fact that he's detoxing. We never talk about any of it.

It's like he's in a foggy daze that he can't quite shake off.

Still, my dad asks nothing of me—he knows that he's already asked so much. I'm Balboa now; I've signed away four years of my life for his debt and mistakes. But I'd do it again in a heartbeat. I'd do anything he'd ask to help him through this. If only he'd ask. If only I knew how to help. This is the first time I've ever really seen him rest since Mom died. I'm afraid to get too hopeful that he'll stay clean this time.

It's of utmost importance for him to be healthy if he ever hopes to get surgery for his hips. It's an awful Catch-22: he drinks because he's in pain; he's in pain because of his hips; he can't get the surgery if he's unwell; then, there's that pesky pain again. It's vicious. But if I can become Balboa, then he can become Healthy Father Figure. I know he can.

This is the one downside of sitting on trains for hours: a whirlwind of thoughts. At least with painting, I can get lost in the motion of my arms. The simple act of moving a roller across a wall. I perfect each brush-stroke; so what if it's a bucket of eggshell white? Montgomery leaves me to wander my thoughts, too busy studying the pages of music composi-tions spread across his lap. I should finish my art school applications. Diego marked up my essay draft with helpful edits and pasted stickers of sushi cats and sassy seagulls on his favorite bits. I've never met a boy who loved sparkly stickers almost as much as I do. I even filled out the FAFSA form. But then I thought about how much my dad is struggling to stay afloat. There's no way.

Besides, could I really get into art school if I tried?

I haven't asked myself what I would want to do in so long that the voice inside my head wavers at the question. Mom's bucket list item number three: *study abroad in a country where art is hidden in every street corner and cathedral.* Was that what she'd wanted or what I'd wanted?

This is a useless exercise. There's too much I have to do to survive.

I sigh and stare at the train doors, willing the package to come through the portal, willing my whole day to yawn open. Open, open, come on. I'd make a horrible monk. I'd probably accidentally burn down a monastery. I stare harder at the doors. I know a watched kettle never boils, but then—I start to feel a rumble on my seat.

"Do you feel that?" I jerk upright, hoping that my train sense is finally starting to develop.

Montgomery shuffles inside his coat pocket and sighs.

"Hello," he snaps at his phone.

Ah, so much for train sense.

"Does it have to be me?" he says.

My question exactly.

I resume staring at the portal doors. Balboa the Monk. Come on, zen, don't leave me hanging.

The doors remain zipped shut. Passengers continue along their routes, completely unaware that anything could come through those doors. Some punk kid is playing music on his headphones loud enough for the whole train to hear. Bet you his mom nags him about hearing loss. Hey kid, don't you know you're going to miss her nagging when she's gone? Your hearing, too.

"Tell Powell to clean up his own mess. I'm done," he says, hanging up the phone.

Montgomery chews his lip for a moment; and suddenly, he slams his textbook shut and leans his head back against the seat. Then, he does something very un-Montgomery-like. He flips off the security camera in a universal f-you and mouths something only an expert lip-reader would understand. I really wish he were facing me, so I could figure out what the heck is going on.

Before I have a chance to ask, Powell stumbles through the train doors as if someone has flung him through. Blue sparks snap and pop around his ears. He staggers forward and skids across the rubber floor. He tries to play it cool, dusting off his burgundy Louis Vuitton blazer and licking his lips, but blood drips down from a crack in his forehead. He touches his finger to the cut and winces. Powell pulls a silk handkerchief from his pocket and blots the spot, daintily.

"Brother," he says, strolling toward Montgomery as if it's a sunny summer day.

"What part of 'no' didn't you understand?" Anger radiates off of Montgomery as he restrains himself on the seat's metal bars. The skin on his knuckles has turned a raw bone white. All thoughts of his music exam have been forgotten as the textbook slides off his lap.

"I heard it loud and clear. Em, on the other hand . . ." Powell shrugs and plops into a seat next to us. He grimaces at a wad of gum stuck to the chair in front of him. "Madame Em has requested your services at Powell station."

"You were supposed to watch the trains so that this would never happen again."

"Not all of us have your magnificent ability to emulate a gargoyle for hours on end."

"Other lines are starting to realize your station is a weak link. They'll keep sending others through if you don't do something about it."

Powell just smirks. "What others?" I say.

Montgomery shakes his head.

"Stay with Balboa," he says to Powell. "Make sure Shen's job comes through. Think you can handle that?"

"You still don't trust me?" I say, grabbing Montgomery's sleeve, but he doesn't meet my eyes. "I don't need a babysitter. I can handle this package on my own. Or I can come with you on your jump?"

"Make sure she follows the rules. I'm serious, Powell."

"And I'm sitting right here," I snap.

"I don't have time for this. I'm sorry, Balboa." Montgomery rises from the seat and towers over Powell. "This is the last mess. Next time, I don't care if Em calls. You're dealing with it."

Without a backward glance, he dismisses me like I'm a little kid who showed up at the grown-up table. His fury with Powell fills the air, sucking the oxygen from my own lungs. As he yanks open the portal doors between the trains, blue sparks snapping along his jawline, he mouths at me, "No questions!"

I stick out my tongue, security cameras be damned. He slides the doors shut behind him. Normally that would at least get me a smile, but now it feels like he's turned to stone. Powell was right about the gargoyle aspect. Even if I have no clue where Montgomery is going, I wish he'd taken me with him. I can't wait to jump through portals again, that rush of opening the doors to somewhere different. I don't want to sit here in the dark.

Always: "No questions, Ruby. No questions!" And look where that got me—a contract to repay a debt I never owed in the first place.

As we barrel through the underground tunnels, wheels gliding across the tracks, no one notices that a man has just disappeared. They're all busy reading email on their phones, or drowning out everything with music, or trying not to fall asleep and miss their stop. Everyone except me.

I'm tired of walking these trains with blurry vision. Montgomery said he would teach me to be the best Balboa possible. And here I am sitting in a time-out with a babysitter who can't get his own job done properly. I rise from my seat. Powell glances over and arches an eyebrow.

"I wouldn't do that if I were you," he says with a mischievous grin.

"You're not going to tell me what's happening?"

Powell chuckles. "You wouldn't ask if you knew how much trouble I'm already in."

"Montgomery is purposefully keeping me away from the whole rail network, isn't he?"

Powell leans close so that the security cameras can't see his lips. "If I were you," he whispers, "I wouldn't let Montgomery hold me back. It's your power, your magic, darling."

Before I have a chance to second-guess myself, I bolt toward the train doors. Powell half-heartedly calls after me, but he doesn't even bother to stand and chase me. He flutters his bloody handkerchief at me as if bidding me farewell instead of reining me back in.

I hurry between the Saddle doors and try to suss out any traces of magic. Maybe I can follow Montgomery like that game where I'd chased him across the bay to Dublin / Pleasanton station. Figure out where he went; figure out all the secrets he won't let me see.

Inside, the glass doors box me in like a phone booth. Vinyl accordion panels give the train enough flexibility to snake and twist through the underground tunnels. The floor dips and bends beneath my feet. All normal, except that scent. It's distinctly Montgomery. If there's one thing that boy loves, it's his expensive cologne. It smells like spicy cedar and patchouli oil. And something else, something *magic* sweet.

I close my eyes and breathe it in for a moment. I know I'm being a creeper, but let me have it, just this tiny thing. I've almost forgotten what it feels like. The way you can crave leaning into someone, like a tree clinging to a sun-soaked cliffside. Do I only crave this because he's someone totally out of my reach? An impossibility. He has no right to smell this good, to spark all my senses with a simple scent. I close my eyes and soak in the tingle of magic he's left behind. *Montgomery.* The word is meant to come out like a command for the train magic to take me to him, but it comes out like longing. *Please, let me see inside this world, let me see inside this boy who smells of cedar and cloves and catastrophe too sweet to resist.*

An icy wind swirls my hair around my face, and within seconds I find myself pitching forward into a different train. I shove the hair from my eyes and keep low to the floor on my hands and knees. Inside the Saddle, I take a moment to catch my breath and ignore the slight headache tingling on the edges of my vision. I don't even feel any nausea, but that must be because I haven't gone far. Or maybe I'm getting better at jumping? Train tracks and voices rumble nearby. I inch upward and peer into an almost empty train car. The cracked glass fractures my view, but it's obviously Montgomery in there. And Merritt. And Em. And a stranger. They've blacked out all the exterior windows with magnets and black paper, latched the train doors shut, covered the security cameras in black bags, and placed an OUT OF SERVICE sign across the windows.

This must be one hell of a situation.

I steady my breathing and crouch low.

I'm really not supposed to be here. I wonder if I turn back now, will they notice the blue sparks and icy wind crackling through the empty train?

"Who told you to sneak in this way?" Madame Em says with a sharp smile. She seems excited for whatever is coming. At first, I panic, thinking maybe she's addressing me. But then the unfamiliar man speaks. He was sitting so still, it's like Em's words have broken a spell. His lungs heave under his damp jungle green raincoat, and sweat drips down his tanned cheeks. He must have jumped from a tropical place. He'll freeze the second he steps into the San Francisco wind. If he ever makes it that far.

"No one," he says.

"And your boy?" Em says. "Don't think I didn't see him on the cameras."

The man shakes his head and keeps his eyes trained on the rattling floor.

"Protecting liars and thieves, are we? Merritt." She waves him forward, and her son lands a hard punch across the man's jaw. The stranger stumbles back, and Montgomery's long arms reach out to keep him upright. Not to protect him. No—to make sure Merritt can land another hit if Em commands it. It makes my stomach twist the way his face doesn't show a shred of emotion.

"Just tell us who told you to cross here," Montgomery says. "And then we'll send you back. Go on, take the easy route."

"My boy . . ." the man says through bruised bleeding lips.

"Your boy will never see you again," Em says, "because there's no way I'm letting liars and thieves cross my lines. Tell me: who told you about Powell station?"

"I . . . I don't know. Please," his voice breaks. "Please don't harm my boy if he tries to follow me back."

"You're assuming we're sending you back."

"Em," Montgomery pleads. "Just send him back."

"Darling, I asked him a simple question." She takes the man's trembling hand and leads him toward the Saddle doors—where I'm currently crouching on the floor. I scramble backward on crab legs and try to conjure Balboa Park station as quickly as I can. Em's blond pixie cut bobs into view, and I hear Montgomery trying to call her back.

Balboa Park, Balboa Park, take me home, but the train groans under me, racing through the underground tunnels, not caring about my plea. I can't focus, not on home, not on my dad, not while Madame Em drags this poor father away from his son.

Powell. I command the train, take me to his cherry lips and his Louis Vuitton jacket smeared with blood. Take me back. A poem I'd memorized in high school comes racing unbidden into my brain—William Blake with his far-flung romanticism and fiery words. I mumble it under my breath as fast as I can:

> Tyger Tyger, burning bright,
> In the forests of the night;
> What immortal hand or eye,
> Could frame thy fearful symmetry?

It feels as if a beast inside the twisting, turning metal hears me, ears perked up in the rustling wind. I take a deep breath and continue calling to it.

> In what distant deeps or skies.
> Burnt the fire of thine eyes?
> On what wings dare he aspire?
> What the hand, dare seize the fire?

Finally, the magic surges through my palms.
My whole body topples backward into darkness.
And into light.

⚔ CHAPTER 23 ⚔

don't have to open my eyes to know I'm back on my original train. I can still smell a hint of Montgomery's cologne between the car doors, that heady cedar and spice smell. Instead of longing, it sends a tremor through my chest. How can the Montgomery I'm with in the quiet moments between jobs be the same person as the one I just saw? How can he blindly enforce Em's rules and still be the boy with music and poetry on his breath? When I open my eyes and peer through the doorway, Powell smiles smugly at me across the train car. He knew what awaited me on the Powell train; he wanted me to see Montgomery like that. Was it to help me or to hurt me? My head spins, but not from the jump. These little leaps between San Francisco stations feel like nothing to me now. Instead, my head spins from all the secrets and rules that fester inside the underground.

I wait inside the Saddle, not ready to hear Powell's ridicule or riddles. I promise myself that once I step outside, I'll snap back to reality. That my head will be completely in the game. That I'll be Balboa and nothing more. It's what I need to do to survive.

I start to pull open the doors but stop midway.

Subtly, my arm begins to tingle like the pinpricks of a sleeping limb coming awake.

A rumble.

I try to listen, try to feel the train's web spreading across the bay, across the world. Maybe Montgomery is on his way back here?

A faint dizziness blurs my vision. Stars creep in at the edges of my eyelids. I reach out to steady myself, but my hand claws at empty air, the door impossibly out of reach. Ice stabs across my arms. My breath hitches, as if all the oxygen is being sucked up by an invisible flame.

And then, a stranger is with me.

Except not a whole man. Pieces of a man. No, flashes of a man, a man far older than me with wrinkles etched deeply into his forehead. Two legs materializing before me, flickering, two arms, a head, then headless, a tattered chest, all of it struggling into reality.

I almost scream.

The impossibility of a dream coming to life.

I try to scramble away, but my feet are frozen.

What if the pieces of his body meld with mine into a Frankensteined corpse? His legs, my arms, our twisted mouth, a yelp escapes my lips, god, get me away. My frozen hands claw at the door, but I can't open the latch, can't feel my fingers.

And then, he's there, in the flesh. A stranger. Breathing on me. He smells of stale onions and soy sauce. Like he ate lunch minutes ago and is about to barf it up on my shirt. I stagger backward. My icy fingers flail on the door latch again. His knees press against mine, and he leans forward, trying to steady himself. His dark, straight hair brushes my face, and I swat it away. The train shudders and takes a sharp turn through the tunnels. The man clutches a messenger bag slung across his chest.

"Balboa?" he says. It comes out more like Ba-Bo with his accent.

I force my lips to move, though I'm still catching my breath. Come on, Balboa, act professional.

"Right, yes. That's me. Shen?"

He nods and passes me the bag. I sling it across my chest. The heaviness pulls my neck forward. He reaches behind me and unlatches the door, so that I can finally step back. Air rushes inside. My fingers scratch across the moist glass.

"Next time," he says. "Wait outside doors."

"No shit."

He nods toward the bag, nudging me to open it. To see inside. I know I shouldn't, but Montgomery always checks the contents before the end of an exchange. I have to look professional, don't I? So technically, I'm not asking questions. I'm not breaking any rules. I'm doing my job. Every successful business needs a quality control department. That's it.

When I peer inside, my breath coils tight inside my chest.

"Something wrong?" Shen says.

I force myself to shake my head. I snap the bag shut and stumble backward.

"Thank . . . thank you," I say.

He stares at me.

The security cameras are watching.

Powell is watching.

Keep calm.

Keep the bag close to your chest.

Back away.

The glass doors slide shut on the man, and his scorpion eyes stare like he's a specimen pinned under glass. Or maybe it's me. Maybe I'm the one pinned in place.

⚹ CHAPTER 24 ⚹

I can't breathe.

My arms clutch the bag as I stagger down the aisle.

"Take it to 1075 California Street. Nob Hill, in case you don't know where that is." Powell doesn't bother looking up from his phone. He doesn't say a word about what's inside the bag or what I've seen with Em and the trespasser. I feel a ripple across the train like a fish threading away in a murky pool. When I glance back, Shen has disappeared.

The train lunges to a stop.

I jolt forward and bang my knee on a bike. Pain pinches up my thigh, but I force myself off the train at Montgomery station. I'm one short stop away from being hurtled underwater across the bay. My eyes are painfully aware of the security cameras watching from on high. I need air, please, fresh air. I shove people out of my way. A woman curses at me under her breath, and I want to curse right along with her. Near the top of the stairs, it smells like someone just took a piss on concrete. Nausea roils my belly, and I keep barreling up the stairs toward the sunshine. A businessman bumps my shoulder, and I tell him sorry, so sorry.

Sorry I spied on Montgomery.

Sorry I signed the contract.

Sorry, so sorry I'm holding this bag of tusks and horns. Broken shards of animals. Heavy as chains wrapped around my wrists.

Aboveground, I lean against a glass wall, blocking a blonde lady's view out of a Starbucks. She glares at me. I should keep moving. Stop drawing attention to myself. Take the package to the drop location. 1075 California Street. Come on, Balboa, this is your job. Still, I'm plastered here against the window while pedestrians go about their business. Sipping their coffee while I hold something I shouldn't be holding.

I think of my mom's gorgeous murals.

Elephants never forget.

There are fewer than eighty Sumatran rhinos and forty thousand Asian elephants left in the wild. Because of poachers. Because of habitat loss. Because of what's in this bag.

I know this because my mom knew this.

Because we watched *National Geographic* documentaries while she painted a jungle mosaic on our living room wall. Because she needed to buy so much emerald green and rain-cloud gray that we had to eat cereal and beans for two weeks straight so that she could save up enough cash. Because a rhino needs its horn. Because she spent a few summers before I was born volunteering on an elephant preserve in Thailand and Indonesia. Because that's what she would have wanted me to do, too.

What would Mom think if she could see me now?

If she knew what I'm holding.

If she knew that I'm helping some nameless asshole sell tusks and horns after sawing them off of a helpless wild beast. If she knew I was breaking international laws, risking jail time. *I'm so sorry, Mom.*

I should never have looked inside the bag. Without peeking inside again, my brain conjures up the smooth ivory—and the maimed animals they belong to. The horns have lost all their majesty, jumbled in a heap waiting to be ground up into medicinal powder or mounted as an intricately carved art piece. The bag's strap rests heavy against my chest. What else has been inside these bags? All the ones I haven't looked inside, busy instead dreaming about running my fingers through Montgomery's hair and living happily ever after in a snowy fairy tale. What other bundles of ruin and greed have I shepherded into my city? They never lied about being the bad guys. Montgomery didn't even flinch when Merritt punched that desperate trespasser. But I've been foolish enough to never allow myself to focus on the bigger picture. I've been trying to survive, trying to grab hold of the reins to my magic. Daydreaming about a boy.

I never wanted to think about what was inside the packages.

I mean, a good person like my father, like Montgomery, couldn't possibly do this, right?

But here I am with a bag in my hands.

An unhoused woman with a mop of shaggy gray hair slides up next to me and holds out a faded Starbucks cup. She jangles the coins and begs for more. She has peanut butter smeared on her cheek and nowhere to clean it off. Everyone ignores her, or steps wide, their eyes focused on their own paths. I want to give her my jacket, maybe buy her another tub of peanut butter at the Walgreens on the corner.

At the same time, my survival instinct thunders inside my head:

I could be out on the streets like her.

I could lose the house.

I could lose everything.

Or I can run the trains.

Your choice, Ruby.

But it's not really a choice, is it?

We just do what we have to do. That's life. There's no point dreaming up something different. I steady my breath and push off against the glass. I toss a few coins into the poor woman's cup, but it doesn't make me feel any less guilty. She thanks me all the same, even though she doesn't know where the money comes from.

Knowing what's inside the bags changes nothing. I signed a contract. I'm bound to this, like it or not. The tusks have already been cut, anyway. Someone else would have brought them across the portals. I'm just the messenger. That's all.

Still, it feels like a ghost haunts my every step.

It's a long walk from Montgomery station to Nob Hill, but at least I can get lost in my burning muscles. Hill after hill climbing deeper into the affluent heart of San Francisco. Multistory hotels and apartments stacked along the hills, intricate designs carved into their facades.

Eventually, I arrive at the address: 1075 California Street. Wedged across the street from the towering Grace Cathedral and a Masonic Temple I'd never noticed before. The shop is crammed into the bottom floor of a fancy hotel. A single giant window displays all manner of jade and rose quartz crystals and apothecary bottles that shimmer gold and indigo in the sunlight. Shelves of exotic powders and tinctures and gems line the walls. A few kids play a game of jump rope on the sidewalk. A tourist saunters inside, eager to buy an elixir for better health, while an elderly man asks for a remedy for arthritis.

The teenage shopkeeper has seven piercings along her left ear and curly hair barely held back by a leopard-print headband. She rings a bell the moment I step inside. She stares at my hands like she wants to read my future. I glance down at my shaking hands, willing them to still. Right, the tattoo on my ring finger. Everyone knows I'm one of the Bartholomew grunts.

A statuesque redhead rushes out from the back room; her pink clogs clomp along the wooden floor. She nods toward my bag without a word. She can barely contain her excitement, bouncing on her toes. The previous Balboa must have been a man of few words. I wonder if my dad hated seeing the elephant and rhino tusks as much as I do. Wordlessly, we exchange bags, and I count the bundled bills. Seventeen thousand dollars. Just like Montgomery said.

We are the bad guys. He wasn't lying.

The woman disappears into the back room, undoubtedly to create another batch of her tinctures to sell to her high-class tourists. An exotic novelty from an exotic city. I turn for the door, my stomach all acid and grinding guilt, but the teenager behind the counter hisses for my attention. My arms tense around the bag of money, ready to fight or flight. I've never held this much cash before, and it feels both a blessing and a curse.

She holds out a small paper bag. This one is feather light.

"For your dad." She taps her hips, and realization dawns on me. Inside, there's a small jar of healing salve. The label says that it helps with joint pain and inflammation.

It feels like she's trying to hand me a get-out-of jail-free card. Ivory powder is rumored to purge toxins from the body. But I still can't ignore the question: did those elephants and rhinos deserve to lose their tusks?

The second I'm outside, I break into a sprint—right into the kids' flashing jump rope. The plastic whips against my face, and the kids stare, shy and wide-eyed.

"It's fine, I'm fine." My cheek throbs something fierce. I can't help but feel like I deserve it, though.

I text Powell.

Done. Where next?

Coffee Cave on Market, he texts back.

I hurry down California Street toward Market, leaving Nob Hill behind and crisscrossing through Chinatown. Red lanterns and incense fill the storefronts. The thick rich smell of jasmine smoke saturates the air. I hurry through the Dragon's Gate, under its elaborate turquoise tiles and serpentine statues. Cash burns heavy in my bag.

I feel like a thief.

⚮ CHAPTER 25 ⚮

When I finally reach Market Street, the sun sits low in the sky, barely bleeding through the skyscraper forest. Darkness always comes early downtown, the tall concrete spires crowding out the sky. I turn left toward Powell station. The blue-and-white BART sign stands like an all-seeing beacon. For a moment, I hesitate on a street corner. People jostle giant shopping bags as they hustle between glittering neon signs. Macy's, Neiman Marcus, Forever 21, Sephora, everything under the sun.

I want to be rid of this bag.

Coffee Cave? Coffee Cave? Finally my eyes snag on a giant red teacup. I hurry into the coffee shop and scan the room for Powell's mischievous smirk. I don't need to search hard. He's cleaned up the cut on his forehead and changed into a honeyed Gucci blazer covered in giant linked *G*s. He wears it over dark-wash jeans and a black T-shirt. He doesn't look at all like trespassers jumped him on his own train or that he's about to conduct a nefarious business deal. I take two resolute strides in his direction before someone grabs my elbow.

"Ruby!"

Who? I hadn't realized I'd grown accustomed to being called Balboa while working the trains. Maybe this is why Dad stuck with "Balboa" all the time. Was it too disorienting to be two different people on these familiar streets, always a chance of running into the people you love?

Diego pulls me into one of his epic caramel-spice hugs, but it feels all wrong. I don't deserve this. Not the girl who has just trafficked illegal tusks, stolen from endangered animals.

"Can we catch up later?" I mumble. "I'm meeting someone."

"Please tell me it's a hot date." He wiggles his eyebrows while balancing two lattes. Cinnamon hearts decorate the foamed milk, and even that feels wrong.

"Hot, maybe; date, definitely not." I force a smile and try for our usual playful tone even though I feel like I'm burning up inside. I don't know how my dad did this, how Montgomery does this. I feel split in two—Ruby and Balboa, both terrible liars.

I finally absorb the fact that Diego is wearing an apron with a gold name tag, and his hair is tied back into a smooth man bun instead of his usual chaotic knot.

"Wait, since when did you work at this coffee shop?"

"New gig. Canvas ain't cheap. And these walls needed *giant* canvases. Look how much wall space they gave me!"

I glance around in awe at his agave paintings. They pop like emerald and amber jewels against the black walls. How did I miss this? Every time I step into a new place, I can't help but soak in the art.

Ruby soaks in the art.

Balboa is here for a job.

With every passing second, I'm flooded with the nauseating feeling that I don't recognize myself anymore.

"You OK, Ruby Tuesday? You look a little pale." Diego reaches to touch my forehead, but I flinch back. I bet his abuela did that for him when he was a kid. I wish I could curl up into my mom's arms and ask her how to deal with this mess. My fingers instinctively reach into my pocket for her bucket list, but that's gone, too.

"I'm fine . . . I just didn't realize you had another art show. You should have asked me to help you hang the paintings."

"I was going to ask for your help after that brilliant Ruby magic you wove above Loretta's ceiling, but for real, girl, you've been busy. Chen told me you turned down the last few gigs. Figured you'd moved on to bigger and better things. You know, finally finishing your college applications. Like I keep telling you, get your ass in art school. Thought maybe you'd finally hunkered down?"

I shake my head. No, no art school. Not in Balboa's future.

"I miss painting with you and the crew," I whisper, afraid my voice might betray the unsteadiness in my lungs. It's the first honest thing I've said all afternoon, and my chest squeezes like a birdcage against fluttering wings.

Powell clears his throat loudly and snatches one of the lattes perched on Diego's arm. He lifts it to his lips and then sighs in disappointment.

"It's gone cold." Powell pouts.

"I am so sorry! Let me make you another." Diego grabs the wide-mouthed mug and rushes behind the counter.

"Sorry," I say. "I didn't realize I'd run into a friend here."

"I did," he says.

"What—"

"You think we don't know who your friends and family are." Powell leans in close and lowers his voice into a steely whisper. "It sounds like *you* didn't even know he was working here."

Heat burns inside my throat as I flounder for something to say.

"Sit down." Powell slides out a heavy metal chair. "Wouldn't want our lattes to go cold again."

Diego delivers the two steaming mugs, gracefully wiping away crumbs. As he's walking away, he mouths the word "hot" and gives Powell a meaningful glance.

Normally, it would make me smile.

Now, I wonder if Diego is in danger because of me. Behind the counter, he hums Lady Gaga songs as he swirls a towel across a stained countertop. He moves like a ballet dancer when he's on barista duty. Powell taps his finger on the tabletop to snap me back to the conversation, apparently irritated that I can barely keep up.

"Montgomery may be a brilliant jumper, and Merritt may excel at turning a person's face into ground meat," he says. "But I'm useful in other ways."

"Why are we here?"

Powell takes a sip of his latte, careful not to spill any milky foam onto his Gucci blazer.

"I can tell you've seen a lot today," he says. "Things you can't unsee. You have that dazed deer-in-headlights look. It's not flattering, trust me."

My fingers clutch the thick leather bag to keep from saying something I'll regret.

"Leave the bag on the chair," he says. "I'll take it when I leave."

I slide the bag to his end of the table.

"Em wanted me to remind you. We know where you live. We know who your friends are. Your family, your dreams, your desires. We're always watching. So, if you get any ideas from that shiny little conscience, I'd suggest keeping them to yourself."

"You don't need to threaten me or my friends, asshole. I signed a contract, didn't I? I promised discretion." I stare him in the eyes, meaning every damn word.

"OK, good," he says, relief in his shoulders as he leans back and crosses one leg over the other. Powell looks like a mallard in a pond, pleased that the rain slides right off his duck feathers. "I do hate this part. I'm not particularly talented at threatening and extorting people. Information, spying, thieving; yes, yes, and yes. But threats? They're just so . . . vulgar. They were going to send Merritt, but they found another stowaway, and so here I am in this rather dull coffee shop. I do like your friend's art, though. He's cute, too."

"He's taken." My teeth grit together. This may be a silly game to Powell, but this is my life. My friend's life.

"I am a rather talented thief." He winks at Diego across the room, and Diego blushes before accidentally spilling espresso grounds down the sink.

"You hurt my friend, and I swear, I'll—"

"I don't know why everyone has to take life so seriously. I'm only playing." Powell waves, and Diego checks behind him first before realizing that Powell means him.

"Is there something wrong with the latte?" Diego scoops up Powell's nearly empty mug.

"No, it was perfect, thanks," he says. "I waved you over to ask—what genius painted these masterpieces?"

Diego blushes again before building up the nerve to say these are his. I've never in my life seen Diego Jose Alvarez acting *shy*.

"How much for that painting?" Powell points across the room to the biggest agave with a flower spike reaching for the clouds—it's almost my height and sparkles with all of Diego's big glittering heart.

"Six thousand," I say before Diego can answer.

"Ruby, that's not—"

"Done," Powell says. "Would you mind wrapping it?"

"Uhh. Yeah. Yes, I . . . OK. One minute!" Diego can barely keep from squealing. "SIX THOUSAND" he silently mouths as he prances away. He rushes to pull the painting down and boots the couple seated at a table beneath it.

"Six thousand?" Powell arches his eyebrow.

"He's worth it."

"Apparently."

Powell twists around in his chair and sends Diego a delicious smile across the crowded room. I bet he's fluttering his long luscious lashes, too. Diego nearly falls off the ladder while he's wrangling the giant canvas off the hook. Discreetly, Powell plucks three wads of cash from the bag and tosses it onto the table. His other hand grazes my knee, and I'm about to twist his grubby fingers off when I realize he's trying to pass me money. Cool it, Ruby. I stuff the cash into my pocket.

"Aren't you going to check if I skimmed any?" I say.

"No need, darling. You've met my brother Merritt, yes? Well, we have ways of dealing with skimmers. Besides, you strike me as an intelligent girl."

I stare at the black bag and glance around at the bustling coffeeshop. Everyone keeps their eyes glued to their laptops and coffee dates. I'm a tiny piece of this illicit web, and no one cares.

"You looked inside the bag." Powell smirks.

"No, I . . ."

"Bags are funny things—all their mystery held inside. Did you know that Pandora opened a *jar* and not a box? At least in the original Hesiod account of the myth. It was a *pithos*."

"What?" My head spins with all his rambling, all my guilt returning to a boil inside my chest. "What are you talking about?"

"Don't worry, I won't tell."

"I didn't look in the bag."

He waves away my words.

"You know"—Powell leans in close as if we're conspiring—"if it wasn't the Bartholomews hustling the trains, it would be someone else. Everyone's greedy. Why not be on the winning team?"

"I don't recall asking for life advice."

"No wonder he likes you."

"Since we're sharing friendly advice," I say, rising to my feet. "Maybe you should mind your own business."

"And you two should learn to flirt less when security cameras are watching."

My cheeks flame red. Damn rosy traitors. "We weren't flirting. We're just bored and passing the time."

"Whatever you say, Balboa. Or is it Ruby? You are so very bad at lying, darling."

"Wait." I grab Powell's money bag before he can walk away. "Be honest for a minute. Where did Em take that trespassing man?"

"Ah-ha, now you're asking the right questions. But that's for clever girls to figure out."

Powell slips on his gold-rimmed sunglasses, standing to take Diego's painting. Miraculously, he doesn't smack anyone in the head on the way out. He slides through the crowd, people rushing to move out of his way like he's a movie star strutting past us mere mortals.

"Since when did you have bougie friends?" Diego says.

"He's not a friend."

Outside, the last of the afternoon light starts to fade. Fog rolls in from the ocean, slowly smothering the sky. The dense foggy clumps look like a herd of lost elephants, searching for somewhere safe. I hurry underground, my hand wrapped around the cash, telling myself it was worth it.

⚡ CHAPTER 26 ⚡

Powell is right—I'm a terrible liar.

That's why I'm freezing my butt off in front of Montgomery station, legs wrapped around my scooter Stella, waiting for a boy who probably does not want to see me right now.

But we need to talk.

I keep an eagle eye out for Montgomery's tall frame, his wavy black hair, his impeccable blue suit. Any minute now, he's going to walk up those BART station steps, emerging from the underground like an apparition.

Any minute now.

Let me preface this with: it's been two hours.

My nose is running from the cold, and exhaust fumes fill the air from cars gunning it down Market Street only to meet red lights at every street corner. The businesspeople hustle from their skyscrapers toward their first Happy Hour of the evening, roaring about their stock market prowess. A burger joint across the street has been tempting me with its delicious French fry torture, but I must remain vigilant.

Now that I've seen the elephant tusks, I can't *unsee* them.

I can't lie about them, either.

That's definitely a no-go in the Bartholomew code of conduct. Absolute discretion, it's written into the contract.

So it's in Montgomery's best interest to remove me from Shen's normal route. I could accidentally spill a trade secret. They should give that job to someone else in the Bartholomew network. Montgomery is a reasonable guy. He's a rulemeister. And if I can go back to being oblivious about what's inside the bags, then I won't feel so guilty when I think about my mom's elephant murals. Maybe.

I chew the inside of my cheek and pick at the white paint still lodged underneath my fingernails. They'll never get clean, no matter how much I scrub.

Two hours of waiting. Freezing my fingers off. Thanks, Karl the Fog—how about a break from your icy chill? I should have brought gloves, but I was in such a rush to catch Montgomery that I only remembered my leather jacket and lavender beanie. The streetlights have kept Market Street glowing bright long after the sun set. My back aches from leaning over Stella like I'm in a horse race. I'll only have a few minutes to catch Montgomery before he strolls home to Em's skyscraper. Only a few short blocks to talk to him outside of the security cameras' watchful eyes. Powell made it clear they're surveilling us. And apparently we're terrible at hiding our flirting.

Here in the crisp unrelenting fog, maybe I can catch the version of Montgomery who will listen.

Suddenly there's a DoorDash driver honking at me. College kid. Cardboard to-go boxes stacked high in the passenger seat. All strapped in with a seatbelt. A red dragon is printed across one of the plastic bags, and a McDonald's symbol is on another bag higher in the stack. It makes my stomach growl.

"Hey, come on, there's nowhere to park!" The guy waves at my loading zone parking spot and then points at the burger joint across the street.

"I'm waiting for someone!" I shrug.

The guy scooches thick-framed glasses up the bridge of his nose and refuses to leave. He parks his car in a driveway and turns his emergency lights on, so I'm surrounded by flashing red and yellow lights. Great, now the dense fog is even harder to see through.

"Some of us have jobs!" he yells in a high-pitched whine.

And some of us wish we didn't have a job delivering packages of a much more nefarious nature.

I hold my breath and grip the handlebars as I watch Mr. DoorDasher sprint across three lanes of traffic for someone else's burger.

Finally, when I turn back, Montgomery is emerging from the subway onto the sidewalk. Except he's not wearing his impeccable blue suit. He's wearing what appears to be jeans and a thick charcoal Henley that shows off his broad shoulders. The shirt has a band's name printed over a stenciled guitar. It's not a band I've heard of before—Harbingers of Hog Pie, or something—but I'm so far removed from the music scene that my last hot crush was on Justin Timberlake.

Montgomery pushes the black curls out of his eyes and crosses the street.

Away from the Embarcadero.

Concert tickets?

Or maybe this is just how he dresses when he's off duty.

It doesn't matter.

I can't sleep knowing that I might have to deliver more bags of endangered elephant tusks. I'd never be able to face my mom's murals again. Montgomery will understand. All I need to do is ask him for a different assignment.

I'm about to kick Stella into gear when Montgomery flags down a yellow taxi cab. Is he so old-school that he doesn't bother with rideshare apps? His family owns a gorgeous Mercedes, which probably comes with its own chauffeur . . . yet, he chose a taxi.

Wait, I get it—all cash. Less tracking.

No questions, Ruby. His deep husky voice rings in my ears.

But I can't wait for tomorrow, when we're under the BART security cameras. I hit the gas. Stella jumps into the crush of commuter traffic. We turn away from downtown, away from the city's ever-competing skyscrapers and into the narrow San Francisco streets that wind through the Panhandle and Cole Valley. I almost lose the taxi through a few stoplights, but it's amazing what you can get away with on a scooter. My teeth chatter, partly from the cold and partly from the adrenaline zipping through my spine.

Finally, the taxi pulls over on Cole and Frederick, and I nearly run over a cat as I skid into a parking spot a half block away. The cat hisses by my boot, its tail standing on end. Sorry, Calico, I can't lose him. Montgomery steps out of the taxi with big headphones over his ears. Both hands fish around his jeans to find a set of keys. 738 Cole Street. It's a lovely teal-and-white Victorian with a pointed roof and intricate patterns that frame the bay windows.

Is this where he lives? I thought the Bartholomews lived in the Embarcadero skyscraper.

I know I shouldn't be here, but Montgomery has shown up on my doorstep unannounced before—in the middle of the night. This isn't so different. Still, my heart hammers as I peek through the stained glass window set into the door. I can only see a staircase, and even that is blurred. My fingers run over the amber and rose glass. Suddenly I catch a flash of sneakers on the staircase. He's coming back down!

I duck backward and crash right into a garbage bin.

The door swings open.

I hide my face under my hands and contemplate jumping into the trash bin, but it's too late.

"Ruby?" he says.

"Uh, yeah, I guess."

"What are you doing here?"

Iced coffee drips down his shirt, and he holds a wad of soaked sheet music. Since he was obviously headed for the trash bin, I lift the lid and gesture to it like I'm a polite servant girl. Flies zip out of the bin and buzz past his face. Montgomery is not amused, to say the least. I've never seen his jaw this tight.

"Did you follow me here?"

"No—well, kind of. Let me explain."

He waits, his hands squeezing the coffee-soaked sheet music into a soggy pulp. Dark liquid drips down onto his sneakers, but his eyes refuse to leave mine.

"I finished that job. With Shen. But you had to leave . . . remember?" I squeeze my hands into my leather jacket pockets. "You were mad at Powell?" I don't know why I'm speaking in questions. Get a grip. My feet shuffle back and squish right onto a half-eaten peach mashed on the sidewalk. "I need to ask for a favor. A reassignment."

"So you decided to stalk me?" he says. "After I've explicitly told you that there are things you are safer *not knowing*."

"I couldn't wait until tomorrow." My shrug is pathetic, but I don't know what else to say.

"Ruby." My name comes out in a snarl, and he flings the sticky sheet music pulp into the trash. I can hear him suck in a breath as he struggles to tamp down his fury. I reach out a hand to his shoulder, but he immediately dodges away.

"Leave," he says. "Forget you ever saw this place."

"Montgomery, I'm—"

"Now."

I step back and knock into the garbage bin. I don't know what else to say, don't know how to fix this. So I run, and I don't stop running. Not when my lungs ache. Not when I pass Stella. Not when my knee hits into a stroller and a mother yells at me for being an idiot. Finally, I stop when the noise of Carl Street drowns out my pounding heart. A bus muscles its way down the narrow avenue. A purple-haired woman plays a melody on her electric keyboard, busking for spare change. Three of the keys are missing, like broken teeth.

How do I fix this?

Forget I'd seen the place.

That's what he said.

But will he forget it happened? He was so furious. I never should have followed him. No doubt from now on, he'll keep me in the dark about the train's real secrets—like he did with the trespassing man, like he does every time he avoids talking about more faraway adventures.

Forget about asking him for any favors. *You've ruined it.*

But he's not the only one who can call the shots.

If I want to change the terms of my contract, then I need to win Em's favor.

A train blares its horn and startles me out of my thoughts.

It snakes across Cole Street, arching wide around the corner. The "N: Judah" Streetcar. Its magic thrums through me like a guitar cord. Heat flares in my freezing palms. I take a step forward without fully meaning to.

The doors are wide open.

Waiting.

Calling.

Powell said I shouldn't let Montgomery keep me in the dark. If I want to impress Em and win some negotiating power, I need to learn faster than Montgomery is willing to teach me.

I'll learn the bounds of the magic *on my own*. I'll figure out how to jump as far and as fast as he can. Better, even.

The bells ring.

I scramble aboard, scaling the metal steps and hurrying into a window seat. These trains don't have the empty space connecting the cars. It's all one long metal tube. Can I use my power without the Saddle to hide inside? Montgomery didn't need an electrified train to take us from San Francisco to Amsterdam.

A graffiti-covered security camera hovers overhead.

I hope Madame Em is watching.

⅀ CHAPTER 27 ⅀

Montgomery said poetry was key. That the train magic is always listening; that the rhythm of words summons them. I'd used "The Red Wheelbarrow" to reach Montgomery; William Blake's "Tyger" to reach Powell. Even in our jump to Amsterdam, Montgomery mumbled poetry beneath his breath. There must be something to this. I dig inside my backpack for the poetry books I'd packed for our boring train rides—books I couldn't fully appreciate when my mom was in the hospital and English Lit homework was the least of my worries. *Let's see what you got, Shakespeare.*

Romeo and Juliet. As if those sappy tragic lovers knew about survival. They died young, after all. Still, they believed in love so fiercely; what if I could call upon my magic in the same way? Something humming and fierce inside myself. Shakespeare's play is in iambic pentameter, so it has a deep steady rhythm like the train, one soft beat and one strong beat repeating five times. Is poetry so different from a spell?

I glance up at the security camera and smile.

You want to see what I'm capable of, Em. You saw how far my father could jump.

You haven't seen what I can do.

I haven't, either.

Yet.

While passengers shuffle on and off the train at the next stop, I read through act 1, skimming Shakespeare's puzzling stanzas until a passage snags my attention. The smell of rich spaghetti and garlic bread and sweet, sweet tiramisu fills the train as an older man settles into a chair near the door. *Concentrate.*

My voice comes out in a whisper:

> ROMEO
>
> I dream'd a dream to-night.
>
> MERCUTIO
>
> And so did I.
>
> ROMEO
>
> Well, what was yours?
>
> MERCUTIO
>
> That dreamers often lie.
>
> ROMEO
>
> In bed asleep, while they do dream things true.
>
> MERCUTIO
>
> O, then, I see Queen Mab hath been with you.

The poetry tingles my senses like pepper spice. A dewy wind creeps across the floor, circling my shoes and brushing against my ankles. I feel like a beast is watching me, eyes peeking through a thicket. Blue sparks snag at the very edges of my peripheral vision.

I hurry through the stanzas where Romeo and Mercutio debate life and love and dreams, but then the magic retreats. Is it bored with my recitation? Maybe it needs more than a poem?

The older gentleman steps off at the next stop, taking his garlic bread and tiramisu with him. I'm tempted to follow him out the door and invite myself to dinner.

Maybe I need to pick something that awakens the train's appetite, something that strikes an emotional chord inside me. Like Powell and the "Tyger" poem. I skim faster through *Romeo and Juliet*, wondering if anything from this disastrous love story will resonate. I've never been in love before. I've never felt so drawn to someone that I wanted us to turn away from our feuding families.

A wind shoves against my back, whipping long strands of my hair into my mouth. I swat away the whirlwind and spin around.

"Hey!" The breeze tingles up my back again as if we're streaking through Norway's snowy fjords, but there's no window open on this train. No air-conditioning pushing through a vent. No one seated behind me at all. Maybe a train knows more about my love life than I do.

"OK, fine," I mumble under my breath.

It's true—I feel too much for Montgomery. And I've already managed to screw it up. Ever since our jump to the snowy fjords, the Van Gogh Museum, the quiet bits of poetry. Ever since we snuck into that tunnel, I've wondered if he might invite me again. Might show me a piece of the world I've never seen before. Might show me more of his true self. The Real Montgomery who seems buried underground half of the time. I've wondered who we could be if I wasn't a Balboa and if he wasn't a Montgomery. I've wondered if we could be something greater together—if only we weren't trapped here, sneaking around in the shadows.

Still, we're no Romeo and Juliet, no Montague and Capulet.

"I'm not reading it," I say aloud, even though I have no idea if the train can hear me. "I refuse to say 'Romeo, Romeo, wherefore art thou

Romeo?' If you can see inside my head, you'd know I'm more of a Mercutio, OK?"

Dear lord, I'm talking to myself on a train.

And Madame Em might be watching.

A white-haired woman farther down the aisle determinedly stares at her romance novel.

Well, since I'm already making a fool of myself, I may as well go all in.

I stand, sore legs and arms wobbling on the rickety tracks. I wedge myself down into the staircase below the floor as if I'm preparing to get off at the next stop. I have two minutes before the doors slide open onto crowded Church Street. Two minutes before passengers try to barrel up the stairs, ruining my chance at discretion. All I see is a door yearning to open. It smells of sweet ocean air sneaking through the cracks. My Shakespeare book lays open to act 2 scene 2.

You want to hear something true?

Here's how I feel about Montgomery.

Here's what I would say if I ever had the courage to ask him to leap into that Verona sunset and never call ourselves Bartholomews again:

```
JULIET
'Tis but thy name that is my enemy;
Thou art thyself, though not a Montague.
What's Montague? it is nor hand, nor foot,
Nor arm, nor face, nor any other part
Belonging to a man. O, be some other name!
```

The train lurches into a turn; the magic twisting into a new direction and running at full speed. I hold my hands out to brace myself, but then realize the physical train isn't lurching. It's me. It's the magic, changing course, channeling through my hands, my words, my sweet longing for a boy I wish had a different name. I push the words through my mouth, even though I don't know where they'll take me.

What's in a name? That which we call a rose
By any other name would smell as sweet;
So Romeo would, were he not Romeo call'd,
Retain that dear perfection which he owes
Without that title. Romeo, doff thy name,
And for that name which is no part of thee
Take all myself.

My hands pull open the sliding doors like thick red curtains in a theater play. The smell of fresh lemon and clashing steel fills my lungs. A moment's steadying breath before I leap—only a moment—then my whole body plunges forward, even though I'm not sure I'm ready to play the part.

The word "Verona" echoes through my ears.

Verona.

⚞ CHAPTER 28 ⚟

I can't believe the train was a hopeless romantic.

As I stumble down the aisle of an empty foreign train, nausea claws at my gut. It tastes like my peanut butter sandwich may or may not veto staying inside my stomach. OK, maybe not so romantic. I rest my forehead against a smooth leather seat. Thankfully, the train is stopped. Likely for a long time, since it's empty. And pitch-dark outside. It was evening in San Francisco when I left. Either I've jumped time zones, or I took a very long time to jump here. Wherever *here* is. I better not be outside Montgomery's window like Romeo creeping on Juliet. He's already caught me once today following him somewhere I shouldn't have.

When I glance out the window, an illuminated sign reads: VERONA PORTA NUOVA. Another sign near an exit reads: USCITA. A closed pizza shop has an Italian flag hung over the doorway with its classic green, white, and red vertical stripes. Pink marble tiles stretch far into the distance.

This can't be . . . Italy?

Did I really jump to another continent all by myself?

My dad has the power to jump from San Francisco to the Philippines on a regular basis. That's way farther than Italy. Magic runs in bloodlines, and I had the help of one very dead, very genius playwright. Maybe I really am in Verona?

"Bellllla," I holler into the empty train. "I'll read you Shakespeare any day you want to drag me to Italy! You beautiful, beautiful beast." I laugh like a maniac and flop into one of the empty seats that smells like bleach and licorice. The jump's made every joint in my elbows and knees throb. My body doth protest. Blue sparks still swirl at the edges of my vision, slowly fading. *OK, breathe, Ruby. Remember what Montgomery said about jumping to different territories*–I need to keep my guard up even if my body is a disaster.

I drag myself up, but then notice a police officer patrolling the empty platform. I duck down, so fast that blue sparks firework against my closed eyelids. A groan escapes my lips from the vertigo. Come on, you're Balboa now.

It's late. Italy is maybe an eight- or nine-hour difference from San Francisco.

So, that's . . . three A.M.?

Which means I'm probably trespassing in multiple senses.

I don't know who runs these lines. Maybe I should jump back to San Francisco immediately. Or if I'm lucky, these crime lords are the friendly type. I dig through my memory to find any hints from Montgomery. We kept talking about poetry, which is information that will save absolutely no one's life when it comes to jumping into unknown territory.

I don't want to relive La Raza station, so I need to turn back.

I've proved I can jump long-distance. That'll impress Madame Em– and hopefully she'll be more willing to negotiate on routes. She speaks in terms of *power*, not weakness. If I want more control over which packages I carry across, I need to prove I'm a force to be reckoned with. Not a grunt or a newbie.

But if it's not me running those endangered elephant routes . . . someone else will.

Oh hell, what's the point of having this incredible power only to be trapped in San Francisco working for crime lords?

I drag my hands across my forehead and swallow down the urge to yell at this stupid empty train.

"You should try these lemon candies," says a man with a deep baritone voice. "They help the stomach. Buona salute."

I bolt out of my seat.

The man smiles and tosses a yellow lemon candy my way. I snatch it from the air and stuff it in my pocket. His laughter sends a ripple across his large potbelly, and a streetlamp illuminates his bald head and muscular shoulders. A scar has left a pale white line from his cheek to his goatee.

"How much do I owe you?" I can't help but chew the paint under my thumbnail. How much is this jump going to cost me? At least this time, I came prepared with cold, hard cash. Anytime I'm on the trains, I keep a stash tucked into my sock.

He shakes his head and laughs even louder. It echoes down the empty train aisle. The man doesn't seem to care that police patrol these platforms. This is his territory—he probably has all the officers on his payroll.

"You young people, always forgetting hospitality." He glances at the sapphire tattoo on my ring finger. "Bartholomews are like *family* to the Stazioni. You think I am a thug here to steal your money. No, no!" He leans forward and pulls me into a wet kiss on each cheek. He smells of garlic and lemon drops.

He unwraps another lemon drop and leans casually against the seat. "You only owe favor. We trade in favors."

"What kind of favors?" I say.

"A favor," he says with a shrug. The lemon candy pops against his teeth, sending a sweet-tart fragrance my way.

"I should go back."

"You ever see the Verona arena. Big stone columns like gladiator colosseum. Built in thirty AD. *Thir-ty* A. D. Can you believe it? Nowadays, they try to build new road, and we wait a century. Billions of euros, et cetera, et cetera. But in ancient times, the arena held thirty thousand people. Now, we use the amphitheater for opera. It's spectacular. You want to see?"

"And the favor?"

"Only small favor, if it is a small trade. You don't have weapons or drugs in your little bag, do you?"

"No! Just . . . a Shakespeare book and clothes, and uh . . . I think there's a, uh, I think a banana?"

"What did you say your name is?" he says, clearly amused the more flustered I get. Cool it, you're supposed to be Balboa here.

"I didn't," I snap.

"OK, OK, none of my business." He throws up his hands. "A Bartholomew is a Bartholomew, just like a Stazioni is a Stazioni. We are all one big family . . . with, maybe, too many knives." The man bursts into laughter and glances me up and down, probably wondering where I keep my knives. "You said Shakespeare? Don't you want to see the city of *Romeo and Juliet*? Or maybe you want to wait until you bring your lover?"

Montgomery's warm lips flash through my mind. My neck flushes, and I take a step back. All that Shakespeare has me tripping.

"No, it's just me this time."

"Come then, I will tell you the secret way," he says. "The amphitheater is closed at this hour, but I know a way. Maybe you take your lover there next time. And maybe you let me visit San Francisco with my Vittorria. She likes the North Beach. The restaurant, The Stinking Rose. You know it?"

"Seriously, she loves garlic that much? You live in *Italy* and you want to go to *North Beach*?"

He chuckles. "We can't help what calls to us."

Like this jump to Verona. Like my feelings for Montgomery. Like the fact that the trains seem to have a hankering for Shakespeare and soapy romances. Like the fact that I know deep inside that I can be as brilliant a jumper as Em or Montgomery—and that I won't let either of them hold back my magic. A sly smile tugs at my lips. I've always wanted to travel to Italy to see all the incredible art and architecture. I don't need a Romeo to take me here—this Juliet can jump all by herself.

"So, this arena—you said there was a secret way inside?"

⚝ CHAPTER 29 ⚝

From the top of the ancient amphitheater, red tile roofs glisten in the moonlight as I gaze outward from the heart of the city. Even though my legs were already aching, I couldn't resist climbing all the way to the top row. City lights flicker all around me, and birdsong chimes late into the night as they catch the last of autumn. Cool limestone presses against my palms. The aromas of citrus flowers and sardines catch on the breeze. It all feels so distant, like I'm standing at the tippy-top of the world. The Stazioni henchman told me they host spectacular operas here. Apparently, the acoustics are sublime. Part of me wants to yell: I'M HERE! I MADE IT! So that I can hear the words echo back to me in the darkness.

Verona.

Halfway across the world.

I jumped all by myself.

Who cares if the *Romeo and Juliet* lore is only fiction; a girl can dream, can't she?

When the contract is done and my dad is recovered, I want to come back here. I *will* come back here. Perhaps I can look up art schools in Italy. A place where broken and burdensome things are treasured. Maybe Diego is right—I should apply and see what happens. Italy and art restoration weren't exactly on my mom's bucket list. But I lost her note deep inside the BART tunnels. Maybe I need to write a new list.

Thoughts spiral in and out of my mind like the endless rows of seats climbing up the amphitheater. Grand stone archways encircle me. They've survived the centuries and stand just as tall as they once did. Montgomery said he loves music. Maybe one day—after I've apologized profusely for spying on him—he'll want to come here to catch an opera with me.

Though, I will never, ever, *ever* be able to tell Montgomery Bartholomew III that I got here by comparing him to Romeo Montague. He'd never let me live it down.

And the trains better not tell him, either.

Giddy laughter dances out of my lips.

I'm here.

By my own magic.

And there are so, so many more places I can jump to.

If only I could break free from my contract.

⚵ CHAPTER 30 ⚵

The jump back to Balboa Park happens so lightning quick that my brain takes time to catch up. It's a swirling vortex of sight and sound. Concrete and stone. Blue-and-white tiles smudging together. Bodies gliding up silver escalators, blurring one into another. A dull thrum of chatter, pigeons and people, and my brain can't separate the pieces. Blue sparks snap and pop and make me flinch.

I take a deep, steadying breath.

A watchful moon burns through the fog.

I've literally traveled back in time, haven't I? Back in time by eight hours with the different time zones. My poor aching bones. My knee joints crack with each step.

When I finally arrive home, I notice that neither of our renters' cars are parked out front. I know I shouldn't, but I pull out my front door keys. My feet glide up the stairs. I wish I could tell my mom all about Verona—*I need to tell her.*

The door creaks open, and I listen for footsteps before rushing into the living room. It smells of fresh oranges and popcorn. It smells like movie nights. A lamp shines amber light onto my mother's murals.

I still can't believe her hands created this.

The jungles she loved with her whole heart.

This wild thing inside our living room, breathing life into this crumbling house.

I feel like I'm starting to forget the exact lines of her face, the exact shade of her copper hair. It's been only two years, but I know she'll keep fading away.

Except these murals.

They're still bright. I gently trace the emerald ferns and press my palm to the parrot's streaked feathers. A shy baby elephant hides between its mother's legs.

If any of the renters ever damage this wall, I swear there will be blood. I don't care that they've left the living room a mess with cereal bowls and sweaters and piles of mail littered everywhere. I don't care that they've hung ugly motivational posters on the rest of the walls. Sayings like: CREATE YOUR OWN SUNSHINE or YOUR ONLY LIMIT IS *YOU*. For a moment, I can gaze at my mom's mural and imagine that she and I still live upstairs. That we're about to sit down to movie night. She'd pull a sourdough pizza from the oven and fill the air with the smell of sizzling meat. I'd sneak bites of her chocolate tart. The wall feels warm against my touch.

It feels alive.

And watchful. Guilt billows inside my chest, reminding me of the ivory tusks I smuggled into my city. The elephant in her mural watches me with distrust. My fingers dig into my palm, pain pinching into my skin. Sure, I want freedom. I want to break my contract with the Bartholomews . . . but it would mean giving up this house. My mom's murals.

Suddenly I hear keys in the front door. I sprint for the garage stairway, but not before Dorothy catches sight of me. Her face crinkles in surprise. I don't stop to apologize, don't say anything at all. I slam the door shut after me and nearly break my neck on the stairs. My lungs pump furiously. Will

I ever learn to tame my curiosity? The upstairs doesn't belong to me anymore, not really.

My dad nearly jumps out of his slippers when he catches me at the foot of the stairs.

"Susmaryosep!" He clutches onto his heart. "I thought you were ghost." When my dad is stressed, his Filipino accent ratchets up a notch and English words slip from his mind. It calms me down to hear his familiar voice.

I glance across the room at the candles lit above the piano. Two Mother Mary votives surround my mother's photograph, along with a rosary. Her eyes appear ever-forgiving, but do I deserve that forgiveness?

"You were thinking about Mom today, too?" I say.

He nods and takes a sip of his dandelion tea.

"Why didn't you ever tell Mom about the trains? She always wondered where you found the money for those expensive flights. She always felt guilty that you had to split your life across an ocean. If she'd known you were just jumping back and forth, she would have—"

"Ruby." He slumps against the washing machine. "The only way to be safe was to keep you separate."

"What do you think she would say about the underground?" My fingers trace the burning candle flame, and the heat bites against my skin. "The dangerous packages we carry across."

"She say, do your best, anak."

Is this the best I can do?

Sleeping in a garage. Ignoring my art school dreams. Shepherding disaster into my city. Falling for a boy who will be nothing but secrets. I don't know a way out of this, and I'm so very tired. Already, Verona feels impossibly far away when I step back into this ramshackle garage. *Mom, what if this is the best we can do?*

As I start to change out of my leather jacket, my phone buzzes. I sigh and pull up the message:

"Mr. Monty: Madame Em requests that you and your father join us for dinner tonight at Embarcadero."

So we've been summoned. Because I stumbled upon Montgomery's secret location in the Haight? Or because of my illegal trip to Italy? The phone trembles in my palm.

"Dad," I say.

He looks up from the spam and eggs he's cooking for our dinner.

"When Em invites us over for dinner, what does that mean?"

He frowns and lets the bottom of the eggs burn on the pan. Smoke starts to tangle in the splintered floorboards above our heads.

"Nothing good," he finally says.

"I figured. Well, you'd better shave. And keep your blade handy."

⊰ CHAPTER 31 ⊱

A car comes for us at eight P.M. sharp. I wear a black dress with a wide boatneck that shows off my collar bones. They're jagged, just the way I like them. My hair is braided into fishtail knots and pinned up. Tonight, I feel like I'm stepping out of a Rembrandt painting. I want Madame Em to look in my eyes and know I'm a worthy jumper in her game. I'm not a grunt.

My dad looks sharp in his white button-down shirt and leather jacket. His jet hair is slicked back. He even took the time to polish his new walking stick. I've never seen the handle of this one before. It's a dragon head made of deep, dark mahogany. It's smoother than the eagle cane Em stole from him. I wonder what else he has hidden inside the pockets of his leather jacket. For a moment, before slipping into the Mercedes, my dad stares at my black ankle boots where he knows I hid my knife.

"You should let me face Em," he says, leaning hard on his cane.

"You're forgetting—*I'm Balboa now.*"

I slip inside before he has a chance to say another word.

When we arrive, Powell leads us from the elevator to the dining room, all the while yattering on about yacht traffic under the Golden Gate Bridge. He doesn't say anything about my father's limp, and he doesn't slow down. I have to keep stopping, pretending to notice a fine piece of architectural detail or antique, upon which Powell eagerly jumps in to mansplain.

"Is that an original?" I say, no idea what I'm pointing at. A squat statue stares at me.

"Oh, god no. That would cost a fortune. It's a marvelous replica, though. In the Egyptology section of the Louvre, you can find this same statue. Bes: protector of home and children. I have a feeling you might benefit from some protection tonight."

I look back to gauge how many more steps my dad needs before he can catch up with us. At least another minute by the look of things. I peer down at the statue. Feather crown, squat body, and a tail dangling between its legs. Powell picks it up and pops open the hollow head.

"Touch up?" he says.

Inside rests black powder. He smudges some around his eyes, which makes the blue irises look even more fierce and ethereal.

"Kohl eyeliner. In ancient Egypt, everyone wore kohl around their eyes, no matter if they were pharaohs or peasants, men or women. They even brought it along into the afterlife. The wealthiest Egyptians mixed in powdered pearls and gold and emeralds."

He flutters his eyelids, and the kohl liner shimmers with a verdigris sparkle.

Rich people pretending they're ancient Egyptian royalty. I sigh and shake my head.

Before Powell can launch down the hallway again and leave my father in the dust, I dab my pinky finger inside the statue and rim my eyes in kohl. I can play pretend, too.

"There she is." Powell smiles. "That's the girl I was hoping would show up tonight."

"Thanks."

"Trust me, you'll need it."

My father finally shuffles up behind us.

"Are you ready?" I say, turning toward him.

He stares at my eyes as if he doesn't recognize the girl standing in front of him.

We gather our strength for whatever lays before us, a pair of stubborn Santoses until the bitter end.

Then, we push open the doors.

CHAPTER 32

The dining room glows with candlelight, and the table gleams with silver platters that look more like mirrors than dishes. Powell and Em sit whispering roughly to each other. Montgomery stares at his phone, his eyebrows together in his usual scowl. No sign of Merritt. I wonder if it's a good sign that the Muscle isn't here. But then again, with the memory of Em threatening to make that trespasser "disappear," maybe muscle doesn't matter.

"Good evening, Madame Em," I say.

She doesn't say a word, only holds out her hand toward the two empty seats.

I push my shoulders back to calm my nerves and make myself appear a few inches taller.

Montgomery looks dashing as usual. Though this is the first time I've seen him in a suit other than blue. This one is a somber forest green. Black foxes are stitched on the cuffs alongside gold *M* cuff links. I suspect he didn't pick it out. Too flashy. It's not the Real Montgomery. Not the boy with poetry books stuffed in his pockets and secret rendezvous in snowy fjords and the same simple blue suit every single day. Judging by the way we were summoned tonight, I won't be speaking to the Real Montgomery–instead I'll have to stare down a statue with a stone fist who enforces Em's rules.

"What a lovely dress," Madame Em says. "It does fine work showing off your shoulders. Doesn't it, Montgomery?"

He glances up from his phone and gives me a bland smile before resuming whatever business he's conducting via text. Probably bossing Six or Dublin around to do their dirty work. So that's it then. Fine. I'm on my own. At least I chose my own outfit, unlike that forest green blazer that screams, fake, fake, fake. I can't believe this is the same boy I thought about to serenade the train to Verona.

My dad finally makes his way across the dining room. Before he sits down, he taps my wrist as a signal to help pull out the chair for him. Thank god it's a heavy teak one. He leans hard on it to lower down on his bad hip. If it were a flimsier chair, it would go flying under his grip. Without any pills or alcohol, there's no way he can hide his pain. I'm proud of him for attending more AA meetings, but it still stings to see him suffering.

When we're all seated at the table, Montgomery stows his phone, and Powell stops his chattering. Everyone sits waiting for Madame Em's command. There's no food on the table, no drinks, only forks, platters, and sharpened knives. Silence settles upon us, and Madame Em looks like she savors every second.

"Why don't you fetch us a few old-fashioneds?" Em says to my father.

"I can do it," I say, already standing so that my dad doesn't have to.

"Sit," Em commands.

"Ice or no ice?" my dad says. He doesn't even blink. His face remains a mask. It's hard for me to see him this way. At home, he's always the first one to burst into laughter or fury. His big brown eyes and wide grin.

"Ice," Em replies.

"No ice," Powell says.

"Nothing for me," Montgomery says.

"Bring him an iced tea," Em says. "Balboa, what will you have?"

"Water," I say softly.

My father lets out a small involuntary groan as he lurches upward from the chair. His cane thumps with every step on the checkered marble. He takes thirty agonizing seconds to reach the bar. He leans his body against the counter as he begins to pour the bourbon and vermouth. A servant gazes blankly from the doorway. My heels thrum against the floor. I want to leap up and help him. I won't say what I want to do to Madame Em.

I sneak a glance at Montgomery's expression. If he really cared about my father, he would have at least a shred of emotion on his face. If he cared about me, he'd stop this. He stares vacantly at the silver candelabras.

"Look," I say. "If this whole thing is about that house on Cole, I–"

"It's not," Montgomery snaps. For the briefest moment, worry flashes in his blue eyes before he hides behind boredom again. My father clinks ice into a glass and balances his broken body against the bar. Let's skip the theatrics so we can all go home already.

"From what Montgomery has told me," Madame Em says. "It seems you've been making very slow progress on the trains. You've barely left San Francisco in all these weeks, and you're still too green for the big jumps, isn't that so, Montgomery?"

"Yes," he says, staring at me intently across the table as if he's trying to send a message.

Still too green for the big jumps. His words burn inside my chest. *Thanks, Monty, way to throw me under the bus in front of the boss. I can't believe he still underestimates me that much.*

My dad teeters back to the table, and I try not to cringe at the ice clinking against crystal. He balances a silver tray with all four glasses in one hand and his cane in the other. Sweat pools on his forehead in this cruel balancing act. My leg staccatos against the chair. *Behave, Ruby.*

I can't tell if Em knows about my Verona jump or not. Is she trying to catch me in a lie? Her pale face gives nothing away as she inches closer to me.

"I'm making steady progress," I say.

"And the rules?"

"Yes, I'm learning all I can from Montgomery."

As my dad nearly topples the cocktail tray, I rise up to help him.

"Sit down," she says, louder this time.

I sink back like iron dropping to the ocean floor.

"Montgomery informed you that there's always a price for crossing portals, correct?"

"Yes," I say.

At this, Powell chuckles, and still Montgomery says nothing. He doesn't look away, doesn't look down at his plate, doesn't look at my father, doesn't look at anything at all. It's like he's transported his soul elsewhere. Anywhere but here.

The cocktails clatter and slosh tiny drops onto the silver tray. My dad lowers the tray onto the table and nearly dumps the whole thing.

"Do I look like a servant?" Em glares at him. "My guests are waiting for their drinks."

My dad nods and delivers a drink to Em, and then moves around the table to set a drink in front of Powell, then Montgomery. Finally, he comes back around and eases a glass of sparkling water by my plate, careful not to spill a drop with his shaking hands. My fingers tremble, too, resisting the urge to splash it in Em's face. She takes a sip of the old-fashioned and then bites into the cherry. A sickly artificial red drips from her teeth when she smiles.

"And yet," she says. "You—*alone*—jumped from Cole Street Metro to Verona Porta Nuova halfway across the world. An unauthorized crossing, in full knowledge of the rules."

My hands latch on to my thighs, and a cold sweat breaks out along my neck. My dad turns to stare at me, speechless.

Montgomery's pupils widen in shock before looking down at his empty plate.

"Yes." I force the word from my mouth, trying to remember why the hell I thought this would impress Em. "I jumped to Italy. I wanted to prove that—"

"You've been lying to us about your talents and whereabouts, is that correct?" Madame Em taps her nails impatiently against the silver platter. "And may I suggest that you choose your words wisely, darling. I don't tolerate liars."

Heat twists inside my chest, and I take a shaky breath. All their eyes are on me, even Montgomery's. There's a plea in his gaze. He must know I'd never tell anyone our secrets. Even after he yelled at me for spying on him on Cole Street. Or maybe . . . he's truly worried about what Em will do to me for this transgression.

"I . . . I was practicing. I just knew I could jump as far as Balboa or Montgomery. And I wanted to prove it to you. I just . . . jumped without thinking. Madame Em, I'm so, so sorry. It'll never happen again. I'll ask first, I promise."

"Indeed. And precisely *how* were you able to jump halfway across the world when you've never been to Italy before? A girl supposedly 'too green' to fulfill her full duties as my Balboa." Madame Em is speaking to me, but her eyes pierce into Montgomery. His long piano fingers twirl a fork in circles, so steadily that I'm in awe of how he's able to deflect her fierce gaze. A lot of practice covering up the truth, I bet.

"I was just . . . lucky, I guess?" My mind flickers to all the secrets Montgomery told me about poetry calling to the trains, amplifying our jumping abilities. The Bartholomews have been in power for decades—there must be a reason Montgomery hasn't told his family about his tricks, and why he still says nothing now. My teeth bite into my bottom lip to keep from saying anything further. I try to remember that I wear the kohl and emeralds of a fierce Egyptian goddess around my eyes, but they're no match against Madame Em's icy gaze.

"Luck," she says. The sound of laughter escapes her lips, but it's not laughter at all. It's more like the thud of a belt against someone's back. Hah. Hah. Hah. Each syllable another punishment. "Then you'll have no trouble taking on bigger jobs now. Buenos Aires, Mexico City, Panama. You'll take over your father's routes. No more of this slow and easy training. There's money to be made, darling." She snaps her fingers in the direction of her youngest son. "Powell, you'll be her handler now."

"Wait," I say. "Montgomery's my trainer, not Powell."

"And who are you to make the rules?" she says.

"I'm not—"

Under the table, my dad's hand clamps around my knee in warning. Through all this, Montgomery says nothing. He gazes out at the jagged skyline, obviously finished with the conversation. Fine, I get it. He's glad to be rid of me and all my troublemaking. I sink back into my chair and wonder how a family can survive in this cold tangle of skyscrapers.

"*Powell* will be your handler," Em says. "And there will be no more fun and games, *from either of you.*" She glares at Powell, who gulps down the last of his sparkling cocktail.

"Of course, Madame," he says. "You know how much I detest fun." Powell straightens his tie and kicks my shoe under the table. Great, I'll have to be the one to keep us *both* out of trouble.

"This is your job, Balboa," Embarcadero says. "You are indebted to the Bartholomew line for the next four years. Do not forget it."

"Yes, Madame."

"There will be no more unauthorized crossings on my lines. I don't care if you're 'practicing.' Your 'practice' is carrying packages across the lines for the Bartholomews—and you will go only where we send you. If I find out you've crossed again without authorization, you'll be headed for the Vanishing Station, where I make our most irritating problems disappear. I do dread dealing with foolishness."

Servants start to bring dishes out to the table, but Madame Em holds her palm up. They freeze mid-step as if she actually has the power to ice their limbs.

"In restitution," she says, "you shall receive no pay for the next three jobs."

"But how will we—"

My dad squeezes my knee again, and I force myself into silence. Three payments gone. All for a practice jump to Verona. Precious cash we could have saved for my dad's hip surgery. How was I stupid enough to think jumping to Italy would earn Em's respect? I'm nothing but a tool to her.

"Understood." I grind out the word between clenched teeth.

"Good. Edward, bring out the quail. It would be a tragedy for our meal to go cold."

The servants burst into motion, swooping in with serving dishes of gravy and potatoes and stuffed quail. They rush back to the kitchen for more.

I rise to my feet. All eyes snap to me.

"Thank you for your invitation, Madame Em, and I'm sure it will be a lovely meal. But, if you'll excuse me, I need some air."

"Ruby, what about dinner?" My dad still sits at the table, and finally, he lets his worry show. Fear for my safety—that's all I read in his big brown eyes.

You want to see my mask? It's nothing but teeth.

"How about we not sit here and pretend this is a social visit? I appreciate your generosity, Madame, but I'm afraid I've lost my appetite. Dad, let's go."

My dad stares in shock. His legs are frozen.

Montgomery finally speaks. "Our driver can take your father home."

His voice makes my heart swell, but I don't dare look him in the eyes.

"Have a pleasant evening," I say.

Before anyone has a chance to say another word, I walk toward the door. I brace myself for strong arms to grab me. To chain me to my chair and force-feed me mashed potatoes. But it never comes. Not when I slip into the elevator. Not when I gulp down foggy air the moment I hit the street. Not when I board the BART train and walk to Popeyes on my way home.

I slump into a plastic booth by the window and order a giant box of fried chicken and Cajun fries. A few people stare at me in my satin dress, my glittering kohl eyes. I don't care that my fingers are covered in chicken grease and barbecue sauce. Whenever my dad eats chicken, he devours every last morsel until there are only thin twiggy bones left. He even rolls the chicken bones around in his mouth to squeeze out that last bit of flavor. Nothing wasted, nothing lost. I take my time. I have nowhere to be. I eat and eat until there's a pile of clean skeletons in front of me.

That's when Montgomery arrives.

He slides into the booth across from me and glances at the pile of bones.

If I'd gotten a lot of stares for my black satin dress, Montgomery draws far more attention in his embroidered blazer and his Rolex watch. He pushes up his sleeves as if he's afraid he might get chicken grease on them. I pick up the last bone and run it through my mouth until there's nothing left on it. Then I spit it out onto the skeleton heap.

"That's disgusting," he says.

"You're disgusting. You just sat there."

"What would you have me do?"

"How about speaking up?"

"You knew Em's rules. I warned you. Why did you jump without me?"

"Because you were mad at me! Because I wasn't thinking properly!"

"Like tonight."

"If I wanted to sit around and pretend we're all nice people having a nice family dinner, then I would have stayed. Unfortunately, I'm not a liar. For god's sake, I thought you people wanted me to be competent at my job. Instead I sit around on trains all day, waiting for little goodie bags of destruction, while you traipse around the world and yell at me for accidentally stumbling upon your secret doorstep. How is that fair? Why even have this power if I can't use it?"

"You want to use your power so badly—go right ahead. Now, Em knows what you're capable of. Good for you; you get to start the big jumps. Don't you notice how much pain your dad is in? You think that's just natural aging?"

"If you recall, I just had the pleasure of watching my father painfully serve drinks because of Em's whims."

"That was cruel of her. And I'm sorry it happened. But that'll be you one day. You can't jump that frequently and that far without repercussions. You'll start to feel bone grinding against bone, your joints turning against you. The poetry helps unlock doors, helps summon the train magic, but it won't stop the pain. Now she knows what you're capable of, and I won't even be there to help. Powell is your new handler, and I can't—"

Montgomery leans his head back and sucks in a breath. When he faces me again, his soft black curls fall into his eyes.

My dad's words echo inside my head. *They're going to use you until there's nothing left.* Rage and grief swell at the edges of my eyes, and everything is too, too bright. I try to cling to that sliver of freedom I'd felt in Verona—that starlit hope burning inside my chest—and a question that keeps echoing: *Why does it have to be this way? Why does my destiny belong to the Bartholomews?* Yes, Montgomery wants to shield me from the pain to come, but he's a Montague through and through. He won't put a stop to his crime family's ruthlessness; he'll keep running the trains even though he knows it grinds good people into bone. It's almost worse that he cares about me, because he still won't refuse Em's demands.

I snap a chicken bone between my fingers.

"What are you doing here, anyway? Got a hankering for fried chicken? Felt like slumming it for a night? Or do you want to order me around some more?"

"I drove your dad home, and I saw you in the restaurant window." He stares at the passing traffic, mainly buses crammed with people too poor to afford cars. Litter overflows from the trash bins, and bright orange graffiti covers the bus stop. "Honestly . . . I don't know what I'm doing here."

"Then leave," I snap.

A busboy comes by to clear my table. He leans close to my ear and whispers, "Is this guy bothering you?"

I smile kindly at the kid. He looks barely a day over sixteen, braces on his teeth and a cute afro puffing up around his ears. I don't know what exactly he would do if this was a bad situation, but it's a small gift that he would even ask.

"I'm OK, thanks."

He nods and walks away with the heap of chicken bones.

"Do they make good Cajun fries here?" Montgomery gazes up at the menu.

"What is this?" I say.

"I haven't eaten yet."

"No, I mean what is this between us? Are we friends? Are we flirting? Are you my boss? Tell me exactly what we're doing here."

He sighs. "I don't know."

"Yes, the fries are good. Best damn Cajun fries you'll get this side of the city."

I slide out of the booth and rush out the door. A second later, he's stalking by my side. It's not fair his legs are so much longer than mine. There's no way I'd outpace him, despite the fact that I'm wearing motor-cycle boots under my satin dress.

"Can I walk with you?" he says.

"It's a public sidewalk. Do whatever you want."

"I'm sorry about tonight. There is so much I want to change."

"OK."

"I don't usually agree with Em's tactics, but the only way we can keep BART safe is to follow the rules. I know she can be cruel sometimes, but there are rivals vying to take control. If it's not the Bartholomew line, there will be another organization in charge, just as vicious."

"OK."

"She's extremely protective of me. If she knew I cared about you, then she'd turn on you. Which means that I can't always act the way I want to around you."

"OK."

"I don't know what the right thing is."

"OK."

"I'm sorry I flipped out when you found my hideaway. No one knows about Cole Street, not even my family."

"OK."

I force my lips to stay still. I'm sorry I stole one of his secrets before he was ready to share it with me, but now is not the time to let my defenses down. I keep walking, even when my toe hits a crack in the sidewalk and sends pain shooting up my already sore knees.

"Ruby—I'm being more honest with you than I've been with my own damn brothers. Will you stop and say something other than 'OK'?"

"OK."

"Please . . ."

"Stop," I say, spinning to face him. "I don't want to hear any more. It's too much. Here's how it goes from now on: I pick up the package; I drop off the package; Powell pays me; end of story. Anytime I want something more, it gets me into trouble. So please do me a favor and keep it simple."

"OK," he whispers.

He turns and walks away without another word.

It leaves me gasping for breath. I grind my teeth together to keep tears from smearing inky kohl down my cheeks.

A man passes me with a bucket of roses strapped to his back.

"Ten dollar!" he yells, glancing around for buyers. "Ten dollar for your love. Roses! Rosas!"

Everything has a price.

Everything.

And the price for me and Montgomery to be together is too high.

I walk the rest of the way home in my black dress, and I don't get a single catcall or lingering stare. I feel people subtly move out of my way, and I think, *Good*—this is the way you survive everything the world throws at you.

⚡ CHAPTER 33 ⚡

Verona, huh?" Powell arches an eyebrow when I jump aboard the early BART train. "You really wanted to see Juliet's balcony that badly?"

My coffee nearly spills onto Powell's pearl Gucci coat when a biker rushes to squeeze aboard. The man doesn't bother to apologize for knocking my elbow.

"What can I say? I love pizza." We slide into a pair of seats and sigh. I'm guessing he's not a morning person, either.

"After all the brilliant insights I've shared with you, you're not going to tell me how you jumped to Verona? I thought we were friends." Powell playfully knocks my knee, so of course, I threaten to dump coffee on his lap. He throws up his hands and grins like a mischievous kid.

"Last I heard, you're my new boss," I say. "Maybe you should start acting like it?"

"Mmm, what shall I order you to do today? Shall I channel my best Montgomery?" He slips into a serious thinker-face for two whole seconds, before breaking down into a smirk.

"Can we not talk about Montgomery?" I chug down the last of my bitter black coffee.

"Fine, fine, let's talk about your friend Diego." Powell sidles close like he wants to hear every juicy detail. And oddly, I want to tell him everything.

He's just so open in every way that Montgomery and Merritt are not. It's a useful skill. And a trap, I'm sure.

"My friend Diego, who is most definitely off-limits."

"Darling, the only one off-limits is *you*, and that's because Montgomery would drop my sorry ass in the Vanishing Station if I laid a hand on you."

"No one has explained this Vanishing Station thing to me yet. Except when Em so eloquently threatened me with it at dinner."

Powell laughs. "Of course our saintly little Montgomery doesn't want to tell you about his dark side." He glances up at the security camera watching over us and threads his fingers through a lock of my long black hair. "Do you think he's watching?"

I smack Powell's hand so hard he yelps. He glances down at his French manicured fingernails and shakes off the pain. Teach him to touch my hair again.

"The Vanishing Station is a place . . . well, sort of." He shrugs. "It's a non-place that only Em and Montgomery can jump to and from. I'm sure there are others in the world who can get there, but I haven't met them yet. No one *wants* to go there. It's pure desolation. A wasteland. It's a place where we can make people *disappear*."

"Has Montgomery ever taken anyone there?" This time I'm the one who glances up at the security camera. I wonder if he is watching.

Powell smirks. "Why don't you ask him?"

"We're not on speaking terms."

"But you have such amazing people skills!"

"You know, if *sarcasm* is your superpower, then you're not going to win this weird competition with your brothers."

"Darling, I'm the *stylish* brother. I always win. So, spill; what's in that ratty backpack you carry around?"

I immediately think of my Shakespeare books and the William Carlos Williams poetry that Montgomery gave me. Secrets he trusted me with.

"Art school apps," I say—the first thing that flies into my head. "Diego wants me to get into art school, so he marked them up with brilliant suggestions. I just haven't done anything with them for months." My fingers trace the fine lines of my palm as if there might be answers there.

"Then apply to art school." Powell shrugs.

"That simple?"

"Yup."

"Have you ever had to worry about anything in your life with Em and Montgomery watching over you, fixing your mistakes?"

His mouth turns hard, and his knuckles knock twice against the metal window frame.

"I'm here, aren't I? Fixing *Montgomery's* mistake for getting too cozy with a certain jumper. What's your excuse for not applying to art school?"

I push my shoulders back into the seat and let out a long sigh. I hate it when *Powell*, of all people, has a point.

"So you're going to apply to art school," he says. "Make Diego proud, and then give me his number."

"He has a boyfriend, remember?"

"I remember," he says. "I also remember those glorious dimples. And those biceps. Who knew painters had so much muscle?"

I flash him a glimpse of my own lean sculpted arms.

"That's nothing," says a raspy female voice. Six appears out of nowhere—well, actually out of a portal that seeps icy air along the back of my neck—and slides into a seat behind us. She flexes her muscled arms and cracks her knuckles. She goes on to crack her neck and shoulder socket, too.

"God, stop that," Powell says, shuddering.

"You'll start to sound like this, too," Six says. "Once Em has you running Balboa's route every week without rest. Wait until you see what your knees will look like in a few years."

"Don't give her nightmares," Powell says. "Hell, don't give me nightmares."

A dark queasiness twists in my gut, roiling up my throat. I touch the smooth, unblemished skin along my inner elbow.

"So where are you sending us today, *boss*?" Six cracks her knuckles again, right next to Powell's left ear. He flinches and smacks her hand away.

"Show her the route to Buenos Aires." He discreetly slides a black messenger bag under the seat toward her. "That's in Argentina," he says, turning to me.

"I know where Buenos Aires is."

"Good, then you know it's the southernmost point of the continent. Good luck, darling."

"You're not coming?"

"And waste my precious joints on a little errand." Powell laughs. "I pay Six extra to do that for me. It speeds up her contract end date, and I get to stay in salty San Francisco. Everybody wins."

"Except Six."

Powell frowns. "There's a man named Córdoba waiting at Callao station on the D Line. He should have a thin tube around twenty-four inches long. Don't open the tube. Understood?"

We both nod.

"Go on, grunts," he says. "The sooner we finish this, the sooner we can go home."

"You mean the sooner *we* finish this," Six says. We rise from our seats and walk toward the connecting doors.

"Devil's in the details, darling." Powell waves us off and flips open his dog-eared copy of the *Meditations of Marcus Aurelius*. The Roman emperor's stone face gazes at us.

"Since you have no idea how to get there, *I'll* jump us through," Six says, jabbing her knuckles into my shoulder. "But that's your one freebie, grunt."

We hover for a moment near the connecting doors, our toes surfing the train's undulating floor. "Back in a flash." Six winks, and before I know it, icy air floods into the Saddle, smothering my breath and filling the thin space with blazing blue sparks. My palms prickle, and my hair whips around my face.

Show-off.

Six hurls me through the portal doors.

Spanish words and strangers' elbows swirl around me. My legs scramble for solid ground. I reach my arms out to grab on to anything and collide into a fleshy shoulder. A sharp high heel slams into my shoe, and I yelp back.

"Perdon!"

"Sorry, sorry!" I scramble back into more bodies who shove against me like I've fallen onto a giant trampoline. Finally Six grabs my elbow and whispers sharply, "I really don't understand what he sees in you."

I swallow a gulp of stale air and shove the dizziness down, down, away.

The southernmost part of South America.

We're in Buenos Aires.

Gorgeous mosaic portraits stare back at me through glass windows. A woman with ivy woven into her hair and face. A little boy with a crown of colorful leaves. All the tiny mosaic tiles come together into one glittering image. I've always been mesmerized by cities that turn their subways into art galleries. Open to anyone who can spare a glance. Apparently, Six is not one of those people. She darts off the train, dodging through the river of passengers heading toward the SALIDA sign. I run to catch up.

"Maybe Powell would like you better if you stop cracking knuckles in his ear," I holler.

"I wasn't talking about Powell."

Damn, have Montgomery and I really been that obvious?

My imagination suddenly snags on the image of Six and Montgomery. I wonder if they ever had a history—I mean, they both have incredible jumping abilities and have known each other for years. *Quiet, brain . . . you've already told off Monty.*

"Memorize this station, this train, this feeling," Six says. "Callao station, Line D. You'll need to come back here on your own next time. Some people need to leapfrog this far south. Maybe try Costa Rica or Panama as transfer stations. The former Balboa didn't need to, but jumping ability doesn't necessarily spread evenly or equally through bloodlines. You might be as pathetic as Powell."

"Why do you take orders from him if he's that pathetic?"

"Because he's still a Bartholomew. And I signed a contract. I need to pay it off as quickly as possible. Before my joints get as bad as your dad's."

"Why did you sign it, anyway?"

At first Six doesn't look like she's going to tell me, her shoulders going rigid under her sharp collarbones. From this angle I can see that her joints have swollen at the elbows. Fiery inflammation pulses under her skin. She catches me staring, and I can't hide the sadness in my eyes—all I can think about is my dad, his poor broken limbs and his alcoholism to mask the pain. It could have all been stopped.

Her maple eyes soften.

"Em finds jumpers who are young and desperate," she says. "All the crime families do. All around the world, they track down jumpers, and then 'recruit' them. Em's offer was better than the life I was leaving behind." She shrugs, even though it looks like a heavy weight rests on her shoulders.

"Where was your life before?"

"It doesn't matter," she mumbles. "I'm never jumping back."

"When I jump, I feel the strongest pull back to Balboa Park."

"Sixteenth Street Mission will never be my home," she says. "Just my tether."

Six locks eyes with a stranger in the crowd. He stalks toward us with a poster tube draped over his shoulder. It must be Córdoba.

A bird scrambles away from his hurried footsteps down the train platform. The street birds in Buenos Aires are subtly different here. White flecks along their charcoal necks, like a splash of speckled paint. I know it's only a plain old pigeon, but the fact that I'm on the other side of the world makes my eyes bright and buzzy.

Before I know it, Six finishes the job without a hitch. Bags exchanged, transaction complete. All the way to the southern edge of the world, and I won't even be able to see Buenos Aires. Just a grimy train station. My heart sinks as I catch a glimpse of the sunlight sneaking down the subway stairs.

"Can we peek aboveground?" I say.

"This is work," Six snaps, rushing toward our waiting train. "Lucky *you* might get away with galivanting around the world for fun, but some of us have livelihoods on the line."

"I just want to see what it's like here."

"Do it on your own time, grunt."

Aboard the D Line, Six is about to shove me through the portal doors again, using all her fury to fuel her. But I grab her wrist before she can do it.

"Wait," I say.

"No tricky business. I promised Powell I'd take you right back."

"It's not a trick." I hold out my open palm. "Let me take you back to Balboa Park. Let me save you a jump. Then we can drop the package with Powell, and mission accomplished."

Six squeezes her swollen elbows and hesitates as the train rumbles down the tunnel. Slowly, reluctantly, she reaches out her hand.

"Don't mess this up," she hisses.

"Let me try it."

She nods, a slight smile on her lips.

Wind howls against my neck as I think about the only home I've ever known. I jump us back—not as swiftly or gracefully as she did—but back in *one giant leap*. Just like my dad could. It makes me smile even as a sharp throb begins in my ankles and spreads up my knees to my hips, until my hip bones scream in pain. I topple into the aisle, but Six grabs me before I hit the ground.

"You didn't have to do that," she whispers.

I shrug, not ready to speak through the nausea twisting in my throat. We hobble off the BART train while familiar pigeons beg for popcorn crumbs. They always seem to find enough to make it to the next day.

"I told you, I always find my way home."

"And Saint Petersburg will always be my home." Six holds out her swollen elbows to keep hurried passengers from knocking into my aching body. "I never want to return to Russia, but I always dream of Saint Petersburg's streets."

My chest warms with this small truth she's shared with me. Even in these dark tunnels, we can find friendship here. I hope.

"Sit for a few minutes. I need to make a phone call." Six jogs down the platform, while sunlight warms my shaking hands. I close my eyes—and then force them open again because the nausea is too much. Breathe, Ruby. I still remember how my dad used to bring back sticky purple Ube Kalamay from the Philippines, and I wish I could bite into sweet coconut rice to calm my stomach.

Six returns and hoists me to my feet. "Wait near the bus stop," she says. "A car is coming to take you home."

"I can walk a few blocks," I mumble as my body sways.

"No, you can't." She smirks and lets me lean on her while we hobble toward the escalator.

"You've been doing this since you were thirteen?" I don't bother to hide the astonishment in my voice. I can't imagine how she's done this so many years without breaking to pieces. Six nods—not with pride or gloating but with the stark determination needed for survival.

"Most jumpers get an inkling of their powers around middle school," she says. "Some are late bloomers and don't fully develop until high school."

"Why didn't I ever get recruited?"

"That's a question for your father," she says.

Thick, gloomy clouds hover overhead as we emerge onto Geneva Avenue. A stopped bus rolls out its wheelchair ramp to let a passenger aboard. Exhaust churns into the sky, and wind sneaks through my knit sweater, sending a shiver up my neck.

"You're going to be OK?" Six says.

"It'll fade." I lean down to massage the pain in my knees. "Right?"

"The pain, yes. The Ruby Santos spirit . . . I hope not."

I give her my first genuine smile of the day.

"Next time you're in Buenos Aires," she says. "You should visit El Ateneo Grand Splendid. It's maybe two blocks from Callao station. They won't notice if you sneak a quick look."

"With a name like Grand Splendid, how could I not?"

"It's a stunning bookstore. Inside of an old opera theater."

"Art books too?"

"Every kind of book." She smiles. "Anyway, I need to go—Powell is waiting, and he hates waiting. Such an impatient brat." She readjusts the strap slung over her shoulder. It dawns on me that there's likely a precious painting inside that poster tube. One I'll never see. One that the public might never see again. Likely stolen. Maybe from a museum, maybe from a church. And we're no better than the thieves.

I'm about to reach for the painting—just to take the tiniest of glimpses—but then I pull my hand back and shove it in my pocket.

No more questions, Ruby. You saw where your wild dreams of free-dom got you. Three lost pay days and more grueling jumps. Keep your head down and do your job. That's the only way to end this contract with the Bartholomews.

"So, what kind of car am I waiting for?" I say, suddenly itching to run away.

"You'll know." She heads toward the underground, her short blue hair twirling in the wind. "I understand now . . . why he likes you." She says the words barely above a whisper before disappearing into the tunnel.

This whole day has felt like a surreal dream, one moment blurring into another, while certain memories—like the Buenos Aires mosaics and Six's sisterly smile—feel stamped into my brain. That's why, when a sleek black Mercedes pulls up to the curb, I wonder if I am indeed dreaming when Montgomery's face appears through the glass.

⚡ CHAPTER 34 ⚡

C an I give you a ride home?" Montgomery hollers over the traffic noise and swings open the door. A semitruck shudders past, probably chock-full of jungle plants to decorate the office skyscrapers downtown.

I want to tell him to get lost, but my body lurches for the passenger seat. All my bravado with Six disappeared the moment the ocean wind crept under my sweaty shirt. After the jump from Argentina, the autumn cold cuts deep into my joints. I try to exhale through the pain. My forehead leans against the dashboard as I massage the backs of my knees. Montgomery blasts the heat. Sweet, sweet mercy, can we move to a tropical island and never come back?

"A concoction of orange juice, glucosamine, and omega-3s helps dull the pain. At least, for me it does." He gently eases my forehead back to pop open the dash. Out fall little white bottles of every supplement associated with joint health—chondroitin sulfate, glucosamine sulfate, calcium, vitamin D3, ginger, turmeric, omega-3, green tea, and a giant bottle of ibuprofen to ease the swelling. All the stuff my dad takes every morning after he drags his legs out of bed.

"I take it you've tried a lot of things for the pain?"

"Not everything," he says. "But I hope I never get that desperate."

I rub my palms over my knees again, desperately trying to smooth out the sharp ache. Montgomery reaches out but stops before he touches me. He pulls his hand back to the steering wheel. His Adam's apple bobs like he's keeping words tamped down his throat. A shiver curls down my spine as the warmth of the car heater swirls. I still remember the way our knees would press together on the trains, that small secret warmth slipping between us. I wish that wasn't my first thought getting into a car with Montgomery Bartholomew III.

I need to shut down those thoughts. It's the only way I can do my job without longing for more. Six is smart to focus on working down her debt as fast as possible. I want out—but I need to play by the rules.

The bright citrus blossoms of Verona fill my lungs when I crack open the orange juice. The smell of freedom. Art waiting to be discovered if only I can jump beyond the Bartholomew confines. Montgomery always makes me crave all the things I can't have.

I turn away from him.

My head rests against the window as he accelerates away from Balboa Park station. The fog erases the sky, erases all the edges of the buildings as if the world is one gray muddle. Montgomery turns to face me at a stoplight, and I squeeze my eyes shut. Please don't say anything.

"Ruby." He speaks so softly, I can barely hear him over the heater. "I want you to know—I wasn't holding you back because I didn't think you could jump that far. Or because I didn't want you to grow your magic. I was training you slowly because . . . I didn't want you to feel this pain. Em will—"

"You don't have to explain."

"I should have been more honest," he says.

Silence stretches between us as the engine rumbles, waiting for release. My fingers tremble against the smooth leather. I open my eyes.

"The light's green," I whisper.

He drags his eyes back to the road. The car lurches forward, and we cruise along 19th Avenue toward the darkening ocean—which is definitely not in the direction of home.

"Wait, where are you taking me?"

"The Sutro tracks." His arctic eyes stare at the road ahead, unblinking.

"Why?"

"You asked Powell about the Vanishing Station—"

"You were spying on us!"

"We're even then." A small smile curls the edge of his lips, and it makes me want to lean in for a kiss. Maybe it's a good thing he's not my trainer anymore. It's too easy to fall into this magnetic pull, even when I'm mad at him, even when my job is on the line.

"I wanted to make sure Powell didn't mess with you on his first day as trainer," he says. "Make sure he didn't send you to Antarctica."

"So you heard us talking about the Vanishing Station?"

"There's something you need to see. Then I'll take you home. No tricks."

"OK."

"You're sure?"

I nod, even as my head spins. I pop two ibuprofen pills in my mouth and wash them down with orange juice. The sharp citrus tang helps clear my mind.

When we pull up to Lands End Lookout, the parking lot is emptier than usual for a Tuesday afternoon. The kids in my high school used to come here to make out. Claire called it Lips End, for obvious reasons. When I was a sophomore, I came here with a boy named Cristian in his dad's pristine black Mustang. We didn't even end up kissing much, with his nonstop chatter about its V8 engine and 480 horsepower and something-something-

239

torque. God, that feels so long ago, but it's been only a few months since I graduated. Sometimes, whiplash hits me when I think about how much has changed since I found out about Dad's debt, since I signed away my life to the Bartholomews.

Since I discovered magic.

Craggy cypress trees cling to the cliffsides. Montgomery points out the trail, and it winds through sand dunes covered in fuchsia ice plants. Ravens caw above us. Laughing, no doubt.

"I thought you said you cared about my knees," I complain. "This looks like a hike."

"It's not far, and I can carry you if you'd like." He spins around and offers me his back. He does it with such chivalric sincerity that I burst into a laugh. Still wearing his same midnight blue suit, he looks out of place in these wild dunes. His wavy black hair catches in the wind, and mischief sparks in his eyes. Half of me wants to jump aboard–the half that doesn't want to admit this version of Montgomery pulls me in every time. The other half remembers our horrible dinner with Em, where he did absolutely nothing to help me and my father.

"No pity rides," I say.

He shrugs and mumbles "so stubborn" under his breath.

We plod through the fine white sand, crisp ocean salt tingling my senses awake.

"You said there were train tracks here?" I say.

"There was an eccentric millionaire named Adolph Sutro who built an incredible bathhouse in the late 1800s. You know those rocks north of the Cliff House? Right there." Montgomery points beyond the ridge to a massive white building that looks like a Greek Revival temple perched atop a rock. "Sutro even built a railroad that could take people from the heart of the city right to Ocean Beach, Sutro Heights, and the Cliff House. He hardly charged anything. Of course, Sutro eventually went bankrupt. And after the San Francisco fires, ruins are all that's left."

Mossy concrete slabs are embedded in the waves below. Every day, the sea steals more away.

"Are there any people like Sutro who rule the train lines? People who aren't in it for the money?" I wrap my arms around myself to keep the wind from cutting through my sweater.

"That's a dangerous question to ask a Bartholomew," he says.

"As far as I can tell, there aren't any security cameras here. Unless that raven is in disguise." I send him a playful smirk, but he doesn't meet my eyes. Instead, he gazes at the ruins below, silent as the waves thud against the rocks over and over. White foam spills between the jagged stones, disappearing back into the sea.

"I wish you didn't trust me as much as you do," he says, finally. "Em will never be a Sutro, and it's dangerous to even speak about other lines. Your contract is with the Bartholomew line. End of conversation."

"So, why couldn't you be a Sutro instead of a Bartholomew? Isn't there any choice in how you rule the lines?"

Montgomery strides forward without an answer. I can't keep up; a sharp twinge flares inside my kneecap with every step. But he knows that. Message received, loud and clear. Stop. Asking. Questions.

A clearing opens up between two cypresses. The trees look as if they've been here since long before San Francisco became a city. We sink and stumble through the dunes. Luckily, we don't have to trek far. Montgomery points to a patch of dark, damp sand, closer to the tide than I'd like.

"This is awkward," he says. "But will you lay here? Next to me. This is the spot." He drops down into the sand, immaculate blue suit and all. I kneel down, close but not touching. My lungs savor a salty breath, and I press my back into the sand. It cushions gently around me like a feather blanket. Lying here reminds me of when Montgomery first took me to Amsterdam. We felt so hopeful then; now, we're dancing around each other, barely speaking. The tide bites up the coast, swallowing more dry land as high tide sweeps in. How much time do we have before it washes over our bodies?

A seaweed mist speckles my face, and the sand's dampness seeps through my thin wool sweater. I'm not dressed for the beach—at least not a San Francisco beach. The bitter wind pushes me to lean into Montgomery's side. His arm jerks, then softens. He doesn't move away, but he doesn't move closer, either. The tide relentlessly inches upward. I dig my left hand into the sand to steady myself, but my palm hits metal. My knuckles graze along an iron bar wedged into the ground. Ah, clever—we're lying between two train tracks.

"Please, not another jump today," I groan.

"We're not leaving San Francisco."

A pelican cackles overhead, almost as if he's calling us to join him. He leaves behind a gang of pelicans dive-bombing for fish in the white-crested waves. He doesn't look back, instead pumping his long wings faster and faster toward the Golden Gate Bridge. I shouldn't be disappointed that Montgomery isn't whisking me to a secret train station halfway across the world. It means my joints won't take another beating today. It also means we're trapped here, in this city we love and hate with every halting footstep. Grim clouds press down on us, and the glaring brightness makes me squint.

"I think I need to hold your hand to do this," he says.

"You think?"

"I've never done this with anyone, except for when my dad first showed me. It was a secret, even from Em."

Reluctantly, I loop my fingers into his, and magic immediately zips through my fingertips and up the tender skin along my wrist. Blood swirls inside my chest, tangling around my heart.

"What's happening?" I whisper.

"Give me a minute, I need to summon the magic. It can be . . . *stubborn* sometimes. Like someone else I know."

Heat streaks across my cheeks, and I'm so glad Montgomery's eyes are closed. It's not the magic sparking; it's us. His warm skin pressed into mine. Sometimes, I wish my body was a better liar.

Montgomery starts to hum a tune that reminds me of a sad Irish ballad played on fiddle by the fire, or maybe a lullaby. His voice rings out, full of longing for family, for home, for something that was lost long ago.

Suddenly the sand drops away, the waves, the gulls, the sea fleas flicking near my ears, the seaweed stench—all gone. Replaced by a foggy haze that isn't actual fog but rather an eerie sea-blue web. It crackles in random patches. It feels like we're swimming in air, the wind tugging thick and syrupy in every direction.

Montgomery squeezes my hand, and I hear his voice nearby, even though I can't see his physical body. I can sense only the deep bass rhythm of his words and his warm fingertips.

"Still with me?" he says.

"Yes." I give his hand a squeeze in case he can't hear me.

"These 'sleeping' lines are different from the ones running under the city. Those are packed full of life and electricity. Those have the power to transport us across physical space. These abandoned trains still have power, though. Power to jump through memories ... and it's hard to tell what else."

"So, we're inside some sort of mind space?"

"I think so."

"Inside a sleeping train?"

I feel Montgomery shrug beside me, though I can't see his physical form. It's like sea water sloshing against my collarbone.

"Maybe the magic just uses the train lines as a conduit to travel like we do? Even though my family has been ruling BART a long time, they've never known the answers—never cared as long as the portals keep bringing in money."

Something bristles along my arm, nudging me before scampering away. I reach out a hand but then realize I don't actually have a hand inside this dream space.

"And our bodies?" I say.

"We're still lying in the sand."

"Hopefully not getting submerged under high tide."

"I'm pretty sure you'd snap back to your body if the waves came in."

"'Pretty sure'?"

The sound of the crashing waves overlaps into the dream space, echoing through our sticky silence. They sound closer than before.

"I don't like to come here, unless I have to," he says, softly. "It reminds me too much of my dad."

"He showed this to you and not to Em?"

"He didn't trust what she'd do with the power."

"But he trusted you."

"Once." Montgomery sighs, and something whinnies in the distance, afraid of the shift in his tone. The blue sparks crackle and pop at the edge of my vision.

"He wanted to show me why he was leaving. He said he didn't have the words, but if he could show me, then maybe I'd forgive him."

"How old were you?"

"Eleven."

"Shit. That's a lot to unload on an eleven-year-old."

"If it's OK, I don't want to visit that memory. Not because I don't trust you; I just can't . . ."

His voice comes out so soft and broken that I wish I could wrap my arms around him. Though, if this is indeed a mind space, then why can't I dream it? I try to remember what it felt like to hug him in the dark BART tunnel; the exact spot where my chin rested on his chest, the reach of my arms around his broad shoulders, the way I had to lean up on tiptoes to kiss his neck.

He gasps in surprise.

"Clever." He smiles into my hair, or at least that's the sensation—warm full lips pressed to the top of my head. The swirling blue sea warms into gentle currents. Curiously, he runs his fingers down my spine, and it's not like my real body, it's like there's no skin, no clothes, no heartbeat separating us. It's intoxicating. I run my fingertips down his spine, too, hoping he might feel a fraction of what he's doing to me.

I hear him swallow hard, his body shivering next to me in the sand.

"Ruby . . . I need to concentrate to make this happen. I don't want to accidentally end up on the beach yet."

"Sorry."

He sighs when I pull away and gives my hand a squeeze.

"You won't want to hold me like that when you see this memory."

"Let me be the judge."

"That's what I'm afraid of."

When he squeezes my palm again, Montgomery's memory blasts into vivid reality. It's like my face is pressed up to a theater screen and I'm watching a film unfold, except everything is in white, yellow, cyan, and magenta, as if I've been dropped into the center of an RGB Venn diagram. It's dizzying at first. But soon my eyes adjust.

A boy is running.

Montgomery's lanky legs pound against concrete.

Three boys—middle-school age, maybe—are playing hide-and-seek in the Ferry Building, hiding behind shelves of knit hats or finely spun pottery or expensive farmer's-market Honeycrisp apples grown right across the bay. They're being brats. The shopkeepers yell at the brothers, barely able to tell them apart with their same wavy black hair, pale skin, bright eyes. Powell, the obvious youngest with his short wobbly legs, runs outside—and nearly hurtles into the traffic along the waterfront road. But then, there's Em tugging him backward by his sweater sleeve.

"Always watch where you leap!" Em grabs Powell and Montgomery's hands, while Merritt sulks behind them. Montgomery knows that Merritt resents being too old to hold Em's hand. Montgomery wishes he were too old, though. He doesn't like how hard Em grips, dragging him where he doesn't want to go. A trolley car is coming. An empty one. Without Em saying so, Montgomery knows it's only for the Bartholomews. Gleaming emerald walls, wheels slowly dissolving into rust in the ocean air. Montgomery hesitates, but Em drags him forward. They're never alone on a train like this, even though his family rules the lines.

An OUT OF SERVICE sign glows in the window.

Powell jumps in and blares the horn. He laughs loud and fierce. Merritt tosses him off the driver's seat, and they fight over a conductor's hat that makes them look like a French cartoon. It all feels familiar and wrong at the same time. Montgomery's legs tremble even though the train is absolutely still.

"Em," he whispers. "Why are we alone on the train?"

She saunters toward the empty space connecting this train to the next one.

"Because only the strongest survive this world. Come, boys." Em spins around and holds her arms open, but it doesn't feel like a hug—no, it feels like a net to catch slow-witted fish. "Show me who will be left standing when our enemies come for us again." Powell runs toward her, giggling; Merritt charges forward, shoulders angled like a quarterback. Montgomery follows his brothers, silently, reluctantly, as if he already knows this is a trap.

Because it is.

⚵ CHAPTER 35 ⚵

Suddenly, the Vanishing Station stains his sight—*my sight*—like wine spilled into a drunk sea. It swirls and roils and sucks everything into its endless depths. It feels like I'm trapped inside of a movie screen.

The Vanishing Station is the exact shade of twilight dusk when red and orange and vermillion have already fled the sky, leaving nothing but a deep bruised purple. Everything is in silhouette. Overhead, all the brothers hear is the sound of flailing flesh bashing against a wall, like birds frantically throwing their delicate bodies at glass. Even though there's no escape. Even though it means hurting themselves. Montgomery's pulse jumps with every sharp thwack.

Squealing train tracks break the silence every few seconds. The boys cover their ears and drop down to their knees. Em has foam plugs nestled into her small, pale ears. None of them can stand upright, as if they're wedged between two tunnels where stone and dirt and millennia meet in a place that has no name. Bodies feel heavy enough to sink below the sea.

"This place," Em says, "is the Vanishing Station. This is where we take our enemies. Anyone who threatens us. It's the only weapon that has saved us."

"Mom," Powell whimpers. "Take us home. Please!"

Em scowls. "Crying will not get you home, my sweet boy."

Powell sobs louder. "Please make the birds stop," he begs. "Tell them to stop; tell them we'll find a window."

Montgomery feels around the ghostly space, searching for doors and exits, moving as if he's wading through waves that shove against his lanky body. Merritt curses at the shrieking trains.

"There is a door," Em says, backing away from her boys. "For those who have the gift." She leans back like she's floating in a pool of water. She knows how to swim out of this place, this cave, this nowhere. A wine-bruised wave sloshes against her body, but she easily carves through it. She arcs an arm back, and then the other, her limbs slicing through the dark sea.

And then, she's gone.

Powell curls his skinny arms around his knees and won't stop muttering about the birds. He tears at his ears, while Merritt punches against the murky darkness. Montgomery ties his sweater around his ears, then presses his hands along the wave-wall where Em disappeared. He tries swimming his limbs, but his long arms hit an invisible barricade. He hums to keep himself calm as this impossible place pushes against his sanity, as it does for Powell and Merritt—Montgomery is just better at hiding it. He hums and whimpers and hums, louder and louder, until his singing rings out like clinking a crystal glass with a silver knife. Calling out to Embarcadero station, calling for home. He shoves his shoulder—*hard*—against the glass, until he's falling, falling through inky waves.

Montgomery collapses onto the train's floor.

Back inside the empty green trolley.

Feathers and bones lay scattered around him. He breathes hard, his fingers purple from circulation cut off for seconds, minutes, hours? He's lost all sense of time. His teeth won't stop chattering. Em doesn't help him up, only smiles, wolfish and proud.

"So I have my Montgomery."

She plucks a feather from his hair. In San Francisco, the Ferry Building's bell chimes, a warning toll echoing across the bay.

"We have work to do, darling, lest our enemies find a crack in our defenses. Come, Montgomery." Madame Em holds out her delicate hand.

"But ... what about ... my brothers." Montgomery can barely speak through his chattering teeth.

"We only need *one* Montgomery. Each boy is another weak link against me, against us. Our enemies will exploit it. If the boys cannot defend themselves—"

"But they're my brothers." Montgomery stares, and Em doesn't even flinch.

"Only the strong survive. We wouldn't be alive if I hadn't sent our enemies to the Vanishing Station when they came for us. After your father left us."

Her heels clank against the trolley's metal stairs, and the exit doors swing open. She doesn't wait for Montgomery to follow. She leaves the cage door open.

But he doesn't follow.

Minutes later, he peers out the trolley's door to where tourists scuttle across the Embarcadero's wide boulevard, and ocean air blasts his already icy cheeks. In the distance, Em disappears down the stairs of a BART station entrance, heading underground. She looks like a dark lord slipping back down into Hades.

Montgomery scans the train for a way back to hell.

He runs at the door, paddles his arms toward that memory of a wine-drunk sea. Bruises burst against his pale white skin. When nothing happens, he slams his shoulder against the walls, every wall, any wall, any way back to his brothers. He can hear Powell crying about the birds. Montgomery's sneakers crunch on bone shards and broken feathers. What if ... but he doesn't wait to think it through. He crunches the delicate bones between his teeth, piece after piece of those desperate birds. He shoves against the connecting doors, until his body pushes through empty air and back into the dense waves.

Powell lays in a ball while Merritt tears at the walls, at his ears, his fists bloody. Montgomery doesn't say a word, his last reserve of energy quickly dissolving. Instead, he pulls them back across the portal while they claw at him like drowning swimmers.

The only thing keeping him steady is his dad's old song ringing through his ears—*the dog's away to Bellingen, to buy the bairn a bell*. He remembers his dad's husky laughter, his calloused hand on their first leap to Embarcadero station.

The brothers' heavy breathing fills the train car.

Em is back, sitting in the conductor's seat, her face unreadable. Her blond hair looks windswept. Powell scrambles across the floor and onto her lap, even though he's too big for such childish things. She lets him sit, his thin body shaking in her arms. Then, as if she's made up her mind, she pushes the train into motion. Montgomery doesn't stand yet; he can't stop his body from shivering. Blood runs down his lips from the bird bones. Merritt glances down at his little brother, at his own bloody hands. A darkness settles into his eyes.

"Why don't you ring the bell, darling?" Em says.

Powell dings the trolley bell as the Bay Bridge looms above them, dividing the bay in two. Steel cables spiral into the ashen sky. Powell laughs, jittery and loud.

"Chase, come see!" he says.

"Darling, don't call your brother 'Chase' anymore. He's Montgomery now."

"Montgomery." Merritt's face scrunches up. Their family has always been ruled by an Embarcadero and a Montgomery. Until their dad abandoned them. Until it was only Em. A mother and three young boys. Boys who each had a unique name, waiting for the day when they would inherit their stations.

Now, it's been decided.

Merritt jumps up, crushing bird bones underfoot. He doesn't help Montgomery up. He leaves his brother bleeding on the floor. Because they're not really brothers anymore, are they? There's a chain of command now.

Merritt pounds against the doors.

"Let me off." His voice is hoarse from screaming inside the Vanishing Station.

Em pushes the train faster down the tracks. "This is our train, boys. Our city." She hugs Powell against her chest. "Let's see how fast and far we can make her run." Merritt grits his teeth but stays silent. He doesn't ask to be let off again.

Powell laughs as they race across the cityscape.

"Chase!" he says. "Montgomery, look how fast we can fly!"

Montgomery's raw fingers grip onto the grates as the train howls through the fog. He pockets the bird bones, for the next time he'll be forced to return to the Vanishing Station.

⟩ CHAPTER 36 ⟨

n an instant, I'm awake in my body at Lands End Beach. My eyes open to stark sunlight. It's a tenuous sun, one that could be stolen from us by passing clouds. It heats my skin, even as Montgomery—no, *Chase*, his name is Chase—trembles beside me.

"Can I call you 'Chase'?" I whisper.

He doesn't speak, doesn't open his eyes. I don't even hesitate before I wrap my arms around him, my legs, too, in hopes that I can fight away his icy chill. He lets me touch him, even though I can feel his lungs struggling for shallow breaths. I shouldn't, but I kiss the soft skin along his temple, and bit by bit, his clenched hands unwind. He hooks his shaky arm around my waist, pulling me more tightly to him. Someone steps in the sand a few yards away—and I almost reach for my blade. Soon, the footsteps disappear, replaced by raven caws as they twirl in the fierce ocean winds.

The sun holds steady against the fog. My body holds us steady. It's always so much stronger than I think it is.

"I would like it if you called me 'Chase,'" he whispers in my ear, and the suddenness sends a thrill down my spine. Now that he's coming back into consciousness, I'm fully aware that my body is wrapped around him like seaweed clinging to a drowning swimmer's leg. Oh god, what if this is too much? I try to give him space, but his arm stays firmly wrapped around my hips. "I like this, too," he says.

"You seemed cold."

"It's worse than cold . . . It's like reliving every second of that memory."

"I'm sorry you had to relive it. You could have just told me."

"It's hard to describe the Vanishing Station. When Em threatened you last night . . . I couldn't breathe . . . I can't let . . ." A chill racks his body, and I hug my arms more firmly around him. "It scares me, Ruby. She means it. Promise me you'll follow her rules. Em's dangerous. Hell, I'm dangerous."

"Em's the dangerous one. You're—"

"I've taken people to the Vanishing Station." He lets his words hover in the salty air, and a deep dread sinks into my stomach. "At Em's command, I've taken enemies there. Jumpers who've tried to overthrow her. I can make someone disappear into that wasteland. It scares the shit out of me that I'm capable of it. If I ever leave the Bartholomew line, what's to stop a rival from using me? At least with Em . . . I can be Montgomery and have some semblance of control."

"You call that control?"

"I can at least keep Powell and Merritt safe, and the other jumpers, too. The ones who stumble onto our lines—I can turn them away before Em sinks her claws into them. If everyone just follows the rules, we'll keep our rivals from taking over, and things will keep running smoothly, and . . ."

"*Chase*—listen to yourself. You're letting her corrupt the trains. You're *enforcing* her rules."

"If it's not the Bartholomews, other lines would do the same, or worse. The Stazioni, the Colectivo, they're as ruthless as Em. Everyone knows I can jump to the Vanishing Station—you think the other lines will just let me walk away if I leave the Bartholomews? There is no out."

"All of the lines are like this?" I say. "You're telling me they're all heartless crime lords? This whole massive network of train tracks around the world . . . and there's no other option?"

He drags his hands over his eyes and lets his head sink deeper into the sand. "I don't know."

"At the very least, can't we stop Em? What if—"

"She's still my mother, Ruby." He bolts up and dusts the sand from his suit. His tall, lean body sways for a moment like a eucalyptus tree in a storm, then steadies.

"Well, that doesn't mean we need to enable her," I say.

He shakes his head and sighs. His hands rest helplessly at his sides.

"Why did you show it to me then? I already can't stomach trafficking the endangered elephant tusks. Ever since Em's dinner, I've been telling myself to stop daydreaming, keep my head low, and just obey the contract. How am I supposed to live with myself if I know that monster is running the trains? That I'm helping her!"

"I've been tracking the abandoned stations all around the world. The other crime families—their schedules, routes, blind spots in their surveillance. I've done a lot of research."

"For an escape?"

He holds his hand out to help me to my feet. I force myself to stand on my aching limbs, my shoes sinking into the uneven sand.

"Ruby, I wanted to show you that memory so you know Em's threats are real. But I also want you to understand why I haven't left yet. My brothers may be brats, but they're still my brothers. They're the only family I have, and they'll never leave this life behind."

"If they knew Em was going to abandon them at the Vanishing Station, would they still obey her?"

"That was a test. To prove I could bring them across the portal. That's how Em operates, in games and challenges. She knew I'd go back for my brothers."

"Are you sure?" I try to wipe away the wet sand clinging to his cheek, but he backs away. "What if she was telling the truth and didn't expect you to go back? What if she's only keeping your brothers around to chain you to BART?"

Montgomery stares out at the relentless waves. The high tide bites at the edge of my sneakers, and I leap away, but not before the icy water soaks into my heel. A shiver shoots up my leg and into my gut.

He's never going to leave them.

"It's getting late." He sighs. Without waiting for me, he starts for the trail. His long legs cut across the dunes, kicking up sand in a wild spray. I hope his dark memories don't haunt him tonight.

"Chase," I holler.

He turns back, an unexpected smile lighting up his face when he hears his real name.

"Can I ask you a question?" I say. "About us."

His smile widens when I say "us." It makes me smile, too.

Chase starts trekking back through the dunes to reach me. His shoes catch on seaweed and driftwood, but they don't slow his steps. When he finally looks me in the eyes, the sunlight dances across his bright blues. It makes my heart thunder—almost as much as the question I'm about to ask.

"Why did you trust *me* with this memory?" I whisper above the crashing ocean waves.

"You have to ask?"

I nod, afraid maybe I'm imagining there's more between us than there really is. I need to hear him say it. Why trust me, of all people?

"Because when I'm around you, you're always Ruby," he says, hooking his fingers around my belt loop and drawing me closer. My breath catches in my throat. "Even when you're trying to be Balboa—you're always *you*. Every bit of you is right there, ready to fight for the things you love. I've never met someone more earnest."

"So . . . you're saying I'm a terrible liar?"

He laughs, but his blue eyes haven't lost their intensity.

"Ruby, I want you to know the real me. The good *and* the bad. Chase *and* Montgomery. I guess it's a good sign that you're not running away screaming after seeing what I can do with my powers."

"All I saw was a scared boy who went back to save his brothers."

"You haven't seen the people I've dragged there." His voice is so raw and sorrowful that a fierce protectiveness burns through my entire body. The sound of birds pounding against glass echoes inside my head.

I reach out and take his hand.

Relief finally loosens his shoulder blades, and he pulls me closer until I can smell his familiar cedar and mint scent. Dark hair falls across his eyes, and I wonder how long he's thought himself a monster.

Madame Em is the true monster, manipulating her own son. And yet he's no longer that scared little boy. He's Montgomery—crime boss, heir of the Bartholomew line. It's up to *him* to break free.

"I'm not running," I whisper in his ear. "Unless your music is *that* bad."

He laughs, relief pouring out in his deep, throaty voice. "I'm good on violin and guitar. Run away if I pick up a set of drumsticks."

"Noted, but you still haven't played me anything!"

"I'm kinda playing in this music show on campus next week. Maybe you want to come?" He's so cute, nervously fishing a postcard from his blazer pocket. It's a relief to lean into this tiny sliver of our lives that is "normal" and leave his memories of the Vanishing Station back in the sand.

"Come, if you want." He hands me the postcard. "It's a free show."

I scan the details: a concert on the Stanford campus. Bing Concert Hall. Friday night, seven P.M. "Passages Through Time," a presentation of honors theses. It's so "normal" that it feels more shocking than if he'd handed me a golden ticket. Just a boy asking a girl to a concert.

He flashes a shy smile. As I watch him walk toward the trail, his fingers tap a rhythm only he can hear. What would it be like to see him onstage? His long fingers gliding across a keyboard or strings. My mind all too easily jumps to how his hands felt on my skin. Damn. It. All. That boy.

I crumple the flyer into my pocket.

The truth is: we're not college kids.

If we ever want that future for ourselves, we need to escape Em's twisted web.

We need to vanish.

But how?

✄ CHAPTER 37 ✄

On Friday night, my dad hums while he shaves, using a mirror precariously balanced over the washing machine. He never hums, not unless . . .

"All right, who is she?" I say.

"What?" He tries to hide his smile.

"Come on, Dad."

"OK, OK, I see her at the Mexican market in the mornings. Her name is Florinda. Oy, break my heart already. Maganda." He says the last word long and slow, savoring each syllable. Maganda means "beautiful" in Tagalog. Lord, he's worse than a swoony teenager.

"Please, say no more."

"We have drinks tonight."

"Drinks?" I arch an eyebrow. AA only works if he can keep abstaining from alcohol.

He waves my worries away. "I know, I know. Only Coca-Cola."

"Why don't you go . . ." Anywhere but a bar. I scan my brain for a good first date—walking in Golden Gate Park, ice-skating, the Stinking Rose (OK, maybe not garlic breath). There are so many things he can't do with his bum hip. So many places he shouldn't go with his alcohol addiction. So many places that cost too much money.

"To the movies?" I say, feebly.

"Then how will we talk? There's karaoke at Harriet's. Maybe she's a Mariah Carey."

"Trial by karaoke? Well, I hope you don't sing a kundiman. Not on a first date. You don't want to come on too strong."

"Oh, anak, you've never seen your dad sing a love song. No woman can resist my kundiman." He takes in a big breath and launches into a serenade, but I throw up my arms to cover his mouth.

"Please! Just . . . save it for the ladies."

"It's Friday night." He laughs, slipping on his coat and shimmying his shoulders. My father, the lover boy. Please make it stop. "Why don't you go out with your friends?"

"I'm too busy for friends."

"And boys?"

"What happened to the days when you forbade me from dating?"

"Anak, I want you to be happy, too."

"I am happy."

"I want you to be happy like when your mom was alive."

My chest hitches, and I look away. I wish it wouldn't still do that, every mention of my mother like an electric jolt through my heart. Dad kisses my forehead before he heads out the door.

"She would want you to smile, too," he says.

"Go on, Sap Master. I won't wait up."

He starts his slow walk, dodging stray chair legs and cardboard boxes that jut into the walkway. Even with his cane, he looks regal. Slicked black hair, smooth coffee skin, leather jacket. He doesn't let the pain show, even without the alcohol or painkillers. It's no wonder he fooled me for so long. Finally, at the door, he lets out a long gasp and then sucks in another breath to keep walking.

When did we trade places? Shouldn't I be the one sneaking out on a date? Do other daughters have to worry about their fathers making it back home safely?

"Good luck!" I holler at him.

"I don't need luck," he says. "She'll hear my kundiman and be hooked."

§

The house settles into quiet. Not a single footfall upstairs or a hint of wind through redwood branches. Which is to say that it's all the more depressing sitting in a garage alone, researching a magic train map that for the uninitiated technically does not exist. All week, I've been a good girl, running the mandated routes with Powell and generally not breaking any of Em's rules. Montgomery and I are keeping our distance—there are too many eyes on us right now. But every night, he leaves sweet voice mails with the music he's been composing. They sound like film scores that match our dramatic lives. I listen to them on repeat before I fall asleep each night, the violin solos stirring too much inside myself.

I want out.

But I don't know how to escape Em's contract. Not without losing my mom's house and murals. Not without putting my dad in danger while he's at his most vulnerable. Not without knowing whether Montgomery will ever leave his family. It feels so hopeless that I spend hours researching maps instead.

Lying in bed, I dig out the crumpled concert flyer and smooth out the edges. Tonight. Bing Concert Hall. I wonder what he sounds like onstage. Is this Montgomery's version of a kundiman, and I won't even be there to hear it?

Follow the rules.

Don't draw Em's attention while you figure out an escape plan.

Skip the concert because they might be watching us.

This is the worst bucket list ever.

I push my head back into the pillow. Cobwebs dangle high overhead, and I try to ignore the tangled webs. I hit play on one of Montgomery's music voice mails. The piano is not nearly as grand on a tiny speaker phone, but it'll have to do. I so rarely have the house to myself. Eighteen, and I still don't have my own room. I curl up in bed wearing the same sweater I wore at the beach. I can almost smell Montgomery's deep cedar and spice cologne, his warm lips along my neck. My hands wander over the soft skin along my hips, my shoulders sinking into the goose feathers.

All of a sudden, a call interrupts with a loud buzz. I scramble to stop the damn thing. Can't I have two minutes to myself? I check the screen in case my dad is in trouble. I always worry that he might fall somewhere. Or worse, that I won't be there to rush him to the hospital.

It's Montgomery.

I don't pick up. There's no way I'd fit in with those college kids. But he leaves a voice mail. His raspy voice whispers in my ear:

"I was wondering if you were coming tonight?"

I sigh and smother my face in the blankets.

6:34 P.M.

If I hurry, I could catch the second half of the show. I could hear him play music on his piano or trumpet or whatever those talented fingers touch.

Then what?

We'll complicate everything. We'll remind each other of the life we can't have with Em ruling over us.

I close my eyes and ask: *What would Ruby Before Cancer do?* I don't even need a second thought before I know the answer.

She'd chase the boy.

Where did that part of me go?

And if I'm totally honest, I'm afraid to stroll the Stanford campus, afraid to feel that longing for art school and all the maybes.

I close my eyes and let the thrumming, wanting part of me beat through the voice inside my head. It's small, but it's there, threaded through my heart, stammering to get out.

Before I lose the thread, I throw on my cleanest pair of dark jeans and a jade cashmere sweater that was once my mom's favorite. It's a tad too big, with sleeves down past my palms. My mom was a few inches taller than me, but I still love her sweaters.

6:42 P.M. I'll surprise him there. Snag him after the show ends.

I rush to the BART station. In the distance, a train roars across the tracks. Shit, I'll have to wait at least another ten minutes.

The show starts at seven P.M.

When the next train finally arrives, it's packed with commuters and the dinner crowd. I gaze at the train map: from Balboa Park to Daly City to Colma to South San Francisco to San Bruno to Millbrae. Then, at Millbrae, a transfer to the Caltrain line, so that I can take a different train farther south to Palo Alto. From Millbrae to Burlingame to San Mateo to Hayward Park to Hillsdale to Belmont to San Carlos to Redwood City to Menlo Park to Palo Alto. And then a ten-minute walk to the Stanford campus.

It'll take . . . forever.

I'm screwed.

And an idiot.

Why didn't I think of this earlier?

I can jump straight to Palo Alto. *A Wrinkle in Time*-style.

I received an invitation this time—direct from the Bartholomew heir himself—so I'm not breaking any of Madame Em's rules. Besides, jumping *within* the BART line is totally acceptable.

The Saddle awaits me. I try to think back to my last time in Palo Alto. Ages ago for a second-grade field trip. We were heading to see an old black-and-white film at the Stanford Theatre, restored to its 1920s glamour. Think of the train station. The blazing bright sun compared to San Francisco's fog. The roof's retro red stripes that Tony Lanni had said looked like his grand-pa's diner where he promised to buy all the girls strawberry milkshakes, so, of course, Brandon Ellis had punched him in the gut.

Stripes, concrete, sun, is that enough to get me across?

I slide the doors shut and double-check Montgomery's invitation. It's real. My heartbeat hammers, and my sweaty palm dampens the postcard. I know it's not the end of the world if I can't make it to his show on time. I know this. Still, some small wanting part of me wonders if he'll play me a kundiman. I don't want to be fool enough to miss it.

I don't want Em to take everything from us.

We can have this.

My imagination summons not only Palo Alto station but all the possi-bilities luring me across the tracks. Sitting in the gorgeous theater, clap-ping when the curtains rise. Malt crunch milkshakes while we wait for the next train to San Francisco. A kundiman with a melody too sweet to forget.

I don't have to open my eyes to know I've made the jump.

I feel it in my bones now.

An electric buzz spreading through my palms.

Palo Alto station. 6:52 P.M. Hey, I might even be able to catch the entire show! I'm about to step into a luminous sunset, warm autumn air soaking into my lungs, when I feel a hand clamp onto my shoulder.

At first I think maybe Montgomery is here to surprise me.

Then I realize how wrong I am.

⚡ CHAPTER 38 ⚡

Sharp nails dig into my cashmere sweater, and I hear threads ripping as the man drags me backward into the train. The doors shut. The sign for Palo Alto station whips by in a blur, and my stomach lurches.

"Wait," I say, before I can think of anything else.

"Where do you think you're going?" the man hisses in my ear.

A few passengers avert their eyes, while others are so immersed in their phones that they have no idea something is wrong. No one wants trouble. Not unless I scream out, and even then, will anyone help me? *Calm down, you can get out of this.*

The man grimaces, and the scar on his chin twists into a furious red. It's not the kind of scar you get from shaving or running into a tree branch. It's a sharp thin line. Undoubtedly from a blade.

"That was my stop," I say. "Let me go, asshole."

"I'm the asshole? Do you know what we do to trespassers?"

"Last I checked, this is a public train. And dude, we're on the same team."

He laughs and laughs—while digging his nails harder into my arm.

Then it hits me.

This isn't a BART train.

This is NOT a BART train.

Shit.

I'm an idiot.

I can't believe I forgot Palo Alto isn't on the BART line. I'm on *Caltrain* now, even though I'm still in the Bay Area. Location doesn't matter, *lines* matter. I remember what Em and Merritt did to that trespasser on BART. My whole body floods with a mixture of embarrassment and fear. Do they have their own version of a Vanishing Station?

The man holds my trembling hand up to the light—the sapphire BART tattoo is undeniable.

"Looks so tender," he says with a mock smile. "Didn't know we'd be welcoming fresh meat aboard tonight."

The man wears forgettable blue jeans and a gray T-shirt. But that's a lie. There's muscle and train magic under there. A "CAL" tattoo snakes up his hairy forearm in thick block letters. He holds his balance easily as the train jerks from side to side. Inside his pockets, there's a blade, or worse. I need to get off this train. Now.

"Montgomery will—"

"So, you're one of Montgomery's pets? Wonderful, let's see how angry we can make that bastard."

He twists his grip painfully around my arm, but then a baby starts screaming, woken from her nap. I stomp hard on his toes and bolt for the portal between the trains. I'm almost to the doors when he shoves me forward, and my forehead slams against the plexiglass. Pain explodes across my skull. The man yanks me up and drags me into a seat with him. We sit side by side like he didn't just shove my face into a wall.

"Oh, honey, I wish you weren't so clumsy sometimes. How about you take a big breath and calm down?" He pats the throbbing bruise on my forehead like he cares about my pain. Like I'm a silly child who fell. I struggle to stand up, but he pinches the back of my neck and pulls me down by my skin.

"Easy now, I just want to talk." He glances at the wary faces around us. With eyebrows scrunched in confusion, a couple women shoot daggers with their eyes. They're not blind, but they also don't know how to help. My only advantage is that he has to ride these trains every day. Portal magic or not, if the police catch on to him, his life will become much more complicated.

"I have nothing to say to you."

"Don't I deserve an apology?" he says.

"I'm sorry I jumped onto your train without permission. I should have asked first. There, happy?"

He laughs sharply in my ear.

"BART jumpers are NEVER allowed on our trains."

"I didn't know."

"Now, that doesn't sound like Montgomery. He's always been brutal about *rules*. So maybe you're not a recruit?" Another train station zips by in a blur, and my neck throbs where his nails dug in. "You know, I always wondered what kind of girl Montgomery would chase, and here we have our answer. What's your name?"

"None of your damn business."

"You're on my train; you're my business now."

"Well, I'll happily get off your train."

"Do you know what we do to trespassers?"

"Bore them with inane questions?"

"You want to go home?"

I nod.

He smirks and chaperones me toward the portal doors. He even opens the doors for me and bows.

"Just like that?" I say. "You'll let me go?"

"Now who's asking inane questions?"

I don't believe him, but what other choice do I have? My only hope is a quick leap. I rush to summon Balboa Park station, but before I have a chance, he crams his body inside with me and slams the doors shut. I kick his legs and scratch at the hand locked around my throat. It's too close contact for the boxing maneuvers my dad taught me. I reach for my blade, but icy air floods my lungs. Blue sparks crack and splinter across the glass. His breathing goes ragged, and his grip around my throat falters. Not that it matters—my brain is thrown into a roller-coaster whiplash.

Everything stills for a moment. Except the train, which seems to skid to a stop, lurching our bodies forward. A conductor yells, "Jyuryo teishi ichi, yoshi!" Is that Japanese? My fingers slide down the damp glass as signs in a foreign alphabet blur across my vision. Black-haired girls with fox backpacks scamper off the train, laughing at each other. Before I have a chance to ask where the hell we are, the man drags me through another portal. My stomach lurches into free fall. I don't know how to stop him.

Finally he shoves me backward, and I tumble onto gravel. A sharp crack, and I don't have to check my back pocket to know my phone is smashed. Mud oozes between my fingers, and tall grass brushes against my cheek. The man stumbles over to me, clutching his own forehead. He trips on a rotten railroad plank. My only saving grace is that he must be reeling from the jump, too.

It also means that we've gone far, far away.

Where the hell are we?

I scramble to my feet, shoving away the nausea. Fists up, feet wide, enough distance between us so that he can't grab me again.

And then I see it.

Crickets and bees buzz in the tall weeds. Lush green leaves surround the railroad tracks and snake their way into the metal shell of an abandoned train car. Two rusted slabs of railroad iron stretch into a forest. Some of the wooden planks have crumbled into rot. Wild ferns cover the steep hillsides surrounding us, hungry for sunlight. Bricks that were once a passenger platform are now overgrown with fluorescent moss and lichen. This is a place that has not seen trains in a long time. At least not moving ones.

A sign reads:

HELENSBURGH

I gaze back at the abandoned train car and the crumbling stone tunnel behind it. It's disorienting standing in the midday heat—the sun blazing overhead—after leaving behind a chilly sunset in San Francisco. Dappled sunlight sneaks through the forest, and the train tracks reach into infinity.

This would be a surreal and beautiful place, if not for the fact that someone brought me here to kill me.

⚰ CHAPTER 39 ⚰

throw off my mother's cashmere sweater. It'll only get in the way now. Sweat drips down my sides. The man's eyes lock on to mine, and a grin flashes across his chapped lips.

"I thought we could use a bit of privacy," he says.

"Where are we?"

"Never been to New South Wales, Australia?" He smirks, but I can still see the wince of pain crease his forehead. That was a big jump *with a passenger*. It must have cost him. He leans back on his right foot like he's a drunken bear trying to balance on a ball. I can use this to my advantage. I can–

Hang on. Did he say *Australia*?

Holy smokes, that's far. Thousands-of-miles-across-the-ocean far. I don't know if I can jump back. Maybe I could hike to civilization, follow the train tracks to a town. And then what? Fly home with no passport, no phone, no money, nothing. But that's only if I can escape first. Steep hillsides and nowhere to run, except down the tracks in a straight line. He'd catch me in no time. All that sinewy muscle; I bet the bastard can run.

The vine-covered train is my only way home.

"It was abandoned in the 1920s for a new route," he says, pulling a blade from behind his back. He grips it fast, like he knows exactly where to shove it. "I've heard this place draws ghost hunters. Shall we find out why?" He lunges toward me, and I dodge at the last second.

This time, I have a blade in my hand, too.

This time, I won't let his hands anywhere near me.

If I can lure him away from the train doors, I might be able to shut them and jump home.

Thousands of miles.

By myself.

From Australia.

Panic rises in my throat, and I struggle to tamp it down. Focus, you need to focus. We move in a half-circle, fists up. Our blades slash through the humid air while horseflies hunt for fresh skin.

"Don't you have better things to do than take me sightseeing in Australia? Wouldn't your employers be pissed that you're wasting your power? You just left Palo Alto wide open for other jumpers. I wonder what your boss thinks about that."

"Shut up," he says, doubt flickering in his eyes.

He reflexively glances toward the train doors, and I use the moment to gain a few steps closer to the portal. He slices through air again. I'm light on my toes, and nowhere near as groggy as he must be. I need a few more steps, enough to slip inside the train and slam the doors shut. Except, I realize there are no doors. The thin metal hinges have rusted away through the decades, leaving the doors heaped in the dirt and overrun with vines.

He stabs again, and this time I plunge the blade in his direction.

The man leaps back, but not before I nick his shoulder.

A line of blood seeps through his gray shirt. His nostrils flare with anger, and then he does something stupid. He lunges. I jab my fist straight for his nose and send him staggering. Now! I sprint for the train. My knuckles burn, but I'm at the doors, and I'm . . . being dragged backward by my hair. A couple knots rip from my scalp. I kick him in the gut and wrench myself inside the train. Jagged metal scrapes against my palm.

I'm in.

Balboa Park, Balboa Park, Balboa Park, come on.

But I can't feel the spark of magic in my bones.

Can't pretend this train is going anywhere.

It sleeps stubbornly under my touch. Rusted metal sways beneath my boots, and rats have chewed through the seat cushions. The forest has crept inside a broken window, vines snaking through glass. Dark beetles and centipedes scuttle in the shadows of this hollow shell.

This isn't a train. It's a graveyard.

"You don't know how to get back, do you?" he laughs, stepping inside. His sinewy body blocks the sunshine—and the exit. "Newbies never do. You probably don't even have the power to jump that far."

"I have the power."

"Be my guest, then. I'll give you one minute to work your magic."

"Liar."

"I swear on my grandma Angie Romanoff's life. Go on—try it."

I think about everything Montgomery has taught me, about my dad serenading his reflection, about paintbrushes poised in my hands, about the pigeons who still come back to Balboa Park even though someone has put up spikes to keep them away.

Still, I can't focus. Not with a man holding a knife, waiting for me to fail.

"Ten," he says. "Nine. Eight."

"Shut up!"

"Seven. Six."

A snake hisses in the darkness, and we both freeze. We glance down at a tiger snake curled beneath a dilapidated seat. Its jaws hinge open. Pale yellow-and-black stripes run the length of its scales. Of course we're in a country with some of the deadliest snakes in the world. Paralysis. Difficulty breathing. A single bite is a death sentence.

"You were counting?" I say, hoping he'd be stupid enough to lunge at me. Spook the snake. Give it a target. But he stands frozen, his jaw twitching. Fear widens his pupils, and the knife trembles in his grip. I try again:

"Scared of snakes, pretty boy? Wait until I tell Montgomery what a coward you are."

Slowly, he reaches his hand back toward the doors.

The snake hisses again.

He freezes.

"Take me with you," I whisper.

He leaps for the door—words rushing from his lips—and rips the portal open with a spray of blue sparks.

The snake attacks, but its fangs catch nothing. His ankle has already disappeared into a haze of shattered blue light. It throws the snake off: this burst of icy air in a sweltering Australian forest.

I hold up my knife. I don't want to kill this beautiful, fearsome creature, but I refuse to die here. Not today. Dappled sunlight glints off of its tiger stripes. It hisses once more, and then retreats. My heart hammers inside my chest. Slowly, it slithers down through a crack in the floor. I let out a heavy sigh before realizing that there are probably all manner of creatures lurking in this rotten train. The buzzing of insects takes over all sound.

Well, I didn't die.

But that doesn't mean I know my way home.

I touch the spot the man had just used to jump home. I still feel a spark of icy electricity. I try to feel it in my bones.

Home, take me home.

Please.

I close my eyes, even though I hear a worrisome crunching in the distance. I push away all thoughts, everything but Balboa Park. My station. My new name. My everything. I start to recite a poem from the William Carlos Williams book, one I've already memorized, one I always thought was too dramatic until this very moment. The words "death" and "barber" and "sleep" roll across my tongue, slippery and dangerous and alive. The words create a pulsing melody, one I hope the trains will hear. *Please, hear me.*

The crunching grows louder outside, and I start to feel ice in my veins. I feel the train shaking awake, a shaggy sleeping beast under all the ruins. I imagine that it might like this forgotten jungle, this overgrown, tangled place. It might like poetry whispered in its ear. *Please, take me home, please. Listen to my words, my intentions. Help me return to Balboa Park.* My breath comes out in a cold mist, and I open my eyes to see the forest slowly dissolving. Ferns melting into molten green. Bricks swirling into snake scales. My mom's green cashmere laying in the dirt.

And this:

Two men hiking, their thick boots crunching on the gravel between the train tracks. They hold up their long-lens cameras. They aim at my face through the glass.

I close my eyes.

My body feels like it's being ripped open and sewn together again. Over and over, a metal needle pounding through my brain. I want to crumple to my knees—if I had knees, if I had a body to crumple, if I had anything other than this searing pain and splintering blue light.

Suddenly the squealing of train tracks roars through my ears.

I stagger forward and knock my already bruised forehead against the doors. The windows are plexiglass and covered in scratches and graffiti. Fluorescent light glows above me, no longer sunlight and a canopy of trees. The train pulls into the station, and I hold my breath until I see the sign BAL-BOA PARK come into focus.

Home, I made it home. The doors open, and I collapse onto concrete. I start laughing hysterically. I can't get up off my knees, and my lungs feel like they might burst. A stranger drags me up onto a bench. They're saying words, but I can't hear anything but flapping wings overhead. I laugh and laugh, saliva dripping down my chin, and I don't think I can get my mouth to do anything else.

I wonder if those ghost hunters snapped a good photograph of me.

A girl disappearing inside an abandoned train car.

An icy mist in the middle of a sweltering Australian forest.

I don't know why I find this so funny.

Maybe because I almost died?

Maybe because I jumped thousands of miles across the ocean?

Maybe my mind can't handle this?

My mouth aches. When I finally notice who's hovering over me, all my laughter evaporates in an instant.

"What's your name?" a police officer says, and I forget about what the ghost hunters caught in their cameras. Instead, I panic about what the security cameras have seen.

⚡ CHAPTER 40 ⚡

oosebumps cover my bare arms, and I can't stop shivering. I left my mother's favorite sweater to rot in Helensburgh. Another thing to mourn.

"Ma'am, do you know your name?" the police officer says.

"Balboa," I say, and then realize I sound insane telling him this while hunched on a concrete bench inside Balboa Park station. "That's my nickname. My real name is Ruby Santos."

"Ms. Santos, are you feeling OK? It sounds like you fell departing the train."

"I'm sorry. I got into a fight . . . with my boyfriend. I'm a little shaken, that's all."

It's easier to lie when your lies are partly true. He analyzes the bruise on my forehead. I start to shake harder as the fog nips through my damp cotton shirt. The last of tonight's passengers leave the station.

"Would you like to press charges?" he says.

"What? No! I just want to go home. Please, sir."

I struggle to pull myself to my feet, and I have to clutch the concrete bench to keep from hitting the floor.

"I can drive you home. Where do you live?"

"No, I can walk. I swear."

"I wouldn't suggest walking home at this hour."

I scan the walls for a clock and realize that the train station is deserted. A BART operator pulls the ticket turnstile gates shut. Finally, I catch sight of a clock. It's past one A.M. I'm damn lucky to have caught the last train of the night.

I left San Francisco around seven P.M.

Where did those six hours go?

The police officer gently lifts me up by the elbow. I lean against his solid frame while he leads me to his squad car. He nods at the BART operator, who only gawks at me. What if the cop is lying? What if he actually saw magic on the security camera and is going to lock me up for questioning? What if I can never go home again?

"Where do you live?" he says.

I gulp down my fear, even as my heart pounds a heavy rhythm inside my chest.

"Cayuyga Avenue. The corner of Cayuyga and Foote."

"That's not far. We'll have you home in no time."

Even though it's only the two of us, he opens the backseat and slides me in behind the metal screen. Before I can bolt, he slams the door shut and climbs into the driver's seat. I stare at the spot where door handles should be, but aren't. I can't open these doors from the inside.

My breath hitches. Trading one graveyard for another. But there's no portal magic to save me inside a cop car.

"Please, sir, I just want to go home."

"We'll get you home."

My teeth are chattering, so he turns on the heater. Warm air streams through the vents, making me sleepy even as fear pulses beneath my skin. I jumped thousands of miles. Or maybe the snake bit me, after all, and I died in an abandoned train car.

When the car pulls to a stop, I jolt awake. I don't remember falling asleep. My shoulders and knuckles ache, my knee joints especially. I jerk around to scan the neighborhood and quickly realize this is my block. He took me home, just as promised.

"Which house is it?" he says.

"It's OK, I'm fine from here."

"I'll walk you inside." He unlocks the door and helps me to my feet.

"It's the lavender-and-white house. But you really don't need to—"

"Nonsense. I wouldn't feel right leaving you in the street in your condition."

He leads me up the front stairs, and I don't know how to tell him we live in the garage below. Or that my father isn't actually a US citizen, just a portal-jumping lackey. That he's from the Philippines and isn't legally allowed to be here. He jumped across an ocean for his daughter.

We hover at the metal gate.

"Did you lose your keys?" he says.

"No, I just . . . don't want to wake my parents."

He doesn't show any sign of walking away, so I fish the keys from my pocket.

Well, let's pray the renters don't have a heart attack. Better that than get my father into trouble. I slip inside the gate.

"See, I'm home now," I whisper through a half-open door. "Safe and sound."

The light blazes on, and Dorothy suddenly appears in her slippers and robe.

"Good evening, ma'am," the police officer says.

"What's . . ."

"Hi, Mom! I'm sorry I'm home so late."

Dorothy's face scrunches up, but she doesn't call me out on my lie.

"I'm glad you're safe . . . honey," she says.

"Sorry to disturb you at this hour, ma'am. But your daughter was in rough shape at the train station, so I drove her home. I know this comes as unsolicited advice, but I think she should stay away from that boyfriend."

We both stare silently at him. Dorothy pulls her robe taught around her chest, and my teeth chatter in the midnight cold. Finally, he tips his hat and turns to go.

"Good night, miss," he says.

"Thank you," I whisper, before shutting the gate behind me.

Dorothy and I stare at each other across the threshold.

"I'll go back downstairs once the cop car pulls away."

Her partner, Shannon, shuffles up in a pink striped robe. Her pixie cut is practically standing on end.

"What's going on?" she says, rubbing the sleep from her eyes and finally taking a long look at the girl shivering uninvited on her doorstep. "Lord, look at your forehead!"

Shannon runs for ice.

"It's OK, really." I quickly turn toward the stairs, but my head spins too fast and I wobble.

"Uh-uh, sit down before you hurt yourself." Dorothy wraps her arm around my shoulders and leads me to their couch. "If you're going to use me as 'Mom,' then I need an explanation. Besides, I don't think you can get down those stairs."

The moment I slide onto the couch, my head nosedives for the pillows. "It's a long story," I mumble into the soft velvet. If I'm not mistaken, I'm talking into a pillow with the colorful face of Frida Kahlo printed on it.

Shannon comes back with a bag of chopped-up butternut squash and a towel.

"Sorry, it's all we had in the freezer," she says.

Dorothy brushes the hair away from my bruise and eases the lumpy bag onto my skin. I can't hold back a wince.

"And you said you were worried you wouldn't make a good mom." Shannon leans in and kisses Dorothy on the cheek. A smile passes between them and calms my heart. It feels so normal. Like this is actually my home. Like she could be my mom. I soak in my real mom's murals in the lamplight and let my neighbor hold frozen butternut squash to my forehead.

"You can sleep here tonight," Dorothy says. "And explain yourself in the morning."

"I can ask my dad to carry me downstairs."

"I'm sorry, sweetie, but I think he's been drinking tonight."

"We don't mind, truly," Shannon says. "Sleep, and we'll talk in the morning."

I'm too tired to feel embarrassed or disappointed about my dad's binge. Maybe retching, maybe swearing as he stumbled over boxes, maybe manically singing karaoke at the top of his lungs. Dorothy runs her fingers through my hair, and scraps of ferns and twigs fall to the floor. Shannon drapes a blanket over me, and someone takes off my boots. Dorothy reaches to turn off the lamp, but I grab her hand.

"Please, I want to see my mom's murals. Even when I fall asleep."

"The elephant one always makes me feel better." Dorothy smiles before leaving me with the murals.

The quiet of the house settles around me. Its edges soft in the lamplight, the mural feels dreamy. Elephants wave their trunks from the corner of the room while a parrot soars through jungle branches. I glance at my mother's signature in the far right corner.

Meredith Murphy Santos.

I always found it strange that my mother adopted my father's last name even though they'd never married. She said she always liked the way it sounded. Like the saints were watching over us.

In my sleep, my dreams are infused with the rich emeralds and ambers of my mother's murals. Spiraling fern leaves and wild sunflowers. I'm running through a forest. Not because someone is chasing me with a knife. Not because I need to jump home from an impossible place.

I'm running because it feels good to run in the sunshine.

I'm running because it feels like flying.

❧ CHAPTER 41 ❧

I wake up to pounding. Both inside my head and somewhere far away. Can someone please just let me sleep? Between work and Montgomery, I've had enough rude awakenings to—wait, I'm supposed to be at work! I bolt up from the couch and nearly topple to the floor. The bruises on my forehead throb, and my skin feels feverishly hot. Dorothy sneaks a glance at the idiot pounding on the door below.

"Is he the man who did this to you?" she says.

I hobble over and peer out the window.

Lo and behold, there stands Mr. Monty in his ever-impeccable blue suit. He raps his knuckles against the door, not a ginger hello, no—this knock means business.

"No, it was a different man. That's Montgomery. He might be angry, but he would never do this to me. I'm late for work. I need to talk to him."

"Oh no, you don't. You're taking a sick day. Use our couch for as long as you need. Besides, I don't trust any man pounding my door at the crack of dawn."

She gives me a fierce mama-bear look, and it makes my heart ache. The fact that a stranger would do this for me—I don't even have words. I've always thought of Dorothy and Shannon as the annoying anonymous footsteps upstairs, the renters who stole my mother's murals from me, the renters who judged us for living in a cement garage, but I should have looked more closely. How many times have I turned my back on help that was only a few steps away?

"My phone broke," I say, nodding toward the cracked screen on her coffee table. "I need to tell him what happened last night."

"Fine, but he's coming up here and talking to you like a gentleman."

I nod, even though my neck aches.

Dorothy swings open the window.

"Hey, Mister! She's up here. And keep it down, people are trying to sleep."

Montgomery straightens his suit as if he's been caught acting like something other than a gentleman. A moment later, he stands in the doorway and has to duck under their hanging orchids. I'm too ashamed to turn around. I can't bear the idea of showing him how stupid I was last night jumping onto a Caltrain.

"Ruby, I promise I'm not mad about the concert." He says the words flat, but I can hear the undercurrent of disappointment. "But this is a *job*. You have to show up. On time. You have to answer the phone. You're under contract, so the next time you decide you want to sleep in—"

I turn around.

"Jesus, what happened to your face?"

He rushes over, and Dorothy blocks his path. He towers over her petite frame, but she doesn't seem to care.

"I'm not going to hurt her," he says, his blue eyes bright with concern. "I promise."

Dorothy reluctantly lets him through, though she hovers by my side. Montgomery reaches to touch my bruised forehead and leaves his hand hanging midair. It drops to his side, and I can see his jaw working.

"Are you OK?" he says, eventually.

A ragged breath tunnels through my lungs. I want to speak, but I'm afraid my voice will break. This is a job. I can't show weakness in front of my boss. He'll never trust me again.

"Dorothy, can we have a minute alone?" he says.

She nods and shuffles away in her fuzzy butterfly slippers. "Holler if you need me. Shannon's a chef. She knows how to use a cleaver."

I let out a little laugh, but it has the unintended effect of unleashing a hiccupped gulp of air. I can't stop my chest from shaking.

Montgomery reaches his strong arms toward me, and when I don't back away, he wraps me into a fierce hug. It's so warm and unyielding. I let him hold me. Worse, I let myself press my aching forehead against the broad muscles in his chest. My whole body shudders. Tears flood down my cheeks, and I wish I could wrangle them back inside.

"I'm sorry I couldn't make it to your concert. I really wanted to go, but I did something stupid."

He glances down at my bloodshot eyes.

"Tell me," he pleads.

"I got dragged . . ." We glance toward the kitchen, the renters undoubtedly listening from the other room. I lower my voice to a whisper. "I jumped to Palo Alto. I wasn't thinking straight. I thought the Bartholomews ruled the entire Bay Area, including the South Bay. I was wrong, obviously."

"Oh, Ruby, I could have sent a car. Or picked you up. Or at least warned you about Caltrain. I was so obsessed with practicing for the concert that I didn't even think—"

"Montgomery, stop. I was reckless. This is what happens whenever I . . ." My cracked lips can't bear to finish the sentence. I was foolish for dreaming of more. It gets me into trouble every time.

"Where else did they hurt you?" His fingers run along my arms, and a delicious heat spreads into my skin. All my nerve endings feel so raw and broken, and yet his touch steadies me, makes me feel alive.

"Only my forehead. But he took me to Helensburgh."

"That bastard—wait a minute . . . How did you get back home?"

"I jumped."

His mouth hangs open, and his wavy black hair falls into his stunned eyes. "You jumped? Helensburgh to Balboa Park? As in *the* Helensburgh? Australia?"

"It wasn't easy. I feel like I've been hit by a train."

"Ruby, that's about as far from San Francisco as you can get across the world. Most jumpers can't do it. Not even if they leapfrog. It's an abandoned train, a boneyard. How did you jump it?"

"A little luck, and a little William Carlos Williams poetry came in handy. Thank you for sharing that with me."

"Even with the poetry, it's a hell of a jump. I know you've been to Verona and Argentina, but this is a hundred times harder. No electricity, rusted tracks, all the way in Australia. How, Ruby?"

"Balboa Park is my home. It's always been my home. I'll always find my way back here." I can't help but glance at my mother's jungle murals.

"They're beautiful," he says, following my gaze. "There's no question your mom was an artist."

"I won't ever leave this house behind. I found my way back here. I'll keep finding my way back here."

"You're going to feel rough for a few days, maybe more. Your best bet is to sleep."

"What about work?"

"Work can wait. I'll cover for you if Powell asks questions. Christ, Helensburgh. I can't believe you sometimes."

"Well, believe that I feel like I've been trampled by a dinosaur. And then hit by a train. And then maybe the dinosaur came back for a second round. I don't even know if I can limp to my bed."

He lifts me off my feet before I can say another word.

"I'll help you downstairs," he says.

Dorothy chimes in from the kitchen. A carving knife dangles from her hands. It's hard to take her seriously in her flamingo pajama pants, but the look in her eyes is dead serious.

"If you get any Viking ideas about carting her off, we'll have more than just words."

"I'm helping her downstairs, ma'am."

"Good. Don't drop her."

"Thank you, Dorothy," I say. "For everything."

Shannon beams with pride, and Dorothy nods but doesn't let her guard drop. Montgomery does his best to not snag my boots on the railing. Every step sloshes sour bile down my throat. It would be horribly embarrassing if I hurled on him right now, so I hold my breath as long as I can.

When he swings open the garage door, we're immediately met with the stench of vomit. I see a pool of brown-red mush dripping from the clawfoot tub. I bolt out of Montgomery's arms to get away from that awful smell. My boots hit the pavement hard, and pain shoots up my spine. I barely make it to the agapanthus plant next to the sidewalk before I start dry heaving into the leaves. Montgomery pulls my long hair back from my face and waits for me to finish. He drapes his jacket over my shoulders and eases me back to my feet.

"You can go now," I say, shoving my hair back. "It's OK, I'll clean up. My dad must have . . . he must have drunk too much on his date last night."

I hover by the door, my feet frozen on the concrete. My heart pounds, unbearably loud inside my chest. I can hear my father snoring from the opposite end of the room. I know it's him. I know that snore. But it feels like there's a monster lying on that mattress, dressed as my father. A big bad wolf waiting for me. Everything tells me not to go inside. To run, to hide, to get away from here. My legs begin to buckle. Most of the time, I can tell myself I'm strong, that I can push through anything; and then I do. But this morning, all I want to do is run.

Montgomery shuts the door before I can enter.

"You're not sleeping in there." He scoops me up and walks toward his car. Part of me wants to protest. Part of me wants to say I'm no damsel in distress. That I can hold it together. Instead, I lean my head against his shoulder as he eases me into the backseat. Is it so wrong to be taken care of sometimes? Why is it so hard to accept help?

"We see you!" Dorothy hollers from the second-story window.

"It's OK, Dorothy!" I holler back.

"You sure, honey?" she says.

I nod, their tenderness dredging up more emotion than I can handle. My body crumples against the leather seat. We start driving, the grays of the city blurring into feathers. The fog, the concrete, the train tracks. Mist, graphite, pewter, iron, charcoal; we live in a world of a million grays. So, what if this feeling between Montgomery and I edges into gray territory?

"Please don't take me to your skyscraper. I hate that place."

We drive in silence for a minute while he chews his lip. I press my palms against my stomach and slide sideways across the seat cushions. The leather feels cool and smooth against my cheek.

"If I ask you to keep my hideaway a secret and not snoop around—can you promise?"

I barely hear his question with my ear pressed against the leather seat, wheels rumbling below.

"Are we going to the house on Cole?" I mumble.

"Ruby, no questions."

"Thy lady be too sick to protest."

"Is that a promise?"

"Yes, Mr. Monty, I promise."

Soon, the car's rocking motion lulls me to sleep, and the minutes slip by like paint dissolving into a glass of water.

It's not until I feel a hand shaking my shoulder that I groan awake.

"Can I just sleep here?"

Montgomery's strong arms lift me from the car. I remember loving the feeling of being carried to my bed after a long road trip. I remember pretending to be asleep so my mom would scoop me up. She always knew I was pretending. It didn't matter; she had strong painter arms from a million brushstrokes. More muscle than Schwarzenegger and The Rock combined. That was my mom. Meredith Murphy Santos. In my sleepy haze, I silently ask her if I should trust Montgomery, and I think I hear her whisper, *yes*. Yes, trust the boy with poetry in his pocket and a glare that could turn enemies to stone. If she were still alive, she'd invite him over for chai tea and blueberry scones as heavy as doorstops (because, let's face it, my mom was a horrible baker). It makes me smile to think of her, even if she'll never meet all the boys in my future.

Stairs creak underfoot as I try to keep the dizziness at bay. I lean my bruised forehead against his shoulder, and his cedar forest scent calms me.

"When we make it to the top floor, please keep your eyes shut. It's safer for you to not see certain things. I'll only need a minute to tidy up."

"After the tiger snake in Helensburgh, I think I can handle dirty underwear."

Montgomery's laughter rumbles beneath my ear. It reminds me of how close his skin is underneath his crisp white shirt. I hook my fingers into the buttons of his shirt, and his heartbeat drums beneath my palm. I wish I could bottle up his laughter and take a swig of it anytime I felt my courage falter.

"I swear it's not underwear," he says.

"Then, what?"

"Ruby."

"OK, OK, I'll shut my eyes at the top."

We're climbing steps up the tower of Babel, up up into the sky, but in reality, we're going very slowly. I don't know how to shape my body to make it easier on his muscles. These are narrow stairs. Smooth wooden panels brush against my knees, and sometimes my boot snags on a railing. Keeping my arms and legs tucked in makes my body tremble with the effort. His breath huffs, but he doesn't complain about the climb. Finally, he jangles the lock on the third-story door and stops.

"Eyes," he says.

"Yes, rulemeister. I'll give you two minutes."

Montgomery eases my body onto a plush feather couch, and we both let out an exhausted breath. It smells like orange peels and pencil shavings, dust and sunlight.

"When can I open my eyes?" I say.

"Gimme a minute—I just lugged a girl up three flights of stairs."

"You going to lug me back down those stairs too?"

"You're on your own, princess."

I smile and hear him rustling through drawers, moving papers. Tidying up, or hiding dirty magazines, or looking for shackles, who knows.

"Don't worry, I won't judge."

"The less you know about the Bartholomew business, the safer you'll be. Em doesn't let us share contacts or maps with jumpers, and if she finds out you know too much . . ."

Great, more secrets, just what we need. I refuse to let Em's watchful eyes come between Montgomery and me. I'm tired of masks and lies and hiding. Montgomery shouldn't have to be two people mashed into one. I want him to be *Chase*, always.

I open my eyes before he tells me it's time.

Bright morning light blinds me from a cinquefoil window overlooking rooftops. Across the street, there's an emerald stained glass window with fish scale shingles covering the front gable. Ah, these gorgeous old Victorians. We must be at attic level. I knew the address already, but I would never have guessed what it looked like on the inside. Its angled redwood ceiling, its dangling raindrop lights crafted with hammered copper. Montgomery crouches to pick up the last of his secret papers. Some look like maps; others seem like long columns of numbers. Dust motes dance in the air, and the space smells strongly of orange peels. It's one long stretch of a room with a farmhouse bed on one end, a couch on the other, and every sort of musical instrument scattered in between. Sheet music, stray popcorn, and pencil shavings lie scattered across the coffee table.

"Chase," I say, and he turns, startled to hear his true name. A hesitant smile flickers across his lips. I wonder if anyone in the world calls him by his real name. Or if it's only me.

"This is your place, isn't it? You live here."

"No questions—you promised."

"What are all those papers?"

He glares with his practiced Montgomery-intensity and stops his manic attempt to hide the confidential BART documents.

"Ruby, please. I brought you here, trusting that—"

"I'm sorry, I'll stop. I promise, I'm only here to sleep."

"You can take my bed if you want. I put you on the couch because I didn't know which you'd prefer."

"Either is fine."

"Bathroom is over there." He points to a door near the staircase. "There's maybe a little food in the mini fridge if you get hungry. Peanut butter and oranges, at least. Water, ginger ale. That sort of thing. You should take more supplements for your joints. I'll be back in a few hours. Are you going to be OK here? I can grab you some takeout if you're hungry. Are you hungry?"

"Wait, slow your roll." All his rapid-fire talking is making my head spin. "Where are you going?"

"The man on the Palo Alto train: did he have a scar on his chin, or a burnt patch on his neck?"

"Montgomery, don't."

"Scar or burnt patch? Or was it the one who likes to hum White Stripes songs all the time?"

"I already did something stupid enough for the both of us. Please leave it."

"I need to know."

I sigh and squeeze one of the couch pillows.

"Scar," I say. "On his chin. Gray eyes like knives."

"Palo," he says. Montgomery leaves without another word.

I'm too tired to follow him, too tired to convince him that whatever revenge he's planning is a bad idea. His footsteps lead down the creaky steps and out into the street.

I nosedive for the bed. It smells so very Montgomery. It's embarrassing how much I like it. It makes me wish his legs were tangled with mine, his muscles pressing into my soft skin. It makes me ignore everything else that aches.

Even if it smells like he hasn't changed the sheets in a few weeks. It's funny to think of these two Montgomerys–the finely tailored suits and clockwork trains, versus the messy musician with more instruments than a twelve-piece orchestra. How is it possible to walk around wearing so many masks? At least it makes me feel less guilty about crawling into his bed with my dirty feet. I nestle deeper into the sheets and finally let my muscles relax.

It feels like home.

⚡ CHAPTER 42 ⚡

When I wake up hours later, I feel halfway human. And when I say halfway, I mean halfway. At best.

The light has faded from the sky, and faint stars are starting to reveal themselves in the skylights. My throat is so dry, I can barely swallow. Inside the mini fridge is every kind of energy drink and super healthy green juice you can find at Whole Foods. The door is also loaded with tiny blue bottles of SKYY vodka like I've walked into a fancy hotel room. It's none of my business, but I wonder how many of these he drinks. At least twenty tiny bottles stare back at me. I slam the fridge shut. My brain isn't ready to process that. He said no questions. I promised no questions.

It's not easy crossing an overgrown jungle of instruments to reach the bathroom. The attic stretches and sways in my vision like I'm Alice after drinking the potion and turning twenty sizes too big.

I need to come up with lies to tell Madame Em. On the security cameras, she would have seen me jump from Balboa Park—and then disappear. No way her enemies would let her have eyes on their trains, so I'm guessing she didn't see Palo drag me to Helensburgh. Unless she has eyes everywhere. Think, what lies to tell her . . . lies I won't crumble under. *Think.*

My forehead pulses and throbs, and I have to reach for a cabinet to steady myself.

Cedar incense. This will help. I strike a match, and sulfur fills my nose until the stick catches flame. Smoke unfurls into the air. The room dissolves into a rich forest smell, ancient redwood bark and clove leaves underfoot. So this is why he smells so Montgomery all the time.

Shouldn't he be back by now?

We need to get our cover-up story straight before Em summons us. Maybe we can tell her we were searching for ways to expand her empire. I've seen that hungry shadow in her eyes, the need for more territory. Maybe we can say we jumped to Helensburgh *on purpose* to see if it's any match for the Vanishing Station.

I tug at the tangles in my hair and realize how desperately I need a shower. No luck finding a fresh towel, but I jump in anyway.

Sweet lord, never underestimate the power of a bath.

My entire body melts into the peppermint soap and hot water. I scrub away the dirt caked around my ankles, the sweat etched on my forehead. I feel like a snake finally able to shed its skin. My mind flashes to the tiger snake's hiss—and the shampoo bottle slips from my hands. Get a grip. You're in San Francisco; you're in Montgomery's secret hideaway. *Safe*, but my body doesn't believe it yet.

I towel off with a mostly fresh T-shirt and then grab another one from his pile. It's far too big on me, coming down to my thighs, but it's comfortable and unbelievably soft. I might have to "borrow" this one. It's blue with a burnt-orange boulder on the front and a teal night sky. Scrawled across the shirt: *Red Rock Amphitheater, Morrison, Colorado*. Music boy, through and through. Maybe we can catch a concert there, one day. Maybe I can convince him to go on a road trip, far away from train territory. Do you hear yourself, Ruby? Stop thinking ahead; stop wanting things. This is how you got into this mess in the first place.

But it's hard being here. His whole hideaway makes me want to explore—a place that feels like bottled-up dreams. I gingerly inspect each instrument, careful to keep my water glass from dripping on them. The smooth wood and fierce strings, the gentle piano keys and gleaming trumpet knobs. The roof beams are polished redwood, and it makes me feel like I'm in a cabin tucked in the woods, far away from everything. After he's finished with Palo, I wonder if he'll still let me slip in and out of this secret place, simple as dipping a paintbrush into any color I crave.

I check my phone, hoping he might have sent a message. That the revenge job—whatever it may be—is done. But it's no use. My phone is cracked and broken. I can't even check if my father called me. Not that I can stomach talking to him at the moment, not after he broke all of his promises. Again. After everything I've tried to do for him, he still couldn't stay sober. All the risks I've taken, and he couldn't risk another night without alcohol. I'd gotten hopeful when he finally tried AA meetings, but he's still the same old dad. A violin string squeals under my touch, and I set it down before I break it.

It's not fair.

A few years ago, there was a kid on my block who stole my bicycle. I'd told my mom that I wanted a boy's mountain bike. Definitely not a beach cruiser with pink handlebars and a flower basket. Not for me. This bicycle was matte black with silver side mirrors. We'd picked it up from a rummage sale and spray-painted it ourselves. Even then, I thought of myself more as a rogue Batman than a Superwoman. When I rode it, I was unstoppable. So, this kid saw me run upstairs to grab a soda. Two minutes, that's all it took. At first I didn't know it was him, but then a couple days later, I saw him riding down the boulevard on my matte black mountain bike. I'm not proud of it, but I imagined tying an invisible string to the frame so that he'd go speeding down Fulton Avenue and get whipped clear off into oncoming traffic. I asked myself, *what would Batman do*, and my caped crusader was being rather mum about the matter. So I asked my dad. Big. Mistake.

I never should have told him.

"Where does the thief live?" he'd said.

Three Johnny Walkers later, we'd left the house. Near midnight. My dad made me show him where I'd seen the kid riding, so we walked eight blocks, all the while my dad fuming at the injustice. It was a time when he was fuming at every injustice—my mom's cancer diagnosis, the fact that we couldn't keep up with the hospital payments, the fact that he couldn't see his family in the Philippines as often anymore. Every couple blocks, he took another sip of whiskey and mumbled what I assumed were curse words in Tagalog.

"Dad," I said in a small voice. "I'll get another one."

He gave me a crooked smile. It was a smile I'd seen only once when he'd busted an opponent's tooth during a boxing match. Sure, the jerk probably deserved it, calling my dad a FOB and all, but that smile haunts me. It's one I imagine he must give to the trespassers he takes to face their fate at Helensburgh.

I know it was supposed to feel good. *Revenge.* You were supposed to savor it on your tongue like a chocolate lava cake. But, honestly, the whole time I worried about my father. What if a police officer drove by and caught his whiskey breath? What if he did something stupid, as his limbs got sloppier with each step?

When we stopped in front of the bike—*my bike*—my dad tested the jumbo U-lock that this kid had latched around the wheel. Another chain wrapped around the tree in the sidewalk.

"Leave it, Dad."

He didn't reply. Instead, he pulled an orange spray can from his pocket. He laughed, not his normal laugh, but the one that spilled out when he had more alcohol than blood in his veins. He shook the can and blasted paint all over the bike. And then on the house. And then on the sidewalk. Until finally, a light blared from the living room above. We sprinted down the block, and I should have known then that his joints were failing him. We barely made it home.

The next day, I saw a family scrubbing their walls. I saw my bicycle tossed on the corner of Mission Street. I could have rescued it. I could have dragged it home and repainted it Batman black. But the truth was, I couldn't stomach seeing it anymore. Not after I'd seen my father's polished veneer scraped down to the raw edges.

That's what I've grown used to feeling about my father with each drunken binge and careless mistake. I want to walk away. And yet, when it comes to my father, I always drag him back from the gutter. I always spray on a fresh coat of paint. Is this what it means to be family? I don't know how it's supposed to be. I don't know how we can change.

I glance at my cracked phone and toss it onto the table. Let him wait. I'm not ready to bust out the paint. Not yet. I flop back onto the shaggy wool rug and rope my fingers through the black-and-white tufts. The moon creeps higher into the sky as the hours pass.

I stare at the door, waiting for Montgomery to return, wishing and hoping and praying that I never ever see him that way. Revenge dripping from his hands, vodka on his breath. I know the Vanishing Station haunts him. And I pray he's not there now.

⚡ CHAPTER 43 ⚡

Keys jangle in the lock, and Montgomery appears as if from a dream. The buttons on his shirt are torn, and he's lost his silky blue blazer. The moon glows watchfully overhead. He kneels next to me on the plush rug where I'd fallen asleep near his treasured violins and drapes a blanket over my bare legs. Our fingers tangle through tufts of soft black-and-white wool. He rests there, as if in prayer; his eyes slide shut, and I want to leave kisses along his heavy eyelids.

A car door slams outside, sending a flash of fear through my chest, but then the fading footsteps leave us in quiet once more.

"Do I want to know?" I say, once again afraid to ask questions.

"Helensburgh will look like paradise compared to where I left him."

"The Vanishing Station?"

"No," he says, his voice parched and crackling. "Never again."

Relief surges through my tightly wound chest. He's not Em. Will never be Em.

Montgomery clutches his ribs as he stands up. I don't want to think about how hard Palo hit him there. His leaden footsteps stagger toward the mini fridge, where he chugs down a bottle of green juice. And then another. And then, a clink of little glass bottles.

"Can you not..." the words stick in my throat as I gather the nerve to say them. "Can you not drink the vodka? Please."

He stares across the moonlit room, eyes hungry and dark. This doesn't feel like the same sleepy boy who draped a blanket over my legs.

"It's been a long night," he says.

"There will be many long nights," I say. "Go ahead and ask my dad."

Montgomery sighs and slumps against the countertop. He shuts the fridge door with a rattle of glass bottles. His long limbs slip under the blanket with me, and I can feel him shivering. Not from the cold, no; this attic stays warm as a bird's nest.

"You didn't have to do that," I say. "I'm grateful, but you don't have to... to be 'Montgomery' all of the time."

"Palo crossed a line. I won't risk him coming back to hurt you again."

"I crossed a line, remember? Jumping onto their trains in the first place."

"And he didn't hesitate to take you to Helensburgh."

"What happens next? Will they come after you now?"

"Don't worry—this is being a Bartholomew. This has always been the way things are."

"But I do worry about you. And I worry about what Em will do when she finds out. How are we going to explain Hel—"

"Don't think about that right now," he says, curling his body around mine, until my back firmly presses into his chest. My hips curve into his, and it feels like warm honey is seeping into all the cracks between our bodies. His hand runs along my thighs, and now I'm the one who can't help but shiver. "I just want to think about how good you look in my T-shirt," he says.

"You know I'm planning on stealing this shirt forever."

"It's yours."

We gaze through the skylights, hoping to catch a star or two brilliant enough to shine through the city lights. I don't know how I'm ever going to fall back asleep with his body pressed into mine. Even with exhaustion weighing down his limbs, it's like Montgomery can't resist touching every inch of my bare legs. When I press my hips back, his whole body feels taut and awake. I'm never going to be able to sleep again.

He starts to hum a melody, his full lips dragging along my neck.

"Is that a kundiman?" I whisper.

"Hmm? *Kuun-dee-man.*" He tests the word slowly on his tongue. It's cute how much he tries to pronounce it perfectly. Like maybe he actually cares what it means to me.

"It's a love ballad from the Philippines," I say, immediately regretting it.

His hand freezes on my hip.

Oh god, Ruby, did you just ask a boy to sing you a love song? Heat floods my cheeks, and I pull the scratchy wool blanket over my head. We lay in silence for a few agonizing seconds, our chests rising and falling under the thin canopy.

"I'm a terrible singer," he says, eventually, as if he was searching this whole time for the perfect song. "But I can play something. What do you want to hear?"

"No, no, I was just kidding. I didn't mean—"

"Ruby, tell me what you want." He tugs the blanket down from my face, so he can meet my eyes. He leans up on his elbow, and the moonlight makes his lips glow. Such lush, kissable lips. What I want? His hand caresses down my thighs again, as if he's already playing ivory piano keys. All the things I want come flooding into my chest—I've never felt such an ache for *everything*. I want him to touch every inch of me, to slip off this shirt I've stolen from him, so that there's nothing between his skin and mine. I want to open my eyes and not have this all disappear. But it *is* all going to disappear. It's all going to shatter. I hide my eyes under my forearm, afraid he'll see right through me.

"What's wrong?" Montgomery says, gently prying my arm away.

"Too often, I've had the things I want taken away. And in the end . . . sometimes it's better not to want them."

"That would be a very sad song, Ruby Santos," he says as he leaves a trail of kisses along my clenched jaw, "and tonight we're playing a kundiman."

Montgomery pulls himself up and clutches his aching ribs as he reaches for the nearest guitar. He does a terrible job of hiding his grimace. I can't help but laugh at the idea of Montgomery Bartholomew III strumming me a love song on a guitar. What a cliché. I'm a terrible person, I know, but a guitar?

"I'm serious, you don't have to play a song right now!" I try to drag him back into the blanket.

"No, no, the lady demands a kundiman. So, she shall have a *kundiman*."

I burst into dizzy laughter, and then so does he, which doesn't help his ribs. He slouches over the guitar and groans. He tries so hard to bury the agony. His knees, his ribs, and all the sore spots he won't admit to. I stagger over and try to grab the guitar. Of course, his grip tightens. He grins at me. We pretty much devolve into two drunken elephants fighting over a banana. We've jumped thousands of miles today, and still, neither of us will let go of the silly guitar. Finally, I wrestle it out of his grip and hide it behind me. Before Montgomery can reach it, I pull him into a kiss. Long and hard. A kiss I've been waiting for, holding back from, leaning into with all the same breath. His hands tangle into my hair and I slip off his shirt without a second thought. He wasn't kidding about the ribs. Plum bruises bloom across his pale skin.

"I'm sorry," I say, my fingers lightly touching the broken bits.

"It was my choice."

Montgomery pulls me into another deep kiss, one full of hunger and pain and longing from many long, dark nights underground. It's a hunger I can taste, honey and tart berries and thorns all in the same bite. He pulls me up to my feet, and we're stumbling through a wildflower meadow of musical instruments. God, my brain has turned into an eighteenth-century Brontë novel. Wildflower fields—really, Ruby? I pull back and smile up at him, and when I do, I can feel more of his mask fade. He smiles at me, at his guitars and violins and trumpets and the other instruments I don't know the name for strewn all over his shaggy rug. I can see the real Montgomery brighter than I've ever seen on the trains. Chase—his name is *Chase*. It makes me want to laugh all over again, seeing him hopscotch through the messy music piles, tugging my hand. We're breathless before we've even made it across the room. I love how I can feel silly and sexy at the same time with him. Like I don't have to choose. Like there is no stage or audience, no right or wrong. When we finally topple onto the mattress, we groan on impact.

"God, why does everything have to hurt?" he says.

We burst into laughter again, which makes our lungs ache more. Still, there's no way we're sleeping yet. When he drags his tongue along my bare skin, I can't stop the ragged breath hitching in my chest. His fingers slip down between my thighs, and I have to bite my lip to keep from yelping.

"Your downstairs neighbors are going to hate us," I say, breathless.

"Lucky for them," he says in between long deep kisses, "the attic is soundproof. Any good musician knows you don't piss off your neighbors."

"Oh, really? Well, in that case . . ."

This time, I pin *him* to the bed. A wave of dizziness dances across my forehead. Not now—I've had enough train hangovers to last a lifetime.

I lean my head back to catch my breath and soak up the stars shining through the skylight. I'm still wearing his Red Rock T-shirt. He smiles when he sees it on me, the way it bunches up around my bare thighs, the way he can easily caress his hands up my sides while I stay cocooned in its warmth. My legs straddle his hips, and I start to move in smooth circles that he can't resist. His breath hitches. I stop and lean down to whisper:

"It's like we've vanished, just you and me."

Chase smiles and takes my hand the way he always does right before we jump halfway across the world together.

But tonight, the only place I want to be is here.

Tonight is mine, and I want it all.

§

Long past midnight, we give our aching bodies a chance to catch up with us. There will be tomorrow and tomorrow, and time for more. I tell myself that's true, that it won't all disappear come daylight. My shoulders and hips meld into his, our limbs tangling together into sleep. He reaches for a remote on his nightstand and flips on a stereo. Classical music dances into the moonlit attic. Slowly, I realize it's the soundtrack to *Star Wars*.

"Nerd," I say.

"Mhm, hmm," he smiles, already halfway asleep. "This one's my favorite. It's called 'Binary Sunset.' You know that moment when Luke is staring out at the twin sunsets in *A New Hope*? I keep watching that scene, wondering how John Williams wrote the score."

"Do you think one day you'll compose music for movies?"

"I can dream, can't I?" He presses his nose to the back of my neck and breathes deeply. It makes me smile.

I wish we could stay here in this attic at the edge of the world.

But I know the world has other plans.

⧽ CHAPTER 44 ⧼

I n the morning, sunlight glares from the skylights. Even though we're near busy Haight Street, I can't hear any traffic through the soundproof walls. Montgomery has a crust of drool clinging to the corner of his lips. It doesn't stop me from kissing his cheek. He yawns awake and stares up at me with those song-worthy eyes. Cerulean and sky: This boy is meant for the clouds. I need to stop staring; I'm already too hooked.

"I should check on my dad," I say, rolling out the pinch in my shoulder.

"Stay," he says, with his face still mashed into the pillows.

"Should I bring you coffee and donuts first? Cole's Creperie has the jelly kind."

He shakes his head and groans. "Ugh, headache."

"Are you sure I can't bring you anything?"

"Just a million years of sleep."

"I'll add it to the list."

"Thanks."

"You shouldn't be thanking me. It's my fault you're crumpled in a ball."

"I'm not crumpled in a ball," he says, stretching his long limbs across the bed. His joints crack, and he cringes when the pain in his ribs catches up to him.

"When are you going to tell Em about Helensburgh? Those lies about us trying to explore more territory for the Bartholomews."

"Just a few more minutes of sleep. Then I'll go."

"Shouldn't I come with you?"

"That'll only make things worse. I'll take care of Embarcadero. Go take care of your dad."

"Thank you," I whisper, slipping my fingers through his messy hair.

He smiles and pulls the blanket up to his chin, leaving his feet bare.

Good thing I can actually stand up without feeling like someone tinkered with the gravity switch. I savor one last backward glance at his sleepy, drooling face before dashing down the stairs. For once, San Francisco grants us a sunny day, and of course, I'm too "hungover" to fully appreciate it. My fingers itch for a pastel pencil, but I'll have to wait until I'm home to sketch these intricate Victorian rooftops.

Luckily, the N train rolls up right quick, and I hop aboard. No more jumping home for me. I'll take the long way, thank you very much. A little boy starts wailing nearby, but even that doesn't bother me today. The train rocks forward into motion, pigeons scattering out of the way, and I'm about to slide into an empty seat when a hand latches on to my arm. Please, not Palo, please, not again. I glance up at the culprit, afraid to see those knife-gray eyes.

Instead, Madame Em towers over me in her stiletto heels.

Surprise twists in my gut as she drags me back toward the Saddle doors, her grip much stronger than I expected. Was she watching us, waiting all night for her opportunity to attack? Her nails dig into the soft fleshy spot between the veins in my wrist.

"Em, stop!" I say.

The wailing boy sees me, and his mouth clamps shut.

I suddenly realize she's walking with my dad's eagle cane, even in her stilettos. The cane is polished to oyster-gray perfection, more weapon than mobility aid. She doesn't wobble a step, even as the train *clu-clunks* down the street. It's broad daylight. People are staring. Wake up, Ruby, this is a slow-motion nightmare, right? I barely find my balance before Em rips open a portal. Lightning quick, ice fills my lungs, and cobalt sparks swirl in my vision. I struggle to stay on this N train, ground my feet in this metal box, stay on Cole Avenue, instead of whatever hell she's dragging me to. I try to push away her magic, but she's caught me in her jagged net. And it finally dawns on me—the memory Montgomery showed me, to warn me of the Vanishing Station. No, no, I lurch out of her grasp . . . but it's too late. The ground falls away, the train, the wailing boy, the grocery store selling overripe bananas across the street, everything falls away, until there is only mind-splitting vertigo.

I'm falling.

My whole body goes numb. Then images of train stations flood my vision. I can't tell if we're actually there or if she's forcing visions into my head. St. Pancras station, the crossroads from London to France and beyond. Brick walls and steel archways. King's Cross with its dizzying purple neon lights spiderwebbing across the ceiling. My breath squeezes out of my throat—how do I know these places? I'm there in a flash and gone again. Em drags me to another, and another; Grand Central's turquoise dome with a map to the stars; Paris's Gare du Nord with its glowing lamplights inside an airplane hangar; a million languages chiming through the tracks; god, my brain is cracking into shards. She rips my body from station to station, until the pain turns into a roaring wind that drowns out my screams.

Em barely breaks a sweat.

It smells like burning oil. I'm a fish caught on a hook being dragged behind a high-speed boat. I thrash through air and space, and I can't feel the edges of my body, where I begin and where the world ends. Only pain ripping into my forehead and ripping out my fish guts.

Finally she stops and shoves me through a doorway.

I fall and slam my shoulder hard against unforgiving rock. It knocks the breath out of my lungs. A wine-drunk sea churns around us, and bird wings crash against an invisible cage. This is a place that is both distinctly nowhere . . . and one that will forever haunt my dreams.

The Vanishing Station.

Another Helensburgh, but without the tangled forest. And without any hope of escape. I lie gasping on the ground, if it can be called ground. My hands spasm across the inky blue static, and sour bile coats the back of my throat.

"Em . . ."

She snaps her fingers, and the howling train tracks *stop*, the birds *stop*, the waves *stop*.

The silence is scarier than all else.

It means she can silence me, just as quickly.

My fingers touch my lips, trembling.

"You know, I didn't become 'Embarcadero IV' because of bloodlines," she says. "I became Embarcadero because I fought for it after my husband disappeared. Our rivals tried to take my family's legacy from us. But I did what I had to do for my boys. I see that sheer determination in you sometimes—when you're not acting foolish."

I crawl on my knees toward the cave walls. Maybe I can find an exit like Montgomery did, maybe I have the power, too. She shoves me back with one of her spiked heels, and I split my lip on a rock. Salt and blood spill into my mouth. Her shadow pools behind her, writhing across the jagged stones.

"Please, Em, I'm sorry," I say.

She smooths her silk dress, and her blond pixie cut fans out like a halo. An immaculate painting—an Angel of Death. I wish my brain wouldn't waste energy turning everything into a painting. I need to find a way out.

"A train only runs if all is in order," she says, swinging my dad's eagle cane in circles. "A perfect dance of conductors and passengers and clocks and cogs and wheels turning. When a train jumps the tracks, it's a very dangerous thing. You must realize that. You must realize the difficult position you've put me in."

"I didn't mean for Palo to happen."

"Excuses do us no good. You've rekindled the grudge with our rivals to the south, and you've placed my son at the center of it. Do you realize what Montgomery has done? The danger he has put himself in? The danger he has put his *family* in!"

She stomps down on my left hand with her spiked heel, and I scream.

Em snaps her fingers again, and my scream cuts out. Silence. My heart hammers inside my chest as I claw at my lips.

In the dim light, her shadow snakes across the ground. I feel like my eyes are playing tricks, the way it doesn't follow her movements. I scramble away, afraid of what haunts this wasteland.

"Do you think he'd come for you in time, if I left you here?" she says.

I try to say something, anything, but nothing comes out. A whimper rumbles in my chest. Tears streak down my face, but even those evaporate into nothingness. In the distance, I hear the sad whine of a creature watching, warning the others that a predator is among them. I want to beg, but Em doesn't even give me the option.

"Hmm...that's what I'm afraid of. All that power, and Montgomery would only ever use it to ensure you didn't rot. Such a waste."

She arcs her neck side to side, and two sharp pops echo into the void. When she crouches down near me, a monstrous shadow looms behind her—*is part of her*, I suddenly realize. It's visible only here in the eerie glow of the Vanishing Station.

"You are a powerful asset, I'll give you that. Helensburgh, Verona, Buenos Aires, Amsterdam. But I see everything on my trains. Which means that I know you're also a powerful distraction for Montgomery. Everyone has a weakness—and I will not have our enemies use *you* to weaken Montgomery. You will not put him at risk. You will abide by my rules, or the Vanishing Station will be the last place you ever see."

My lips move before I have a chance to stop them; and this time, the words echo into the darkness. "I'd do anything to protect Montgomery."

At this, she smiles, wicked and wide.

"Good, I was hoping you'd say that." She spins her cane in a shimmering arc. "Darling, sometimes you remind me so much of myself. It's a shame you were born to Balboa, when you have far more talent than my other sons."

"I'm nothing like you." A sourness roils in my gut, and I rise to my feet.

Madame Em laughs and floats her arms out into the sea-blue waves. She leans back, and a gaping hole appears behind her like an ink blot. It's like no portal I've ever seen.

"*Next time*, I won't leave you a way out," she says.

Em disappears more quickly than I can blink, all ballerina grace and precision. A glimpse of my father's cane spins through the portal, holding the doorway open for the briefest of moments.

I lunge for it.

It's the last thing I see before my mind slips into darkness.

❧ CHAPTER 45 ❧

When I was young and my mom didn't have enough money for vacations, we would ride the trains. I don't know why we never stepped off. The idea never crossed our minds. The one and only goal was to glide along the tracks. The feeling of soaring high over the rooftops, or deep down underground, sneaking under bridges and barreling across the bay. It was always sunnier in Berkeley than it was in San Francisco. We'd bring sketchbooks and balance them on our knees, perfecting the art of a steady hand. My favorite was to sketch my mother's face while she gazed out the window, sunlight glowing on her cheeks. When she'd ask to see it, I'd always be too shy to show her—it would never live up to the real woman. It reminded me of the way so many master artists have tried to paint the Virgin Mary. A million variations, and yet none come close to capturing all of her contradictions.

I wonder if someone has sketched me yet. I'd make the perfect subject, still as a statue, pale as a dead girl.

I've been sitting here long enough.

Hours, maybe.

Back and forth on a local subway line . . , in a city I've never visited before. I hear snippets of Spanish, or is it Portuguese? Sound wavers in and out, as if my ears have become waterlogged.

Leaping after Em has drained every ounce of energy left in me. I blink in and out of consciousness. Mostly I press my forehead against the glass, pinned to my seat. At least the headache has subsided slightly. We're coming up to a bright patch where orange flaming leaves scratch against the windows. I tug my sweater over my eyes and wince.

Growing up, I'd gotten used to the tragic image of unhoused men and women curled up on the BART trains, desperate for a moment of peace. I used to complain about the smell—that rancid, unwashed stench—but my mother snapped at me. *They have nowhere else to go. They have nowhere to wash, nowhere to heal. Let them sleep, let them dream.*

And so I sleep.

And so I dream.

⚗ CHAPTER 46 ⚗

The next time my eyes blink open, a man is sitting next to me, knitting a beanie. Correction–*crocheting* a beanie. His crochet hook loops and threads through thick yarn. His deft, pale fingers make quick work of the hat. It's a color I'd choose for myself–a deep turquoise yarn interwoven with feathered pearl. It's in the pattern of snowfall.

"Er hodet kaldt?" he says, when he catches me staring.

"I'm sorry?" My throat is parched and raspy.

He smiles and holds the hat close to my head to check the sizing.

"Is your head cold?" he says.

I stare at his squarish face for a long moment before I recognize him. The spiky blond hair, the nearly translucent eyes, the hairy knuckles.

"Håkon?"

"At your service."

"What are you doing here?"

"Waiting for you to wake up. And trying not to get bored. There are only so many things one can do on a train for hours." He holds up the crocheted beanie again. "I hope I got the size right."

I stare out the window at the unfamiliar landscape. At least if we were in Norway, Håkon's presence would make slightly–*only slightly*–more sense. But I'm at a loss. The countryside sprawls with vineyards and ancient churches and stone walls. Cattle grazes in the fields beyond.

"This isn't . . ."

"Norway?" he says. "No, it's not."

"Then where are we?"

"Is that really the question you want to ask right now? I think you should be asking a far greater question—*where are we going?*"

"Where are we going?" I whisper, fear of the Vanishing Station twisting up my spine.

"That's for you to decide, Balboa." Håkon starts up his crochet hook again, loop and pearl, loop and pearl, the turquoise hat slowly materializing from a ball of yarn.

Like magic, in its own way.

"Håkon, can I go home?"

"Where's home?"

"You know where."

"But does it have to be?"

I tangle my fingers into the thick ball of wool, squeezing it in my palm to keep tears at bay. I'm so tired. Can we please stop these cruel games?

"I just want to go home."

"I'm here because the trains called me. I felt them rumble and crack open a portal that led to you. As it does for all the lost jumpers I find on the trains. Don't ask me why. Why me? Why you? But here I am. Offering you a choice."

"There is no choice." My voice breaks when I say the words. "I can't lose my home. I can't escape the Bartholomews."

"You've done a lot of things that you once thought impossible."

Håkon hands me a thermos full of warm chai tea with milk. It's such a relief that I would hug him if I could. *So* hygge. Warmth surges through my chest, a flicker of energy where I thought none was left. He doesn't look up from his crocheting, just keeps moving down the woolen chain.

"There are other train lines in the world," he says. "And other jumpers looking for escape. There's an *underground* to the underground. If you choose it."

"But Montgomery—"

"Montgomery and I are friends, despite it all. He has a choice, too. One he has not been ready to make. "

"My dad—"

"Knows more than you think."

I take another gulp of chai tea, its sugar and spice bringing me back to the living. Honey settles beneath my tongue, but my brain still feels too raw to think.

"Can you take me back to San Francisco?" I say.

"I can."

"Will you?"

"I will."

"And what will you get in return? What's the price?"

"You've been spending too long with the Bartholomews and the Caltrain and the Stazioni, and all the other fools. The only thing I ask is that you consider my question: *Where are you going, Ruby Santos?* It doesn't matter where you've been; where you are now; or whether they call you by your true name. When you know the answer to that question, give me a call." Håkon ties the finishing loops on the hat, cuts the yarn with a craggily tooth, and tosses it onto my lap.

"And don't catch a cold," he says.

A faint smile crosses my lips, and my thumbs trace the subtle snowfall pattern in my new hat. It makes me crave a walk in the snowy fjords with Mont–with *Chase* again. Could we have that life if we want it enough?

"Hold my hand," Håkon says, slowly rising from his seat. "I will take you back to Balboa Park. And don't forget–det går så bra, skal du se!"

"What's that mea–"

But I don't have a chance to ask another question before the wind roars through my ears and the ground dissolves under my feet like thin ice.

⚡ CHAPTER 47 ⚡

Håkon dropped me off at Balboa Park station after we leapfrogged from god-knows-where Spain, to Madison, Wisconsin, of all places, and finally to foggy San Francisco. And the hat fit perfectly.

But when I finally arrive home, my father doesn't mention all the missed calls and lost hours. He doesn't mention my absence or my sunken eyes or the fact that I found him passed out in his own vomit. He doesn't mention that there's a half-empty bottle of bottom-shelf vodka hidden under the sink. It smells almost as nasty as the bleach beside it.

Instead, he asks:

"Do you think I could fit inside our balikbayan box?"

My father crouches near the giant cardboard box and mimes twisting his body into a pretzel. He gives me a boyish grin. "Maybe if I try the yoga, na?" He hands me a can of Spam to stuff inside a shoe. I flick the Spam into its cavernous cardboard belly without a glance.

My father clicks his tongue at me. He carefully slips it into a Cole Haan boot that used to belong to my mother and is tragically one size too big on me, like everything she owned. Every inch of space counts in a balikbayan box. It will travel thousands of miles across the ocean to our relatives in the Philippines. It's like Christmas year-round, but instead of fancy presents, the box is filled with hand-me-downs and enough Spam and chocolate to survive the apocalypse. This is our way of helping the family we left behind. I scan the declarations list to keep myself from losing my cool. It goes like this:

1. Five Starbucks coffee bags (dark and smoky like Tita Rosa likes it)
2. Four pairs of Lucky Brand jeans (that have grown too stretched out for my hips, though they'll fit Cousin Allysson's just fine)
3. Six bars of Dove soap (because apparently the twins are going through a no-baths phase)
4. Twenty cans of Spam (for emergencies, or not)
5. Twenty Toblerone chocolate bars (definitely for emergencies)
6. Five tubes of Colgate toothpaste (in sincere apology for the chocolate)
7. My father's unspoken memories of the home he left behind for me

Of course, he picks *now* to pack a balikbayan box, as if he could hide under a saintly halo in service to the Santos family. This is my father: binge and forget. Binge and forget. He'll buy supersweet donuts that make you feel sick after eating them, and then pretend like nothing happened the previous night. When I was younger, I'd play along. I'd smile and eat the donuts, even though I couldn't look at my father without anger chewing my gut. Truth was, I didn't know how to play the game. I didn't know that I could change the rules. But I'm not a kid anymore.

"You promised," I snap, even though my bones ache, even though all I want is my bed. Anger surges through my fists, giving me a reserve of energy I didn't know I had left. It's a bottomless anger that can only be kindled by the ones we love, the ones we'd reach into the flames for, if only they'd take our damn hand.

"Do you think we should send the Cheetos? It's Glenn's favorite."

"Don't you dare change the subject. You promised you would work on you while I took over the trains. What happened?"

He turns away. "I'll add the Cheetos."

I grab the chips and throw them on the ground. When I stomp down, the bag pops, spilling sickening neon crumbs all over our floor. It's stupid and childish and I don't know why I'm doing it, but I keep smashing my foot down until nothing's left except orange powder smeared onto concrete.

"Ruby. Ruby! We go for walk."

I march down our hallway of junk and leave orange footprints in my wake. I wait outside. I wait and wait, until finally I snap my head back into the darkness, only to nearly knock foreheads with my father. He inches his cane forward, takes a step, drags the other foot forward, cane, step, forward. My muscles are revving to go—fight, flight, anything but this. Even after Em's mind-splitting punishment, fire churns inside my veins. We take three agonizing steps toward the sidewalk. We'll never make it around the block.

"I don't want to go for a walk," I say, chewing my lip.

"Come on, Little Hamboorger, your daddio needs exercise."

Watching him walk: it's like the top half of his body is dragging the bottom half. Almost like a soldier carrying a wounded man to safety, but instead it's one body, one man, and his sheer determination. He twists and grunts with each step. His knuckles go white with how hard he grips the cane. And yet, he keeps moving forward. That Dylan Thomas poem loops through my head. Damn Montgomery and his poems. Its chorus builds as I wait. As I walk. With my father, failing. One long step for his every three tiny inches forward. We walk. A man sporting shiny red Nikes jogs past us and averts his eyes. My father doesn't pay him any mind. He smiles, grits it out through his teeth. How can so much strength and weakness be wrapped inside one man?

In ancient Greece, Nike was the goddess of victory. Laurel leaves for her crown, wings on her back. She'd fly across the battlefield, granting speed and strength, fame and glory. What victory can my father ever expect if he never heals, if he never sobers? If you think a pair of fancy sneakers will fix him, you're wrong, you're so wrong. Hip surgery might not even fix the problem. It might take away one source of pain, but not the addiction.

An older woman leans on a fire hydrant while her Scottie dog inspects it. He pretends he's Sherlock Holmes, dog detective. The dog side-eyes my father and seems nervous that he's not walking "normally" like the rest of us humans. The dog yips at him, and the woman tugs on his leash.

"I'm sorry, Winston always makes a fuss." The woman scoops Winston into her arms and taps his chocolate-chip nose. The dog huffs and stares at my father suspiciously as he inches toward us. "When's he getting his hips done?"

My mouth goes dry.

Whenever we can save enough money.

Whenever my dad can finally cut back on the alcohol.

Maybe soon, maybe never.

Maybe only after all the fight has left his body.

"Soon," he says through a long breath. There's that smile again. That foolish fake grin.

"You know, the longer you wait, the longer it takes for you to recover. The more complications there could be in surgery. Trust me, I had mine done back in 2009 and it was the best thing that ever happened to me. Sure, I was down for a couple months, but Winston would never have forgiven me if I couldn't take him on walks anymore."

"He'll have them done soon," I say.

"I can recommend a doctor." She eagerly pulls out her phone to look up a contact.

"We got it, OK!" My anger spills onto this poor lady with her Scottie dog pedaling in her arms, but I don't care. She should mind her own business. I'm itching to walk away, but that would mean leaving my father here to fend for himself.

The lady steps back and drops her dog onto the pavement. The Scottie huffs at my dad's feet before they cross the street. Good riddance.

"Ruby, manners, na?"

"She should mind her own business," I growl.

My eyes scan the street for anyone else in our path, any more obstacles to pummel into the ground. It's not fair—none of it is fair. My father's limp is not something we can hide, not like his binge drinking or the cancer that ate away at my mother's insides or the fact that we live in a garage. This is a weakness anyone can see. I can't bear the thought of anyone thinking any less of my father for his limp. I can't bear the thought of him never healing, never jumping trains again, never championing a boxing ring. Not my dad.

This is all because of Em and her demands for more jumps, more riches. Her festering greed corrupting the BART lines. I remember when my dad said the Bartholomews would use me, just like they used him. Until the magic makes my joints crumple, until there is nothing left of my body to take. But we can still put up a fight. *Come on, Dad, fight! I can't be the only one fighting for you. I can't carry this burden alone.*

My whole chest shakes. I'm not strong enough to carry it all.

When he finally reaches the corner, he wraps me into a tight hug. Even on his broken limbs, he helps hold me up sometimes, too. I let all of my disappointment and anger drain away into his hug. He holds me even as strangers walk by with heavy groceries slung on their arms, hiking their way home to the people they love.

"My Little Hamboorger," he says into my ear. "I'm sorry I failed you." My dad grips hard on his cane as his lips tremble. When he looks away, I can still see the flash of emotion in his eyes.

"It's only failing if you stop trying," I say.

"Your dad is a strong old man. He's a Santos. He keeps on fighting."

"Your daughter is a fighter, too."

"I know. She's stronger than her dad. More stubborn, too. I promise I will try more AA meetings. It's just . . . sometimes the pain is too much." He rubs his palms along his ailing hips and winces.

Another baggy-jeaned teenager approaches and crosses to the other side of the street to avoid our tears. Let him watch. These tears will slide right off my cheeks. After Mom died, after Em threatened to take the house, after Palo left me in Helensburgh. We always find a way.

Where are you going? Håkon's words echo in my ears.

Not where we've been, but where we're *going*. As my chest slowly loosens, new ideas start churning like electricity flickering on in a blacked-out train.

"We need to find a way for you to get hip surgery sooner. We need to bring down the pain, so you have a fighting chance against the alcoholism. I know the surgery won't cure your addiction, but at least it might give you a level playing field. One you might win, if you try hard every damn day."

"Maybe you send me home in a balikbayan box and we go on a 'medical vacation.'" He says it as a joke, but my brain starts to draw a rough sketch.

A train.

A jump.

Send him home.

Of course.

What haven't we thought of this sooner?

Surgery is much cheaper in the Philippines. He has loads of family there who can help him recover, and our money will stretch further. There's an old house in Baguio that my dad always talks about when he feels nostalgic. It's simple, tin roof and concrete walls, but right near the beach. He could hide away there temporarily. We won't have to worry about plane tickets or illegal visas; we can jump the portal straight to the Philippines. And maybe, just maybe, he'll finally have a fighting chance to beat his alcoholism, without the chronic pain dragging him down. It might be possible.

Maybe.

Before the dream can disappear, I paint the words aloud:

"We're taking you on a medical vacation. We're taking you home, Dad."

⚡ CHAPTER 48 ⚡

Back in the garage, my father stares at the balikbayan box and all the things we'd meant to send to our faraway family. Little did we know that my dad could be included along with the Spam and Cole Haans.

"I can't ask this from my brother." His fingers jitter through his hair, for once not slicked back like Elvis. "Rodrigo has five kids. He has no time to care for an old man recovering from surgery."

"Maybe we can hire one of the cousins to help afterward? I can wire you money. Do you think this might be enough down payment for the surgery?" I crouch behind the washing machine and tug out my stash of cash. Cobwebs catch on the plastic bag bulging with green Benjamin Franklins. It's grown larger than I thought. My dad stares at the bundles of hundred-dollar bills with his mouth wide open.

"That's yours," he says.

"I've been saving it for you."

"It's not enough. Maybe for the surgery—but what about the jump? Em will not let me. She worry that I will work for her enemies."

Memories of the Vanishing Station come roaring into my ears, and I have to force my hands to steady.

"Let me deal with Em. I can ask Montgomery to convince her if she won't listen. I can tell her it would be only temporary. If . . . I mean *when* . . . you recover."

Even if the entire plan works—the jump to the Philippines, the hip surgery, the Santos family watching over him—there's no guarantee his hip will heal, no guarantee his alcohol addiction will end. It's one giant leap into the unknown. It might end up being a complete and utter waste of our savings. I try not to let my doubts show, but they hover like moths.

"I can't leave you here alone," he says. "Who will watch you?"

I swallow down my panic and hand him the cash. I want to say Montgomery will watch over me, but that's not true, even if he promises to write me a kundiman song. It'll be me and this makeshift garage and my own two feet when it comes down to it.

"I'm a fighter, remember?" I say.

But my dad catches the waver in my voice and pulls me into a bear hug. His cane clatters to the concrete floor.

"I'm not leaving you here. Not with those devils."

"I can take care of myself." I don't dare tell him about the turf war I've riled up or about Montgomery's bruised ribs. I don't tell him about my near-death jump at Helensburgh station or even about the Vanishing Station and Em's threat to leave me there if I break her rules and endanger Montgomery again. I don't tell him that it makes me sick to think about what's inside the packages I carry across the portals. Elephant tusks and bags of heroin, stolen paintings and unmarked cash.

I tell him to leave.

Please.

"No," he says, his wide chin jutting out. He digs his heels into the ground like I'm about to drag him onto a train portal right this instant. I couldn't, even if I tried—there's no way I'm strong enough to drag someone across the world against their will. I'm not Madame Em or Montgomery. I have absolutely no idea how to force someone into a jump. Especially someone as stubborn as my dad.

"No? That's it?" I pull away from him. "You won't even try?"

"I am trying," he says.

"Not enough."

I realize too late how much those words sting. His eyes flare in betrayal, and his cheeks flush red. But it's the truth. Madame Em rules our lives. We live in a garage, and the floor still smells like vomit despite all the bleach Dad scrubbed it with.

"Not enough!" He spits the words back at me, his anger flooding to the surface. It's so rare for me to see his rage. In Filipino culture, you keep the negative stuff bottled up inside. You don't talk about your problems. Not until it's too much to bear.

"Do you know what I've sacrificed for you?" he says.

"No, *I don't know*—because you kept it all a secret! My whole life, you only told me lies."

"The contract was for you!" His eyes bulge and spit flies across the room. "I jump back and forth from Philippines to San Francisco, back and forth until my joints ache, until everything is broken—so I could be here with you and your mama. Em threatened to recruit you. To use you! She knew you had my blood and would inherit magic. She knew exactly where you lived; she knew you loved drawing your mama on the trains. But I said no. I said—*take ten years*. I signed a contract so those mga demonyo would never recruit you, so I could jump here anytime to see you. I told Em, I will watch over Ruby and keep one life in San Francisco, one life in Philippines. Then your mama got sick, and I asked Em for a loan to care for you and Meredith full-time—no jumping, no commissions. But the cancer dragged on; the bills were too much. Now, I can't keep jumping like I promised. Now, I can barely walk. I broke my promises to Em. And you tell me it's not enough?"

He's breathless by the time he finishes his tirade, and I feel like I'm falling through the portals again. Vertigo floods my forehead.

The joint pain, the alcoholism, the debt.

All because of me.

I stumble back into the washing machine as if I've been physically struck. My mouth gapes for something to say, but what could I ever say to this?

Already, he's trying to pull me into a hug, regret in his dark eyes. I push his arms away, but even the concrete feels unsteady.

"Ruby, no . . . It's not your fault. Come here, anak."

He pulls me into a bear hug again, and this time I sink my forehead into his steady shoulder. I think of all the small and big sacrifices my dad has made to be with me in San Francisco. All so he could watch me grow up and protect me from the forces that wanted to use me. I clutch the cash in my pocket and remember that there is something I can do for him now.

"I'm not leaving you behind," he whispers. "I promise I will get better."

"You can't promise that."

Not unless something changes.

❧ CHAPTER 49 ❧

My scooter barely makes it over Twin Peaks as hungry fog sneaks into Stella's poor sputtering engine. Wind bites at my bare ankles, and I wish I'd remembered gloves.

Here I am again.

Loretta's coffee shop.

That forever-ago art show, losing my mom's bucket list, *discovering magic*—it all felt like the start of something. But what's truly changed? I still feel caught in a spiderweb.

I shove open the door, ready to demand a triple-shot espresso because I have no idea how I'll get through this day without it.

I stop mid-step.

All of Diego's life-size canvases are gone.

All his brilliant jade agaves with their spiked flowers reaching skyward.

The walls are blank.

Diego rushes over and pulls me into a hug.

"Girl, I thought you died!" he yells into my ear, not caring that the entire coffee shop can hear. This boy has no idea how close he is to the truth.

"It's been, like, five days," I say.

"You ever heard of texting?"

"My phone died."

"Details," he says, waving away our conversation. "Anyway, I have something more important to show you."

"Wait, wait, what happened to your art? If someone stole it, I'm coming after them with a machete."

This time, he leans in to whisper—which, frankly, is something I thought Diego Jose Alvarez was not capable of. "I sold. Every. Last. One. Your friend Powell is a miracle worker, a Medici patron of the arts, a Greek god, a cute—"

"Hold up, what?"

"He had his bougie friends buy my art. Every last painting."

Diego is positively glowing. His brown skin turns to bronze in this light. I want to be happy for him, but it worries me that Powell might be up to something. After Em and the Vanishing Station, every mention of the Bartholomews sends a sharp twinge deep into my bones.

"Wow, that's . . . wow."

"Very wow," he says.

"And, Powell . . . he didn't make you sign anything, did he?"

"Like an autograph?"

"Like a contract?"

"Ruby, are you feeling OK?"

I nod, trying not to think about the Bartholomews sinking their claws into every aspect of my life. Like they did with my dad. I came here to ask him what he thinks about sending my dad to the Philippines for surgery. It'll mean one less thing for me to worry about while I plan an escape from Em's rule. I don't know who else to talk to. But here, under these twinkling fairy lights, Diego looks so happy. If I want to keep Diego as a friend, I can't go around burdening him with my family drama. It's mine to bear.

I force a smile, and he tilts his head in confusion.

"¿Que pasa?" he says.

I want to say: everything. Everything has happened. And yet, nothing has changed.

"OK, fine, go all emo-Ruby on me." He slides two chairs out and drags me down into a worn wooden seat. "But I have news that will make you smile."

"You won the lottery?"

"Girl, if I won the lottery, you ain't never seeing me again. I'd be on the first flight to Costa Rica." He slides a giant envelope across the table. "This is better. Open it."

My eyebrow arches, and he shoots one right back.

"¡Ábrelo!" he hollers.

"You know I despise surprises."

"The news in that envelope will surprise exactly no one."

My finger digs under the flap and snags on the sharp paper. Blood pools on the tip of my index finger from the tiniest of cuts. The lamplight brings out the startling sea blue in my BART tattoo. Diego is about to ask about it, but then he sees my frown when I open the envelope.

It's early admission.

To the Rhode Island School of Design. To RISD, one of the top fine art schools in America, with a campus in a near-imaginary place called the East Coast. Artists like Dale Chihuly with his dreamy glass art sculptures went there, along with a load of other real artists.

I feel like a complete and utter imposter.

The name says Ruby Josephine Santos. The scholarship says partial coverage. The letter says CONGRATULATIONS in big, bold type.

But I didn't even apply.

"Diego, that's forgery."

He jerks back as if I've slapped him across the cheek.

"Come on, *you* earned this," he says. "You'd pretty much finished the entire application. You were just too scared to submit it. So, I mailed it out–that's it. I thought you'd be . . . happy?"

I stare at the letter–this should be my golden ticket out of here. A dream come true. A promising future. But what about my dad? What about my BART contract? My mother's house? Rhode Island feels impossibly far away. And I'm a fraud.

"Which art pieces did you send them?" My raspy voice wavers between fury and fear.

"Your murals from Chen's painting gigs. It was all your art. The Best of Ruby Santos. They even gave you a partial scholarship. Look."

His finger taps hard against the paper, but my vision has gone blurry.

"I told you I wasn't ready for art school yet. My dad . . . the house . . . it's all, too much. And now this."

"It's an opportunity, Ruby. Can't you see that?"

"It's a lie."

I push my chair back too roughly, and it slams against another chair. A girl squeals and scoots out of my way. I can barely hear her through the blood thundering in my ears.

"How could you do this?" I say. "I thought we were friends."

"This is what friends do," he says, softly. "Believe in each other, when we refuse to believe in ourselves."

"This is never going to happen."

Diego frowns and leans back in his chair.

"You know," he says. "I kept wanting to blame your dad for the way you shut out every possibility. Every hope, every dream. But maybe you're too scared to let go. Too scared to leap. You're acting just like him."

"If I wanted judgment, I could have looked in a goddamn mirror." I snatch my bag and start for the door. I don't have to listen to this bullshit.

"I care about you, Ruby Santos," he says, rising to his feet. "I won't sit back and watch you throw away your talent because you're afraid to dream of more."

Diego dashes to a far corner and rips a curtain from the wall. The entire coffee shop has been eagerly savoring our argument, and now that the white velvet comes crashing down, they let out a collective gasp. There, staring me down, are architectural shots of Chen murals—*my murals*. All commissioned for cash. The giraffe reaching toward a baby's cradle, the ceiling with dreamy clouds drifting over a lone table. Even a bike-shop mural I painted more than a year ago: a wall of endless Monstera plants, entire universes painted in between the Swiss cheese holes in their leaves. One of the bullet points on my mom's bucket list—achieved.

I don't know what to say.

It obviously shows off his photographer's eye. And with everything that's happened, I feel like I'm staring at my own artwork through a stranger's lens.

"This is the portfolio I sent in," he says. "You wrote the essay. You filled out the application. It's all you, Ruby. Why won't you believe it?"

I shake my head and back out the door.

How can I ever hope to live *that* Ruby's life without giving up on the people I love?

Sirens howl past me as I struggle to start my scooter. Please, Stella, come on. I give the ignition a rest and squeeze my hands on the handlebar to stop shaking.

I need to talk to Chase.

He understands how hard it is to let go of family, how impossible it is to chase our dreams.

When Stella finally starts, I rush along Golden Gate Park down John F. Kennedy Drive, past its sweeping lime-green lawns where, tucked into a paddock, a herd of shaggy bison roams, blissfully, impossibly. Here, in the middle of my city. I've heard bison can run thirty miles per hour, almost as fast as my scooter right now. Another fire truck barrels down Lincoln Way, drowning out all sound except for their sirens.

When I park at Chase's hideaway, I realize that this is where the fire engines were headed.

All I can imagine is Chase asleep while Palo arrived with a gas can and a match. Could Palo have possibly found him? The stench of burnt wood and melted plastic fills the air. It's sour and acidic and all wrong. The whole house didn't burn—only the attic, only Chase's hideaway. All his instruments, his sheet music composed during sleepless nights, his secret maps and intricate timetables. The stench nearly makes me double over, and I grip onto Stella for support.

This is all because of me.

Ambulances have already come and gone. Firefighters oversee the rubble and embers while neon yellow caution tape barricades the doors.

I reach into my pocket, but then remember my phone is still cracked. So I sprint into Cole's Creperie and tell them it's an emergency, that I'll buy a dozen, two dozen, a hundred jelly donuts if only they'd let me use their phone and look up the number for the Embarcadero skyscraper.

I ask the operator for Montgomery Bartholomew III.

He answers—thank god, he answers.

But he doesn't say anything.

I just hear his breath, the way it hitches and breaks.

"I'm coming," I say, running for the nearest train.

§

Elevator doors open to a cavernous marble room. No stars hang overhead, no light at all, except a dim lamp in the distance. I wonder if Montgomery Bartholomew III can hear my hollow footsteps.

His apartment is one floor beneath Madame Em's.

Antique mirrors line the walls, and sleek modern furniture comes in every shade of black and white. Thick glass windows shut out all noise, all humanity. I can see the ocean, but today it's only a thin, gray haze.

Montgomery sits in one of the blocky leather chairs. He stares at a blank television screen, completely still. His face looks exactly like the first time I saw him here, in the long hallway of portraits. Like a figure in a Caravaggio painting, he sits frozen and contemplative . . . and burning under the surface.

I linger over him, but he doesn't glance up.

On the table, there's a crumpled note—the only trace that a human being lives here.

"This is your home. Remember where you belong."

Suddenly, it dawns on me that it wasn't Palo at all.

The fire, the ashes, Chase's dreams up in smoke.

"She . . ." I can barely say the rest of the words before my knees buckle. I steady myself against the armrest and force the words out of my mouth. "Your *mom* did this?"

Montgomery starts laughing, a jagged, broken laugh. His hands grip so hard to the leather cushions that I can still see his thumbprints when he lets go.

"I'm so sorry." I kneel down to take his hand, but he doesn't squeeze back.

"Don't be," he says. "This is my home. It's . . ." He gazes around like he has woken up inside a crypt. Except he's not screaming. Come on, Chase, *scream*. Roar, yell, anything. Don't give in to this.

"This place is not you," I say.

"But I'm Montgomery. I was always meant to be Montgomery."

"Chase," I whisper.

His jaw clenches.

"This is where I belong," he says. "This place is . . . home."

"You can't let her control you like this. Please, Chase, please don't let her take away all the beautiful, worthwhile pieces inside yourself. I know you tried to hide inside that attic."

"It's all gone. My maps, my music." His voice breaks before he goes silent.

"No, it's here." I press my lips against his forehead, against the soft fabric of his shirt. "You can build it again. You don't have to stay here."

He shakes his head and rises to his feet. I gaze up at the stony face towering over me.

"What choice do I have?" he says.

"Do you remember when you took me to Norway? To Amsterdam? Do you remember when you told me to not sign the contract? That I had so many ways forward if I would just open my eyes." My voice starts to take on a manic fervor, a train hurtling down the tracks, unstoppable. "You knew then that I deserved better. That *we* deserve better. You'll hate yourself if you keep pretending to be Montgomery. But you can start over. I saw your maps on the floor, all the portals and hideaways you've discovered around the world. Why can't we just . . . *vanish*?"

I can't believe those words have tumbled from my mouth. Diego was right—about me, about Chase. Already, I can see all the ways Chase can carve his own path, can carry his own name. Why is it so much easier to see the truth in other people's lives than in your own? My father, Chase—I can see their futures brimming with potential, if only they'd take the leap. And for once—finally, *finally*—I can imagine my own bright blazing future.

"We can both start over." I grip his hand fiercely and remember the way he'd grabbed mine in that long-ago hallway of dead-men portraits. All the faces of Embarcaderos and Montgomerys in his family's long legacy. He was desperately trying to lead me to an escape. I can do this for him now. I can do this for *myself* now. "We don't have to stay in San Francisco. We have the power to jump *anywhere in the world*. For a fresh start. We don't have to use that power for crime or rival families."

His eyes finally start to focus on me, the storm clearing from his sky blues.

"Em won't let you go," he says. "And she definitely won't let me go."

"She hasn't heard what I'm offering yet."

⚡ CHAPTER 50 ⚡

I go upstairs alone despite Montgomery's protests.

He gave me his keys.

The star-shaped lights dangle overhead, their jagged points aimed downward. A chill runs through the marble entryway as if I were walking through forest shadow. I don't call out. I don't stumble. I know where to go, which room she'll be in. I force my legs to walk; I force my tongue to prepare for all the things I need to say. Down the ghostly hallway, all the Montgomerys and Embarcaderos in an unbroken line. Pale white faces from decades of jumpers who have chosen this path, this narrow walkway, this chain and curse. I can imagine Montgomery's portrait at the end, and it makes me smile that it's not there yet. It might never be there–if Montgomery finds the strength to carve his own path.

But this isn't about Montgomery.

This is for me.

For my own path forward.

Montgomery told me where to find her. Down the long hallway, third door on the left. Her precious library. My body shivers as I turn the crystal knob. The San Francisco skyline glitters beneath us, almost toylike from this high up.

Madame Em glances up from her book and flashes me a look that can only be described as triumphant. The book slams shut with a loud crack. She grips the obsidian cane in her fist, and I have to resist the urge to grab it. That belongs to my father. His pride wrapped up in the eagle carving, all his hopes and dreams about coming to America, being here with me—ruined because of Em.

"Hello, *Balboa*." She leers. "Did my son send you here to speak on his behalf?"

"No, I'm not here for Montgomery."

"Good. I taught him to fight his own battles."

"Though, for the record, I think you're a total witch for burning it down."

"That was not his home. It's better he doesn't delude himself."

"I thought you were clever, but you of all people should know that if you burn it down, it'll rise back up."

Em sighs and leans the cane against her armchair.

"So, what foolish thing are you here to beg for?" she says.

"I'm not begging, Em. My home—it's yours. I forfeit it. My contract and my father's contract are over. We will no longer serve the Bartholomew line. Take the house, and leave us in peace." I half-expect my heart to implode the moment I say the words aloud. Instead, I feel a shackle lifted from my ankle. Blood rushes through my veins, alive and beating. This is the right decision. My mother would understand—she'd want this for me. Freedom, finally. A future, finally.

"Darling, don't bore me." Madame Em laughs and picks up her book again. It's a book of maps, train lines zigzagging around the world. Her fingers trace over more territory to steal, as if she needs more wealth in this shimmering skyscraper. "Have you forgotten you've made a promise, Balboa?"

"It's over. You can take my house, my mom's murals, everything. It's yours. I refuse to run the trains. My dad and I are leaving, and we promise not to work for any other lines. We're starting over. It's what I should have done when you first threatened to take the house."

Again, I expect the words to knot and stick in my throat, but they come out smoothly. The truth always does, in the end.

Madame Em rises from her velvet couch and gestures to the gold-framed maps lining her library walls. Every inch is covered in faraway places that she foolishly believes she can control. I realize suddenly that it's her attempt at armor, while she hides here, in her tower. She's afraid to seem small, unimportant, bare. But I don't care if she can see my every scar. It's my past, not my future.

"And what would your dear mother think?" Em purrs. "I'd order my men to roller over every inch of her murals in bone white. Even the one in your precious little closet."

Her words hit me straight in the gut, and I struggle to swallow the guilt and anger threatening my resolve. My hands shake as I ball them into fists, but then I let go. Remind myself of the freedom I feel when a paintbrush is in my hand instead. A flicker of hope kindles inside me when I think of my art school acceptance. That maybe I do have a talent worth sharing with the world. Even if I don't choose RISD, there's a future waiting for me.

"The contract isn't what my mother would have wanted for me, even if it means losing her murals. The crime, the lies, the garage–I deserve better."

"You can't break a binding contract."

"The contract was to save our house. I forfeit the house."

"And your father's life?"

"That wasn't part of the contract."

"Darling, even before you signed the contract, I would never have let you and your father walk away. I knew full well that you'd come groveling back here for a job." She pounds the eagle cane on the hard marble. "No one walks away from the Bartholomews."

I can't help but laugh. She's just as afraid as I am to lose what we have left. But here she is, the grand Madame Em, hiding in her skyscraper and forcing us grunts to protect her empire. What is she without her magic, without her loyal sons?

"Without the trains," I say, "you have no power here."

At this, she laughs. "Merritt, take her."

Merritt leaps out from where he was hiding behind the door and blockades my only exit. His muscled arms fold across his chest, and he looks at me like I'm one of the dead rats he'd delight in throwing into Montgomery's bed. I snatch a gold painting from Madame Em's wall and hold it hostage. It's an ancient map from the early railroad days in Great Britain. It must be very old, very valuable. Irreplaceable, maybe. How many abandoned stations must be hidden in its labyrinthian lines? Has she found them all? Gold foil glimmers in the paint, making the stations glow like pinpoints.

"I'll destroy it," I say. "If you don't let me go."

"I'll buy another." She shrugs and tosses me a letter opener. "Go ahead."

Sweat coats my fingers, but I don't hesitate to dig the letter opener into one of the painting's corners. It saws through the delicate canvas.

Em flinches, her lips drawn into a hard thin line.

"Merritt!" she yells.

He takes a step toward me, and I see the gap of light behind him in the doorway. My only escape.

"I've been looking forward to stepping into the ring with you again." Merritt tosses me a lazy grin. "I wonder how many scars Montgomery can stomach before he breaks up with you? Maybe I should start with your pretty face?" Merritt flicks out a flash of steel. The blade's edge looks sharpened to perfection.

This letter opener is no match. But my father's blade is tucked inside my boot. Do I have any chance of beating Merritt in a knife fight? Blood rushes to my head when I realize the answer. No, no chance at all.

"Please, Em, let me go." My chest squeezes tight and my sweaty fingers nearly drop the painting. "What good am I to you as a prisoner? My entire value to the Bartholomews is as a jumper."

"Darling, you must always think of the competition. My rivals would love to get their hands on you and your father. You know too much about the Bartholomew lines and you have considerable power."

"We promise, we won't work for anyone."

"Says the Balboa who is breaking her contract. You're a fool. Search the world; there are no free rides. You either rule an empire or you serve one."

"That's not true. There are other paths."

"This is the only path."

She's wrong.

Håkon said there were others like me who want a life without the contracts and corruption. I have to believe that's true; otherwise, what's the point of having all this power?

I glance at Merritt, his knife still pointed at me.

"You know," I say, "she would have left you in the Vanishing Station if Chase hadn't gone back to save you. She's a snake. She'll get rid of you when you're no longer useful."

Merritt shakes his head in denial, but there's a flash of hurt in his eyes. I fling the painting at him and sprint toward the door. He slashes at the canvas midair, and it collapses in a heap at his feet. His giant hand grabs my wrist before I can slip past. Merritt twists my arm back, shooting pain up my elbow. God, I wish we were on a train right now. I could jump farther and faster than he could in a heartbeat. Merritt hooks his arm around my throat and drags me toward Em. I slam my elbow into his gut. Not even a grimace. Shit.

"Take her down to the trains," Em commands. "It seems someone wanted another chance to visit the Vanishing Station."

Panic floods my chest as Merritt's grip tightens. *You're a survivor, Ruby Santos, a survivor.* I chant the words inside my head as I kick and flail and scratch.

And then, release.

I'm coughing on the velvety rug, my knees buckling beneath me.

I see his leather shoes first, then his midnight blue suit.

Then the thick iron fireplace poker at his side.

"Chase?"

He takes my hand and pulls me up, so much like that day he found me, when I'd lost my mother's bucket list on the train tracks. Madame Em's mouth hangs open as she glances at Merritt sprawled unconscious on the floor.

"Stop this, Em," he says. "Let her go."

"You would do this to your own brother, your own blood?" Her lips tremble, and soft wrinkles halo around her eyes.

"My own blood?" he grimaces. "*You* left them in the Vanishing Station. *You* burned down my hideaway. You knew what it meant to me."

"I burned down your delusions!"

"You're deluded if you think being your 'Montgomery' isn't killing me a little every day. I can't do it anymore. I can't be Chase *and* Montgomery. I won't."

Tears rush to the corners of her eyes, but Madame Em doesn't allow a single one to fall down her cheeks. She blows out a ragged breath before her eyes sharpen.

"It's over," he whispers.

But Em looks nowhere near done.

Chase pulls us out of the map room, slamming the door behind us and barricading its intricate handles with the fire iron. He leans his head against the thick mahogany and sucks in a shaky breath. This must be pure torture, betraying his blood. His family.

"Chase," I say. "We need to run."

We break into a sprint down the hallway of dead men. My throat burns almost as badly as when Em dragged me through the portals. We wait for the elevator doors to open. Come on, open, open, open. There's only one way out of this damn tower.

"Leave San Francisco quickly," Chase says. "Em will lock down the trains if she hasn't already."

"Wait, what about you?"

"You're not experienced enough to drag someone across a portal against their will. Your dad will need to agree to jump. Here–" He hands me his electric-surge device and a crumpled map. The elevator doors slide open.

"You're staying?"

"There are things I need to finish." His jaw tightens, and his hand squeezes mine, like in the sand, like on our jumps, and I don't want to let go. "I'll buy you as much time as I can."

"But . . ."

"I'll meet you where we first kissed."

I desperately pull him into a kiss now, our lips melting into cinnamon and salt and too many maybes. A knot coils inside my chest knowing that

Montgomery might not make it out of San Francisco. He might not leave his family, after all.

"Oh, now who's being dramatic?" a voice says.

We break away, and Chase raises his fists at the man stepping from the shadows.

Powell emerges, wearing a blazer embroidered with jagged silver branches. His loafers barely make a sound on the marble. He drags a hand through his marvelously sculpted hair. Even in a moment of disaster, he comes dressed in his finest.

"Come now." He holds out his empty hands. "That's no way to greet a gentleman."

Still, Chase clutches his hands steadfastly.

Powell inches closer and closer until he wraps his brother in a warm embrace. He whispers, loud enough for me to hear. "A proper farewell in case you never return, you bastard. Don't say we were never brothers."

Powell reaches for the elevator doors and holds them open.

"What did you expect?" Powell says. "A stab in the back? We're not all Bartholomews."

Chase blushes and finally lowers his fists.

I step inside, and Powell steps in after me.

"I'll make sure she arrives safely at Balboa Park. But that's it." Powell flips the collars up on his velvet blazer and hits the button for the ground floor.

"Thank you," Chase says. "I'll tell Em you put up a fight."

Powell winks before the elevator doors slide shut, and we drop down to earth. The moment the doors close, he lets out a ragged breath. "I can't believe I'm doing this," he mumbles. "You better be worth it."

My heart lurches into my throat as gravity collapses beneath us.

When our feet touch down, we break into a run for Embarcadero station. Well, I break into a run—Powell tries to keep his dignity. As the train rushes into the tunnel, I can feel its roaring pull, its reins ready and waiting. Powell almost doesn't catch the train but still manages to jump with me from Embarcadero to Balboa Park. We're there in a flash. Powell keeps an eye out for any incoming henchmen. Either Em hasn't called them yet, or they think Powell is escorting me somewhere on her orders. When we arrive, he doesn't step off. I push my way through the crowd and glance across the doors.

"Won't she punish you?" I say.

"I'm all she has left." Powell dusts off his blazer, and light gleams on the fine silver threads. "Merritt is no leader; Montgomery is the fallen son. Win-win. If I ever see either of you on my trains again, you'll find yourselves in a fate far worse than Helensburgh."

"Powell." I catch his sharp, glittering eyes before the train doors slide shut. "You do mix a divine Last Word."

"Cheers." He raises an imaginary glass and grins.

Slimy bastard.

I break into a run, hoping no one has gotten to my father first.

ς

When I shove open the garage door, I don't see my dad behind the dusty boxes and plastic-wrap furniture. No spam and eggs and steamed rice. Not even footsteps from the renters upstairs.

"Dad!" This reminds me too much of trying to catch him on the train. That mournful kundiman song haunting me. "Dad!"

"Hoy!" His voice hollers from the back garden.

I rush past our faded travel posters and rip them off the walls. We deserve the real thing. When I throw open the garden door, sunlight streams down, bright and clear. No fog today, no chill in the air. My dad sits smiling under our favorite redwood tree, and it breaks my heart to imagine we might never see it again.

If my dad agrees to come with me.

"We need to leave now. There's no time to explain. I broke the contract."

"But the house?" He sloshes his mug of mint tea as he struggles to rise. I pull him up, but the crumbling dirt and bark make it difficult for him to find steady footing.

"It's not worth trading our futures for."

"Ruby . . ."

"Dad, trust me."

My voice is a train moving in only one direction–*forward*.

For once, he doesn't contradict me, doesn't give me excuses. He takes my hand and lets me lead him through the darkness.

The only thing we take from our old life is the stockpile of cash we'd saved up for his hip surgery and addiction recovery. Neither of us dares to take a backward glance at my mother's murals. We know we'll turn to salt if we look. Instead, I hold her murals wholeheartedly inside my memories, for a future when I can paint my own.

⅀ CHAPTER 51 ⅀

My dad leans on his cane while we wait for the Millbrae train. On our way underground, I'd stood in front of the sliding elevator doors to keep them from closing on him. It's hard for me to imagine him nimbly flying across these portals, job after job grinding down his joints until the pain became too much to bear without painkillers. Without alcohol.

If I'm brutally honest, there's more than hip pain causing his trouble. The hip surgery might help his joints, but it might not help his addiction. I don't know all the reasons he drinks. I can guess it has to do with losing Mom, with leaving his family behind in the Philippines, with the corruption Madame Em made him carry across the world. Maybe he'll never tell me. Maybe it's just genetics. Maybe he doesn't even know all the reasons.

But I have to hope that if we fix one problem, more good will follow. My dad once told me what it was like to carve a path through a thick jungle. You swing your machete at one swath of vines, take a step, swing, step, swing, step. That's it. My dad's BART contract was one swing, the hip surgery another, and the alcoholism will be another swing, and another, and another for the rest of his life. I hope he makes it out of that jungle, but I truly don't know if he will. All I know now is that I can't clear the path for him. He needs to cut his own path. He needs to believe there's a way out.

"When we're in the portal, you'll have to guide us to Manila. I can jump, but I don't know how to find the station."

"Yes, you do." He gives me one of his wide grins, the one he saves for singing. "You're a Santos, too. I found you here; and you'll always know how to find me."

I smile at him as the train swoops into the station. He braces himself against the eager crowd. Kids jostle each other to be the first one through the doors. One boy jumps inside like he's clearing an invisible hurdle at a racetrack. Excitement rises in my bones, another world opening up, even as one is closing behind us.

We have to hurry before Em's henchmen catch us. My dad takes my hand and draws on everything in his reserves to bring us to the Saddle doors. The plexiglass slides shut, and muddled silence swallows us. Only the sound of the train rumbling on the tracks. *Clu-clunk, clu-clunk*, and my heartbeat's hammering in my ears.

"Tell me about the Philippines," I whisper.

"I miss my home, anak. One day you will see Tito Rudolfo's jeepney. He painted it bright red and pineapple yellow. Mother Mary and Mickey Mouse on the inside. Oh, he drove like a maniac. We pray the rosary every time. Your mama, she loved it. Rudolfo drove us everywhere. Your mama, she danced on the beach in Boracay and drank from coconuts, until she was so sunburn we call her 'kamatis.' You know, 'tomato.'" He laughs, loud and fierce, and I can feel warmth flooding in through the train doors. Island heat and humidity. It feels so different from the icy chill I usually feel when I jump. It makes me smile thinking of my mother, young and beautiful and gallivanting around the islands with my father. It makes him smile, too.

But then my breath catches.

Merritt materializes on the other end of the train car. Those broad shoulders and boxer fists. A bloody gash bulges from his temple. I feel the train pulse with magic, like it's a horse wanting to buck a rider. My heart rattles inside my chest. My father must have felt it, too, but he keeps talking, and the heat rises into our palms. It feels like the train can hear our stories. Like it wants to hear more.

"I remember Lola's photos," I whisper, quickly. "There was so much food at Christmastime, I thought it could feed an entire village. All the ripe mangos and piles of pancit noodles. My aunties singing and laughing so hard I could almost hear it. And I thought, how does my daddy live with his heart split across the world?"

Blue cracks zigzag across the doors as Merritt tries to yank them open. He's stronger than I am, and I can't keep the doors shut. My feet slip. The magic can't hold. Merritt reaches his arm through and clamps down on my wrist. I hit the electric-surge device in my pocket, and the train dissolves into complete darkness.

In that moment, small as a wing beating in the air, my father croons his love song: to home, to family, to all the things he fights for every day.

"Dahil sa iyo," he says.

Because of you.

And it pulls us through.

⚜ CHAPTER 52 ⚜

Except not quite the way we'd hoped.

With our magic combined, we make the jump in one staggering, breathless leap.

But something is wrong.

My joints ache like metal screeching against metal. Joints that haven't been oiled in centuries and are now creaking into motion. I hear my father gasp beside me. A strangled breath escapes my mouth as we rip through a portal in Manila. Solid gray walls materialize around us, boxing us inside a physical space again, bodies everywhere, but my hands don't feel like my own and my knees start to collapse inward. Legs shaking. His legs? Our legs? Oh god, I remember the way Shen had materialized in his jump from Shanghai to San Francisco. It was as if his body couldn't come through in one piece, like a werewolf struggling between man and wolf. Except our bodies are struggling in this same space, our memories mixing together, my blood, his blood.

I think of everything that's uniquely my own. Mine and only mine. The way paint digs under my nails and I love to chew it out. The way Montgomery gives me poetry books and I read them on repeat before falling asleep. The way I'll cover tacos in cilantro while my dad wouldn't dare touch a leaf. The way a drawing burns inside my head and flows out my fingertips. The fact that I just got accepted into one of the most prestigious art schools in the country.

Finally, I start to feel the space inside my chest expand again. Beside me, my father topples to his knees. I lean my face against the glass. The aisles are much narrower here. In this train car, it's too crowded for us to go unnoticed. Dozens of eyes peer through the glass, unsure if they really saw what they think they saw. A ghost, a spirit, a demon. I drag my father up to his feet with shaky arms. He leans heavily on his cane. The crowd parts for us, mouths agape. We can barely get off the train before a flood of incoming passengers nearly crushes us back inside. The crowds are incredible, a mishmash of elbows and polo shirts and black hair.

We need to find Tito Rudolfo—my dad's family on this side of the world. *My family.*

"Quick," I say, elbowing our way through the bodies. "We need to run before Merritt follows us."

"Merritt cannot jump this far. Only Montgomery." My dad squeezes the words out of his mouth as his lungs struggle. "Others need many jumps to follow us. And the jumpers in Manila know me well. We have time."

I waver in the sweaty crowd. Shoulders knock into mine, and I growl under my breath anytime I see someone knock into my father. He gives my hand a soothing squeeze while he sends SOS text messages to his brother that we made it. Sweat drips down my neck, so unused to this humidity and heat. My brain can barely soak in our surroundings, the bodies pressing in on all sides, the blazing sun outside the station. I'm still spinning from the magic, but my body is slowly acclimating to long jumps. I don't know how the vertigo hasn't knocked me to my knees yet. It must have been–

"Dad," I say, staring at the way his arm presses so firmly on his cane. "I could have jumped us both here. The pain in your joints–"

"The pain is always worth coming home." He smiles at the bustle of the market stalls and the sea of brown faces. The sweet smell of mangoes bursting from the smoothie shop. I shake my head and laugh.

"So stubborn," I say.

"You need rest, Ruby."

Another train rushes into the station. Oh, how I long for a nap right now. Except . . .

"Once Tito Rudolfo arrives, I need to check if Montgomery made it out OK. We said we'd meet at the place where we first . . ." I blush and turn toward the vendors selling bright orange shaved ice. "We promised we'd meet at an abandoned train."

My dad stares at me, all his usual protectiveness flaring in his eyes.

He knows he can't protect me forever.

He knows the world awaits me.

Wanderlust.

In the distance, we catch sight of Tito Rudolfo's brightly colored jeepney pulling up to the train station. He honks and waves a cup of melting purple ube ice cream.

My dad pulls me into a tight hug, no sign of weakness in these old bones.

"You know how to find me, anak."

I take a step back, and my breath hitches. I'm about to leave behind the only family I have left. The separation feels all the more crushing after the train magic almost smashed our bodies together. But now it's my turn to explore all the world's shimmering possibilities. My dad can easily blend in here, disappear into the secret Santos family hideaways. If Chase and I stay, we'll be easy targets for Madame Em. I need to give my dad a chance to recover.

"I'll see you soon. I promise."

"Mahal kita," he bellows in his loudest singing voice. He doesn't care if strangers hear the Sap Master proclaiming his love for his only daughter.

"Mahal kita," I whisper back.

Another train rushes into the station, and I start pushing my way through the crowd. My dad hobbles in the opposite direction where his brother will drive him to the family's secret safehouse near the sea. I wonder how many jumpers Tito Rudolfo has hidden away. There are so many secrets I still don't know about the Santos family. My dad pulls out a couple crumpled dollars and buys an Ube Kalamay. Before the train stops, I see him stuff the sticky purple rice between his Cheshire cat grin. I burst into bubbly laughter. I burst into tears, too, but I don't let them stop me as I climb aboard the train. Passengers give me a path to reach the space between the cars. The Saddle, awaiting another ride. A few people gently pat my shoulders; too many of them have known the bittersweet tang of the diaspora. My body sways as the train barrels forward. I squeeze my eyes shut and think about all the things still alive and thrumming and waiting to be discovered in my life.

I imagine the place where I first kissed Montgomery, the place I'd dared to reach for more. With shaky hands, I grab the reins of this beautiful, wondrous beast and pull open the portal doors.

CHAPTER 53

Everything depends on
sunlight
breaking through the fog.
Will he find me here?
Will he brave the leap?
Of faith, I have little.
But it is enough to dream.
A flicker, a heartbeat in the beast below my feet,
Waiting for us to grab the reins.
He comes,
A nameless boy,
A haze of gray through the glass,
Then,
blue eyes
brighter than any sky.
We leap.

⅀ CHAPTER 54 ⅀

The video screen freezes so many times, it feels like we're playing charades. Every third word, every fourth freeze-frame, who knows if we're understanding each other. Maybe my dad is trying to tell me to grow a mustache; maybe he's telling me the meaning of life. Best guess, he's telling me not to worry. At least it's a good distraction from thinking about whether the Bartholomews will ever find us here. Now, the screen freezes on my dad's surefire grin. It's what I miss most about him—he grins with all his teeth, even the gold molars in the far back.

"Frank Sinatra . . . [*gaaaarble*] . . . karaoke."

I catch the last word of his sentence before it dissolves into static again. I don't need him to fill in the rest. Always and forever a crooning Sap Master. That's my dad.

Tito Rudolfo has been keeping the mic warm and the piña coladas alcohol-free. Five more weeks until the hip surgery. This is the prep stage, when my dad will have to stay healthy and sober. When the time comes, I'll sneak through the train lines and hold his hand before they wheel him into surgery. Five weeks. I know he can do this. Still, I worry about the next binge, the next temptation to throw away everything for a single icy sip of San Miguel—and worst of all, he might lapse after the surgery is done.

"What . . . [*garble*] . . . up . . . [*garble*], Little Hamboorger?"

"Dad, how many times do I have to tell you to stop calling me that."

I smile anyway.

The frame freezes again, but it still lets his laughter bubble across the thousands of miles that separate us. On the video feed, my face is as blurry as a passing train. I cling to his laughter as worry churns in my gut.

I ask the questions I'd normally be afraid to ask if he could actually hear me.

"What if the hip surgery doesn't change anything? What if you can't get over your addiction? What if Tito Rudolfo doesn't want to take care of you if the drinking gets worse? What if—"

"Ruby," he says, catching all my words despite the freeze-frame video. "It's my turn to try harder. For myself. It's your turn to live. Go, bahala na."

The shakiness in his voice spurs tears at the edges of my eyes. I know he must be terrified, yet he fights his battle, anyway. For himself, this time. I tilt my head back to gaze at the geckos crawling across the ceiling like mini Spider-Men come to save the day.

"Dahil sa iyo," he croons softly into the microphone.

I hold the song deep inside my chest. It's his kundiman to me, his family, to all the people he loves. To everyone who motivates him to stay healthy and safe. There is no end to this part of the story. It's a battle every day. It's up to him to keep making the right choices. It's up to me to dream up a brighter future.

Tito Rudolfo appears in broken fragments on the screen, all smiles and awkward pixelated noses caught mid-blur. Gaudi would be a fan of our abstract family portrait. No one hits "end call," all of us stubbornly waiting for a moment of genuine connection, until finally the screen clears and my dad flashes his biggest grin.

"Until tomorrow, Little Hamboorger."

⚚ CHAPTER 55 ⚚

You sound like an elephant," I say.

"That's the point, isn't it?" Chase blows hard into the khaen's bamboo pipes, his ears flaring in a cute, geeky sort of way.

"Save your brilliant experimenting for later. You'll scare them away!"

My sandals smoosh into wet grass while I reach my palm out to an elephant, as if it were a stray cat instead of an eight-thousand-pound creature descended from mammoths. It has orange speckled freckles across the top of its trunk. My mother somehow left out the fact that they have hair–actual hair!–sprouting from the tops of their lumpy gray heads. My fingers itch to rub its scalp. Yes, I realize I'm a weirdo. The gentle giant pays me no mind and continues to chomp on leaves under the shade of a banyan tree.

Every inch of jungle is slathered in green–emerald, olive, shamrock, sage, chartreuse. My mother nailed every shade. I try to memorize the greens for later when we're back in our hostel bunk beds, where I can sketch her beloved murals from memory. Yet, I'm realizing I don't quite care about the jungle the way my mom did. Instead, I keep finding myself drawn to the ancient fading murals in the Buddhist temples and reading articles about art restoration.

Maybe one day I can help save murals from disappearing.

I'm researching art schools abroad. Venice, Prague, Paris—cities that seem to care about history, about keeping art alive through the centuries, about bringing ruins back to glittering life. Every time Chase catches me browsing, I feel a tinge of embarrassment. Who am I to pursue such a ridiculous dream? I'm not a real artist. And every time, he swoops down to kiss my neck and whispers, *Ruby, you belong there*. And I know it's true. I already have an application ready for this admissions cycle, thanks to Diego, so I can still meet the deadlines. Yes, his handiwork earned me early admission into RISD, but we all know I'm a stubborn beast. I need to do this for myself. And I've always wanted to study abroad. I've been sending Diego postcards, hoping he'll forgive me. Something tells me that he already has.

"Are you sure Em won't find us here?" I say, offering a banana to a mama elephant, who quickly snatches it with her trunk.

"The Bartholomews don't have connections in Thailand." Chase smoothly ducks away from an elephant who tries to run her trunk through his hair. "We're in a distant *jungle* where the mosquitos are eating me alive, and there are absolutely no train tracks nearby. Let's worry about the Bartholomews later. I think we could use a little break."

"This coming from the most serious gargoyle I've ever met?"

Chase laughs. His smile lights up his eyes, the lush emerald backdrop reflecting a hint of jade inside a sea of blue. I wish I could paint this moment. He's fully himself here, like the Montgomery mask and burden have finally lightened. None of it is gone—our history, our families, our traumas, our misdeeds—it's never gone. It still haunts his nightmares, as his body tangles into a mosquito net surrounding his bed. He still flinches at the sound of metal squealing against metal or when he sees chicken bones piled on a plate. And yet, our burden grows lighter the more we reach toward a brighter future.

I snap way too many photos—Chase serenading the elephants; Chase struggling to hold the bamboo khaen pipes between two large hands; Chase nearly dropping the instrument into a pile of elephant dung. I can actually call him Chase in public. Though I have to admit I still call him Mr. Monty when he's being a pain. Like now, when he's so enamored with a new instrument that he won't let it go. Not until he puzzles out how to play it. Still, I cheer him on. These are his dreams, and maybe one day he'll create something as beautiful as a John Williams score—after *a lot* of practice.

"Come on, Mr. Monty, let's leave the khaen on the scooter," I say. "You need two hands for baby elephants."

He thankfully shakes out the saliva before strapping the bamboo pipes across our scooter.

"You can serenade me later when the elephants are out of earshot."

"You sure?" he says.

"Me—definitely. Our roommates—they might need some convincing."

He laughs and leaves a soft kiss along my neck.

His latest instrumental obsession is as long as his torso and has eight bamboo pipes to blow into. Even though we arrived in Thailand only a week ago, he's already picked up a frachappi, a taphon, and a chap yai, which almost made our hostel roommates kick us out from all the cymbal clanging. When we're riding our scooter through the crush of traffic, Chase straps it to his back and nearly knocks us sideways.

I check for text messages on my temporary phone, using a new number that Madame Em can't trace. My dad's usual Friday night disaster calls are blissfully absent. Tito Rudolfo keeps chiding me—*why didn't you reach out for help sooner? We're family after all.*

Not like the Bartholomews.

Not with our knives out.

Not hiding behind false names.

No more Montgomery or Balboa.

It's Chase and Ruby now.

You heard me.

Chase and Ruby.

That simple reality still makes me smile. Chase laces his fingers through mine and gives me a perfectly kissable grin. It sends heat spreading across my already hot skin.

I don't reach up on tiptoes to kiss him, though; I'm waiting for later, when I can give him much more than a kiss. Later, when we have a chance to shower off all the bug spray and sweat and Tiger Balm. Later, when the mosquitoes aren't nipping my ankles, when there isn't an elephant trying to comb his hair. Later, when I can paint the perfect shade of chartreuse and pretend I have no idea where his chap yai cymbals are. *Later.* It feels so good to have a "later."

"Sah wah dee khaa!" a woman hollers from under a golden sign that reads CHIANG MAI ELEPHANT SANCTUARY in beautiful Thai script.

"Sah wah dee khaa!" I holler back, bowing my head and pressing my fingers together in polite greeting.

She holds up a fresh bunch of bananas and winks.

I'm not the only one who notices. A mother elephant and her baby catch sight of those yellow morsels and hurry over for a snack. I'm about to snap a photo when I hear my name crash through the frenzy of jungle noise.

"Ruby!"

I spin around and startle at the familiar face weaving through the banyan trees. The lush leaves are big enough to blot out patches of his pale face, but I'd recognize him anywhere. My heart rattles, and my hands clench into fists.

The man trips over a gnarled root and rights himself. His tan explorer boots seem purchased for this trip alone. To find us here, deep in the Thailand jungles.

Chase freezes, his face already morphing into his Montgomery mask. His lips press into a grim line, and his fingers twist around a switchblade he still keeps in his pocket. His broad, muscular shoulders straighten, and it's as if he's grown even taller beside me.

"Man er ikke norsk med mindre man kan navngi fem typar snø," the man says with a smile.

Chase shakes his head. "Not here." The words come out in a hollow growl. Håkon's grin doesn't falter.

To find us at this exact elephant sanctuary—nowhere near train tracks—must have been one hell of a mission. Håkon's face is bright pink from the sweltering sun, and he itches at the mosquito bites covering his right hand. No knife, not yet.

"True," Håkon says. "This isn't the place for snow."

"It's not the place for old friends, either," Chase says.

The sting shows in Håkon's translucent hazel eyes. He should be wearing sunglasses, but maybe he's done with masks, too.

"How did you find us?" Chase ignores the elephant plucking at his hair. The jungle cacophony continues with its fever pitch of insects and cawing hornbills with their guttural barks.

"It was difficult," Håkon says. "But the trains led me here."

"What do you mean *the trains* led you here?" I say, finally snapping out of this surreal moment. I slap the mosquito sucking blood from my elbow, and it leaves a throbbing bump. This can't be happening; I thought we were safe, at least for a little longer.

"You have a fan club." Håkon shrugs. "And I'm only a humble messenger."

"What's the message?" Chase says.

"We've known each other many years, yes? As friends."

"Yes, and we're still friends, but—"

"*But*—since you were a Bartholomew I could not be entirely honest with you. Maybe now you're ready to listen?"

Chase nods.

"Well, I help jumpers *escape*, for lack of a better word. The train magic helps me find them. When I'm on board the lines, I get flashes of memories or clues. And that's how I'd found Ruby the first time. I told her that there's an alternative to the rivaling gangs, and it's the truth. There's an alternative to the contracts and the debts and the corruption."

Chase glances at me and doesn't hide the hurt in his eyes—how can there still be so many secrets between us? I squeeze his hand and pull him closer.

"After Em dragged me to the Vanishing Station, I jumped to Spain," I say quietly. "Håkon helped me get home. I . . . I didn't think you'd want to talk about . . . that place."

Chase swallows hard and lets his shoulders slacken. "Thank you, Håkon, I owe you a big favor."

"Still thinking like a Bartholomew." Håkon laughs. "You owe me nothing, friend." He quickly bats at a mosquito on his soon-to-be-sunburned cheek. "It should come as no surprise that the underground has an underground. We help jumpers escape their contracts and the gangs exploiting them. Jumpers like you. We could use your help."

"I'm done jumping," Chase says. "I'm sorry, friend, but I'm done with the underground." He doesn't wait to hear another word before he stalks deeper into the jungle. A baby elephant trails after him, lured by the left-over banana in his back pocket. I want to run after him, too, but I can't walk away before hearing more about the other underground.

"Chase, wait!"

He doesn't turn, doesn't falter. A monkey howls in the distance, warning his family of the disturbance to their sweet equilibrium.

"He just left the Bartholomews' gnarled web," I say to Håkon. "And Madame Em is probably hunting us down as we speak. If I were him, I wouldn't want to hear anything about the trains for a long time, either."

"And you . . ."

"Also need time."

"You know, Montgomery—sorry, I mean Chase . . . you said Chase, right?"

I nod.

"We've been friends ever since we were kids. And honestly, I never thought he'd leave his family. He cares for them, whether they deserve it or not. I'm glad you had a role in helping open his eyes. But . . . I would also suggest that you keep your eyes open. Blood runs deep."

"So do dreams."

Håkon smiles, his endless enthusiasm flaring inside his hazel eyes. "You, Ruby Santos, are exactly who we need in the underground. You've seen Madame Em's Vanishing Station. Well, she's not the only one who can help people vanish. You know where to find me."

I watch as Håkon weaves through the tall grass and back to the gravel road. He walks without looking back, and my chest thrums with the familiar pull of train magic. The way it sparks in my palms, as if I can summon a beast and grab hold of the reins.

Chase's laughter echoes through the banyan trees. The baby elephant is trying to wrestle with him. He doesn't want to hurt her, so he lets her lightly squish him against a tree trunk. I burst into laughter and rush to his rescue.

"Need some help?" I holler.

"Save me!" he laughs.

I pull the last banana from my pocket and waggle it in the air like a magic trick. The baby elephant races over.

That's the beautiful thing about magic.

You never know when you might need to pull it from your back pocket.

⚡ EPILOGUE ⚡

t is said that within the tangled vines of the Taman Negara jungle, in the narrow land between Thailand and Malaysia, there lie train tracks leading to nowhere. A project abandoned, forgotten, grown over with decay and fierce new life.

It is said no one jumps from such a place.

It is too far, too forgotten.

The hum of electricity has been replaced with the hum of industrious beetles; diesel smoke replaced with rainforest mist.

The iron tracks barely rise above the jungle floor.

Still, the trains can hear you.

If you listen close for their rumble.

⚵ ACKNOWLEDGMENTS ⚵

D earest reader, thanks for giving my novel a chance to inspire a little magic in your life!

It feels like an impossible task to thank everyone who helped along this journey, but here goes:

Mike, thanks for always listening to my rambling ideas—sometimes even before you've had your first coffee. For that, I am forever grateful. Thank you for always taking care of our two scoundrels when I jet off to a writing retreat. You are my home, my love, my blue-eyed adventurer who always reminds me when I need to slow down. Without you, I would never be able to reach the tall shelves. Thanks for always supporting my dreams, and I hope to always do the same for you.

To my incredible agent Kerry Sparks & her brilliant assistant Rebecca Rodd at LGR—I can't thank you enough for discovering my manuscript in your slush pile and taking it all the way to auction! You've been the best imaginable champions of my writing.

To my ever-insightful editor Maggie Lehrman and the entire Abrams Amulet team (Emily Daluga, Megan Carlson, Andrew Smith)—thank you for taking the leap of faith. Every step of the way, your advice and astute questions have made my novel stronger and more nuanced. Your editorial notes have taught me a lot about writing, and I can't wait to work with you on my next book. Let's see what other magic we conjure up together! To designer Natalie Padberg Bartoo, Micah Fleming, and illustrator Tim O'Brien—thanks for the gorgeous book design. It makes me want to leap into the portal and see what adventure awaits.

To my MUG Writing Group—Brianna Bourne, Aleese Lin, JC Peterson, Taylor L.W. Ross, and Genevieve Sinha. I would have lost myself on this winding and perilous publishing journey without your support and inspiration. You're the best travel buddies, brainstormers and crit partners. Cheers to many more writing retreats together, and I can't wait to gather around a roaring fire and laugh about all the ways we sneak writing into our hectic lives. I owe you each *one* Jellycat, *two* perfect glasses of wine, and *endless* hugs. (And I can't forget Anthony Lanni, may you rest in joyful peace).

To author Nova Ren Suma and the talented cohort of writers in the 2021 Tin House YA Workshop—you gave me such generous revision notes on those early chapters. Special thanks to Emily Young for keeping us connected and for her helpful critiques.

To author friends I've met along the way who have given me invaluable publishing advice: Nikki Barthelmess, Zoraida Córdova, Lilliam Rivera, Seina Wedlick, Emily J. Taylor, Grant Faulkner, Misa Sugiura, Laekan Zea Kemp, and so many others. Thanks also to Kristy Boyce for organizing her Harlaxton London Retreat; it was a revision haven for me.

Big thanks to NaNoWriMo for making me believe I could finish a novel—even if those first ones were terrible! There's a power in *believing*.

Loving thanks to my great, big Ellickson family—from Wisconsin to NY to Australia—for supporting my debut novel.

Dad, I'd hoped you would hold this book in your hands. But God had special plans for you, and the grief is still so raw that I've had to start and stop writing these lines at least seven times. You would have been that cowboy in the bar telling everyone, "You have to buy my daughter's book! It's brilliant!" Thank you for being proud of me, and for working hard to support your family. All the Ellicksons miss your singing and laughter, and I hope you're up in heaven surrounded by that peaceful, easy feeling . . . and maybe a vintage VW Beetle and a toolbox to keep you busy.

Mom, thanks for being strong and fierce in the face of every challenge. This publishing journey required a lot of grit—and you taught me to never give up.

George, I couldn't have asked for a better childhood dreaming up Lego worlds and running wild in the redwoods with you.

Mike, I need to thank you again because we all know I'm right back to drafting at dawn. I promise, I'll write a book about "Jurassic Park in space" for you—as long as you promise to explain the astrophysics. Thanks in advance for supporting all the books I have yet to write!